Joan Hessayon was born in Louisville, Kentucky but grew up in Missouri. In 1949 she went to Paris where she met her husband, Dr David Hessayon, the creator of the bestselling *Expert* series of gardening books. They married in 1951 and share a love of history, plants and writing. Joan Hessayon's first novel was published in 1983. Her most recent novels, *Capel Bells*, *The Helmingham Rose* and *The Paradise Garden*, are also published by Corgi. She lives in north Essex and has two daughters and four grandchildren.

Praise for *The Paradise Garden*:

'I thoroughly enjoyed *The Paradise Garden*. Joan Hessayon's knowledge and interest in the world of business . . . the registration of old houses and particularly her vast knowledge of gardens and gardening, all touch upon real interests and influences in my life. I hope others enjoy this book as much as I did'
Sir John Harvey-Jones

'A good yarn about a lifestyle with which I could identify'
Daphne Ledward

'A delightful novel . . . a book of great charm'
Katie Boyle

'Her best yet – she is a born storyteller'
Fred Newman

www.booksattransworld.co.uk

SEASON OF MISTS

Joan Hessayon

CORGI BOOKS

SEASON OF MISTS
A CORGI BOOK : 0 552 14868 7

First publication in Great Britain

PRINTING HISTORY
Corgi edition published 2001

1 3 5 7 9 10 8 6 4 2

Set in 11/12pt Sabon by
Kestrel Data, Exeter, Devon.

Corgi Books are published by Transworld Publishers,
61–63 Uxbridge Road, London W5 5SA,
a division of The Random House Group Ltd,
in Australia by Random House Australia (Pty) Ltd,
20 Alfred Street, Milsons Point, Sydney, NSW 2061, Australia,
in New Zealand by Random House New Zealand Ltd,
18 Poland Road, Glenfield, Auckland 10, New Zealand
and in South Africa by Random House (Pty) Ltd,
Endulini, 5a Jubilee Road, Parktown 2193, South Africa.

Printed and bound in Great Britain by
Cox & Wyman Ltd, Reading, Berkshire.

This book is dedicated with love to Gill Jackson

ACKNOWLEDGEMENTS

I am indebted to a number of people for their help in producing this book. Cathy White, arboriculturist of Harlow, Essex, got me off to a good start. Melvyne Crow, Manager of Braintree Landscape and Countryside section, gave me so much of his time that he must be glad this book is finished.

As always Dr Steve Dowbiggen, chief executive of Capel Manor, has been generous with information and suggestions, as has Andrew Deane.

I am very grateful to Dr Mark Lyne, Dean of Science at Writtle College, and to Martin Stimson, head of Horticulture, for a wonderful day out at Writtle. My medical guru was Dr Timothy Baylis.

Angelina Gibbs set me on the right track in my researches into post-traumatic stress disorder.

Two policemen, PC Barry Schultz, Gosfield, and PC Steve Smith, Ipswich, and an ex-member of the Met, Dick Goodwin, were all very helpful on the subject of policing. Of course, in the end I had to make my policemen behave in a way that suited my story, rather than the more complex truth about the police.

As always, I am grateful to Gill Jackson for her

help and to my husband, Dave, who has made writing this book possible. I am fortunate to have Averil Ashfield as my copy editor, someone who is sympathetic to my style and intentions. Finally, my thanks, as always, to Di Pearson for her good advice and guidance and warm support.

PROLOGUE

12 September

September was proving to be as hot as August had been, and with as little rain. The polluted air was perfectly still, the temperature an exceptional eighty-one and thunderstorms had been forecast.

North Essex is a pretty, gently rolling part of England, without dramatic peaks and valleys, just hills that never exceed a few hundred feet, no matter how steep they might appear at times. The houses fit into the landscape with sensitivity and make the towns and villages a picturesque part of the country.

However, the three men sitting shoulder to shoulder on the bench seat of the old lorry were not in the mood to appreciate East Anglia's virtues, being more interested in its narrow roads, particularly the one that stretched up through the small town of Homestead, taking more traffic than it could hold and relying entirely on the goodwill of drivers to prevent disaster.

'Ought to build a ring road,' said Mel, a little weasel of a man with a shaved head. 'Bloody place.'

'That's typical of you, that is,' said Duggie.

'Just thinking of your own convenience, never mind the countryside. What do you care if the government bastards are always cutting down trees to build more roads? There won't be any trees left one of these days.'

Duggie had twisted his thick yellow hair into skimpy dreadlocks, had a gold stud through his nostril and a ring through his lip. There were eight coloured rings on his left ear, marching up the lobe. He fancied the idea of being an eco-warrior, but he played the part only occasionally, at weekends or when he had nothing better to do. In truth, he thought that camping out in the branches of a tree or tunnelling underground were activities too uncomfortable to be considered. He was, however, very articulate, able to bellow the warriors' view to police and journalists, which made him a welcome recruit at any protest.

'They're only doing their job. Making the roads safe. What we pay our taxes for.' Little Mel was squeezed between the two bigger men on the front seat of a 1985 four-wheel Leyland freighter with a rusty crane resting firmly at the back. The ride was uncomfortable and the cab smelled of fifteen years of sweat and grease. Along its side were the letters FRU, giving anyone who might be interested a chance to test their inventiveness in completing the name.

'You? Pay taxes? When did you ever pay taxes?' said Tommy the Turk. Neither Duggie nor Mel had any idea how Tommy acquired his nickname. As he was large, dark and of uncertain temper, they didn't intend to enquire.

'When I had a job I paid taxes. Couldn't help

10

it.' Mel sank further into his seat, keeping his eyes straight ahead as they turned left onto the Gorham Road.

Duggie wiped the sweat from his forehead with the back of his hand. 'Some oaks are hundreds of years old. They can live to a thousand and—'

Tommy slammed the flat of his hand on the dashboard. 'Shut up, for God's sake! You can hug a tree later. There it is! Just there! See that little lane? Turn there. Drive up to the lodge and let me off. Go on to the house and get the lorry close to the pool at the back of the house. The four statues are at each corner. Then wait for me. I'll have a word with the old man, then come down and do it.'

'We could get started,' offered Mel.

'Look,' said Tommy, putting a good deal of menace into his voice. 'Just because you stole this old thing don't mean you know how to operate it. Now do as I tell you.'

They reached the red brick lodge and Tommy leapt from the cab without waiting for the lorry to come to a full stop. An old man in black trousers, a collarless shirt and an unbuttoned waistcoat had opened the lodge door and now stood, all five feet of him, peering open-mouthed at the lorry. He seemed to have very few teeth.

Duggie kept his face averted as he sped on towards the beautiful but neglected Georgian house. A forest of six-inch-high sycamores had grown up in the rough grass to the east, but he noticed a fine old wellingtonia on the front lawn, a cedar of Lebanon to the right of the house and a number of oaks, some of them suffering from dieback, others dead, a few with trunks that could be ten feet around or more.

Turning right, he gunned the engine and drove over the hard dry lawn that someone had recently cut with a badly set mower, then up towards the lily pool behind the house. The pool, which must have been very beautiful at one time, was now half empty and clogged with leaves.

What he liked about the place was its air of decay, giving the trees a chance to grow unhindered by the hand of man. He thought this neglected garden must be a paradise for wildlife. Climbing down from the cab, he peered around, taking in the isolated position, the sheltering trees higher up the hill.

Unseen by Duggie, there was a movement among the trees to the north, a rustling among the undergrowth. But Duggie was too busy fighting his fear to notice that he and Mel were being spied upon.

The girl had been walking among the trees fifty feet higher up the hill from the pond, but she quickly hid behind a very large chestnut when she saw the men. Her heart pounded fiercely, for she was truly terrified. She had been led to believe that *they* had gone away for a few days. If she were found to be trespassing by the madman who owned Gorham House she couldn't imagine what would become of her. She therefore kept perfectly still behind the tree and stole only one or two glances at the new arrivals. It soon became obvious that the madman was not among them. These were three workmen come to remove some garden ornaments. Nevertheless, she was so shaken that she slipped down to sit on the warm

September earth for twenty minutes before she felt strong enough to continue her walk in the arboretum.

Four statues, apparently representing the four seasons, two males and two females, all fully dressed, stood sentinel at the four corners of the pool, each one six feet tall, blackened with age and splotched with green and gold lichen, their features weathered to a blur.

'How much did Tommy say these statues are worth?' asked Mel.

'Twenty thousand each, maybe more.' Duggie scanned the horizon, then turned to look at the house. He decided he wouldn't want the responsibility of this old place. It looked like it was falling down. Must cost a fortune to heat. Probably had lots of open fireplaces. There was a stack of firewood by the back door and lying on top of the logs was a chainsaw. Some bastard was committing the crime of cutting off the branches of beautiful trees just to keep himself warm and his fireplaces looking romantic.

Duggie was wondering what sort of trees had provided the logs, but just then Tommy rounded the corner of the house. He sprinted up the slope and joined Mel and Duggie at the back of the lorry by the levers which operated the crane.

'First you've got to anchor the lorry, let the legs down. If you don't anchor it, it could fall over. Then you can swing out the crane to pick up the statues. There. Now go over to the first one and put the straps around the waist. I'll lift.' They hurried to do his bidding and soon had the first of the statues on the back of the lorry.

They worked frenetically, sweating and

cursing. The ground was hard, perfect for their task, but Duggie, who could not concentrate on any task for very long, thought some of the plants were suffering from the month-long drought.

Having covered their treasure with tarpaulins, Mel and Duggie took a breather while Tommy brought the crane gently to rest on its plinth. Tommy reached the steering wheel first and Duggie glowered as he was forced to seat himself on the far side. Mel still got squeezed in the middle. It was a bumpy ride as Tommy drove at speed back onto the driveway, but the hard ground was scarcely marked by the lorry's sixteen tons, plus cargo.

As they left, their observer broke cover and ran up the hill, past fallen branches, brambles and tumbling leaves towards the neighbouring property.

The three men passed the lodge without pause; the old man was nowhere in sight. Tommy drove at a steady pace away from rural north Essex, down to their rendezvous at a caravan site on Canvey Island, manoeuvring his way south through the heavy traffic while never exceeding the speed limit nor drawing attention to the vehicle. Tommy gave every indication that he had done this sort of thing before, the cool professional compared to the excited amateurs. Tommy wore gloves. The others had not thought of this precaution.

There was virtually no conversation along the way, but what there was centred on the coup they had just pulled off. They were all high on adrenaline, all thinking about their share of the sale.

Duggie had never stolen anything more valuable than a few rolls of lead in all his nineteen years. He scratched his armpit and thought about how he had this day stolen not only a lorry but also four statues worth eighty thousand pounds.

Mel had been in trouble with the police in his teens, but now picked up whatever small jobs he could find on what he liked to call the Black Economy. At twenty-two, he was headed nowhere, like his friend Duggie. They lived in different parts of Bishop, had known each other for several years and got along very well. Nevertheless, Mel was baffled by Duggie's passion for trees and had never been converted to the cause.

Tommy the Turk was not known to either man. He had met them at their local, had taken their measure quickly and offered them a commission: steal a lorry with a crane and meet him in Homestead the following day. Duggie and Mel were anxious not to annoy Tommy who seemed to be somewhat unpredictable, a man who would be quick to express his annoyance with violence.

In little over an hour Tommy was once more operating the crane, this time unloading the statues into a lock-up before approaching a Portakabin to see the person he identified only as the Fat Man. Duggie and Mel hung about awkwardly, waiting for their money. Fat Man earned his nickname by being enormous, probably incapable of walking more than a few yards before he was out of breath, unable to turn his head because of the fat on his neck. He was also well over six feet tall with a mean expression. So when he gave them each fifty

15

pounds and waved them away, they were torn between greed and fear.

'But – ' said Duggie. 'We was promised a grand.'

The fat man looked at them with contempt. 'Not by me, you wasn't. I've lost my buyer for these things. I'll have to hold onto them. That's a risk.' He peeled off a ten-pound note for each of them. 'Go on. Get rid of the lorry. Put some petrol on it and burn it. Make sure there are no prints left. Take it back close to where you stole it.'

With that they had to be satisfied. They understood that they had taken part in a robbery of goods worth eighty thousand pounds for which they had been given a mere sixty pounds each. They had risked their freedom and they had been cheated.

Duggie drove away furiously, clashing the gears as he swore loudly. There followed a short, bitter quarrel about who had been responsible for getting the other involved in such a fiasco. Nothing resolved, the men fell silent for half an hour.

Duggie broke the silence. 'Bastards!' But he was speaking more to himself than to his companion.

'You said it. I'm never getting mixed up in anything like that again. No way.'

'I was talking about the Chinese.'

'Chinese!' cried Mel. 'For God's sake! What have they ever done to you?'

'Long-horned beetle. Comes in from China in infected wood, crawls out, starts drilling holes in trees. There's no cure and it could be a worse disaster than Dutch elm disease. We lost fifteen million trees from Dutch elm disease.'

'Go on. Must be more like one and a half million. You got your decimal point in the wrong place. Can't have been fifteen million. Anyway, it was before my time. Wasn't it? Forget about it. We get along without them all right, don't we?' He began to bite his nails. 'I was counting on that money. I've got a few bills to pay.'

'It's terrible in parts of America and the first beetle was spotted here ten years ago. Bastards!' Duggie was silent a moment, then brightened. 'I got an idea. I know where there are some garden ornaments. Not big like the ones we just lifted and not old, neither. But there's some big urns and that. We could take them, store them in my lock-up garage and after a while sell them at a car boot sale.'

Mel sucked his lower lip for a moment. 'Risky. How do we know the people won't come home while we're doing it?'

'It's perfect, really. These people go away for the whole of September, stop their mail, have no deliveries. They don't even trust their gardener to come in and tidy up. We could take the stuff and sell it before anybody reports it missing.'

'How close to Bishop? It's not in Gorham, is it? We wouldn't want to turn over two places in Gorham.'

'The house I'm talking about is sort of in Gorham, but set well back. My lock-up's in Sible Hedingham. We can unload real quick.'

Mel beamed. 'Hide the lorry somewhere until after dark, then unload when nobody's around. Then dump the lorry like that Tub of Lard said.'

'Yeah, make ourselves a few quid. I can get my uncle's pickup. We'll take the stuff to Hertfordshire. Won't sell it around here. Show those bastards.'

They talked animatedly for the next half an hour, reliving their recent adventure and planning what they would spend their money on, until they reached the turn-off that Duggie said led to the unoccupied house. The Hoo, though every bit as secluded as Gorham House, was a totally different sort of property. A Tudor-type red brick mansion which had been built at the turn of the century, it had been renovated with much money and imagination within the past year. The stoneware which decorated the grounds was all new, all of it of the ground stone variety produced by mass-market manufacturers.

Duggie knew, however, that many of the pieces were worth hundreds of pounds. And there were at least twenty items worth stealing, none of them very heavy. He knew this because he had picked up a little cash by helping the gardener to put them in place. There was no need to tangle with the complexities of the crane, as they could carry the items away quite easily. He mentioned as much to his mate.

'Aw, now, I'm not so sure.' Mel was six inches shorter than Duggie and half his weight. He looked unfit. 'I've had back trouble for months. I'm not about to cause myself any more aggro. We've got the crane. We should use it.'

Duggie shrugged. 'OK. I'll drive down to the walled garden. That's what I helped to fix up. It's a formal garden. Lots of little curlicues

18

of hedging about a foot high and all sorts of classical figures and urns and things.'

They reached a wrought-iron gate in the wall and Mel jumped out to open it. The garden needed weeding, he saw, but it was pretty with narrow gravel paths and spaces created by the hedging, which were filled in with pink geraniums, now past their prime. In the centre of the design stood a naked figure of a woman clutching a towel which she held between her breasts, partially hiding her non-existent pubic hair.

'I can get her from here!' cried Duggie excitedly. He would send the crane out over the six-foot wall, but had positioned the lorry so that he could operate the controls while keeping an eye on progress through the opened gate. 'Don't worry!' he called. 'The crane will extend that far.'

He jumped from the cab and went to the controls at the back. Slowly, the crane swung out about ten or eleven feet, but this was still short of the distance needed. Duggie found the lever which controlled the boom extension and quietly the business end of the crane inched its way towards the statue. Even with the boom fully extended, they were a foot or two short of their goal. Mel said not to worry, he could manage. He took the lifting straps and stretched them to encompass the naked lady's waist.

'Hoist away!' Mel looked skywards. 'Better make it pretty quick. I think it's going to rain.'

Duggie squinted at the black clouds that were rapidly gathering. 'Piece of cake.'

He operated the lever. The straps strained but the statue showed no signs of giving way. He pulled harder. 'Must be stuck!' Suddenly, he felt some movement. The lorry's offside wheels had left the ground.

'Christ!' yelled Mel. 'It's going to fall over!'

Duggie panicked, caught so completely by surprise that he couldn't for the moment think what to do. By the time he remembered that he should have lowered the legs, it was too late. The lorry toppled over on its side knocking down the garden gate, fifteen feet of the beautiful old brick wall and, incidentally, two very nice stone urns. The naked lady, however, stayed safely on her plinth, unmoved by the drama being enacted around her.

'Aw, shit!' said Duggie. There was a clap of thunder and it began to rain.

CHAPTER ONE

5 August

The village of Gorham, north Essex, rests on rather flatter ground than does the neighbouring town of Homestead. It has about a thousand residents, two pubs, a village store, a newsagent, a splendid village hall and a broad recreation ground. Trees abound. Drivers take the winding roads too fast for safety, but generally the residents feel secure among their neighbours. The sense of community is strong.

On the whole Edwina Fairfax, at twenty-one, and three days into her first job since gaining a qualification in tree work, was pleased to have taken a small mortgage on a bungalow among Gorham's quiet citizens. Her office was just ten minutes away in Bishop, but her duties would often have her out and about in Gorham and Homestead and several other villages, giving her what she considered to be a perfect way of life, one spent mostly in the open air.

Her boss, John Blue, was manager of the landscape and countryside section of the planning department. She had been employed on a one-year fixed contract to look after the trees in this relatively small area, but she had been given reason to believe that the short contract would lead to a permanent job if she performed well.

Bishop council, John had explained, covered a large area, from the outskirts of Chelmsford, widening up to Sudbury one way and to Haverhill the other. Two hundred and fifty square miles. This was a lot of territory for the staff to cover. Therefore, they frequently gave short contracts to promising young people. The pay was low, but everyone benefited. The young person gained experience, while the council gained an extra pair of hands.

The landscape and countryside section dealt with all statutory work related to trees and land-scaping within the district. Naturally, they dealt with tree preservation orders, trees in conser-vation areas, the new hedgerow regulations and legislation relating to dangerous trees. The section also advised on development sites. And they offered advice to the general public which added to their workload, but provided tree owners with sound guidance.

As if that were not enough, they implemented environmental schemes and operated a country-side management project in the River Colne Valley. The work of the section was so far-reaching that Edwina really believed her one-year contract would lead to a permanent job. Council employees were always overloaded. She was fortunate not to have been given more responsi-bility than she could handle. For the moment, she was delighted with her comparatively small area and limited remit.

She was passionate about the environment and

impatient with those who had other priorities. She knew that 1999 had been globally the hottest on record, knew that the trees were coming into leaf earlier than ever before, that birds were nesting earlier in the year. She could see around her the stress caused to trees by years of drought, but she knew also that she loved to feel the hot sun on her back, responding to the warmth, feeling more alive because of it. So happy was she that sometimes she forgot to worry about the well-being of the world and for hours at a time revelled in the beautiful East Anglian countryside, so different from her native west country, before guiltily remembering that she should be deeply depressed by the destruction of the environment.

The Escort was second-hand, a major purchase which took a sizeable bite out of her grand-mother's legacy, so dark a green that it looked black except in strong sunlight. As she waited to make a right turn, the narrow Gorham Road held a few cars – one, impatient to be off, was revving its engine behind the Escort as two others rounded the bend at high speed from the opposite direction. When they had passed, she turned into Bread Lane and parked a few yards from the corner, hoping that anyone wishing to drive down the lane would be able to do so while keeping well away from her paintwork.

Like the heroine in an old spy movie, she glanced furtively in all directions, making sure that there was no-one in sight before opening the car door. A mild contortion to collect a three-rung ladder from the back seat, then a neat one-handed vault over the four-foot-high brick and flint wall and she was almost upon her objective, a beech of about sixty feet which on this beautiful day of the fifth of August had lost most but not all of its leaves. Bare brittle branches reaching upwards were outlined bleakly against the cloudless sky. The lower branches stretched horizontally and hung over the lane and over the grassy footpath along Gorham Road. Beech trees were notorious for being unable to withstand strong winds, as they were shallow-rooted. When growing on open ground, they expanded so that they had a sturdy canopy. When, as here, they were closely planted with other trees, they stretched upwards towards the light, making them less stable. This one had been fortunate to escape the storms of '87 and '89 in the days when it was healthy. Now that it was dying, the owners wanted to have it felled.

It was within Edwina's power to recommend giving permission to fell or withholding it, but she was not sure what to do. While she should have knocked on the door of Barleytwist Hall and told the Brooms that she had come to take another look at their beech tree, she didn't feel confident enough to do so, preferring to sneak around like a criminal until she could come up with the best reply to their request. On the first occasion that she had seen the tree, Mr Broom had not stopped talking for one minute. New to the work and anxious to do well, she had felt pressured to agree to its felling. Just five minutes' close inspection in peace and quiet should reassure her that she was not sacrificing a valuable tree by coming to this decision.

As the property was defined on two sides by roads, one a sleepy lane which drew those who loved to walk, the other a busy thoroughfare, the trees on the boundary were an important part of the scenery, seen by those passing by, and therefore subject to council restrictions. But a dangerous tree on such a busy corner could spell disaster. Dangerous trees had to be felled, and if the owner was disinclined to fell it, the council would do it for him and send him the bill. On the other hand, what if every slightly unsafe tree were sacrificed? The countryside might soon look ugly and bare. The decision was Edwina's and she felt the full force of her power as she tried to come to the right one.

Many people believed they had a right to decide for themselves when to cut down one of their own trees. They thought the business of getting permission was irritating red tape and interference in the lives and property of honest citizens.

Needless to say, Edwina thought all trees belonged to the entire country, their value to the environment too important to be left in the unsafe hands of amateurs. Many varieties lived far longer than people did, yet couldn't speak up for themselves, so why shouldn't they be protected by the law? Trees had rights. In her new job she intended to be a scourge to the ignorant, and would do her best to ensure that her part of north Essex continued to be leafy and beautiful.

She had been given strict, detailed orders about her duties and powers during the term of her contract. Therefore, she knew perfectly well that she had no business on private property without the owners' permission. Yet she was certain that if he discovered her, Mr Broom would not be angry. He seemed a very nice man, if a trifle garrulous.

Barleytwist Hall was a sixteenth-century red brick farmhouse that must have been quite humble at one time, but had been added on to during the nineteenth century so that it was now a hotchpotch of styles and building materials, its middle black and white work, its two ends built, most likely, of the ugly beige brick that was predominant in the area. Over the years, the owners had tied the whole together with a bright white paint that would not have been known in the sixteenth century. Only purists were likely to cavil, however, since the dazzling paint blended the different parts together so that it now made a rather grand, attractive home. It was surrounded by a dozen acres, all of them landscaped in the manner of Capability Brown. Flowers didn't figure largely in the scheme, but there were many rare old trees, all of them well managed.

The owners were a retired broker and his wife who had sold their Mayfair flat several years previously and come to live in this large property. Edwina had liked both Mr and Mrs Broom, who were a trifle more obviously 'countrified' than their neighbours who had lived in Gorham all their lives. They were gracious and welcoming, touchingly determined to abide by the law.

As she had taken this job in defiance of her parents' wishes, she must now be seen to have succeeded beyond all doubt, and hoped for quick promotion or, failing that, a commendation from someone for some act of brilliance, perhaps even a small piece with photo in the local paper.

Unfortunately, there were not too many ways for an arboriculturist to gain attention, so she must exploit what opportunities there were.

Hence the stealthy approach on this hot day. The crown of the beech was no more than ten feet above ground, an easy climb. Properly, she ought not even to consider climbing a tree that might be dead, unless there was a ground man controlling the ropes and she was wearing a regulation harness and hard hat. That was the textbook approach. However, she thought she could make her inspection easily enough by hauling herself up from the top step of the little ladder, then be gone before anyone saw her.

Quickly, she mounted the light ladder and pulled herself up to stand at the crown. Holding on to the main stem, she put one foot out to test the strength of the lowest branch. The tree, she decided, could be trimmed to make it safe and might even have a few more years of life left in it. She would send the Brooms a list of approved tree surgeons, secure in the knowledge that she had done the right thing. The point had been made to her most forcefully that the resident must be happy to do as she suggested while the council must be convinced that she was preventing the rape of the countryside.

Moving further out on the branch, she gave one last little bounce for good measure. There was a crack like gunfire and the branch broke away about a foot from the trunk. Although she still had her hand on the main stem, it was too large to clutch effectively. She couldn't save herself. Landing on the ground with a yelp, her spine badly jolted, she hardly dared to hope that she had escaped unhurt. Mercifully, neither the branch nor the ladder had come down on top of her.

Several seconds elapsed before the pain started. She tried to move her left leg, but it was trapped. With shaking hands, she felt along her lower leg. Nothing broken, surely, but on impact her foot had driven directly into a rabbit hole and was stuck fast well above her ankle bone. The direction of the hole meant that her foot was pointed downwards, causing the collar of her boot to dig into the back of her ankle. Her head was spinning and she wished desperately to lie back for a moment to catch her breath and wait for her heart to stop racing. Yet her only relief was to lean forward. She tried to raise herself to her hands and knees, but seemed to have lost her co-ordination as well as her strength. Cars whizzed past the Broom property at dangerous speeds. From her position on the ground, she knew no-one could see her. Her hands began to sting, informing her that she had landed among nettles, and her right cheek throbbed where twigs from a nearby holly had grazed her. Her fingers came away from a delicate exploration smeared with blood.

Her first thought was to thank God for small mercies. Her father had not seen her climb a rotten tree without proper safety precautions, had not seen her fall as a result of her own stupidity. Several things, it then occurred to her, could happen next. She could get her foot out of the rabbit hole without help or she could be discovered trespassing by the Brooms or she could be left here all night.

The panic these thoughts induced caused her to writhe ineffectually like a rabbit in a snare. The hole was so small she wondered how her foot had ever managed to penetrate it, but by tearing feverishly at the turf and soil she managed to free herself within a couple of minutes.

Wincing, she bent over to gather up the ladder from the ground. She had been on the Broom property for some minutes and was very worried that Mr Broom would come out to see what was going on. Hobbling as fast as she could, she dragged the ladder behind her, then managed to toss it over the wall. It landed some distance away, quite close to the car. Now all she had to do was to get herself over the wall and she could be away.

She had vaulted over the four feet of brick and flint on arrival but the return journey was not to be so easy. Her ankle was extremely painful and her arms were quivering. If only she had not thrown the ladder out of reach! The wall was very old and leaning at such an angle, she wondered if her weight would cause it to collapse. Nevertheless, she would have to lie across it and let herself down on the other side. To be caught trespassing would be bad enough. To cause some damage to a very old wall would probably end her budding career.

As it was too unpleasant to bring her full weight to bear on the tender left ankle, she lifted that leg first, lying at full stretch on her tummy along the wall before managing to squiggle over. Her tender ankle was now the one on which she had to put her weight. It failed to support her and she landed in a heap on the ground where she gathered a few more scratches.

But from this position she had an excellent view of the police car that had drawn up directly behind her Escort. She tried to get to her feet quickly, but her body would not co-operate as a young policeman got out of the car and came over to offer her a hand up.

'Is this your T-reg?'

'Yes.'

'What were you doing on this property?'

'If you will just bear with me . . .' She limped to the car, opened the door and retrieved her heavy black handbag. It took her only a minute to find some identification. 'My name is Edwina Fairfax and I am an assistant to John Blue at Bishop council.'

He returned her card with a smile. 'You're limping. Is it your ankle?'

'Yes, it went into a rabbit hole. I fell out of a tree.'

'Shouldn't you have been wearing a harness and hard hat? And shouldn't you have parked your car in the Broom driveway and let them know you wanted to look at their tree?'

'Yes, I know, but trespassing isn't a crime, is it? A misdemeanour, perhaps, but not a crime.' She smiled at him, hoping to charm him out of a scolding. 'I'm new to the job. I just wanted to have a little peek at this tree to make sure I can give the right advice. I didn't want the Brooms to know that I was coming back to check again, because I think an experienced professional would be able to come to a decision on the first visit.'

He grinned broadly. 'Probably a wise move. You live at 22 Plumpton Avenue, don't you? I am Felix Trent, your community policeman, and I was planning to call on you today or tomorrow. We're neighbours. Besides, I make it my business to try to know everyone on my beat. Can you drive, do you think, or shall I drive you home?'

'Oh, yes, my ankle doesn't bother me at all.' It was throbbing. 'I'll phone the Brooms on Monday and tell them what I have decided. I've finished work for the day. It's that beech over there that they want taken down. But I'm just going to let them top it. There might be a few more years left in it.'

He squinted up at the tree. 'It looks dead to me and it's right by the road. I'd hate to be called to an accident here and find that tree lying across a car.'

'No, but . . .' Edwina was now struck by doubt. Perhaps he was right.

'Bob Broom has spotted us.' Felix Trent nodded towards the house. 'You can tell him your decision right now.'

'Hello there!' called Mr Broom, panting up the slight incline. A handsome man in his early seventies, he walked with a slight stoop, his legs bowing with age. Wearing brown cord trousers and a yellow waistcoat, he looked like a wealthy weekend countryman.

Edwina turned to face him, taking a deep breath before pinning a smile on her face. 'Hello, Mr Broom! I was just driving round, getting to know the area, when I thought I saw that a branch had come off the tree we discussed yesterday.'

'Dear me, it is dangerous, then. Do say we can take it down.'

'Er, yes, all right. Do you know of a tree surgeon? Someone you use regularly?'

'Yes, old Hargreaves and one of his sons.' He walked over to the tree. 'Good God! Did this come down? It might have killed someone. I don't know what my insurers would say.'

'Yes, well, take it down.' She chewed her lip. Not exactly the cool, calm way she had intended to make a decision.

Barleytwist Hall was not so large as Gorham House, the old mansion several hundred yards along the road, but it was certainly in better condition. There were hundreds of trees on the property. One beech, at the end of its useful life, would not be missed.

'Well done!' said the policeman when they were alone. 'I thought you would refuse to have the tree down. Sometimes people lose sight of the broader picture. You did what was best in the circumstances.'

She blushed with pleasure. 'Do you think so?'

His remarks convinced her that she had made the wrong decision, because who would take the advice of a policeman about saving a tree? Yet she was anxious to avoid a quarrel. 'I guess I can see his point of view. Insurance. Danger to passers-by.'

'Look,' he said. 'Why don't I follow you home? I'd like to get to know you. Because you're on my beat and . . . and . . .'

'We're neighbours,' she finished for him, smiling. 'I promise not to go over the speed limit.'

They got into their cars and were home in three

minutes. The policeman parked in the drive of his own home and walked down to hers.

'Very nice,' he said, nodding at her bungalow. 'The Stouffers were an elderly couple and they kept it in good condition. Mine needs painting on the outside, I know. But that will have to wait, because I've done a lot on the inside. Have you found your way around Homestead yet?'

'No, everything was done in such a rush. I mean the bungalow came up for sale and I grabbed it, didn't even get a survey. My parents were . . . You know, I didn't catch your first name.'

'Felix.'

'Well, Felix, tomorrow being Saturday, I thought I'd have a wander round.'

'It's quite a good shopping area. Not many chains.'

'I like small shops.'

'More variety, keeps the community alive,' he said, doing his best, it seemed, to keep the conversation going.

'I'll have to let you know what I think of them.'

'Good idea! Well, I'll be off.'

She watched as he walked back to his home, then went directly to her kitchen where she made an ice pack from six cubes and a tea towel to put on the tender ankle, made herself a cup of tea and hobbled to the settee. At half past six when the doorbell rang, she was able to walk almost normally to the door.

PC Felix Trent, now in civilian clothes, smiled at her. 'It occurred to me that you might not know many people in the neighbourhood.'

She laughed. 'I don't know anyone.'

'I could call for you tomorrow evening about half six. Saturday night is usually pretty lively at the Prince of Wales. We could have dinner, meet my best friend and his wife. Harriet and Greg Squiller. He's a sergeant, CID. You'd like Harriet, I imagine.'

'Yes. OK. I'm not doing anything on Saturday night, needless to say.' She giggled nervously, then nodded her head, trying to sound cool. 'That's very kind of you. What time?'

'Still half past six.'

'Oh yes. I'm sorry. You did say.' She could feel the heat in her face. Why did she have to sound like such an idiot, just because a man was asking her out? 'Six thirty. Here?' He nodded. They stood looking at each other, two strangers with nothing much to talk about. Perhaps he was already regretting his invitation.

Eventually she mumbled her way to a second goodbye and Felix walked back towards his home. He seemed very self-possessed, which probably was the result of being a policeman. As for herself, she needed a cup of tea to accompany her sense of delight and amazement. This was a turning point, the beginning of a proper social life in the real world. He liked her! Liked her well enough to ask her for a meal, at any rate.

What would her parents think of that? Her father had always called her boy crazy, saying she was desperate for approval from the opposite sex, but this was surely different.

During this past week, she had been lonely. Living in a home of one's own and driving six or seven miles to work each day was not at all like living at college. At Capel Manor there had always been people around, and after classes she had been able to tuck herself in among her fellow students, to stand on the fringes of the crowd, laughing when others did and, always, volunteering for any sporting activity. Sport was Edwina's way in, her passport to a sense of belonging.

But like all good things, her one-year course had come to an end. She had moved into this house in a quiet neighbourhood and had already begun to wonder if she would ever meet anyone. It was a bonus that the policeman was very good-looking. However, if he had two heads she would still have said yes.

Zena Alway had enjoyed a reputation for elegance for the best part of eighty-five years and old age had not dimmed her interest in looking smart. She straightened the collar of her black linen dress and touched up the aqua chiffon scarf at her throat as she took the empty seat at a small table in Maureen's Tea Room.

'How nice to see you, dear,' she said with more warmth than she felt. 'How are you today?'

This casual question was a mistake, she knew. Claris Binns was a year younger than Zena, at eighty-four, and irritated her friend by never missing an opportunity to remind the world of her complaints. Zena thought it was rude and boring to go on about one's physical state. Who, in her eighties, could boast of perfect health?

'I've had rheumatism in my right hand for a week now. I can't sleep at night sometimes. I had to have two paracetamols before I went to bed and two more at two o'clock this morning.'

'I'm sorry to hear that. Have you seen Prunella lately?'

Prunella Jenkins was the absent member of the little trio of school chums who had survived all the others. They had gone their separate ways in their youth, Zena to marry a solicitor, Claris to marry a butcher and Prunella to marry a vicar and move away. But old age had reunited them. The Reverend Jenkins had come back to Homestead as vicar of St Bartholomew, but two years later he was dead, leaving Prunella back where her life had begun.

The three women had survived their various sorrows and adventures and now they needed each other. Zena had bought her meat from Calvin Binns in the days when there were several real butchers in the town. She had worshipped in the church of the Reverend Jenkins in the days when the town could sustain two Anglican churches. They had come together on many a charitable committee where class and money played no part. However, only in the past five years when Claris joined the other two in widowhood had they sat down at the same table.

'I spoke to her on the phone. Her asthma's bad. She's getting old, a bit forgetful.' Claris picked up the menu and studied it carefully.

'Getting silly, you mean.' Zena didn't like Prunella very much although – or perhaps because – she had known her better than Claris. 'She ought to take care of herself. She's got a moustache like Fu Manchu.' Claris gave no indication of having heard this little witticism, so Zena repeated it. 'Like Fu Manchu. I could never let myself go like that. Are you going to have a full tea or just a pot and a cake?'

'Well,' wheezed Claris, 'if I have a full afternoon tea now I won't have to bother cooking this evening. Just some fruit and some pot noodles. I do like pot noodles. So easy to fix. Do you eat them?'

'No, I don't! How disgusting. Really, Claris, you ought to eat more healthily. I—' Zena broke off to smile at the Baxter girl who had started working in the tea room three weeks ago. 'We'll both have the full afternoon tea, Mary.'

'Tracey,' corrected the girl gently. 'Two full teas.'

'I don't like sitting by the window,' said Zena. 'I feel as if I'm on display, like the spider plants. They shouldn't put them in the window, by the way. Too sunny. Isn't it hot? But you like the hot weather.'

'Yes, I do.' Claris took an embroidered handkerchief from her handbag and gently patted her forehead and upper lip. 'I'm fortunate in having such a cool apartment. You must be sweltering in your tiny rooms.'

Zena sucked in her breath, trying to control her annoyance. 'I'm perfectly comfortable in my tiny rooms, thank you, and I can always step outside onto my patio or move into my garden, under the trees. Gardens always have somewhere cool to sit.'

Claris, having lost this little exchange, looked out of the window. The tea arrived and the two elderly women sat quietly as the Baxter girl (Teresa? Mary? Zena couldn't remember) laid out all the paraphernalia of afternoon tea – pot, milk, hot water, sugar, small plates, and a large plate of sandwiches, all crowded onto the small round table that could not comfortably accommodate so much.

Zena, whose treat it was, reached for the pot. She refused to put the milk in the cups first because it was common. Claris always did so because she knew no better. I'm getting cranky, thought Zena. I shouldn't notice such things.

On the other hand, she felt she was perfectly entitled to notice that she had not put on weight all her life, as Claris had, and could wear attractive size ten dresses, provided they didn't have tight waistlines. They always needed shortening, of course. Zena had shrunk by about four inches and was now less than five feet tall. Claris, on the other hand, always looked a mess and had to buy her clothes in an outsize shop. And the outfit she had chosen today was a polyester print in shades of orange, yellow and lime! Zena suppressed a smile as she held out the plate of sandwiches.

Claris helped herself to three. 'Tomorrow I'm going on the coach to London to see *Les Misérables*. Would you like to go?'

'Been there, done that, got the T-shirt,' said Zena.

Claris glared. 'You won't eat pot noodles, but you do use the most awful slang.'

'I enjoy keeping language fresh. English is . . . what are you looking at?'

'There! Aren't they your new neighbours? Look, look! Just crossing the road. We call them the odd couple. Some of the women in my block of flats do at any rate.'

'Well, they don't look odd today,' snapped

Zena. She wondered why she had such a short fuse these days. She wished she had thought of calling them the odd couple, because it suited them perfectly. 'They're a striking pair, don't you think? She is absolutely gorgeous. I call them beauty and the beast.'

'Hmm. Undernourished, but I agree with you. She is beautiful. Tall and with that long blond hair, she could be a model or an actress. He gives me the creeps, though. He's sort of like a wolf. That jawline! My goodness, but he's a frightening character. I wouldn't want to live near them. Why on earth did they buy Gorham House? It's falling down.'

Zena wondered the same thing herself. Mr Cartwright had previously owned the mansion. He had died six months ago at ninety-five, having failed to make any repairs on the house for the past forty years. It had lain empty since his death, and Zena had not seen it advertised in *Country Life*. Then one day the odd couple had moved in. She supposed the deal had been completed privately with whoever had inherited it. And they probably got it for a song. There was no central heating, she knew that for a fact. The wiring was probably in a dangerous condition, too.

Zena certainly wouldn't want it. She had bought the pair of estate cottages further up the lane from the House just after James died six years ago. She had the two knocked together and now lived cosily in crowded rooms, surrounded by her possessions from a much larger house.

'I can't remember their names, but—'

'Good heavens!' crowed Claris. 'How can you forget a name like Midnight?'

'I meant their first names,' lied Zena. 'Of course I couldn't forget a name like Midnight. I just wonder if it is an alias. Midnight. Sounds fishy.'

'They're Leo and Cassandra. Millicent told me. Can't think of *her* last name, I admit. Works mornings in the bakery. Anyway, the odd couple are from London. Probably won the Lottery. He doesn't do anything, but they're hardly the sort to have inherited money from Mummy and Daddy.'

'He could be a trader in the City. City types used to be gentlemen, but they aren't any more. Nowadays they just have to be young and predatory. They make obscene sums of money and I'm told they like to buy places in the country. Not that Homestead is exactly in the country. It's a market town, however, and—'

'Gorham House is not in Homestead!'

'I know that,' snapped Zena. 'I live next door, remember? But the village of Gorham practically runs into Homestead. That's what I meant. More tea?'

As she poured, she glanced at the Midnights strolling down the High Street, gloomy and seemingly as unaware of other people on the pavement as they were of each other. She shivered. They were going to be trouble. He was tall and rangy with black hair and eyes and a permanent five o'clock shadow. Somewhere between forty and forty-five and capable of violence, she felt sure. The wife was much younger. Early twenties and with a distracted, vague air about her.

'Charmless,' said Zena. 'Let me tell you what they did to me as soon as . . .' she struggled for the name. 'As soon as the Baxter girl brings us the cakes.'

Homestead High Street was very steep, probably had a gradient of one in ten. Leo Midnight took the sunglasses from his shirt pocket and wearily put them on. Damned small town. None of the chains you'd expect to see, except Boots. Cassandra had been moaning all morning. She liked shopping. Thought of little else. But even Colchester was too small for her taste. They'd have to go to London for everything they needed for the house. Or so she said. He just might have something to say about that. He shouldn't have moved to the country and was already seeing the disadvantages. And he certainly shouldn't have taken on a huge responsibility like Gorham House.

Cassandra stopped and turned round. 'It's no good, Leo. We are going to have to go into London. I don't care if it does take two hours to get there. I'm used to the big city and—'

'I know what you're used to.'

She had glorious hair, long, blond and absolutely straight, thirty-four-inch hips, perky breasts and a face that had photographers gasping. Before they met, she had earned a bit of money posing in the altogether for amateur photographers, but it had never earned her enough even to keep her in make-up. These days, of course, she preferred spending his money.

Dressed now in a strappy blue patterned dress that reached her ankles, she was turning heads. He lusted after that body, but he had long since learned to hate the person who owned it. Stupid bitch. Hadn't a thought in her head. Cared for nobody but herself.

Leo knew he was different from Cassandra. He cared for nobody and that *included* himself. The world had lost its taste for Leo Midnight, unemployed, not a damned thing to do in this world, and sufficiently well off not even to have to think about it. It was enough to make a grown man weep and sometimes, when Cassandra wasn't around, he did.

'If there's nothing you want, we might as well go home,' he said, taking her by the arm.

She smiled up at him, moving close enough to rub her breast against his arm. 'Only if you take me out to dinner tonight.'

'Too right!' he laughed. 'I've no intention of sampling your cooking.'

Cassandra liked his old low-slung MG. She always giggled like a child when he gunned the loud engine. They drove the short distance to Gorham House, turning into the unmade lane too fast for Leo to keep full control. The car skidded slightly, sending up a cloud of dust. Within seconds they were within two feet of the rear of Zena's Rover as she drove at five miles an hour towards her cottage further up the lane.

Cassandra reached across and sounded the horn, keeping her hand on it for several seconds. Zena's car sped forward.

'Jumped like someone kicked her in the arse,' she said, giggling.

'She's too old to be driving and that car's too powerful for her.' Leo drove close enough to touch her bumper.

Zena put her foot down, lurched forward and

42

drove the car into the nearside hedge where she turned off the engine and waited for the Midnights to make a left turn onto their own property. She was shaking so much she had trouble restarting the engine once they were gone.

'Swines!' she muttered. 'Why do they do this to me? I've never harmed them. It's getting so I'm afraid to drive to and from my own house.'

The remainder of the day didn't go any better for her. She sat down in her recliner in the sitting room, intending to read the paper. However, sleep overtook her and she dozed until it was time to watch the six o'clock news. Afterwards, she went into the kitchen to prepare a sardine salad which she ate with a glass of red wine and a piece of wholemeal bread.

There was nothing to watch on television as usual. She surfed the terrestrial channels, then the satellite ones, but nothing appealed. Suddenly remembering that she had changed the sheets that morning but forgotten to bring the dirty ones down from the bedroom, she went upstairs to fetch them. The steep cottage stairs left her breathless so that she was not totally in control of her legs as she started back downstairs with her arms full of sheets and pillowcases. Her foot caught on the corner of a dangling sheet, causing her to sit down heavily on the edge of one stair. Somehow the bulk of the sheets got under her and she slid the rest of the way down, finishing up at the bottom of the stairs having travelled all the way on her backside. She was in pain but seemingly not seriously hurt. She burst into tears of anger, fear and frustration. If she had broken her hip, would her neighbours have come to her rescue? Not that she had any way of letting them know if she were hurt. Nothing broken, she thought, but she bruised easily and would be very stiff the next day.

'I don't want to be old and I don't want to be alone,' she said out loud. 'If I can't have James, I want to be dead.'

A small sherry revived her. She was rather too inclined to turn to alcohol, but she didn't care. She was tired of living, sick to death of doing today what she had done the day before, what she would be doing tomorrow. Standing at the mirror that morning to arrange her scarf, it had suddenly occurred to her that she had arranged a thousand scarves in front of a thousand mirrors and that she was rather bored by it.

The television quickly sent her to sleep in her recliner, and she woke only when her head had flopped to the side and the strain on her neck had become too great. Straightening her head slowly, her eyes gradually focused on two undressed young women simulating the ecstasies of sex on the television.

'Been there, done that, got the T-shirt,' she muttered, reaching for the remote control. It was two o'clock in the morning. Nevertheless, she took one of her sleeping pills, dreading the possibility of a few hours of miserable wakefulness.

The remainder of the night was filled with vivid dreams: James was alive but fading away, her daughter was with her in the cottage instead of far away in Kuala Lumpur, although even in her dreams still heartbreakingly argumentative. This most disturbing dream seemed to go on for ever and was broken only by a loud high-pitched buzz outside.

Zena opened her eyes and squinted at the large figures on her bedside clock. Five in the morning and the sound was that of a chainsaw! Throwing off the light blanket, she staggered to the window. There was activity, but she couldn't see what was going on. She had two acres of land, most of it between her cottage and Gorham House. Elsewhere she was surrounded by ploughed fields. Fred, the elderly gardener who had tended the grounds at her previous home, came once a week to tidy the beds near the house and mow the small lawn, but the rest of the property was covered in trees. Until this moment, she had rejoiced in the privacy they gave her. Through her own small clump of conifers and laurels, she could see some of the trees on the Midnight property. Several tall trees were dead and would have fallen down if not held at a perilous angle by their proximity to other, living ones.

She needed her binoculars which sat on the kitchen counter so that she could watch the birds from the window. Still fuzzy-headed from the sleeping pill, she staggered down the steep stairs, clinging to the handrail, then shuffled barefooted into the kitchen to retrieve the glasses and hang them around her neck.

Upstairs once more, she had an excellent vantage point for spying down on the Gorham House property and soon focused on the sound of the chainsaw. That evil-looking Leo Midnight was sawing a branch off one of her trees! Outrage made her dizzy. Why would he do such a thing? And at five in the morning! He *was* evil. Perhaps he was coming for her. Chainsaw massacre. But no, that was ridiculous. It was all just part of the plot to get her out of her cottage. That was it. They wanted her out so that she couldn't see what they were up to. She was very, very afraid of them.

However, she vowed she would not be beaten so easily. After all, she had nowhere else to go. She must show the bulldog spirit and fight back. She knew a few tricks. Heart pounding with excitement, she contemplated her revenge for all the times he had harassed her as she drove up the lane. She would sue. She would take him to court. She would, at the very least, inform against him.

Whatever was he doing now? Taking the branch of her tree and dumping it back on her property! The swine! The animal! She dropped the binoculars to her lap, so filled with rage that it was difficult to draw breath. All the anger she had felt for the past few years, as well as the unending sorrow over the death of her favourite daughter, Alice, at twenty, Flora's angry departure for Kuala Lumpur, James's death, were now focused on one man, her arch-enemy, Leo Midnight.

CHAPTER TWO

Returning from an early visit to Homestead on Saturday morning, Edwina stooped to pick up her post. She was grateful for the first junk mail. It was too early to expect letters from her friends, so the brightly coloured brochures advertising outsize clothes, bedroom slippers that opened like sardine tins and discreet commodes were proof that somebody knew where she lived and cared enough to pay the postage.

The small sitting room with its big picture window led directly into the pine kitchen, and there were two bedrooms, in one of which she had already set up her computer. Flat-pack bookshelves and two tea chests of belongings had not yet found a proper home.

Her mother had pressed furniture on her, not only from her old bedroom which she could have cheerfully scrapped, but also a wildly patterned carpet from the Seventies that her parents had put in the loft when styles changed. The spindle-legged pale wood Seventies furniture had also come from the attic and was not to be refused. In vain did she protest that the small tables with their three splayed legs were both ugly and un-steady.

'Save your money for a while,' Mona Fairfax had said. 'You can refurnish when you've been earning for a year or two.' Then she had sighed hugely and murmured, 'If you're still here, that is.'

Entering into the Seventies spirit, Edwina's first task had been to paint one wall of the living room orange, while her mother, who had come to Gorham for a weekend, had shortened the curtains with their pattern of eighteen-inch orange and brown swirls. The garish effect was reinforced by the gold, brown and orange flowers in the newly cleaned carpet. Edwina's mother said that originally the carpet had been in the dining room, partially obscured by the round dining-room table which seated twelve, while the curtains had hung in the barn-like living room of the family home outside Cheltenham.

To put both in Edwina's small room was per-haps a terrible breach of good taste, but they were in excellent condition, and her mother had become quite misty-eyed remembering her youth and good times she had enjoyed in the Seventies.

The brown settee and armchair appeared to float eight inches above the carpet, but they were comfortable enough. All that could be said for the room was that it looked larger than it might otherwise have done, and the decor appeared intentional rather than haphazard.

Edwina planned to spend a good part of the coming afternoon deciding what to wear, which in the past had always been the best part of going out with a boy. Expectation was invariably better than reality, leaving her at the end of the evening depressed and vaguely aware that she had somehow bored her partner beyond endurance.

However, there was work to do before she could dream in front of the mirror. She was very excited about having dinner with Felix. With luck, she would soon know a number of people and the frightening sense of loneliness and isolation would pass.

Edwina was superstitious about some things. She dared not think about this evening as a 'date', for instance. Such presumption could spoil everything. She wasn't popular with men, didn't know how to be feminine and cute. Her brothers had always treated her as one of the boys. Growing up, she adored both boys and often moaned that she didn't want to be a girl. She had seldom worn skirts, had copied their speech and swagger, while attempting to imitate their prowess in assorted sports. This was unfortunate as she could never match their strength and speed. Later, she discovered that she couldn't match their academic achievements, either.

Her father, Matthew Fairfax, a man of striking presence with a full head of silver hair, was headmaster of a grammar school near Cheltenham and probably never gave his students the feeling of awe and terror that he instilled in his only daughter. Her glamorous mother taught biology at the same school and was adored by her students, seemingly finding nothing to criticize in their style of dress, while Edwina could never get it right. Her brother, Robert, her senior by seven years and a younger version of his father, taught physics at a private school in Cheltenham. Her botanist brother Thomas, not so handsome but by far the best athlete in the family, was just three years older than Edwina and had a good position on the staff of a west country agricultural college.

After leaving school, Edwina had spent a year doing odd jobs, first at McDonald's until the pressure from her family forced her to give it up, then as a temp at an estate agency.

In response to six months of relentless nagging, she announced that she had no intention of studying for a degree, preferring to take a one-year course in arboriculture.

'Trees!' her father had exclaimed in amazement. 'You intend to dedicate your life to a chainsaw? Mona, where did we go wrong?'

Despite the fact that everything she did or proposed to do brought on the contempt of the entire family, the vehemence of her father's anger had come as a surprise.

She was wasting her talents, they all said. She could get a degree if she tried. Or why not teach? She could go to teacher training college. She would enjoy it. With her connections she could get a really good job in Cheltenham, they were all sure of it. Besides, there wouldn't be anyone intelligent on the arboricultural course with whom she could become friends.

And her father, in particular, was angered that she had chosen to study at Capel Manor in north London, instead of a horticultural college closer to home. What, he asked at least twice a day, was wrong with the west country?

For once, Edwina had held out against the pressure. This was to be her bid for independence and she needed to get far away. She could not compete with her brilliant family. She simply had to do something where no comparisons could be drawn.

The truth was, she felt like an elephant beside her dainty, beautiful mother and a fool beside her distinguished father and handsome brothers. She needed to escape from their scorn to become a person in her own right. It turned out to be the best decision she had ever made. During her year's study at Capel Manor she changed from a plump, uncertain young girl to a confident woman. Or so she chose to believe.

Having decided to take an arboricultural course instead of, say, floristry, she found herself once again competing with men. In fact, she was the only woman on the course, but this didn't bother her. Better to pit herself against strong young men than to compete with other women in the charm and beauty stakes.

After her very first serious hangover caused by attempting to keep up with the men's beer consumption, she stopped trying to be like the lads. Although she had given up the competitive drinking, she fought for her grades, studying harder and longer than anyone else, and was rewarded by coming top of the class, except for tree-climbing where her reckless attitude brought some serious criticism.

Yet the praise she had hoped to earn by her good performance was not forthcoming. Matthew Fairfax had simply pointed out that she would have been perfectly capable of getting a good degree. And no-one in the family came to see her receive her certificate.

The mockery of her family had worked on her

so thoroughly that she couldn't feel confident in any situation, academic or social. So this evening was a very special test. It had to go well.

In the absence of a better plan, there was nothing for it but to imitate her mother's rituals for entertaining. First of all she went shopping and filled her cupboards with snacks in case Felix should wish to have a drink before they set off, and biscuits in case she could persuade him to come in for a late-night coffee after dinner. She bought every sort of drink, alcoholic and non-alcoholic, that she thought might appeal, before going outside to wash down the front door and the large window sill. The furniture was re-arranged several times. The kitchen was scoured. Air-freshener was sprayed around liberally and the pot plants she had bought at the supermarket were tried out on every surface in the living room before being placed in the hearth next to the television.

At last it was time to start getting ready. Her coarse mid-brown hair reached her shoulders and she had a heavy fringe which she blow-dried to one side for the evening. There followed a struggle to twist the rest into a French knot, but she finally gave up and let it fall. A pleasant face with even features didn't add up to sex appeal, but she thought a little make-up might help her to look more feminine.

She tried and discarded half a dozen outfits before settling on her first choice. A smart black trouser suit in a thin fabric and a pale blue cotton blouse looked, she hoped, feminine enough. Naturally, she was dissatisfied with her figure. Nothing about herself pleased her. Broad shoulders, a modest bust but with no waist to speak of above narrow hips did not seem to appeal to the opposite sex. After all, that was pretty much how men looked, provided of course that they were extremely fit. Curves were girlish and she hadn't any. Briefly, she considered wearing a broad black belt cinched in to give herself more shape. However, the belt was constricting and Edwina always dressed for comfort.

Harriet Squiller gave the baby a kiss, then lowered her into her cot. 'Night, night, darling.' She backed off slowly, keeping her fingers crossed behind her back.

Hannah stood up immediately. 'Where Mummy going?'

Harriet sighed. Hannah was two and sharp as a button. She had seen her granny arrive and knew her parents intended to leave the house. 'Go to sleep, dear. Lie down. Lie down, now, Hannah!'

'Kiss Daddy goodnight.'

'Right! Good idea!' Harriet stepped into the hall. 'Greg, Hannah wants to say goodnight to you.'

She heard Ben squealing. At four, he was allowed to stay up another half an hour. 'Go downstairs with Nana,' Greg said to him. 'I'm going to kiss Hannah goodnight. Be a good, quiet, grown-up boy.'

He strode down the short hall, a good-looking man in his thirties, giving the impression of someone who could deal with any emergency except his wife's nagging. 'You're not dressed,' he whispered to her.

'I can't before Hannah's tucked up!' she hissed

and whirled away towards their bedroom. He raised his eyes to heaven, then put on a smile and went to kiss his raven-haired daughter a fond goodnight. She was the image of her mother, blue eyes, black hair and two adorable dimples. He hoped she wouldn't have Harriet's insecurities.

'Night, night, darling.' He picked her up and kissed her fat cheek, but as he tried to lower her into the cot she clung to him fiercely and began to whine. It was going to be one of those nights! 'Lie down, Hannah. Daddy's in a hurry.' She continued to grizzle. He shouldn't have said he was in a hurry. He did know better. 'Hannah, don't cry.'

Ruth, Harriet's mother, came into the bedroom, ignoring him completely. 'Come on, Hannah. Five minutes more with Nana after Mummy and Daddy have gone, then you will go to bed for Nana like a good girl.'

Hannah gave her father a triumphant smile as she put her arms around her grandmother's neck. Greg backed out of the door without a word, not trusting himself to speak. Of course he didn't mind if Ruth put Hannah to bed, but she had told Harriet to go ahead and do it as she was tired. Now the old bat was undermining his authority and, what's more, she would keep Hannah up to all hours and the child would be fretful the next day.

He stopped in the doorway to his bedroom and reined in his temper. They were lucky to have a babysitter who was willing to come over at the drop of a hat. 'That's nice,' he said, indicating the outfit Harriet had decided to wear. The coral

54

short-sleeved jacket suited her colouring and the full skirt was very flattering.

'Athletic type, did Felix say? She won't like me. We'll have nothing in common, I'm sure of it. Watch for my signal. If I begin to talk about not feeling well, you back me up and we can leave early. Felix has terrible taste in women. Why should this one be different?'

'He seems pretty keen,' said Greg. 'Give the evening a chance. It's nice to be getting out of the house. I, for one, am curious.'

'I suppose she has a degree.'

'I've no idea. She's not going to look down on you, if that's what you're thinking. Relax.'

They said goodnight to Ruth and the children and got into the car, Greg behind the wheel of Harriet's little red Hyundai. Harriet would drive home.

'And another thing,' she said. 'She's bought a house! How can a very young woman who's on a short-term contract with the council afford to buy a house? Tell me that.'

'I expect she's a beautiful heiress.' He switched on the ignition, put the car into reverse and backed down the driveway in a manner which was definitely not approved by the police. He could sense Harriet pumping herself up to meet a challenge. She always did. She would walk into a room as if she owned it, start talking, make jokes, generally behave like a clown. And he hated it. She didn't have to perform to be liked, but he couldn't convince her of that.

Edwina was ready at six o'clock and forced herself to sit reading a book on dendrology until the doorbell rang. Hastily putting the book aside, she stood up, murmured, 'Please make them like me,' and went to the door.

Felix had called for her on foot. 'You didn't expect me to drink and drive, did you?' he joked when she looked around for his car. 'But I forgot. How's your ankle? Can you make it?'

Her ankle had eased considerably, allowing her to answer with perfect honesty, 'I'm not so delicate, I assure you. I'll be happy to walk.'

'The pub's only down the road. You must have seen the Prince of Wales. Very old. Plenty of atmosphere. Good food. You'll like it.'

They walked slowly, giving her time to take quick, assessing glimpses at his face. He was handsome, she decided, very masculine with his short-cropped hair, his strong nose and generous mouth. Felix, she guessed, had no doubts about himself. Perhaps his job gave him confidence.

He was right about the pub, too. The low-ceilinged structure apparently dated back to the sixteenth century. It had a mass of exposed beams, a huge fireplace which was now filled with greenery and a long bar on which rested the elbows of two men, both of whom seemed to have taken root close to the beer taps. Fred was in his early seventies, small and wiry. Tim was a year or two older, a huge man with a benign expression which quickly broke into a broad grin whenever anyone spoke to him. They sat on high stools and greeted each newcomer, somewhat like the characters in *Cheers*, she thought. She liked the pub immediately, approved of the way it was lit by orange wall lights and decided she had found her home from home.

Felix's friends, Harriet and Greg Squiller, were waiting for them in a far corner, seated at a large table for four. Greg stood up to greet her, stretching himself to over six feet. He looked just like a tough TV detective, with a slightly crooked nose and receding sandy hair. His heavy-lidded brown eyes took in everything and seemed to bore into her, which made her feel a bit uncomfortable, as if he knew exactly how stupid she was and how gauche.

Harriet was scarcely older than Edwina, a vivacious brunette in a full printed skirt with a toning coral short-sleeved jacket. She had short nearly black, curly hair and vivid blue eyes with amazingly thick black lashes. Her dimples and Cupid's bow lips gave her a deliciously feminine look. Desperate for some flaw in this gorgeous creature, Edwina saw that she was far from being enviably thin. Harriet was a comfortable size sixteen, so Edwina decided that they could be friends, after all.

'How nice to meet you,' said Harriet with real warmth, 'I hope you've had a better day than I have. My God! Life is just one booby trap after another and I'm the booby who falls into them.'

'Why, what happened to you this time?' asked Felix.

'Well, I was just leaving the car park of the supermarket, and moved slowly – I promise you – slowly up behind a four-wheeler ready to turn right, when he suddenly started to reverse. Didn't even look in his rear-vision mirror! I laid on the horn, but he bumped me just the same. He jumped out. I jumped out and I had just about convinced him that he was a lousy driver, but that I wasn't going to claim for damage, because, of course, there wasn't any. When up comes this busybody and says to me that I was in the wrong lane. Couldn't I see that he had just pulled forward prior to backing into a parking space? Golly! I hadn't noticed at all. Several other people came over and a couple of them added their tuppenceworth. I ended up apologizing and was glad to get out of there. I've told Greg we didn't exchange names or anything, but the chap might have taken my registration number. He was the size of a house, had his hair cut close to his scalp and you could see a tattoo on it.'

Greg made a snorting noise. 'It was nothing. I've told you to forget about it.'

Glancing quickly at Greg, Edwina saw that he spoke to his wife with a mixture of affection and irritation. Perhaps he had heard versions of the story several times before.

Felix grinned. 'You're going to get bonked with a tin of peas one of these days. Why can't you give way gracefully? What's so important about winning an argument in a car park?'

'Oh, you silly male-type man,' said Harriet. 'You don't understand the gender politics of these things. A gal's gotta do what a gal's gotta do. I'm defending the so-called weaker sex. We mustn't let the bastards grind us down.'

She might on occasion be very amusing, but Edwina thought Harriet could be rather trying in large doses – or taken alone when there was no-one else to dilute her incessant joking. She turned her attention to Greg, who seemed to her to have just the right combination of machismo and civic decency that was her idea of a good detective. Like Inspector Morse, perhaps.

Felix sat back in his chair, relaxed and happy. Edwina envied them all their confident air. Felix, especially, knew who he was. He wasn't searching for a personality. Edwina knew only who she wasn't. She was definitely not like her brothers or her parents, but she knew it was stupid to be defined only by a negative.

'Come on, Edwina,' Felix said now, placing his hand over hers. 'You're the newcomer. We want to know all about you.'

'There's nothing much to tell, really. I'm the dumbest member of my family and a great disappointment to them. Dad's a headmaster. Mum's a biology teacher. Both my brothers are teachers. But I hate the idea of doing that. I want to be out of doors. You see, I have loved trees since I was nine or ten and I consider I'm privileged to be able to work with them. I see my role in life as helping to preserve the eleven per cent of the countryside which is covered in trees. This is a much smaller percentage than any country on the Continent. Does that sound pompous?'

'Certainly not,' said Harriet. 'It's good that there are people like you in the world. You're doing something really important. I wish I was making some sort of contribution. I certainly couldn't have afforded to buy a house when I was your age.'

'You're looking after our two kids,' said Greg wearily. 'I wish you could see how important that is.'

'I think we all love trees,' said Felix quietly. 'And we're all grateful for people like you.'

Edwina smiled. 'You know, I've discovered that most people feel strongly about trees, especially those belonging to other people. They want them trimmed or they want them left alone. The trees cast a shadow, they say. Cut them down. Or they provide privacy, so don't let anyone cut them down. Whatever the tree owner proposes, the neighbour opposes. Poplar roots and lime residue, overhanging branches and lifting paving stones are grounds for war. No other plant life arouses such strong emotions.'

'Well said!' cried Harriet. 'You've got a great turn of phrase. I notice these things.' There was a slight pause as Harriet kept her eyes focused on Edwina. 'So how can you afford to buy a house?'

'Harriet!' growled Greg.

'Are your family pleased about what you're doing?' asked Felix.

Edwina smiled, looking embarrassed. 'That's a very shrewd question. No, they are not pleased at all. It was awful to disappoint my dad once again. Unfortunately, I never succeeded in communicating my passion about trees to any of my family.'

Harriet thumped the table. 'Then to hell with them.'

'Harriet!' said Greg. 'Who are you to talk? You always want to impress your mother, you know you do.'

'My dad died when I was sixteen,' said Felix. 'And yet I'm still trying to please him. I went into the force because I thought he would have wanted me to. Every time something good happens to me, I think I must tell Dad. Then I remember. The funny thing is, my mum is always supportive. But it's different. Perhaps we try harder for fathers. Do you think?'

Edwina did not wish to go so deeply into her feelings about her family. It embarrassed her to be talking about them at all. 'Yes,' she said shyly. 'I guess so. I didn't know other people felt—'

'I think that developers of housing estates should be forced to leave the trees,' said Harriet.

Edwina smiled her gratitude. 'They usually are but we keep being told that the nation needs houses. Anyway, they cram in these houses on a plot that is too small to hold them all, leaving enormous trees in the small back gardens that cast terrific shadows so that nothing will grow. Then everybody is unhappy, especially the insurers who don't want trees close to houses and eventually the council lets the new residents pollard them or chop them down. You said you have children. You've heard quite enough about me. How about you two? Where did you meet?'

Harriet and Greg said that they had a very ordinary history. They had both grown up in Bishop, had known one another slightly at school and had met again when Greg came to work at Bishop police station. Harriet had been a civilian secretary there. They had been married for six years and had two children.

'Boring really,' said Harriet. 'I think I'll invent a more interesting life for us, Greg. How about we met on safari in Africa? You said you always wanted to go on safari in Africa.'

Greg gave a short, cynical laugh. 'But you wouldn't ever want to be that far from the shops, would you, love? So, you two, how did you meet?'

'Now there's a story,' said Felix. 'Edwina, you see, had sneaked onto the Broom property. You know, Barleytwist.'

Harriet clapped her hands. 'You devil!'

'And she had climbed one of their trees to see if it should come down. What came down was Edwina.'

'You fell out?' asked Greg, concerned.

'The branch I was standing on broke. It's rather unusual for a beech branch—'

'Hurt her ankle. Decided to get out of there quick. Meanwhile, I saw this Escort on the lane and pulled up behind it. Over comes this woman, having to lie on the wall and let herself fall onto the other side because she'd got a dicky leg. She fell in a heap, swearing like mad.'

'I didn't.'

'You did,' laughed Felix. 'Never heard such shocking swear words in the whole of my sheltered life. I was ready to arrest you on the spot. Very suspicious. And with a ladder, too!'

'Don't let him tease you, Edwina,' said Harriet. 'Felix never arrests anyone. He's so laid back he'd apologize to a murderer for troubling him and let him off with a caution. You're probably twice as daring as Felix is, any day.'

Both Edwina and Felix were slightly offended by Harriet's remarks, and Greg had to step in and tell the young couple that his wife needed a padlock on her mouth.

Edwina didn't believe for a moment that Felix was afraid to arrest anyone. Nor could she see why some people thought of her as a ladette. Harriet was not the first person to jump to this conclusion. Of course, there had been moments of stupid impulsiveness in her past. In certain circumstances she knew no fear, whereas in others . . .

Remembering some of her misadventures at college made her feel slightly queasy. Thank heavens there was no-one around to tell Felix about the time she failed to secure her knots properly and had slid down the trunk of a very tall tree, taking a little skin off her face as she clung on for dear life. Then there was the occasion at college when she led her team in pruning a tree that leaned dangerously over a small stream, only to be told two hours later that they had pruned the wrong tree.

The four of them had an excellent three-course dinner, but by the time coffee was served conversation had begun to lag. The Squillers and Felix had spent some time in police gossip; the men had discussed the cricket; Edwina had been asked about her taste in music. All possible topics seemed to have been used up.

Harriet and Greg had a short strained conversation about who was going to take her mother home, after which everyone was silent.

When Greg next spoke it was in a desperate attempt to lighten the mood at the table. 'How about a game of darts, Felix? I'm still sober enough to find treble twenty.'

'That'll be the first time, then. You're on.'

Edwina tapped Felix on the arm. 'Can the girls play, too, or are you two sexists intent on a serious game?'

Harriet giggled. 'You'd have to give us a handicap. Greg knows I'm lucky to hit the board at all.'

'I don't want a handicap, Harriet. I'm happy enough to lose. Anyway, they've had a few beers, so their aim probably won't be so good. You and I should be able to beat them.'

Felix grinned at her. 'I'm delighted that you want to play, but I think we'd better play in teams. The two of us against the Squillers. Come over here and I'll give you a few tips.' He took her by the shoulders and guided her to the narrow brass strip which had been screwed to the carpet. 'That's called the oche. You have to stand behind it to throw your darts. It's almost eight feet from here to the board. Up at the top is the number twenty. Do you see that little red band in the twenty segment? That's double twenty and the smaller red band further down towards the bull is treble twenty. I hope you're good at mental arithmetic. The bull is double twenty-five and the green part around it is twenty-five.'

Greg had stayed behind to have a brief word with his wife. 'Do you like her?'

'Of course. I like all women with thirty-four-inch hips.'

Shrugging, he walked over to the younger couple and handed Edwina three darts. 'Don't bother with all that, Felix. You just have to know, Edwina, that the game starts with five hundred and one points and you work down to nothing. What's more, you have to finish on a double number with the exact score. Let's get going.'

Greg gave his wife a quick peck on the cheek. 'Harriet will be lucky to get below four hundred. However, I feel hot tonight, so I'm fighting for the family honour. And, incidentally, Felix against me. Want a side bet, mate? A quid says I can beat you. But go on, Edwina, let's see what you can do.'

Felix dashed over to the board and pointed at double twenty. 'Aim there, Edwina, but not until I'm out of the way!' He stepped back a full ten feet before giving her the go-ahead.

Edwina threw the first dart, aiming as instructed at double twenty. It hit the wire just below the segment and bounced onto the floor.

Greg smiled. 'Carry on, my dear, you can't pick up the ones that fall.'

Edwina squinted, threw the second dart and had the satisfaction of seeing it land solidly in the treble twenty space. The third dart came to rest right beside it. There was a cheer from those seated or standing at the bar.

'A hundred and twenty! Well done!' Felix walked over to the blackboard and under Edwina's name put three hundred and eighty-one. Greg gathered the darts which he handed to Harriet. 'Your turn, Harriet, you're up against it, I think.'

'You know why they score backwards, don't you?' she said. 'So that dumb clucks like me can't figure out the score.' Her first dart missed the board altogether and stuck in the box which housed it. Her second and third netted her a total of six. She laughed a lot and the men spent some time in reassuring her. Edwina began to feel slightly irritated.

Felix took his place at the oche, clearly tense and anxious to perform well. He managed a double twenty, but followed it with a one and a five. Greg did only a little better, putting three darts just below double twenty for a score of sixty.

The small crowd around the bar were now all watching. 'Show 'em how it's done,' wheezed Fred. 'Sock it to them, Edwina.'

Edwina could feel her face burning. She wanted to win, but beyond that she wanted to win spectacularly. Show them. Wipe out the memory of her fall from a tree. Adrenaline pumping through her veins brought a faint shake to her hands, but it also enabled her to deliver a perfect score: three darts in the small treble twenty space.

'A hundred and eighty!' cried Tim.

The perfect game consisted of just nine darts, but twelve darts would be a good game at pub level. Anyway, her first fallen dart ruled out a nine-dart game. As the others struggled, she plotted her triumph.

Excitement and a tendency to a jerky throw when she wasn't concentrating meant that she just managed to make a hundred in her third time at the oche. She needed a hundred and one to finish and she had to go out on a double figure.

Harriet, no longer smiling and carefree, managed to place all three darts on the board. Felix, having got down to three hundred and ten, needed one hundred and ninety-one. He couldn't finish in the next round. Nor could Greg, who had only managed to lower his score to two hundred and eighty.

As the two bartenders stopped serving to watch and the drinkers, mostly male, came over to form a noisy supporters' group, so Felix and the Squillers became more and more subdued.

When it was Edwina's turn again, the pub fell silent. 'I suppose you could go out with those three darts. What are you going to do?' asked Felix. He had a slight smile, but he also looked a little hurt. She should not have allowed him to explain the game to her, because it made him look foolish. She should have told them all that she was pretty good.

The silent admission of bad behaviour in no way lessened her determination to win, however. 'I'll try for treble seventeen, ten and double twenty.'

'I have every confidence in you.'

Nor was it misplaced. She played her three darts exactly as she planned, going out in a twelve-dart game. The pub erupted and everyone, including the landlord, offered to buy her a drink. The Squillers and Felix sportingly applauded her.

Greg also patted her back. 'Why didn't you tell us darts was your game?'

'It isn't. Golf is.' That brought a roar of laughter from everyone.

Fred was saying something to her; his voice was not very strong and she couldn't concentrate on his words. She heard, instead, Greg's joking remark to Felix.

'Don't tangle with that girl, mate. One false move and she'll have you on your back and out for the count in thirty seconds flat.' Felix said nothing, just nodded his head and smiled.

Edwina's emotions were always turbulent, but never more so than this evening. Euphoria was replaced by despair. She had blown her chances of ever going out with Felix again. She could imagine the look on her father's face had he been present. Although she would not have won if her dad had been watching.

Greg thought she was a ball-breaker and Harriet probably thought she was a man in drag. In her mind hissed the waspish voice of her mother, criticizing her choice of dress, hairstyle, manners and eating habits. It was a voice she could never quite shake off when in the company of others her own age.

Later, as she and Felix were walking home, she struggled for something meaningful yet witty to say, something that would restore their easy camaraderie and make him forget her bravura performance at the oche. She could think of nothing. The silence lengthened. 'So tell me. What is this new community policing scheme?'

To her surprise, her desperate stab at conversation was on target. Felix loved being a policeman and loved talking about his work.

'We're doing beat team policing, that's all. I'm still the community policeman for Gorham, but I'm now part of a team working out of Homestead station. We have a team of seventeen constables and two uniform sergeants and we're led by an inspector. Greg is the only CID man. There will still be a nominated officer for each area, but we can offer help to each other. It's a good system.'

'And you like your job, I can see that.'

'It's the best. I wouldn't change it for anything.'

'Here we are,' she said. 'Will you . . . will you come in for a coffee, or something?'

'Great, thank you.'

She unlocked the door and led him in. 'My house is the mirror image of yours, you know.' He threw his jacket onto the sofa. 'But you've done it up really nicely. I just bought some stuff from a house-clearance place.' If he thought it strange that her home looked like a throwback to the flared-trouser era he didn't say so.

She made filter coffee and, while this slow process was going on, removed the clingwrap from a plate of dainty smoked salmon and brown bread sandwiches she had made earlier. Half a dozen shortbreads on a small silver dish that had been her grandmother's were made from a recipe given to her by her mother. They had turned out perfectly. There was a bowl of olives and one of crisps in the fridge, waiting to be served, but at the last minute she thought she might be over-doing the hospitality.

Normally she never drank coffee this late and was sure it would keep her awake, but she couldn't expect to sleep at all if she didn't make amends for earlier boorishness.

Felix was studying the small pile of paperbacks on a side table when she entered the living room with the tray. '*Murder Most Miraculous*, *The Dead Drone*, *The Loving Death*! Whodunnits!' he laughed. 'You don't believe all this rubbish, do you? It's not like real police work at all. Couple of men from the force or some old spinster solve the problem in a few days flat.'

She put the tray on one of the side tables and handed him a cup of coffee. 'I love whodunnits. They're puzzles. It's not like real life. They're very relaxing.'

'And these chaps from CID, moping about,

thinking about the meaning of life, or their messed-up love lives or writing poetry. Does Greg seem like that to you?'

'No, but he's only a sergeant, not a DCI. If he wrote poetry, perhaps he'd get promoted.'

'Well, as far as murder is concerned, you're right. He wouldn't be put in charge of a murder investigation. What makes me mad is that people get the wrong idea. They think in the first place that every murder can be solved. How the press went on and on a little while ago because the Met only clears up eighty-four per cent of murders. Do you know what the rate is in New York?'

'I haven't the slightest—'

'Forty-two per cent. And in some of these books three murders a week occur in some small village. Can you imagine how the press would be down on them if that happened?'

Edwina laughed. 'I get the message. You don't like whodunnits. What do you like to read?'

'Well, sci-fi—'

'You idiot!' she cried, laughing so hard she spilt her coffee. 'There are no little green men.'

He grinned at her as he mopped coffee from the table with his handkerchief. 'You don't know for sure. Some sci-fi writers are brilliant, and they're real scientists. They've got imagination and they invent other worlds. They . . . what's the matter, love? Have I said the wrong thing?'

She shook her head, looking suddenly very solemn. 'It's just that I've had such a wonderful time tonight, but there was a reason why I invited you in just now. I must get it off my chest. I shouldn't have done what I did tonight. I have to apologize.'

'For what?'

She put her cup down very carefully, keeping her eyes on the tray. 'Winning. You know.'

'What do you mean? Did you cheat? If you did, I never caught it.'

'No, don't be silly. I mean, not letting on that I'd ever played before.'

He grinned. 'I think we're pretty robust. We really don't mind losing. At least Greg and I don't. Harriet is better at golf. Plays all the time, but she does get a bit competitive at times. Greg was saying we should have a game next weekend. Could you bear it?'

She offered more coffee and pressed him to try a biscuit, but he refused. 'That would be fun, but I meant I shouldn't have let you tell me the rules. I've played since I was old enough to go into a pub. With my brothers. I've never beaten them. Well, a few times and they didn't like it. Dad says I'm always showing off.'

'Edwina.' He squeezed her hand. 'We're tough guys. I've never met them, but I think I can safely say that we are not at all like your brothers. We tease each other a lot and play practical jokes and still manage to keep smiling. I thought it was funny. Don't worry about it.'

'Harriet wasn't too pleased. And she kept asking me about buying this place. I should explain that—'

Felix shook his head. 'It's none of our business. Let it go. As I said, she's competitive. I've no idea why she gets that way. Greg is the best mate I've ever had, but Harriet can be a bit trying. How do people get into the sort of constant bickering the Squillers go in for? I'm not going to sink to that sort of thing ever. If I thought it was inevitable, I wouldn't get married. Sometimes it's so bad between them that I don't know where to look.'

'You're very sweet,' she said. 'You could never be so petty. I know Harriet can be trying, but you must admit that Greg rises to the bait every time. Somebody should call a halt.' She thought for a moment. 'I do some strange things at times.'

That made him laugh out loud. 'I believe you. I'll bet you're game for anything. I mean, not just anything, but—'

'You mean, in a sporting, active way. I wanted to be like all the fellows on my course. So, on the first Saturday night, I went drinking with them. Then on the Sunday I felt absolutely awful, but I was invited to come out for the evening, the whole crowd of us. On Monday morning I was still so hung-over no-one would let me touch a chainsaw. I couldn't have lifted it anyway.'

He laughed. 'That's exactly what I mean. But I noticed you only had one beer tonight. Learned your lesson, have you?'

'And how. I took them all on at darts. They thought I was refusing to drink because I wanted a clear head, but it wasn't that. I don't mind losing. It's just that I hate headaches.'

'My mother's coming up to stay with me for a weekend before Christmas. I can't wait for her to meet you. You'll like her, I'm sure. She's great. She's bleached her hair so much it's stiff and she wears too much make-up and clothes that are a little too youthful. But she's fun, you know? Like you. Always ready for a laugh. She gets a lot out of life and all the chaps were chasing her after my dad died. Mum's even done a bungee jump! What a woman. And you remind me of her, or at least of that kind of spirit. I don't care for my stepfather all that much but I have to admit he's good for her. A steadying influence and he's got plenty of money so Mum can take her courses and try new things all the time. He thinks she's great and he's very good to my sister.'

'Is she like your mum?' asked Edwina, trying to take in this description of a loving mother.

'No,' laughed Felix. 'She's five years older than me and a real nerd. Works for some insurance company on a computer. I'm not sure exactly what she does. However, she tells me she's got a nice bloke, so that's all right.'

'My mother is not so much fun, I'm afraid. A typical schoolteacher, I suppose. Anyway, the school is their life.'

'And your dad gives you a hard time.'

'I can be such a fool at times.'

He seemed totally relaxed in her home. Having asked permission to turn on the telly, he had begun reading the news on teletext. She supposed he liked to keep up with who was killing whom and where. This gave her a chance to study him, to decide that he had a strong, characterful face, to wonder what it would be like to kiss him. She could do this without going into specifics, without wondering how on earth she would ever get herself into a position where Felix would think it all right to kiss her, or be close enough to do so. The whole sex thing worried Edwina. There were too many opportunities for making a fool of oneself.

Half an hour later he kissed her on both cheeks in a friendly but undeniably platonic fashion as he said goodbye. It had been a glorious day, the beginning of the greatest happiness she had ever known. Clearing away the dirty cups, she allowed her mind to create little scenes – Felix in her bed. Felix on holiday. Felix being introduced to her parents. *See, Mum*, she would say. *I can get a boyfriend, after all, and we're going to have fun together and go places and I'll be part of a crowd of people and I won't be the only one without a date.*

It was pleasant thinking about her social life. Her new job with its new responsibilities scared her, and she had been trying not to think about it all day.

Next week she would be facing another day of not knowing what to do or when to do it. She would feel sick inside and probably make more rash decisions like the one to allow the Brooms' tree to be felled.

The important thing would be to hide her feeling of uncertainty from the outside world. This would be her secret. She would act like a much older person, be positive in her decisions and not take any nonsense from anyone. That way, she hoped to go unchallenged until she had learned the ropes.

On Monday morning, having spent a restless night, she drove to the office where her first call was from a woman with a frail voice who said a madman was cutting down her trees. The madman, it turned out, was the woman's next-door neighbour. Would Edwina please come and arrest him?

She said she would be there as quickly as possible to try to sort something out. When she

74

had hung up, she studied a map to see where this Mrs Zena Alway lived and what sort of property her neighbour, Mr Leo Midnight, had. There were no tree protection orders on either property, but Mrs Alway had only a couple of acres. Mr Midnight's property, on the other hand, was extensive – over twenty acres – and she assumed that there were some precious, very old trees in the grounds of Gorham House that should be protected from a maniac with a power saw. She would have to pay him a call. But first, she would take up Mrs Alway's invitation.

The drive took her just over ten minutes and she found the unmade road quite easily, coming shortly after the driveway of Mr and Mrs Broom of Barleytwist. All the properties that were reached by this lane were well hidden from the road. First was the old lodge, a red brick, single-storey structure whose small front garden was defined by a green-painted wrought-iron fence. The front door was also green, but was faded and flaking.

Further along, Gorham House was scarcely visible even from the beginning of its private drive. What she could glimpse of it shocked her because its true state had not been visible from a distance. A suitable location for a haunted-house film, it was in an advanced state of decay. It looked as if every window frame were rotten.

Further up the lane, Mrs Always' cottage was a delightful contrast, being a modest two-storey brick box with small windows. Yellow roses clung to the walls in romantic abandon. Various containers stood on either side of the doorway filled with geraniums and petunias in profusion

75

and the front door was a glossy black with a bright brass knocker. Edwina didn't get the chance to use it. The door flew open as she approached.

'Oh, dear,' said a birdlike woman. 'You're so young. He'll eat you for breakfast. Come in. Come in. Mind the umbrellas. I had a stand for them but it broke and I haven't got around to replacing it. Yes, that's a lovely painting, isn't it? It fell down last year. The plaster just gave way. I thought it safer to just stand it on the floor here in the sitting room. Do sit down. I've made coffee. I'll just get it.'

Edwina sat down on a sagging loose-covered sofa and looked around her. The small room had clearly been two even smaller ones before someone had knocked them together. A single fireplace remained and it was a handsome Victorian one of cast iron painted black. There was scarcely any wall space free of prints and paintings, some of them quite delightful. A huge walnut secretaire stood in one corner, its top almost reaching the ceiling, while other large pieces, including a very large round table with a chenille cloth on it, indicated that Mrs Alway had once lived in a far grander house. The old lady shuffled into the room, burdened by a large tray. Edwina jumped up to help her.

'Thank you, dear. Put it on the butler's stand,' said Mrs Alway. 'Just there. Watch out for the china on the side table. It's Sèvres. My lady-what-does doesn't come until Friday, so I'm afraid everything is a bit dusty. My last home was in Pebmarsh. Much bigger. It had eight bedrooms and a five-acre garden, but what does an old lady want with a place like that? And isolated. Well, I'm a bit isolated here, but I didn't mind when old Mr Cartwright was alive. He lived in Gorham House all his life. He didn't bother me and I didn't bother him. Had a nurse for twenty years. Why he wanted to go on living when he was so crippled up puzzles me. I wouldn't. Not like that. And he'd been gone scarcely six months when these two common creatures came to roost like cuckoos. London types. Everybody thinks they probably won the Lottery and wanted a big house. Didn't know enough to buy themselves a decent one. Well, no-one has taken to them around here. People know what those two have done to me.'

'But you said he was just chopping down the tree this morning!'

Zena thought a moment. 'No, Saturday morning. Five o'clock. I would have called sooner but it was the weekend. He was at it again on Sunday morning. No thought for others. Doesn't know the difference between my property and his own. Do you know, every time I drive up here from the Gorham Road, if he happens to be behind me he drives up and hits my bumper! I'm quite terrified. I should tell Felix. Maybe I will. He's no right to hit my car. And I can't believe it's just coincidence that he's always just behind me. How does he know when I'll be coming in or out unless he spies on me?'

Zena sat down on a chair opposite Edwina and poured out the coffee. She was a little clumsy about it as her eyes were full of tears. Edwina had taken note of the age of her hostess, her frailty and her tendency to dramatize. This Mr Midnight probably had a different perspective on the whole business. She would telephone him, speak nicely to him and charm him into refraining from up-setting Mrs Alway, while at the same time making sure that he looked after his trees.

When they had finished their coffee, they walked across the lawn and through the copse to the Gorham House boundary. There was no doubt about it. A large branch of a chestnut had been lopped off, leaving an eight-inch snag which needed the services of a proper tree surgeon.

'Did he have a ladder to reach the branch?' Edwina asked. 'It's pretty high, even for a tall man.'

'He held the power saw straight up above his head and just sawed away. Look, he did this one next. It's smaller and he had to stand on some-thing and lean right over to do it. That branch hit him on the head.' Zena laughed bitterly. 'Pity it didn't brain him.'

Edwina nodded. 'Then whatever fell on his side he picked up and threw here over the fence. The owner is entitled to the branch. These trees do need to have some work done on them. Some of these branches are so heavy that they are going to snap off, perhaps in the next high wind. And there are several dead branches. He may have been trying to be helpful and behave properly.'

'Then why not work on his own?' squeaked Zena. 'Heaven knows there's enough work for him there.'

Indeed there was. Several tall pines had died and would have fallen to the ground but for the support offered by other trees. Some of the finer specimens had dead branches. Sycamores were crowding out some of the rarities. Clearly this had been a fine arboretum at one time. Possibly planted at the turn of the last century, they had matured without tender loving care, and she could see through the dense wood a cedar of Lebanon which must have been planted two hundred years ago. There was also an abundance of yews which needed urgent protection from an amateur with a power saw.

'Will you leave this in my hands, Mrs Alway? I'll telephone him and then go round if he's in. Best to do it straight away.'

'Yes,' said Zena. 'You attend to it. I don't want to get involved. He frightens me. You may use my telephone. I'll show you where it is.'

'No.' Edwina slipped a hand under Zena's elbow to help her up the steep slope. 'He might dial one four seven one and trace the call and realize you put me on to him. I'll telephone on my mobile. It's in my car.'

Zena clearly thought this was the best policy. She stood in the cottage doorway and watched, wringing her hands, as Edwina sat in her car with the door open and dialled the number Zena had given her.

'Hello?' The man's voice was very deep and sounded rather sleepy. It was a voice so reminiscent of her father's that Edwina actually flinched.

'Hello, Mr Midnight?' The words came out breathy and timid, not at all the way she had intended.

'Uh.'

'I'm Edwina Fairfax from Bishop council. I understand you've just moved to Gorham House.

I would like to drop in to see you and have a look at your trees if I may.'

'You may not.'

'Mr Midnight, I have a legal right to—'

'Look, you silly little woman, you may think you have a right to invade my life, but I've some rights, too. All you council types want to do is stick your noses into other people's business and throw your weight around. I know your sort and I'm not having it.' The phone went dead.

Edwina sat in the car with her mobile in her hand for several seconds, until Mrs Alway called to her. 'He was rude, wasn't he? I can see it in your face. You've gone all red. It's not healthy to get so upset. I should know. He's kept me awake a few nights.'

Edwina got out of the car slowly. Normally, she could stand up to anyone. But Mrs Alway was not to know that the mysterious Mr Midnight had a voice remarkably similar to her father's. What was more, he had called her a silly little woman, a chilling coincidence, although in her youth the epithet had been 'silly little girl'. Her father frequently used those very words when he was angry with her. She had learned to be afraid of his icy anger as a very small girl. Once she had been so frightened by his blast of fury that she had wet her knickers. She had been five at the time and still felt ashamed when she thought of it. The stranger with his brutal manner and deep voice had tapped a deep well of dread.

She refused the offer of a sherry to revive her, advised the old lady to stay well away from her neighbour and said that she would discuss the matter with Felix Trent. 'That's the way to handle it,' she assured Zena. 'Leave it to Felix. He's the law. That man can't argue with him.'

Reversing to drive away Edwina faced up to her cowardice. Leo Midnight was not her father and she was no longer a little girl. There was no reason why she should allow a complete stranger to frighten her. She drove slowly down the narrow lane and turned in at the Gorham House driveway, but had not gone more than a few yards when an old man leapt from behind a laurel waving a small garden fork. She slammed on her brakes.

'Hello, I'm coming to see Mr Midnight.'

'Just gone out.' The gardener, if that was who he was, looked to be in his seventies. Mrs Alway had not mentioned him.

'I just spoke to Mr Midnight.'

'Just gone out, I said. Said not to let anyone drive on to his property. Told me so not five minutes ago. Who are you?'

'The Avon lady.' Edwina reversed out of the drive, crashed the gears and drove off in a cloud of dust.

She had a few calls to make over the area allotted to her and planned to keep busy so that she would not have to think about Mr Leo Midnight and his short temper. She had said she would speak to Felix, but in fact there were other steps she could take before that. For instance, she could go with a Bishop planning officer, all of whom had a warranted right of entry. Unfortunately, the policy of the council which had been explained to her at length was to be very diplomatic, not to rush in and start antagonizing owners. She would be advised to wait, to approach the matter carefully. There was no question, she had been told, of issuing blanket tree preservation orders. Individual trees which affected the landscape could be protected, and those within a property if of special value.

First, however, she would have to look round the property. Perhaps, after all, she should discuss the Gorham House trees with John Blue. Then she would write a letter that would singe Mr Midnight's hair.

Her first call was to a modest property on the outskirts of Bishop which had probably been built within the past five years. The owner had rung to ask for advice about some trees she had put in which were not thriving. There was a substantial semicircular drive to the property and it had been planted with an avenue of ornamental cherries. They were small and spindly, and several were showing signs of distress by losing their leaves, but as Edwina drove to the front door she could see no obvious signs of disease.

Mrs Hurst came to the door and greeted her very warmly. She was in her early forties, an attractive woman who looked perfectly turned out in tailored white trousers and a pale blue cotton tunic. 'The trees were planted by the old boy who comes in once a week to cut the grass. My husband and I do all the rest of the gardening. We're new to it, though. We lived in a flat in London for fifteen years. Never had a garden before. We were lucky to get Tom, but I'm not saying he knows much about gardening. He certainly doesn't know what's wrong with the trees.'

They walked down the drive and stopped by the first tree. 'It's a fact,' said Edwina, 'that if you buy a six-foot tree from a nursery, it is unlikely to grow at all for three years. You see, they dig them up from the nursery bed and, when they do, they chop off about half the tree's roots. On the other hand, if you buy a stripling for a few pence, it won't need staking. It will grow like one found in the wild with a good root system. In three years it will have caught up with the more expensive tree. But you absolutely must keep the grass away from the stem. Grass competes with the tree for nourishment. Give each one a circle of free soil about a metre across.'

Edwina bent down to pull out the grass growing right up to the tree and scraped away at the soil, then laughed loudly. She stood up with a broad grin. 'Mrs Hurst, your gardener has planted these trees in their polythene containers. The black plastic should have been stripped off before they went into the ground. They are probably terribly root-bound. That's why they haven't grown at all. They couldn't possibly thrive. The plastic doesn't rot away, you know.'

'Oh, how stupid . . . I'm really . . . I don't know what to say.' Mrs Hurst was blushing and put her hands to her face in embarrassment. There were tears in her eyes.

'It's an understandable mistake,' said Edwina hastily. She had seen two members of the public this morning and both had been reduced to tears. She really must try to be a bit more diplomatic. 'Look, if you can give me your garden fork and get out your hose – do you have any compost here? I'll replant one. Then you can show your gardener.'

'Yes, it's in the shed. I'll only be a minute.'

She returned promptly, handed over the fork and said she must get a pencil and paper so that she could take notes. Edwina quickly lifted the small tree and set it on the driveway, then waited for the owner to come back. It was several minutes.

'I've been on the phone to my husband and he's furious. Wants me to fire the old boy, but where will I find someone else? He works for several people on this road. It's so embarrassing, but we do pay him to be the gardener. We don't know anything.'

'Let me show you how this tree should have been planted. You dig a hole at least six inches wider and deeper than the soil ball. Then you need some compost . . .'

'Oh,' said Mrs Hurst and ran off like a child who has been very naughty and wants to make amends. She returned struggling to push a wheelbarrow with a bag of soil-based compost in it.

Edwina had used the time to dig a large hole. She now placed some compost in it, set in the tree in its black ten-litre container, ripped the plastic with her knife and carefully slipped it off.

Teasing out the roots which wound tightly round the soil ball, she cut a few, being careful not to break up the soil ball. Then she tipped in some compost and firmed it all down.

'You mustn't be too upset, Mrs Hurst. Most people don't know how to plant a tree properly. In fact, it has been estimated that half of all amenity trees die within five years due to lack of proper care, and nine out of ten trees planted in urban areas. Yours are all still alive, so that's terrific. Your best bet is to teach your gardener how it's done, then keep him on to do it. You don't want to lose him if he's good at mowing the lawn.

'These trees shouldn't need staking after five years, but since you're going to replant them all, you could put in stakes for the first year. I haven't time to stake this tree, but you need to drive the stake down at least a foot below the planting hole, place it low down and at an angle. The tree should be held at the base but allowed to be whippy at the top. That way it will grow strong.'

Mrs Hurst did not seem to be listening carefully. 'This is going to give your friends on the council a good laugh. We've been such fools.'

Edwina sighed, wondering how she could convince the woman that this was not so. 'In the first place, there is no-one to tell, no-one would be interested and if I were to tell all the stories I know about people's ignorance of trees, I'd do nothing else. Most people don't know about trees. That's why I'm doing this job. Please don't let it prey on your mind.'

Belatedly, she remembered that she hadn't told Mrs Hurst about watering the tree. She pointed out that she had left a depression around the tree which should be filled with water during hot dry spells, at least during this first summer after their replanting. 'Five litres of water per tree every two weeks. I know we're in the middle of a drought, but if your gardener is careful, it should be all right.'

Mrs Hurst thanked her profusely and waved her off ten minutes later, after Edwina had drunk the coffee her hostess urged upon her. She had now had two cups of coffee, it was almost noon and she was still thirsty. As the Prince of Wales was only fifteen minutes' drive away, she decided to have a sandwich and a diet cola before going back to Bishop to do some paperwork.

Fred was seated on a stool at the bar. 'Hi,' she called. 'I think you must live here.'

'I think you must,' said Fred. 'Every time I come in here I see you.'

Edwina told the girl behind the bar that she would have a ham on white, but hadn't decided finally what she would have to drink. It was a hot day and a cola drink didn't seem like a very refreshing idea.

'There's someone in here been asking about you,' said Fred softly. 'Over there. John Hargreaves. He's a tree surgeon and a great darts player. Probably wants to challenge you to a match.'

Edwina turned to see a huge man in old jeans and tartan shirt. He was in his early sixties and his face was that of a man who spends his days out of doors. Thin lips, iron grey receding hair and eyes so deeply set they couldn't be read made John Hargreaves a little intimidating. Nevertheless, she smiled and crossed the room with her hand extended.

'Hello, Mr Hargreaves, I'm Edwina Fairfax. It's nice to meet you!'

He shook her hand, but he didn't smile. 'I've been wanting to have a quiet word with you to get a few things straight. Mr Broom called me in to see to a tree you said was dead and had to come down. As it was a hazard, I took it down immediately.'

Edwina's smile froze. She knew she had been right to order the tree felled. John Blue had said she'd done the right thing as mature beech is intolerant of change, and of the drought summers of late. Beech bark cracks and decay enters. The trees are shallow-rooted and when they go, they go quickly. Not like oaks which deteriorate slowly. So it wasn't her decision that was the problem. Something terrible must have happened. Someone hurt? It was by a busy road so maybe it fell on a car . . .

'Police put up traffic lights and she came down a treat.'

'Oh, that's fine. I thought – '

'Now I know it's me, the tree surgeon, what can be fined, not the arboricultural officer from the council, but – '

'No, no, I gave permission. I thought the tree should come down. And it presented a hazard, so . . .'

Mr Hargreaves took his time, drank deeply from his pint, put down the tankard, wiped his mouth on his sleeve. 'Bats.'

Edwina put a hand to her pounding heart. 'Oh, God.'

CHAPTER THREE

'Ordinarily I wouldn't be able to get round to it so quickly. But I knew I'd be free this morning. We started at half past eight. Felix Trent was there. Said he knew the tree was to come down and to get a move on as it was holding up the early morning traffic. I know my job. It was down in no time.'

'Bats,' said Edwina, barely above a whisper. 'There were bats in the tree?'

'You said it was to come down. Mr Broom wanted it done this morning. Felix wanted it quick. It's not my fault. I don't see why I should be held to blame. We had shifted all the wood away before we even saw that there was a roost in it. Some were injured but the others flew off. Sort of.'

'It's not your fault. It's mine.' She sat down heavily and put her face in her hands. Her first big decision and she had blown it because of a fall from the tree, because an attractive man had come along to distract her. She had visions of a raft of complaints. She had laughed at Mrs Hurst. Mr Midnight thought she was an interfering bureaucrat. Mrs Alway was convinced Edwina had failed to protect her trees, and now the bat preservation people would want her scalp.

Hargreaves leaned close to give her a rough pat on the shoulder. 'Too many bloody bats as it is,' he murmured. 'I'm prepared to say nothing if you are.'

Edwina looked up and smiled slightly. 'I won't be so stupid next time. Let's just keep quiet about this.'

'I'll buy you a drink. By the way, that Bill Juggens gets all the council business even though we're cheaper than what he is. I'd appreciate a chance to work for the council occasionally.'

'I understand.'

'What are you drinking?'

'A whisky and ginger ale.' He looked surprised and she shrugged. 'Better make that ginger ale without the whisky. Too early in the day.'

As Hargreaves went off to get her drink, Edwina clasped her shaking hands. Bats were protected by law. The correct thing was to inform the Bat Conservation Trust when a bat roost was threatened in order to give the experts time to advise and, if necessary, to make arrangements for the care of the bats. Major tree work should not be carried out in June, July and August if possible because bats were present in trees and vulnerable. She knew it all, had studied it on her course.

She should have left the dead tree standing, minus dangerous branches. It was illegal to intentionally kill or injure bats. It was even illegal to deliberately disturb them or damage, destroy or obstruct access to bat roosts whether or not bats were present at the time. She knew the law. She also knew that it could be damaging for her future career if it were known she had been so careless.

She could put the blame on Hargreaves. He should have looked for evidence of bats. What kind of tree surgeon was he? Or maybe, she sighed . . . he had just made one stupid mistake as she had, an error that could bring not only a hefty fine but embarrassment. So she wouldn't judge Hargreaves harshly if he didn't judge her.

Even so, when he had returned with a ginger ale for her and another beer for himself, she eyed him with resentment. Who could she depend on if not a professional tree surgeon?

'If that old bat sent you, you can just turn around and get out of here,' said Leo.

Felix blinked. He had driven to Gorham House in order to introduce himself to the new residents. Mrs Midnight was nowhere in sight, but Mr Midnight, all six feet something of him, was standing in his doorway with an expression that said he'd be willing to take extreme measures to preserve his privacy. He was wearing a faded blue T-shirt that fitted his long torso well and very old jeans. His shoulders were square and broad. He gave the impression of having the stringy muscles of a long distance runner. While he was three or four inches taller than Felix, he was probably a stone lighter.

Last year there had been a poor devil who'd wandered away from Clover Nursing Home. Wearing bedroom slippers and a vacant expression, he had got himself into the beer garden of the White Hart where he had suddenly turned nasty, swinging out at anyone who came near him. He was angry with the world, suffering unknown inner torment. Felix and two others from the station had arrived to take him away. He proved more dangerous for being totally unpredictable and it had taken them fifteen minutes to subdue him and lead him off. Leo Midnight brought to mind that mental patient, being potentially violent and dangerous because his actions couldn't be predicted.

'Which old bat would that be?' asked Felix mildly.

'Mrs Alway. She called you to complain about me, didn't she?'

'I've come merely to introduce myself. I am Felix Trent, your community policeman, and I like to get to know everyone on my beat.'

'What? Everyone? My, my. In the real world, real policemen don't have time to trot around introducing themselves to all the citizens. They're out catching the bad guys. Still, I suppose you have to fill your day somehow. Anyway, I'm sure villains would be too much for you to handle. You're nothing but a bloody social worker.'

Felix was wearing his uniform white shirt and dark trousers with his radio clipped to a shirt pocket, looking smart, looking a valued member of the establishment, looking sane. The radio spilled out a few tinny words which both men ignored.

Felix put on the slow smile that he always wore when annoyed, determined never to give others the pleasure of seeing that he was riled. 'You are right, of course, Mr Midnight. There are no

91

big-time villains living on my beat, just a few naughty boys. But I know them. I'm here to protect you and your property. I want you to know that you can call for me by name.'

'I don't need to have my hand held and I don't want you on my property. I'll make a deal with you. I won't break the law. You don't come creeping round here.'

Felix made no move. 'Not even to discuss Mrs Alway? Care to tell me about it?'

'I'll leave that to her. She'll make a good story of it.' Leo stepped back and shut the door in Felix's face.

The young policeman shrugged and returned to his police car where he sat a moment to make some notes. Two cars on the drive, both sports cars, both fast, one black and in good condition, the other a rather dilapidated old red MG. This interested him. Who laid out for a classic car and a MG at that, then failed to maintain it? He made a note of both number plates, then drove directly to see Zena Alway.

Grimacing, he reminded himself that he knew a remarkable number of very pleasant people and was usually welcomed wherever he went. There had to be a few rotten eggs, and Leo Midnight did not frighten him. Probably a harmless nutcase, that was Felix's opinion, to be revised in the light of any new evidence in the future. For the moment, he was more concerned to protect Mrs Alway from herself. She was quick-tempered and inclined to say what she thought.

'He makes my life a misery,' she said when he asked her about Leo Midnight. 'I'm terrified of him. He tries to make me have an accident as I'm coming up the lane. Hits my bumper with his car, that sort of thing.' Zena wiped away a few tears. 'And then Saturday morning he woke me at five o'clock. Five o'clock! And it was the noise of his chainsaw and he was cutting branches off my tree! Leaned right over to do it. Then he dumped the branches onto my property. I haven't phoned him to complain, I can assure you. I'm too frightened.'

Felix remembered the angry man he had just left and thought Zena was right to be cautious. 'Stay away from him. Don't get his back up. He seems a little unstable. I'll keep an eye on him. By the way, what is his wife like?'

'Very young and incredibly beautiful. Long blond hair. Everyone in Homestead seems to think she's a sweet little thing. But I tell them, she leans out of the window and uses the most terrible language to me. For no reason. What have I done to deserve this at my time of life? I wish now I hadn't telephoned that new tree woman from the council.'

'Edwina Fairfax? You rang her? When?'

'This morning. She was here within the hour. Such a sweet thing. She said she would telephone him from her car, then go round and have a word with him. Well, I couldn't hear the conversation, but as she was talking her face went bright red. She switched off her phone and just sat in the car for a minute. She wouldn't tell me what he had said, but I could tell it was rude.'

'Zena, listen to me. Stay away from him. Having a feud with a man like that can only end in misery for you. You're not up to fighting somebody like him.'

Felix thought that he had Edwina sussed out. Any man, no matter how bad-tempered, might well come off second best in a confrontation with her. Nevertheless, he would warn her when they met on Saturday to play golf. Meanwhile, he intended to head back to Homestead station and look up this character on the PNC, the Police National Computer.

The information available on the computer was strictly for police use only, but what it told him about the new resident would help him to know how to act towards Midnight. He could keep an eye on things, maybe issue a gentle warning to others as he had done to Zena. He would be able to find information about the man if he had ever been convicted in court.

At the station he went immediately to the computer. Greg strolled over to join him.

'Anything interesting?'

'Just going to look up a new resident. Leo Midnight. Sounds like the sort of nickname you might be given by the tough boys – or maybe the kind of thing a nutter picks up at the movies. Funny thing is, he acted a bit like a cop. I don't know what makes me say that. He was bloody rude. Not afraid of me. Full of his rights. You know the type.'

He tapped in the name and, to his delight, there was a listing. Leo Midnight, six feet two inches tall, weighing one hundred and eighty pounds, forty-four years old. His last known address was in Islington and he had one conviction for obstruction of justice three years earlier. He'd been given a two-year suspended sentence. Not at all what Felix had been expecting.

'Could happen to a cop,' mused Greg. 'Especially one from the Met. Maybe there was something very important to hide. You never know.'

'Yeah, but he seems totally unstable to me. Acts very strangely. He's scared old Mrs Alway half to death and told off Edwina for daring to want to visit him.'

'Lied in court, probably. Well, possibly. Of course, he could have criminal connections, but maybe not.'

Greg was, in Felix's opinion, a very fine detective who had settled early in life for a quiet existence. Harriet did not want to leave the area. It was probably a poor career move to stay in a largely rural area officially classed as 'low crime'. Nevertheless, Felix thought the force was lucky to have him.

Greg rubbed his chin. 'He may have got thrown off the force because of the conviction. I admit we're doing quite a lot of guessing here. Then he wins the Lottery or the pools and never has to work again. Or, and it is a possibility we've got to bear in mind, maybe he's up to something naughty. Could be.'

'I think he's crackers. Round the twist. You haven't met him.' Felix closed down his computer and swivelled round in the chair to tell Greg about Midnight's antics with Zena Alway.

Greg was unimpressed. 'She is a bit too frail to be driving and her motor is too big and powerful for her,' he said. 'Besides, maybe that's just her version of events. Perhaps she did something stupid and he got annoyed.'

'He told me to get off his property, said he

wanted his privacy. Wouldn't let Edwina come to look at his trees.'

Greg smiled. 'I'm not saying you're wrong. We'll bear him in mind. So far, he's just been unpleasant. We don't put chaps in jail for that. Even if we want to.'

Felix laughed. Away from Midnight's strange expression and menacing attitude, he recognized that he had overreacted. Shortly afterwards, he left the station.

Greg watched him leave. He was fond of the kid, but that didn't mean he was prepared to share his every thought with him. He picked up the phone to speak to an old acquaintance of his who was now a police sergeant in Islington.

Leo woke in a sweat, as usual, his heart pounding, his hair clinging to his scalp. He slept in the second best bedroom which faced south, down towards the Gorham Road and, beyond that, rolling farmland to the horizon. It was probably a desirable view, but he would have preferred traffic noise and a view of massive buildings no more than fifty yards away, neon lights reflected in greasy streets, the wail of sirens, the screech of brakes. Leo was a city man born and bred, and he liked to know that his fellow man was not too far away. The countryside gave him the creeps.

He had given Cassandra the main bedroom, a crumbling room of massive proportions with an ornate plaster rose in the ceiling and an equally ornate cornice with half a dozen sections missing. The place was filthy and smelled stale. The late owner's furnishings were still in place and needed to be cleaned, especially the carpets, but

Cassandra had no interest in housekeeping, was not the type to lift a finger. Leo, himself, was incapable of sustained effort. Yet he didn't feel safe having a cleaner come in.

His own room was down the corridor from Cassandra's and, for safety's sake, he kept his door locked. Less likely that way to walk in his sleep, to commit some unspeakable act, to say something he would regret.

The shower head in the bathroom next door to his room was full of limescale and therefore sent out only a thin stream of water, but it was enough. He lathered his body, washed his hair, towelled down, all the while wishing that he could feel refreshed and clean, wishing that he could take any pleasure in anything.

An electric razor was not up to handling his dark beard. He filled the washbasin and scraped his chin with a safety razor, seeing but not seeing his face, manoeuvring the blade around the curves and planes while managing to ignore the bitter expression of a man living on the edge. Except for those few brief moments while shaving, he never looked at himself, couldn't bear it. And this was the same Leo Midnight who used to stand in front of the mirror for hours posing, making faces, trying on his trendy gear. But that was in his carefree twenties. Probably the best years of his life.

Not wishing to sleep on ancient, possibly damp beds, he had bought new ones for Cassandra and himself. The rest of the furniture was simply that which had been in the house for generations. He had not bought so much as a teaspoon. The curtains were dusty, rotted by the sun, but he wouldn't be calling in a curtain maker. Let them rot. He chose a white T-shirt from the untidy pile in the chest of drawers, gathered up socks and underpants, began to dress, with fingers still shaking from the previous night's drinking session.

It occurred to Leo that with the exception of those few golden years he had never lived in decent surroundings. His mother had not thought that cleaning a house was important. His father, when he had been sober, had never considered putting himself to the trouble of tidying up. Not that anyone in the family did anything sensible after his little sister died. That had finished off what scant family feeling existed.

Leo's older half-brother, Reggie, might have taken some pride in a home, might have given the young boy some comfort and companionship. It hadn't happened. Leo would never know what sort of relationship he and his brother might have had. Reggie had left home after Sissy died when Leo was ten, had gone to Canada and never been heard of again, except once to say he had arrived.

When Leo was eleven his father had one day crossed the road in a drunken stupor and been knocked down. After that, he and his mother had lived from hand to mouth until he was fifteen and he had gone out to get a job working for a local garage. A month later she went off with a new man, leaving her son to fend for himself. The memory still brought him near to tears.

Suddenly, he brought his fist down on the chest of drawers. Why couldn't he stop thinking about the past? Why had he been condemned to relive his life by day as well as by night?

He took a deep breath, commanded his brain to pay attention. Getting out his laptop computer from its hiding place beneath his underwear, he plugged it in and tapped in an e-mail address.

'No progress,' he wrote. 'Maybe we shouldn't have come here. The house is falling down and the neighbours are nosy. Would you believe it? PC Plod came round to introduce himself! I told him to piss off.'

Cassandra came down for breakfast at ten o'clock. She was wearing the clothes she had bought the day before in Homestead, a skirt so short it hid only her crotch, a blouse so low it showed her cleavage. She modelled the outfit for him, turning this way and that, flicking her hair back, making a provocative little pout.

'I bought some underwear too.' She lifted her skirt to show him that the knickers were the thong type. She was a beautiful girl, desperate to be noticed, desperate to be loved and lusted after. She couldn't return the love or the lust, didn't have it in her. She'd flirt with a man, really turn him on, then walk away satisfied. Until the next time when she needed another fix of admiration. Pathetic. He had to give her one thing, though. She had taste in her own adornment. No plucking her eyebrows to extinction, no bleaching her hair until it was like straw. Her choice of clothes was sexy, but no more so than many a young woman wore. No, Cassandra was a class act. So long as she kept her foul mouth shut and refrained from expressing her many cock-eyed opinions on a large variety of subjects, people were inclined to assume she was a refined young woman from a moneyed, middle-class family. The thought almost made him laugh out loud.

She was still preening for his benefit. He turned away. 'Leave it off, Cassandra, and have your breakfast.'

Her body slumped and the bright, sexy look disappeared. She had her own demons, her own dark thoughts that had to be kept at bay. Cassandra shopped to forget. He knew that. She was pathetic, but he could not feel pity.

The phone rang at half past eight on Saturday morning. Felix had been busy all week and had not had a chance to see Edwina, even briefly. He was afraid the call would be to cancel their golf date. However, it was just a resident of Gorham, Alvin Copse from Singleton Road, asking him to check on a car Alvin proposed to buy. Felix explained that he could only tell him if the police had an interest in the car, that is, if it were stolen. Otherwise, if Alvin was later unhappy with his purchase and felt he had been cheated, he would have to contact the office of fair trading. These phone calls were frequent and Felix was happy to make sure that no-one was being offered a stolen car.

He was very proud of his bungalow and had done a fair bit of work on it. Every room had cupboards which he had built. In fact, the kitchen had more cupboards than his meagre kitchen equipment and crockery could fill.

In the matter of decorating, he was a complete idiot and knew it. He painted every wall and all the woodwork white, bought brightly coloured ready-made curtains and hoped for the best. His furniture came from house-clearance sales and had not cost him very much. It was comfortable and solid. What more could a man want? He spent as little time in the house as possible and had only bought it because it was a bargain, having been allowed to go to seed.

He washed up the pan in which he had fried two eggs, a couple of pieces of bacon and a tomato. Three pieces of toast and two cups of coffee had completed his breakfast. There was just time to call his mother before driving to pick up Edwina.

'Hi, Mum! How are things? How's Frank? That's good. Tell him to take care. And Sharon? What, another new boyfriend? My God! I thought she was settled with what's-his-name. Me? Well, I'm glad you asked that. I've met this girl – ' For the next ten minutes Felix talked about Edwina, told his mum about her skill at darts, asked her advice about where to take the new girlfriend. But when his mother made the mildest of remarks about hoping that this time Felix would be prepared to make a commitment, he said bluntly that he wasn't ready for that sort of thing. She recognized the annoyance in his voice and changed the subject, simply wishing him a pleasant day.

Felix hung up feeling refreshed as he always did after talking to his mother. He loved her dearly and knew that the only possible objection to a decent chap like Frank was that he had taken his mum and Sharon down to Devon. He was just jealous, he told himself, and tried briefly to concentrate on liking poor Frank. It was a difficult task.

When he called for her, Edwina looked ready for business in a white golfing skirt and navy T-shirt. Her hair had been pulled back into a ponytail. She was the picture of health, youth, happiness and decency. He liked her a lot, but he was not ready to get seriously involved. He just hoped she understood that.

Harriet did not look quite so good in her skirt, but she, too, gave the impression that she meant business.

'You'd better be good, Edwina,' she said cheerfully. 'I can't play darts worth a damn, but I practise my golf regularly. Are you really better at it than you are at darts?'

'No, of course not,' lied Edwina. 'That was just a joke.'

Greg wasted no time in pulling Felix aside. 'I rang a friend in Islington and we were right. Leo Midnight had been on the force at some time. The thing is, my friend never knew Midnight, but when he made a few enquiries it became clear that nobody would talk about the man. I have to assume he has disgraced the force and let down his mates. He may now be into something dicey, but there is no telling. If, as everyone thinks, he's won some money, he may just be prepared to settle down and live quietly. Either way, he's unlikely to want you sniffing round. Probably had enough of the police. If old Mrs Alway wants to make a complaint, we'll deal with it. Otherwise, we'll leave him alone.'

'I advised her not to. Of course, if he goes too far – '

'Put it out of your mind, Felix. There's nothing further to be done. Trouble is, there's not enough crime in Gorham to keep you busy. On the other hand, I've got a real problem. Harriet is determined to do well today. My life has been hell since the other night at the pub. She's been out and bought a dartboard, been practising every day. Bloody woman! She's declared war on Edwina.' He laughed as he said it, however, and Felix was able to feel reasonably relaxed about Harriet's competitive spirit, since he could see the two women deep in conversation and finding much to amuse them.

'Well,' he said. 'Let battle commence. Harriet seems to be in a very good mood. Edwina will soon charm her.'

Unfortunately, Felix quickly saw that he was wrong. Even before she stepped up to tee off, Harriet's pleasant expression had disappeared and she was in deadly earnest. There followed several embarrassing minutes while she chose a club. Then she stood addressing the ball for a full minute, wiggling her ample bottom, pulling back the club only to change her mind about carrying through.

Greg urged, 'Come on, for God's sake. What's the matter with you? It's like you've never played before.'

'If you don't shut up, Greg Squiller, I'm going to go home this minute. Now leave me alone.'

Eventually she hooked the ball to the right halfway down the fairway, where it landed in the rough. Edwina's ball was not much better. It occurred to Felix that she had made up her mind to lose, but with Harriet in her present mood and playing badly, it was not going to be easy. Greg sighed deeply, gave Felix a helpless shrug of the shoulders and stepped up to the tee. Now thoroughly put off his game, he, too, hooked the ball.

Felix, probably the poorest player of the four, hit his ball two hundred yards straight down the fairway. He couldn't help laughing, but he was the only one to do so.

The morning didn't get any better. Two hours later they were back in the clubhouse, having recorded some of the highest scores the course had seen in recent weeks. Edwina and Felix won by three holes. Greg and Harriet were no longer speaking to each other, but they remembered almost simultaneously that they would not be able to have lunch with the other two. Baby-sitting was given as the reason.

'What is the matter with that woman?' asked Edwina when she and Felix had found a table upstairs in the clubhouse to have a sandwich. 'Why is it so important to her to win? I tried to lose.'

'Everybody knows you tried to lose which probably made Harriet furious. I'm sorry. I've known her for almost a year. Not well, mind you. Just slightly, but I've never seen any of this competitiveness in her before. It's like a disease.'

Edwina sighed. 'I could do with a woman friend. I don't know many people and . . . I could just do with a woman friend, that's all. Somebody to go shopping with, to gossip with. Women need women. It's really annoying.'

'I'll introduce you round. In fact, I'll have a drinks party and introduce you to a dozen more people. Of course we'll get together with Greg and Harriet again some time, but not for any competitive games. Perhaps it will all blow over. Greg was really angry. He's going to give her hell.'

'Felix, let's forget about them for a while. I have a little problem and I need your advice. There's this man who lives in Gorham – '

'Leo Midnight.'

'Yes! Do you know him?'

'I met him the other day. He was extremely unfriendly. Wanted me off his territory. He mentioned Zena Alway so I went up there. I have advised her not to get involved in a war with Midnight. Is it absolutely necessary that you see the trees? I doubt if anyone went there to check on them for years.'

'Not even after the great storm of '87, so I've been told. Planning officers have a statutory right to get onto the property. But I don't want to go down that route.'

'Is the house listed?'

'No. It's old enough but it's been messed about so much there's nothing worth preserving. No help there. I'll get my courage up and visit him.'

'Why not write to him first? Give it a little time, coax him a bit. If that doesn't work, threaten him with the law. You can do that, can't you?'

'I can get tough eventually. I'm going to write him a stinking letter, see if that works. I suspect there are trees of national interest on that property. The house is set just as if it's in a clearing in the woods. There's bound to be something of interest. I saw signs from Mrs Alway's property that there was once a fine arboretum at Gorham House. Mrs Alway says rumour has it that a lot of trees were planted around 1900. But there's been a house on that land since the year dot. I imagine there are some very old yews and oaks, at least. I must see it, but I can wait a few weeks, I guess.'

'Good idea. Let John Blue handle it.'

Edwina sighed. She did not think waiting for John was a good idea at all. She wanted this very unpleasant man to respond to her threats, not his. Leo Midnight dominated her thoughts to such an extent that she knew she must do something positive if she was ever to free herself from his evil spell. She was already composing the letter in her mind. She'd show the ogre a thing or two. He'd be sorry he ever tangled with Edwina Fairfax. It was just terribly bad luck that he reminded her so forcefully of her father.

Greg and Harriet drove away from the county golf club and were silent for several minutes. 'We've got to eat something,' said Greg eventually. 'Do you want to go home or shall we stop off somewhere?'

'Fish and chips. Take them home,' murmured Harriet. 'I can't face anyone.' She found a tissue and wiped her eyes.

'I don't know what the hell's the matter with you. Why are you making such a fool of yourself over Edwina?'

'She's too good for him.'

'What are you talking about? No woman is too good for Felix.'

Harriet sighed. 'It's just . . . she's got everything. A really good career, her own money, a

106

great body. And confidence. Have you noticed how much confidence she has?'

Greg sighed. 'It's not confidence. It's bluster to cover her uncertainty. She's just a kid in her first real job, for God's sake. Have some sense.' Nevertheless, he understood now. This was about Harriet's old feelings of inadequacy, expressed as antagonism to Edwina. 'You wanted kids. You wanted to raise a family. I give you an allowance and you can spend it any way you want to. Don't go back to work just yet. Wait till Ben and Hannah are in school. It's not that long.'

'Go back to what job? I wouldn't want to work in Bishop doing clerical work. That's not a career. I want a career.'

'What as? A professional golfer?' Greg knew that he shouldn't have been so cruel, but even so he was unprepared for the floods of tears that followed.

'Your work is interesting. You don't know what it's like spending the whole day in the company of young children. There's no stimulus. I need something that will challenge me.'

Greg didn't know what to suggest, but he soon discovered that Harriet had given the matter some thought. 'I want to study floristry. My mother says she'll have the children. I could start in September but I need to register soon. Eventually I'll open my own shop. We could use the money. You'll be glad of it.'

Greg objected violently, imagining his children being raised by Harriet's overly cautious mother. They argued about it for half an hour, calling a truce only while they were actually in the fish and chip shop. Eventually, as usual, Greg gave in. He was no match for Harriet in determined mood, but he made no attempt to hide his bitterness. They ate a silent lunch at home, then he went to pick up the children from Harriet's mother. It turned out Hannah had been sick all morning.

Cassandra was hot and sticky. She had spent the morning waxing her legs and bikini line, a difficult task she preferred to perform for herself as they always hurt sensitive skin so much at the salon. She had then painted her toenails before slipping on a pair of flip-flops and shuffling down the uncarpeted stairs. The kitchen was full of dirty dishes, but she knew that Leo would do them eventually. She could outwait him, calculating that if he were left with the dishes often enough, he'd relent and buy her a dish-washer. They lived in a big house, and she had expected to be treated with consideration. Luxury, that's what she had been expecting. Not squalor. She knew all about squalor.

Walking out onto the veranda, she looked for a chair sufficiently clean and sound to take her slight weight. There were none. The wicker chairs were rotting and the metal ones were covered in rust. For a moment, she was undecided whether or not it was worth staying out of doors. There was absolutely nothing to see except trees. Leo had been hacking away at some of them, trying to cut out a view of the countryside to be enjoyed from the veranda, but he hadn't made much headway. Leo, she suspected, just liked to use the chainsaw. He said it helped his nerves.

'We should buy some chairs!' she called to him as he approached from round the back of the house. He was sweaty but seemed pleased with himself. She adopted a pout. 'Why can't we have some new furniture?'

He joined her on the veranda dressed in navy shorts and a grey T-shirt. He was carrying two cans of beer. 'Why don't you bloody well wash one of these old things down? You do nothing but creep around the house in your latest new clothes. I've not seen you wear the same thing twice.'

'Liar.'

He sat down on a wicker chair. There was a tearing sound as the seat gave slightly with his weight. 'You are the laziest bitch I've ever seen.'

'We live in a big house and we should have servants. They're the ones should do the cleaning. I'm not a skivvy. I didn't hitch up with you to be a skivvy.'

'We could work together to clean up the place a bit.'

She chewed on her thumbnail, an annoying habit that he had not noticed before they came to Gorham House. Her thin pink singlet and sarong-type skirt suited her well. She was breathtaking this morning, with eyes of a luminosity he had not seen on a woman before. Her figure was perfect. He was amazed that she could keep it looking so delicious merely by maintaining a disinterest in food. She never indulged in any form of exercise.

Cassandra saw that he was studying her and smiled, running her tongue over her lips. 'You fancy me, don't you?'

'Of course I fancy you.'

'But you can't do nothing about it, can you?

You're nothing but a goddamned eunuch.' She stood up, stretched elegantly, then stuck her tongue out at him. 'You get me some help around here or you're going to be sorry. I just might leave you. How would you like that?' She went through the open doorway to the dark hall.

He leapt up to follow her. 'Don't you threaten me, my girl! You do some work around here and I might, just might buy you that dishwasher you've been going on about. Come down here! Don't go upstairs.' He grabbed her by the arm as she reached the bottom step.

Suddenly afraid that she had gone too far with her insults and threats, Cassandra cried, 'Don't hit me! Don't!'

Felix was at the station when the 999 call was relayed. Domestic violence at Gorham House. Cassandra Midnight calling for assistance.

'I knew it!' said Felix. 'I put him down as the type. He's a big man. He could break a woman in two, especially as everybody says she's a frail little thing. I'm on my way.'

Chelmsford police had a polaroid camera with which to photograph victims of domestic violence. The officer answering the call could photograph the person, showing exactly what had been done to the victim. Later, if they were reluctant to make a statement, the polaroid could be used as evidence. But Felix had no camera. Mrs Midnight must be persuaded, for her own good, to come with him to the station to make a full statement. Leo Midnight must be taught that he was being watched very carefully.

The house was as he remembered it from a few

days earlier. A broom had still not been taken to the veranda. Cobwebs hung everywhere and the garden furniture was ready for the scrap heap. Leo Midnight was seated in an old wicker chair calmly drinking from a can of beer.

'Ah, PC Plod,' he called. 'What brings you back here?'

'A 999 call. Request for assistance.'

Leo leapt to his feet, tossing the empty can on the chair. He looked utterly bemused. 'What are you talking about?'

At that moment Cassandra staggered out the door, her mascara running down her cheeks. 'Oh, officer, please help me,' she murmured. 'My husband . . . assaulted me.' She pointed to numerous bloody marks on her arms, to a red weal on her cheek. She tottered to a seat as Leo looked on, his mouth gaping.

'Hello, Cilla,' said Felix quietly. 'You're not up to your tricks again, are you?'

Cassandra gasped. Leo made a sound as if he had been punched in the stomach.

'Oh, God!' she moaned. 'You! What are you doing round here?'

'I've been stationed here for the past year.'

'I knew you was a cop,' she said, wiping the mascara stains from her face with a tissue. 'But if I'd known you was living anywhere near I wouldn't have come.'

'You scheming little bitch,' said Leo quietly. He didn't seem to be particularly angry. 'Did you dial 999 to say I'd hit you? The other way around, more like.'

Felix bent to look down on the beautiful face which did not seem to have aged in the past few years. 'Look at me. Did this man hit you? That's quite a mark on your face. How did it happen? Will you come down to the station and make a complaint of an assault?'

'What's the use?'

'Will you make a statement now?' He pulled out his notebook. 'Who is responsible for the wounds on your face and arms?'

She was silent for a moment, then jumped up and headed for the door. 'Why don't you bugger off, Felix? I hoped never to see you again.'

When she had gone, he turned to Leo. 'Do you care to make a statement?'

'The lady can be rather spiteful. We argued, briefly, about her unwillingness to do any housework. I can't even remember what I said to her. She said something like "don't hit me, don't hit me," and ran upstairs. I didn't give it another thought. It never occurred to me that she might be planning to set me up. I was having my beer and you turned up. How long ago did you know her?'

'She was sixteen. I was eighteen. I took her out a few times. She was living with a foster family. The Reeds. My mum didn't like her. Sorry. I'm not saying she isn't a wonderful wife to you, although – '

'Did you hear about her boyfriend? The one who died eighteen months ago when she was pregnant? Did you know she lost the baby as well? All within the space of three weeks.'

'I heard about it. I'd left the area years earlier, but an old mate rang me. She's had a terrible life.'

'My point exactly,' said Leo. 'Make some

allowances. Don't you lot come round here in droves. She had enough of that when her boyfriend drowned. She's emotionally rather fragile and she does dramatize things. I have never laid a hand on her, and never will. I promise you. So you never knew her boyfriend?'

Felix sighed. Leo Midnight always seemed to take charge of any conversation they had. He decided to surprise the older man. 'What a lot of personal questions! Be careful. I might get to thinking you were once a policeman yourself. You interrogate like a cop.'

Leo registered shock followed by extreme anger, but he did not speak. Felix knew he had scored a direct hit.

'As you well know,' said Felix, 'you're not investigating me. It's the other way around. So keep your size elevens under the bed and forget you were once a cop. We don't need your Met ways around here.'

Leo took a step closer. Felix sensed the menace in the man and braced himself for a set-to. 'I suppose you looked me up on the computer. By God, if anybody round here comes telling me they've heard I used to be a cop, I'll know where it came from. That's against the rules, sonny. You open your big mouth around town and you won't be PC Plod for long.'

'I may be Plod to you, but I know the law. Nobody will be told what was found on the PNC.'

Leo eyed him critically. 'You know, I don't hold with this community policing. A cop should be at the sharp end, fighting the villains, not holding the hands of a bunch of middle-class sods

113

who think they're upset. Surely that's not what you became a policeman for. Oh, it's all right for the older guys, the ones who are waiting out their retirement and need to do anything useful, but not a young bloke like you. You should be doing something challenging. If you're happy here, there's something wrong with you. You're not a bloody social worker, even if you like to act like one. And take a bit of advice from someone older and wiser. You cross one of these middle-class types, don't say "How high?" when they tell you to jump, they'll soon give you a mouthful. They pay your salary. They want value for money. And don't make that face at me. You haven't got an answer because you know I'm right.'

'I know nothing of the sort, *sir*. But I have no intention of arguing with you. Despite your opinion of community policing, you may one day be grateful for my help.' He smiled. 'Do give me a call any time.'

Having failed to get a statement from Cilla who was now Cassandra, Felix drove to the parking area by the Gorham sports pavilion. Too restless to sit in the car, he got out and paced the ground, hoping to look gainfully employed if anyone happened to be watching.

The sight of Cilla had knocked him for six. He couldn't think straight. He had lost his virginity to her all those years ago. A gangling boy of eighteen, he'd been grateful for her considerable expertise. She had led him through his initiation, making it a wonderful experience. It was not until much later that he began to worry about how he compared with the other lads, to wonder if she were cheating on him. Long before their bust-up, he had been eager to break away. His mother had nagged him about it for weeks. Cilla was unpredictable, vengeful and, worst of all, so sweetly pretty that people believed her, no matter what she said.

Voices were growing nearer, two women with pushchairs heading for the children's play area. He returned to the car and went to the station where he would have to make a report. But that could be done later. It was lunch time. He put his hand on Greg's shoulder. 'Let's go out for a bite. I need a quiet word.'

Seeing the young man's troubled face, Greg immediately closed up the file he was reading and grabbed his jacket.

'So what happened?' he asked when they were on their way to The Bull, seven miles away from Homestead. 'Is she coming in to make a statement? Had he beaten her up? Hospitalization? Don't let him bully you.'

'I know her, Greg. She's changed her name to Cassandra. Used to be Cilla, like, you know Cilla Black. Maybe it was a different name before I met her. She's a funny girl. Hasn't changed much since she was sixteen.'

'Was she badly hurt?'

'Big red mark on her face. Cuts all over her arms.'

'But that sounds a bit like – '

'Self-mutilation,' said Felix. 'If a man's going to beat up a woman, he punches her, slaps her a few times, maybe throws something at her. He doesn't go making little scratches on her arms. And I saw no signs of any punches. She didn't want to make a complaint. Shut up as soon as she recognized me. He was out of it, had no idea she was going to put in a call.'

'Do you think he'll hurt her in future?'

'No, I don't. Mind you, she might drive him to it. I'm damned sure I'd wring her neck within the week.'

Greg turned on to a winding back road towards Blackmore End. 'But you'll make out a full report, cover your arse. You know, these things can be tricky. He might be playing mind games with her, pushing her beyond what she can stand. She might be hurting herself as a plea for help. You mustn't dismiss the whole business that easily.'

'I know her!' shouted Felix, and his voice reverberated around the interior of the car, making Greg wince. 'She was sixteen. I was eighteen. I said I was going away to police training. She was pissed. Banged herself about a bit then staggered into the station and made a statement accusing me. They hounded me to death. I was scared, I can tell you. Nearly didn't get to Shotley, my whole life in ruins. I didn't know how to defend myself against the charge. My mum hired a lawyer, but there was a really great sergeant at the station. He asked Cilla all the right questions, disproving her claims. You know, "Tell me again how he threw a plate at you. Where did the plate land? Did it break? How many pieces?" She finally got fed up and told them she had made it up. Then they wanted to know if I had put pressure on her. Greg, I know she's screwed up. Had a hell of a life. In and out of care. In and out of foster homes. That sort of thing. But just

116

looking at that beautiful face makes me feel sick inside.'

'Here we are,' said Greg. 'I'll buy you a beer.' This was all he could think of to say, so startled was he by the turn of events, the amazing coincidence, the potential for trouble. He had no genuine words of comfort for Felix, who was still clearly suffering from having false claims made against him. This was one dangerous woman. She might do anything. He would take great care where Mrs Leo Midnight was concerned. And he would keep Felix well away from her. Come to think of it, he would keep Felix well away from Leo Midnight, as well.

Felix didn't move immediately, just sat in the car brooding. 'You know what he said? Said I'm a social worker. He said community policing is a waste of time.'

'Typical Met,' said Greg.

Felix knew what he meant. London policemen tended to look down on their rural comrades, seeing them as less efficient, less likely to have to face real trouble. Of course, those in other forces had equally unkind thoughts about the Metropolitan Police Force. The rivalry and the jokes were largely good-humoured, but feelings ran deep.

He remembered that he had let Leo know the Homestead police knew of his career. Perhaps Felix should confess what he had done. Yet he felt a little sheepish about having mentioned it to Leo. He decided that what Greg didn't know wouldn't hurt him.

CHAPTER FOUR

Cassandra was standing at the foot of the stairs when Leo returned from having seen Felix off the property. She hung her head and looked at him through her lashes with a sly smile on her pale lips.

He took a deep breath, controlling the urge to do exactly what PC Plod had accused him of. Her cunning chilled him. She wanted to be the centre of attention at all times, and if he didn't dance attendance on her she would see to it that someone else did. 'Now what was that all about?'

'That's to teach you not to ignore me. You piss me off sometimes, Leo. You don't appreciate me.'

'Did PC Plod piss you off?'

'He was leaving me. I don't like it when people leave me, but I didn't really love him. He was useless in bed and he wanted to be a policeman.'

'Did he know your boyfriend?'

'Carl? No. Carl was different. He was older and more mature. Carl wouldn't have liked Felix. He was a real man.'

He approached her and, with a tremendous

effort of will, placed a kiss on her neck. 'You really loved Carl, didn't you?'

Her eyes filled with tears. 'Yeah. Oh God, Leo. I did really love him.'

'And you lost your baby.'

'I didn't want the baby without Carl. I'm not sad about that, not really.'

No, thought Leo, she wouldn't have wanted a baby, especially not one she had to bring up on her own. Cassandra was not the maternal type, but he could imagine her falling apart after Carl's death, needing a man to lean on, someone to tell her she was beautiful and loved.

He told her he would take her out to dinner in Chelmsford that night if she got herself all dressed up. She squealed and hugged him, then started up the stairs quite happily, having forgotten her attempt at causing him serious trouble.

He called up to her. 'You know, if you knock yourself around on a regular basis, you're going to lose those great looks.'

She turned on the stairs and beamed at him. 'I never thought of that. You're absolutely right. I won't do it again.' She paused. 'But you better treat me right or you'll be sorry.'

Leo went upstairs to his own room, removed his laptop from its hiding place and plugged it into the phone line. 'They're on to me,' he wrote. 'Looked me up on the PNC. Cassandra shopped me to the cops, rang in to say I'd beaten her up. PC Plod turned up. Seems he knew Cassandra in their teens. She had pulled the same stunt on him. His name is Felix Trent. Works out of Homestead station, but I don't think this young bloke was smart enough to rumble me. Only one

119

member of CID stationed there. Must have been him. Don't know his name. I'm in the spotlight which is very bad for our plans. Hope you are having a decent holiday.'

He paused, his fingers resting lightly on the keys. Then with feverish haste he tapped out, 'I have often thought that I would try to tell you how much I love you, how you brought me some happiness and sanity at a bad time in my life. I guess I never really loved anyone else, not really loved them. I thought I did, but it never lasted. You have given me everything I hold dear and I will try to give you the one thing left in this world that you want and need. I miss you.' He read it over, then carefully erased everything in the final paragraph before sending the e-mail. Some things could never be said.

Leo hoped that he and Cassandra could rub along quietly in future, without drawing attention to themselves and, above all, without quarrelling. The next morning, however, they received an invitation in the post. Mr and Mrs Eric Hebard requested the pleasure of their company at a drinks party at their home in the village of Elton Magna on the following Friday.

Leo tossed the invitation across the kitchen table. 'We'll not be going to that!'

Cassandra read it quickly. 'They invited us? They want us? Oh, Leo, you are an old meany. You're trying to keep me in a cage. I want to go. Please say yes.'

He sighed. 'What do we have in common with these people? They're probably old farts and they'll look down their noses at us.'

'They want to know us because we've got a big

house and they think we're grand. Please, Leo. I can put on one of the pretty dresses you bought me and make all the men wish they could get me into bed. We've got to see somebody sometime. We're buried out here.'

He threw up his hands in mock despair. 'OK. I give in. But don't blame me if you're bored.'

Edwina arrived at the office early each morning to collect her mail, to see who had applied for permission to lop a branch, cut down an old pear tree or remove a leylandii hedge. There were letters, too, from neighbours who wished to complain about infringements of the law as they perceived it – the tree cut down without permission, the neighbour's hedge that stole all the light. There were accusations and counter-accusations of spite, anonymous tip-offs about trees brought down in the dead of night. The necessary paperwork was particularly irksome. She preferred to be out of doors, promising herself each day that in the very near future she would sort out the chaos on her desk.

There were always a few phone messages, mostly from Zena Alway which supplemented the letters she scrawled in blue ink on blue paper, her writing so spidery that Edwina had trouble reading them. Zena had a talent for getting her very worked up and angry about the Midnights. So angry was she on several occasions that she almost found the courage to visit Gorham House and confront Leo Midnight. This mood always passed before she could act on it, but the problem of the trees at his home simmered away at the back of her mind.

On Wednesday morning there was less than usual to deal with, so she decided to visit Grover's Court which had a courtyard around which fourteen ancient single-storey almshouses had been built on three sides. One of the duties of the section was to visit sites to see if a particular tree was dangerous. The council could do the work and send the bill to the owner, or order it to be done by the owner immediately.

However, as John had explained, the almshouses belonged to the council, so the landscape section would be handling the problem. 'Visit the site and write a very brief report,' John had said. 'Then we'll talk.'

The almshouses were home to a number of elderly people, most of them women. The courtyard area was small and the grass was sparse, struggling to survive under the large lime tree that grew in the middle. Its spreading branches and interesting bark gave the development a leafy rural air that removing the tree would totally destroy.

Yet the tree was massive with a root spread to match, and it was well known that limes growing twenty metres or less from buildings could sometimes cause problems with foundations, if the soil happened to be a heavy clay.

Recently, Westminster Council had been saddled with costs of a million pounds because they refused to give permission for a London plane tree to be felled. Properties were damaged. The residents had sued the council and there had been a messy and expensive court case. Although London clay presented particular problems, this case had a disturbing effect on all councils which were naturally anxious to avoid a similar disaster.

The tree's roots were not the only hazard. Limes were usually infected by aphids which produced a sticky honeydew that fell on cars and benches and anything else that lingered too long beneath their branches. A black fungus then fed on the honeydew and some people were allergic to it.

The answer might be to remove the tree, then plant in its place half a dozen urban trees, something, Edwina thought cynically, that the neighbourhood children could vandalize with ease.

On the other hand, removing the tree would probably have serious consequences. The public did not fully understand the question of tree roots and subsidence, nor, occasionally, did the representatives of insurance companies who demanded that some unoffending tree be removed immediately.

Subsidence and its opposite, heave, occur on clay soils. It is not the actual roots of a tree that cause a building to move, but the water taken up by those roots which causes the clay to shrink. Huge trees take huge amounts of water. A forty-foot tree, for example, takes up about fifty gallons of water a day during its growing season. Take out the tree and the water loss ceases, of course. The water that was being removed will now slowly collect in the clay soil which in turn will expand. Heave occurs. A building might, for instance, be lifted at one corner, causing very expensive damage. All of this takes a long time to happen, twenty years in some cases. But the cost of repairing the damage of heave is even greater than that for repairing subsidence.

The right way to go about it is to prune the tree progressively more severely. This will cut down the water uptake and so lessen the chances of subsidence; heave will not be caused.

The branches of the lime, she quickly decided, should initially be cut back to about fifteen feet. The appearance of the courtyard would be marred only until the following spring when it would come into leaf once more. Who could object to such a simple remedy? She had been on the site barely ten minutes, but was confident that pruning would do the trick.

Returning to the council offices, she interrupted John who was in conversation with a man she had never seen before. He was not pleased to be stopped in mid-sentence.

'I've seen the lime tree at Grover's Court. Now what should I do next?'

John sighed, excused himself and stood up to speak quietly to Edwina. 'Look, you know exactly what to do. Can't I trust you to get on with this one quickly without further input from me?'

'Yes, oh, yes, John. Thank you very much. I'll deal with the whole thing. Trust me.' Edwina apologized to the unknown man and almost ran back to her desk to get in touch with a tree feller.

Unfortunately, all the approved tree surgeons were fully employed and there was a growing waiting list. Perhaps Hargreaves could be given this simple job, thus fulfilling any obligation she had to him over the bats. She spoke to him briefly. Hargreaves expressed his gratitude for the work and said that he would get on with it. Edwina, he said, would be glad she had put some work his way.

She believed the residents would thank her in nine months' time when they had an attractive tree that didn't threaten their homes nor take their light. At the moment, however, they might not be so grateful. Some of the old dears would be unhappy, no matter what was done, and that could be unpleasant. Edwina, disliking confrontation with elderly ladies, had solved this difficulty by not speaking to any of them when making her assessment.

Satisfied that she had done a good job on the Grover's Court tree, she realized it was no longer possible to put off the question of Mr Leo Midnight. John Blue had explained the situation to her very carefully. She had a perfect right to knock on his door if she had reason to believe that there was a dangerous tree or that protected trees were being damaged. Mr Midnight, for his part, had a perfect right to tell her to get off his property. She could write to him and demand admission, stating the reason, and giving him forty-eight hours to agree. If he still refused, it would be necessary to obtain a court order which took about six weeks.

Her problem was that she had seen no dangerous trees and there were no tree protection orders on any of them. She had no cause.

If it were any other home owner, she would have left the matter. However, given her irrational fear of the man, plus her determination to do something outstanding that would prove she was doing valuable work, she had to act decisively. Leo Midnight had become her bête noire, a challenge and a threat to her self-respect. She couldn't bring herself to face him. Therefore, writing a strong letter was a satisfactory alternative.

Turning to her computer with a grim smile she drafted a letter:

Dear Sir,
You must arrange a date for me to enter your property within the next forty-eight hours. If you fail to allow me access to your property within the stated time, a court order will be taken out against you.
And what is more, if you do not comply, I will place Tree Preservation Orders on all your trees of whatever size and age. I advise you not to engage in a battle you can't win.
Sincerely yours,
Edwina Fairfax
Landscape and countryside section

She read over the letter, feeling satisfied that its message was strong enough to frighten Mr Midnight into complying with her demands. After all, she had the force of the law on her side. Quickly, lest anyone in the council should see what she had written, she sealed the envelope.

After work she went to Sainsbury's, as Greg and Harriet and Felix were coming to dinner. She and Felix had begun spending each evening together. He would drop round, ring the bell and say something casual about perhaps going out for a drink or driving to the coast. She might invite him in for a meal of some sort. Another time, he might pick up fish and chips and bring them along. Their relationship was very relaxed, so she felt no pressure to be on her best behaviour. She didn't have to examine her every word and compare it against the way the most popular girls back home or at college behaved. And the inner voice that was her mother's sharp soprano had been silenced almost from the day she met Felix.

Naturally, she had her little dreams. Dreams of Felix making love to her, of his telling her she was beautiful and that he loved her. She pictured the setting in some detail. There would be dozens of candles glowing everywhere, like a seduction scene in the movies or one of the makeovers in *Changing Rooms*. They always had candles, especially in the bedrooms.

He would slowly undress her and lead her to the bed. Then he would take her passionately, without the awkwardness that had accompanied her two brief affairs. And, most important of all, she and Felix would be together for a long time. If any dumping were to be done, she would do it.

He would not cruelly send her on her way as Brad had done, with a few words about there being nothing serious between them and their going to bed together not meaning a thing. He had said it was just a laugh and now it was time to move on. As she had slept with him on only four occasions, she felt used. There was no escaping the fact that she had been cynically seduced. He had taken advantage of her desperate desire to be loved.

It was a full year before the opportunity for further pain presented itself. Jack had been intense and possessive. He had not wanted her to have any friends but himself. So eager was she to have a special boyfriend, she had agreed to this. Six claustrophobic months followed before they quarrelled and Jack moved away.

After that, Edwina vowed never to look at another man again. She would be a spinster, very happy on her own. This attitude did not last long, of course. In reality, it had been the other way around. Other men had not looked at her. She was too abrasive, her mother kindly pointed out. She went to the wrong sort of places and consequently met the wrong sort of man. She didn't take enough trouble with her appearance. She was too much of a tomboy.

With so much helpful advice from her elegant mother, she could not help but fail socially. Only college provided her with a chance to be herself. No wonder that brief period had been the happiest in her life.

Until now. In the frequent visits Felix had made to her home, they had come to know each other, to argue without heat about politics or sport, to share their fondness for silly sitcoms. They often watched cop shows together. Felix would keep up a running commentary, pointing out errors and inconsistencies until she laughingly silenced him with a cushion. Such action always ended in a welter of kisses. Edwina was beginning to love cop shows.

She was well aware that his companionship was a gift from heaven, giving her a chance to grow into a confident woman. Sometimes, when she thought how awful it would be if Felix ever said goodbye, she actually felt faint.

This particular evening marked a special step in their relationship. Felix's friends were coming to dinner. She was a fair cook, and what she didn't feel capable of cooking she knew how to purchase from the supermarket. Dinner was going to be splendid, and Felix would be in charge of the wine, even though he and his mates seldom drank anything but beer.

Everything – or at the very least her entire future happiness – depended upon creating a good, relaxed atmosphere. She must get on with Harriet and impress Greg, for it had taken her no time at all to discover that Felix thought a great deal of the older man.

She had the roast well under way when Felix turned up half an hour early. They worked together efficiently to finish preparations. At seven, Greg and Harriet arrived, seemingly determined to have a good time.

'Oh, my God, Edwina!' cried Harriet, looking around. 'Retro Seventies! Isn't it brilliant? You are a very clever designer. I'm surprised you didn't take it up professionally. Is there nothing you can't do?' Harriet turned to her with a sly look. 'It must have cost you a fortune to do this place up.'

'Harriet,' murmured Greg.

Edwina looked around her living room in amazement. Retro Seventies had not occurred to her.

'Do you like it? I'll let you in on a secret. When I realized I was going to have to sit on packing cases for a year or two, my mum dragged this stuff out of the attic. I can't say I like Seventies furniture. I've just tried to make it all go together.'

'You're too modest,' said Greg. 'It's great.'

Edwina glanced at Felix and saw his approval of her honest answer. She knew him well enough to be aware that nothing but the best behaviour was good enough for him. If Felix had a fault, it was that he was a trifle stuffy about people's conduct. Although tolerant of the weaknesses of those he met in the course of his work, he would expect nothing but the best manners from her. She was his girl, an extension of himself in a way, so even to take a little undeserved praise would seem second-rate.

The evening was a great success. After everybody had helped with the clearing away and washing up, Greg pulled two brand new packs of cards from his jacket and announced that they would see how good Edwina was at poker. She had never played it before, but it turned out that Harriet was quite accomplished. It was one of the most enjoyable evenings Edwina had ever spent.

The irate phone calls started Friday morning at half past eight. Edwina barely had time to put her heavy handbag on the floor and sit down behind her desk. The first call was from old Mr Hargreaves. He was pruning the lime as requested and the residents were furious. Hadn't Edwina told them the tree was going to be trimmed, and why it needed doing? No, Edwina had not, but she covered up her mistake by pointing out angrily that he could not have received the papers authorizing him to do the work. He should not have begun.

'Tell the residents,' she said, 'that we are just cutting the branches back to fifteen feet. The tree will look very good next year and there will be no danger of the roots damaging their homes. I'm on my way and will be there in about fifteen minutes.'

There was no answer. 'Mr Hargreaves? Hello? Mr Hargreaves?'

'Did you say fifteen *feet*?'

On hearing the faint sounds of Hargreaves's stricken voice, her heart plummeted. 'Tell me you haven't cut the branches down to fifteen inches. Please tell me you haven't done that.'

'I thought you said—'

'Stop all work. I'm coming over.' She hung up the phone and sat in her chair fighting back the tears. Disaster was staring her in the face. Pollarding a tree could extend its life by many years, but there was always the chance that shock would kill it. If it died, the almshouses might well suffer serious heave. North Essex was a mixture of clay soils and sand, but this lime was growing on pure clay.

John Blue had a deep voice that filled her with dread, although he did not seem to have that effect on anyone else. Coming up behind her chair, he said angrily, 'What in God's name have you been up to? I've received five phone calls complaining about Grover's Court and it's only a quarter to nine!'

'Hargreaves started work on the lime before I sent him authorization.'

'Hargreaves? Hargreaves?' His voice was rising with each word he spoke. 'Show me Hargreaves's name on the list of those authorized to do tree work for the council. Where's your common sense, Edwina?'

'All the others were busy. I just thought I would give him the one job. He wanted work.'

'He wanted work because no-one with an ounce of intelligence will employ him. Besides, I told you exactly how to proceed in my memo. You were to telephone Jim Bassington. He's an authority on these matters and we often consult him.'

'Memo?' she said faintly.

'You didn't read my memo? Oh, Edwina, look at your desk.'

Edwina began scrabbling through the papers on her desk as John ran his hand through his thick blond hair. 'We cover our backsides by doing the paperwork, putting down what we plan to do and when we plan to do it. You simply must keep up with your paperwork. I know people think bureaucracy is a waste of time and money. The point is, the money is the taxpayers' and we must account for it. If you don't like keeping records, you shouldn't work for a council.'

'Hargreaves—'

'Hargreaves jumped the gun. Why do you think we don't use him? The man's a walking disaster. Now, what were your instructions to him?'

Edwina took a deep breath. 'I told him I would want him to cut all branches back to fifteen feet.'

He slapped his forehead. 'But the residents say he's cutting back all branches to stumps!'

She couldn't speak, able only to hang her head and wring her hands.

John insisted on driving her to Grover's Court, which meant that she would have to return to

Bishop with him. Two opportunities for him to lecture her in circumstances where she could not escape the sound of his voice.

They had not gone more than halfway when her mobile rang. It was Hargreaves, deeply offended. An elderly lady had come outside and thrown a bucket of water over Junior. He didn't think the lad deserved such treatment. Where the hell was Edwina? She had promised to come to his aid.

John could hear the tree surgeon's voice and tried to snatch the phone from her, but Edwina was too quick for him. 'It's dangerous. Against the law to drive and talk on a mobile,' she reminded him. 'You wouldn't want to break the law.'

She knew as soon as the words were spoken that she had gone too far, but John merely said, 'Break your neck, more like. You know, you've only been here a few days and already you've put years on me. Why do you have to get everyone's back up? You're a nice kid. Underneath. Those who don't know you very well speak highly of you.'

As these last words were spoken in a light tone, Edwina hoped that the storm was over. 'Sorry,' she murmured, and settled back in her seat a little more comfortably than before.

But her improved mood didn't last beyond first sight of Grover's Court, nor did his. Huge branches of the lime lay on the lawn. It seemed that every resident was out of doors and shouting. Hargreaves was yelling at an elderly woman who was dependent on her Zimmer frame for support while she gave as good as she got. The

tree looked grotesque, still in full leaf but with a
dozen gaps in the canopy on one side. Old man
Hargreaves had been acting as groundman, carefully lowering each branch which had been roped
before Junior began to cut. Even the Hargreaves
family didn't allow branches to fall freely.

'Look at that idiot,' said John. 'His son is
not even properly dressed. No helmet and that
harness is outmoded. No leg loops. If anything
went wrong, he could fall out of it.'

Edwina sighed. 'I noticed that. Very bad
practice.'

John Blue had a degree in forestry and years of
experience. His quiet confidence as he moved
across the courtyard to soothe the residents made
her feel very young and totally inadequate.

She didn't follow him, preferring to approach
Hargreaves to give him a piece of her mind. The
elderly woman raised her Zimmer frame as if to
hit Edwina with it, only to stagger backwards.
Her friends rushed forward to help her and to
add their voices to the woman's in castigating
both Hargreaves and herself.

Edwina turned away. Hargreaves's son, Junior,
was sitting on the ground. He was very wet.
'What's the matter with you, Junior?' she asked,
concerned. 'You're going to have to lay out for a
proper harness. You could fall out of that old
thing if you were ever knocked unconscious or
injured and unable to help yourself.'

'This harness was good enough for my grand-
dad and my dad and it's good enough for me. We
haven't got money to splash about. Besides, all
these precautions are for people too stupid to do
it any other way. So why don't you piss off?'

She considered pursuing him to continue the exchange, but gave up the idea. She didn't need more abuse.

'Edwina,' called John. 'I was just explaining to these good people why it is necessary to prune the lime. Perhaps you can help. What do you plan to do?' He smiled, as false a smile as she had ever seen. 'You will carry on with the pollarding and . . .'

'And get this tree in good order,' she finished brightly, hoping she had picked up her cue. 'We don't want any subsidence, do we? In fact, we may get some trouble, anyway. It may already be too late.'

John, she sensed, knew that she was preparing the residents for the possibility of heave now that the tree was being so ruthlessly pruned. As this could take years, she reckoned that some of them would be dead by the time there was trouble – and that she would be working somewhere else.

She found the courage, under his confident protection, to talk to the residents, to dwell on the evils of the honeydew that fell from the tree, to exaggerate a little the dangers from the fungus that grew on the honeydew. She even found the courage to make a full apology for not having discussed the plan with them before work began.

Somewhat mollified, they gathered round to insist that some other tree surgeon should be employed to finish the work. Having found a scapegoat in Junior for their displeasure, they treated Edwina with more courtesy than she felt she deserved.

On the other hand, Hargreaves told her in a menacing tone of voice that he had better be paid for the work done so far. And Junior, never one to waste words, held up two fingers as she was getting into John's car.

John, to his credit, did not berate her on the return journey. Instead, he patiently explained that she was a public servant, her salary paid for by the taxes of residents. It might, he said, be a good idea if she were to bear that in mind when dealing with the public. Discuss, explain, smile, cajole. Only in the direst circumstances should she bring down the full force of the law on anyone. Only when all other avenues had been explored.

It was just nine thirty when they returned to the council offices. Edwina sat down to open the mail she had not been able to look at before the Grover's Court disaster. There was only one letter of any importance. It came from Leo Midnight and while it was not so blunt as Junior had been, the message was the same. Leo was lifting two fingers to the council. He was prepared to defy her for ever. He did not believe she could impose blanket tree preservation orders. Gorham House was not a conservation area. She might try learning her job before sending him silly letters that were totally pointless.

Five minutes after reading his letter, when her breathing had just begun to settle back to normal, John returned. He was holding a sheet of paper in his hand and she knew that Midnight had written to him as well. She glanced at the clock. Not yet nine forty-five on the worst day of her life.

'All right,' he said, gently. 'I've heard about this man. He is unpleasant. We'll slap him with a

136

court order. No more letters of this nature. Is that a deal?'

'I'm sorry, John.'

He patted her shoulder, shaking his head as he walked away.

At half past eight Felix was on his way to the station in Homestead where he would exchange his own Astra for the distinctive Sierra police car. The road was momentarily deserted, narrow and winding like so many in the district. All the country roads were perfectly safe so long as everyone observed the speed limit and no-one became impatient. The trouble was that farm vehicles so often turned from the land onto the road and trundled their ponderous way to the next field. It was almost impossible to overtake one safely and motorists tended to get angry. They raged like spoiled children and overtook in the most dangerous of places. On the other hand, if the road was clear, they speeded through Gorham like demons.

He saw in his rear-vision mirror that a Jaguar was coming up behind him at speed. As the two cars approached a blind corner, the Jaguar pulled out, gunned its engine and overtook.

'What the bloody hell?' said Felix aloud, forgetting that he was driving a civilian car. No-one behaved so aggressively in the vicinity of a police vehicle. And, he realized, he recognized the car! Not a resident of Gorham, but a business-man from the industrial estate in Homestead whom he had seen at a few local events. 'I'll have you, mate,' he thought and put his foot down.

Before he could round the bend to close in on

his quarry, there was the sound of prolonged impact as steel crunched into steel. He braked hard and skidded to a stop in time to see a small red Hyundai from the other direction turn over twice and the driver of the Jaguar fight with the steering wheel as the car spun on to collide with a tree. He thought no-one could possibly get out of either car alive, but miracles did occasionally occur.

With a pounding heart he reached for his mobile and called in the collision, requesting fire, ambulance and police, then hurried forward to see how many people were involved. The business-man from Homestead, Mr Drinkwater, was dead. Felix could not find a pulse. The man had not been wearing a seat belt and had been thrown halfway through the windscreen.

Felix turned to the other car, reading the number plate upside down as the H-reg Hyundai rested on its roof. He knew the owner of this one, too, and tears stung his eyes as he took in the mangled metal. Marisa St John was – had been – fifty something. She was a widow and lived with her unmarried daughter, Janice, who was beside her in the car. The smaller car had been totally crushed, and had been, without a doubt, the innocent party in the collision.

Neither woman showed any signs of life. Janice's long black hair covered most of her face, but Marisa's short grey style performed no such service. Her injuries were hideous, her face a bloody pulp.

Felix took a deep breath and ran back to his own vehicle which was in danger of being hit by other cars rounding the bend. In his boot he had some warning triangles and these he put at either side of the accident area. Already he could hear sirens. The police would be first to arrive. Nothing to do but wait.

His hands were shaking and he felt sick, but the necessity to act in a professional manner held him together. He had dated Janice twice. They didn't really hit it off, but they had remained friends. She had been a bright young woman who loved dangerous sports. Climbing was her passion and she went often to Wales where she had probably faced death on many occasions. Her mother, Marisa, had been active in half a dozen clubs and organizations.

He thought the businessman was in his early forties. Beyond that he knew nothing about the man who had killed two women while taking his own life.

Police cars were coming from both sides of the accident. Apparently other forces had sent help. The traffic department would send out a Traffic Investigation Unit who would do skid tests and check out the vehicles. There would be a Scenes of Crime photographer, too, and already the police were setting up diversions so that the area would not be violated by cars.

He heard the unmistakable beat of a helicopter rotor and looked skyward. Helicopters took videos at the scene of the accident in major incidents. The evidence of the video would be very important.

Ambulances did not carry the dead. He thought he might go back to his car and retrieve his mobile, tell emergency services that there were three fatalities and no-one injured, but his legs would not take him. A terrible lassitude possessed his body.

He was a witness and off duty. Eventually he would be asked to tell them what he had seen, but he would not be expected to participate in the hours of work that followed such a serious accident. The road, he calculated, would be closed for at least four hours and possibly longer. There would be traffic jams and angry motorists. Yet the sense of horror and outrage that always attended the scene of a murder would be absent at the scene of an accident. There was no evil intent to mull over, no motive to perplex the living, just another example of human folly. But the whole of Gorham would mourn this act of slaughter.

Walking towards him was Dr Flawn who had been called from his surgery. He would certify that the three were dead and notify undertakers to take away the bodies. Afterwards, Dr Flawn had a word with the senior traffic investigator. They both looked in Felix's direction before the doctor came over to him and peered into his face.

'All right, Felix? Are you coping?'

He heard himself say yes. Was he? He thought not. Time passed, but he couldn't concentrate. A police car screeched to a halt and Greg burst from the driver's seat, leaving the door open behind him.

'Felix!' he called. 'Is it Harriet? Is it?' Two of his colleagues ran forward to restrain him.

'No, not Harriet. You know them, but it's not Harriet's Hyundai.' Greg's distress increased his own. He took out his handkerchief and blew his nose.

140

'I thought . . . Harriet travels on this road in the morning. I forgot nursery school doesn't open until September. I had to come and see. Tone just said it's Marisa St John. My God, you dated her daughter, didn't you?'

'Yes, didn't they tell you? Janice was with her.'

'Don't feel up to looking more closely.' He gave a slightly unsteady laugh. 'Forgive me. Got all wound up. These bloody fools!'

'Greg, I'm supposed to report for duty, but I'll not be able to remove my car from the scene. Can you give me a lift?'

'Of course. Let's get out of here. I've had enough.'

At half past ten Edwina had received a brief phone call from Felix asking her to meet him at the Prince of Wales for dinner. She was there at seven, but he was fifteen minutes late which was most unusual. He looked haggard.

'Bad day?' she asked, hoping he would then ask her the same question.

'Fatal accident on the Homestead Road. Three dead. No survivors.'

'Oh, poor you. I wondered why the road was blocked. I had to go the long way round to see a tree this afternoon. You were on traffic duty, I suppose. Nasty. What will you have to drink?'

'A pint of the usual. And you?'

She thought for a moment. 'It's so hot, I think I'll have a white wine spritzer.' Taken up with his own drama, he was not going to ask about her day, so there would be no opportunity to recount the farce of the lime tree. She sighed. It would have been nice to pour it all out to a sympathetic ear.

The Prince of Wales made very good fish and chips. They ate the enormous portions in silence and had not quite finished when they were approached by a woman whose face was familiar, but whose name Edwina didn't know.

'Excuse me. We haven't met. My name is Ulrika Kennet and a bunch of us are just getting up two ladies' teams to play darts. We always have three people on each team, but one of my side can't come. Will you be on my team? The others are all so much better than my friend and I.' She turned to Felix. 'You don't mind, do you, Felix? I won't take her away for long. We'll slosh them, I'm sure.'

Ulrika Kennet had a flushed face and broad hips. She also had a most engaging smile and was about Edwina's age. Determined never to pass up an opportunity to meet new people, she looked at Felix and raised her eyebrows.

He said, 'Go ahead. Give them a lesson in losing.'

She was introduced to four other women and quickly summed up their ability as they each threw a few practice darts. She turned towards their table to give Felix a smile, but he wasn't there. A frantic scan of the room located him at the bar just as he was being handed a third beer. She was momentarily distracted, because Felix never drank more than two pints. He might have his faults, but alcohol played no part in them. Solemnly, he lifted his tankard in salute and began making his way over to the dartboard where a small crowd had gathered.

Despite being distracted, she went out in fifteen darts and her partners soon joined her. They won every game to take the set. The opposing team demanded another set, but Edwina sensed Felix's restlessness and firmly declined.

'Let's go,' he said softly when she was by his side. He put an arm around her waist and held her close. 'Edwina, let me stay tonight.'

She sucked in her breath and counted to five before answering, not wanting to seem too eager. 'Yes, of course.' Her voice sounded all wrong, but there was no point in feigning a sophistication she didn't possess. She smiled up at him nervously as he guided her from the pub.

They reached his house first. She waited on the porch while he gathered a few things and crammed them into a sports bag.

She had trouble putting the key in the lock, so he did it for her. She pushed open the door, switched on the light and quickly assessed the state of her living room. All reasonably neat. Stumbling over the doorstep, she turned to him with a bright smile.

'Do you want a coffee or anything?'

He shook his head. She went into the bedroom and shut the door, trying desperately to think what she should do. Should she get undressed? And what about the candles? There were three scented candles that she had never lit sitting on the dressing table in small glass cups. She took a match to all three. She was in and out of the shower in seconds, turned down the bed, turned out the lights, realized the only nightdress that wasn't in the laundry basket was the Snoopy T-shirt. There was no time to wonder what he would make of such an unglamorous gown.

'Edwina? Can I come in?'

She wiped the sweat from the palms of her hands and managed to invite him into the bedroom. 'I could light more candles—'

'No . . .' He sneezed several times. 'That smell . . .' he gasped. He sneezed again, then four more times before she could get to all three scented candles and put them out. The glass cups were hot as she gathered them up. Felix was still sneezing and gasping for air. They bumped into each other as he made for the bedroom window and she headed for the kitchen with the candles. Now her eyes began to sting. It seemed as if the entire house was drenched in the cloying smell.

Cool night air wafted through the bedroom window and Felix stopped sneezing. He even managed to make a little joke about it. And she even managed to laugh, but it was an effort. All thoughts of passion had left her. She would have preferred half an hour in front of the telly to wind down.

Somehow he undressed her. Somehow she helped him to undress and they made love. Or perhaps, she thought later, they just had sex. Silent and hurried, it was unaccompanied by any sign of deep affection from Felix, and he gave her no opportunity to set the pace or to tell him that she loved him.

For reasons she couldn't quite fathom, she wanted to cry. Momentary release, the joy of consummation had not wiped out the follies of this day. Once again, she had been used.

Later, they showered together. He unpacked

his bag, finding no uncluttered space for his shaving gear and toothbrush and paste except the top of the cistern. She laid out blue towels for him, a bright contrast to the white ones hanging on the rail.

'Ah,' he said, laughing. 'So we won't get mixed up.' She didn't know if she had done something foolish or not.

He fell asleep almost immediately, turning his back and lying well over to his side. But sleep eluded Edwina. Strangely, it had taken this night for her to discover that she didn't know Felix at all. It had all happened too soon. Oh, not for some. A few of her friends felt cheated if they didn't get into bed on the first date. But she had wanted something deeper. She decided he was unsympathetic and self-absorbed, not her ideal man. She had to admit he was good company, but—

He woke suddenly and sat upright in bed. 'What is it?' she cried, startled out of her reverie. 'What's happened?'

Felix swung his feet to the side of the bed and put his head in his hands.

'Was it the candles? Are you ill?'

'Nightmare. Oh, God, a terrible nightmare. I can't go back to bed just now.' He fumbled for the switch on the bedside light. 'Do you mind? I'm sorry, darling. It's been a terrible day, but I thought I could put it out of my mind.'

'For God's sake, what happened? You're trembling.'

'I'll be all right in a minute. It was just the dream.'

He reached for his underpants and shirt. She

145

sucked in her breath, appalled. Was he going to go home? 'Please tell me. It must have been a terrible dream.'

'You know there was an accident this morning. I saw it. I was there. And I knew everybody who was killed. The man in the Jaguar, the one who actually caused the accident, I knew just by sight. But in the other car were two residents of Gorham. Marisa is . . . was a widow who lived half a mile from here. I dated her daughter, Janice, a couple of times. Their bodies were mangled and when I went to sleep, I could see them being ripped up. It was as if I was there and going through the whole thing. In reality, I was close enough actually to see the accident, but not to see their flesh being mangled. Marisa's car somersaulted. The Jag hit a tree.'

'Post-traumatic stress disorder,' she said knowingly.

He was anxious not to be labelled. 'No, no. Just flashbacks like anybody would have. The funny thing is, what I saw in my dream, I couldn't have seen in real life, because it was all in slow motion. Images have been coming back to me all day, but I could cope because I was awake. Now, I can't clear my head. I had to see Janice's sister, go to her house and tell her how they died, offer my condolences. She had been officially informed by someone else, of course, but I had to see her. She lives in Elton Magna. God, it was awful to see her grief. What must it be like to lose your mother and sister in a split second? I think Marisa has a sister or two and her ninety-year-old mother lives on the south coast. Three grandchildren.'

Edwina moved across to put her hand on his back. 'You poor darling. I am a selfish sod. You were going through hell and there I was playing darts. Come here and talk to me. Tell me all about it. I want to hear. Poor you. You've got a rotten job. I would hate it. Better still, let's get up. That's what I do when I've had a nightmare. I'll make us a cup of tea.'

They went into the kitchen and Edwina put the kettle on while Felix talked. 'Do you know? There are about seven hundred murders in this country every year. But over three thousand people die on the roads, and tens of thousands are injured. If we try to stop murders by taking away the weapons of the bad guys, everybody applauds. If we try to stop the much greater slaughter on the roads by bringing down the speed limit, we're villains, infringing the rights of citizens and all that crap. But if the average person had seen as many deaths, as many lives ruined as I have in my short time in the police, they might not be so critical. Speed and drink have got to be targeted.'

Edwina nodded, not choosing to mention the many times she had been stopped for speeding or her feeling of being harassed by the police when they should be out chasing proper criminals. Yet, having seen his distress, she knew that she would drive a little more carefully in future.

'I needed you so much tonight,' he said. 'Do you mind? I needed you. I couldn't talk to Greg or anybody else. Well, especially not to Greg. He rushed to the scene, because the report said a red Hyundai. He thought it might be Harriet. The doctor asked if I was all right. What could I say?

A bobby who can't take it at the scene of an accident? It wouldn't do. I had to keep it to myself. I didn't want to let it all out on you, but I needed to be with you. I'm a selfish brute. A bad lover. Forgive me.'

'Oh, Felix, I should have been aware of how you felt. My dad always said I'm the most self-absorbed person he's ever met.'

Felix put down his cup. 'Your father sounds like an absolute shit. I hope I never meet him. I really do.'

'Oh, no. He's terribly clever and I'm sure he's right. I was totally absorbed with myself tonight. I had a few upsets at work and—'

'You know, I read this book once.' He finished his tea and set the cup down. 'It said that sometimes in families one child becomes the scapegoat for everybody else's unhappiness. It could be that—'

To his astonishment, she leapt up from the table and burst into tears. 'It's not true. He loves me, I know he does. And so does my mother.'

'Of course . . . I didn't mean. Really, it was a thoughtless remark.' He came round the table and tried to take her in his arms. She struggled a moment, talking incoherently about her parents, their many acts of tolerance and their love for her. But suddenly she sank her head on his chest and the sobs died down.

Appalled at what he had uncovered, Felix had no idea how to reassure her. He stroked her hair, kissed the top of her head, vowing to mind his stupid tongue in future.

She spoke softly. 'Only, when I was about seven, my parents had some friends over for dinner. I heard my dad talking. He said he'd been offered a good position at a school in West Africa, but Mum had found herself pregnant with me and wasn't feeling at all well. In fact, she had to go into hospital and when she came home she had to stay in bed for five months. So he had passed up the challenge of a lifetime. I remember those exact words. And all because of me. I've always felt that I spoiled their lives.'

'I'll tell you what happened. Your parents were screwing and got careless, so your mum got pregnant. That's not your fault in any way. If these mysterious employers had really thought he was so marvellous, they would have found a job for him after you were born. Your parents are using you as an excuse for your dad's failure to get on.'

'I know they love me, but I do such stupid things. You wouldn't believe.'

'Come to bed. Let's forget them, Edwina. I'm the man in your life now.'

'They're good people, really. I didn't mean to make them sound . . . It's just me being stupid.'

'Shut up, darling.' He led her into the bedroom.

Felix sighed. He was growing close to Edwina. She was a splendid person, a woman he could admire. But her parents would be the in-laws from hell. He must bear that in mind.

CHAPTER FIVE

Cassandra had been happy all day. She trotted around the old house in a pair of shorts so small they could not possibly be comfortable, and a T-shirt that did not reach her waist. The long hair had been plaited into a single pigtail and she looked absolutely magnificent. Leo found her at half past ten running the vacuum cleaner over the faded carpet in the gloomy drawing room.

'Oh, Leo, we must do something about this place. I've decided to start in the lounge. Is there an attachment for cleaning the furniture?'

'I suppose there is. What's got into you?'

She made a little face, wrinkling her nose. 'I think I'm allergic to all this dust. Can't you get the Quayles to come up and do some house-work?'

'Queenie and Reg? They're in their seventies!' The Quayles lived in the lodge where they had spent the past thirty or forty years, devoted servants of the previous owner, their home secured during their lifetimes. Reg operated the old power mower occasionally and weeded most of the beds in return for twenty pounds a week.

He worked when he felt up to it and Leo asked nothing further of him. But Queenie, so far as Leo knew, had not worked in the house for many years. Despite her age, she seemed fit enough. 'OK. I'll ask her. Maybe she'll come in for a few hours a day.'

'And the windows need cleaning.' Cassandra turned off the vacuum and began banging cushions together, which raised a fog of dust.

'I'd better get the vacuum attachment before we choke,' he said, and left the room. He could hear her sneezing as he crossed the two-storey hallway with its dark, panelled walls and broad, uncarpeted staircase.

Queenie, it turned out, would be quite happy to come in each morning and do a little light housework. Leo offered her the legal minimum wage and Queenie was so delighted, she said she would just nip up to the big house straight away and give Mrs Midnight a hand. She went into her little kitchen, snatched a pinny from behind the door, bedroom slippers from under the kitchen table and declared herself ready for work.

Watching her walk up the drive, Leo thought he had been stupid not to ask earlier. Queenie would not gossip. Furthermore, she was a tall, well-built woman who probably had more energy than Cassandra did. With Queenie's help, they might begin to live a more civilized life.

On the other hand, the Quayles could not be expected to clean the many huge windows. If Leo and Cassandra were ever going to get a clear view of their property, he would have to employ a proper window cleaner. And that could be inconvenient for a man who wanted his activities to be kept totally private.

He solved the problem by driving into Bishop and visiting a pub in a run-down part of town. Ordering a pint, he chatted idly with the landlord and after a few minutes, asked him if he knew of a window cleaner who might be willing to travel over to Gorham. To his surprise, the landlord said immediately that he knew just the man. What's more, Tommy the Turk happened to be standing over by the pool table. With one hip resting on the table, arms folded across his chest and a cigarette between his lips, he looked both strong and villainous as he talked to friends.

'Oi, Tommy, come over here a minute.'

Tommy was a big man, dark and grubby. He frowned fiercely. Leo put out his hand and smiled. 'Good morning. I'm Leo Midnight and I'm looking for a window cleaner for an old house I've recently moved into.'

Now Tommy's face relaxed. For a moment Leo had feared that Tommy would guess that he was or had been a cop, just as he had known immediately that Tommy was probably a villain. Yet the swarthy man seemed friendly enough, not on his guard, not expecting trouble.

'Yeah, glad to help you out. I can come on Monday. Where is this place?'

Leo told him where it was and also gave Tommy some indication of the size of the place. Tommy said he'd probably have to spend two days on the job, if he was to do the job properly, cleaning the windows inside and out. That would be a hundred and fifty pounds. Leo agreed and they parted quickly.

On the drive back to Gorham he wondered what he had got himself into, but decided that he had not done anything too stupid. Those window cleaners who were villains were looking for valuable items which could be easily stolen from inside a house. Gorham House clearly had none. Even if Tommy were an experienced criminal, he would not find anything worth stealing. More importantly, he would be unlikely to gossip to locals about the Midnights' way of life, because he lived too far away. Leo shrugged. Occasionally, it was necessary to take a few chances.

Before returning home he bought mops and bleach, a new vacuum, a packet of cloths, window-cleaning fluid, soap powders and anything else he thought might be used in the cleaning of a house that probably covered ten or twelve thousand square feet.

Queenie was working hard when he returned. She had found some furniture polish and had the entrance hall looking less gloomy and smelling of lavender. She also had a list of supplies she said were badly needed. Her urgent requests were only partly met by his purchases. He would have to make another trip into town.

Cassandra, it seemed, had gone to bed exhausted. She had left a message that she was not to be disturbed as she wanted to rest before the drinks party that evening. She hoped that Leo had a clean shirt. If not, he must arrange with Queenie to get one washed and ironed.

Leo had a good arrangement with a Homestead laundry and dry cleaners. His worries about the evening's entertainment did not centre on clean shirts.

That evening, as he drove to the Hebards' home, he felt quite sick. Posh people in the country filled him with unease. Well acquainted with the moneyed set in London, if only through his work, he thought of these people as a breed apart: smug, happy in their routines and rituals, a community looking inward and determined to keep out the intruder.

He had no idea how he should behave. Not that he cared about doing the right thing. It was simply that he could not bear the thought that others might be laughing at him. Straightforward aggression, a knife, a gun, a brickbat caused him not a twinge. The knowingness of others left him feeling defenceless.

'What are we doing, going to the home of complete strangers?' he asked suddenly.

'Going for a laugh, that's all. You look pretty good in a suit and tie. I've never seen you that way before.'

'I'm uncomfortable. When I retired, I figured I'd never wear anything I didn't feel comfortable in.' He turned to her and smiled. 'See what I'm willing to do for you?'

'For a quiet life, more like,' she laughed. She was excited, anxious to arrive and dazzle them with her beauty.

The Hebards had sent him a little hand-drawn map which was accurate enough. However, it didn't indicate the narrowness of the roads, some of which could take only one vehicle at a time. Fortunately, they met no-one coming the other way and turned into the long drive behind two other cars.

They were just five minutes late. Apparently,

arriving on time was the proper thing to do. The muscles in his jaw tightened as he manoeuvred the car onto the neighbouring field next to a familiar Rover. He could see several dozen people on the lawn. Zena Alway must be among them.

'I'm overdressed,' wailed Cassandra, suddenly unsure of herself. 'Everybody's looking quite ordinary! Why did I wear this silk thing? Leo, take me home. I've got to change.'

'You'll be a knockout. Don't worry. They're dowdy and you're not. And why shouldn't you wear a few sparklers? They're not real. It's not as if you're shoving real diamonds down their throats.'

She got out of the car and her stilettos immediately sank into the soft earth. 'Bugger!' she snapped. Leo turned away so that she couldn't see his smile.

Her dress was of palest pink silk, heavily encrusted with diamanté around the neckline, which plunged invitingly. There were not many inches between the low neckline and the hem of the short skirt. The whole thing floated as she walked and was held up only by diamanté shoulder straps.

He reached into the back seat and pulled out a soft cashmere wrap. 'Here, put this stole around you. I think we're going to be outside the whole time. They've got a table set up to serve the drinks.'

She snatched it from him. 'It's not a stole. It's a pashmina. Anyway if I put this on, they won't be able to see my dress.'

When he laughed, she turned and gave him a

cheeky smile. 'Let's see how many husbands I can steal.'

'Give it up, my girl. They're all way past it.'

'They can dream, can't they?'

As they approached the house, a woman of about fifty-five came towards them with a bright smile. She had short grey hair and a most enormous bosom that bulged only a few inches above her waist. She might have a brilliant smile, thought Leo, but she had no taste whatsoever in clothes. Her flowing two-piece outfit was in some splodgy shades of green. It didn't occur to him that it might be silk; he assumed that it was made of polyester.

Her welcoming remarks could not have been warmer. 'You must be Cassandra and Leo! How nice of you to come. Oh, what a beautiful gown, my dear. It's exquisite.'

'Yeah,' said Cassandra with a self-deprecating laugh. 'That's what you get for inviting townies. I'm overdressed and my heels keep sinking into the lawn.'

'Such a lovely dress,' said Kitty. 'You'll make the party go with a swing.'

She's done it again, thought Leo cynically. Charmed the pants off some old bag who could not possibly have any idea what Cassandra was really like, and wouldn't believe it if you told her.

'Come straight away onto the terrace, then. You won't sink into that. Oh, here's my husband, Eric.'

Eric, a sleek weasel of a man with receding hair plastered to his head, registered the amazed approval that was common with people meeting Cassandra for the first time. He spoke briefly to

Leo, then placed a hand under Cassandra's elbow and guided her away to meet other guests.

'I must introduce you to a few people,' Kitty said to him.

'First, tell me who they are so that I can get a fix on them.' Anything to delay the ordeal.

'Oh, that's a good idea. Well, over there, the older couple. He's in a blazer and she's wearing that pretty floral dress. They're your neighbours from Barleytwist.'

'I thought Zena was our only neighbour.'

She gave him a conspiratorial look. 'I shan't introduce you to her. She's getting a little cranky.'

'And you know she can't stand us.'

Kitty laughed. 'Everybody knows she can't stand you. No, the couple I mean are the Brooms. They live at Barleytwist next door to you, although there are quite a few acres separating you. They're terribly sweet. Wonderful gardeners. I'm afraid our little garden must strike you as being quite pathetic. We've only got an acre.'

'But so beautifully kept.' God, how long could he keep this up?

The Brooms seemed quite friendly. They asked Leo how long he had lived at Gorham House and wondered what he thought of the village. Leo made some reply, convinced that his answers would be of no interest to them.

Kitty pointed out others, mostly farmers, then steered him towards the drinks. He saw with acute disappointment that there was only champagne, orange juice and mineral water. How was a man expected to get drunk in a hurry on that lot?

157

Before he could pick up the first glass of champagne, he met half a dozen couples, all of whom knew who he was and where he lived. Never had he so regretted coming to Gorham House. In his ignorance he had imagined that he was going to ground, hiding out in the country. Instead, he might as well have advertised his whereabouts on billboards. If it weren't so irritating, it would be funny.

He downed his champagne, put the glass on the table and allowed the waitress to hand him another. Within minutes he had finished the second. The third glass made him feel a little more at ease, but he was getting funny looks from the farmer to whom he was talking at the time.

Mercifully, Kitty returned. In the space of twenty minutes he had come to regard her as his lifeline. 'Eric is showing Cassandra around the house. I hope you don't mind.'

Leo picked up another glass from the table. 'Naw, I don't think she'll seduce him.'

He gestured with his glass towards a smartly dressed couple in their forties. 'Who're they? I smell money.'

Kitty laughed nervously. 'Oh, he's a trader in the City. One of the new breed.'

'Not a gentleman.'

She glanced at him briefly, then looked away. 'Let's just say he buys his furniture from Harrods.'

'As opposed to where?'

'Oh, dear.' Kitty reached for a glass of champagne, although she had been drinking orange juice all evening. 'The saying is, you know, that you're not a gentleman if you have to buy your own furniture. It's a joke.'

'I'll bet it is.'

'I've offended you. I'm sorry.'

'Kitty, old girl. You're just educating me. Anyway, I inherited my furniture. Haven't bought a stick. I guess that makes me a gentleman.'

Leo was not a gentleman by any yardstick Kitty had ever heard of, so she made no reply. Fortunately, at that moment, an old friend joined them.

'Leo, may I introduce you to Warwick Provender who farms quite a few acres hereabouts.'

Warwick was probably in his eighties and was heavily dependent on his cane. He shook hands firmly and refused the glass of champagne Leo held out to him. 'Dreadful business on the Elton Magna road this morning,' said the old man in a weak voice.

'Some sort of accident, was it? I knew the road was closed.'

'Yes,' said Warwick. 'Poor Felix witnessed the whole thing and he knew all three people who were killed.'

Leo was startled out of his alcoholic haze. 'Felix the policeman? You know Felix?'

'Yes, of course. Fine chap. He'll be on to you if you drive home after all you've been drinking.'

'I'm amazed that you take so much interest in what I'm drinking. Oh, dear.' He looked round with a comical expression. 'I'll bet you've been talking to Zena Alway. Yes, there she is. Hello, Zena!' Leo waved, but she turned away quickly.

'Take pity on her,' said Warwick, quietly.

'Not a chance.'

Leo walked away in search of someone to insult, but the urge wore off after a minute or two. Where the hell was Cassandra? He wanted to go home. Some people were already drifting off. He helped himself to half a dozen cocktail sausages and four little sandwiches. The City trader was talking loudly, so he walked up behind the man and slapped him on the back.

'Hi, mate! I understand you buy your furniture at Harrods.' He moved on before the confused man had a chance to reply.

Two people emerged from the house, talking intently. 'Cassandra! Where you been?'

She joined him, laughing. 'Boy, have you hung one on! Come on. We better go. I'm driving. Bye Eric, bye Kitty. I had a wonderful time and so did Leo by the looks of him.'

It was getting dark. They stumbled over the soft ground, swearing and giggling in equal measure.

'Oh, what a hoot!' said Cassandra when she had manoeuvred the car onto the narrow road.

Leo slumped down in his seat. 'Thank God we never have to see them again. I'm sure they'll forget us as quickly as we will forget them.'

Cassandra glanced nervously at him but made no reply to this, but Leo didn't notice anything amiss. He had fallen asleep.

Kitty said goodbye to Zena Alway and left Eric to guide the old lady off the premises in the gathering gloom. She flopped down on her favourite chair in the sitting room.

Eric walked into the room and took his usual place opposite her.

'My God, that woman should not be behind the wheel of a car.'

'Leo Midnight is one of the most objectionable men I have ever met. I have every sympathy with Zena. Poor woman.'

'Somebody ought to tell her she's too old to drive.'

Kitty, who hoped to go on driving for the rest of her life, bridled. 'I know half a dozen people Zena's age who drive perfectly well.'

'So do I,' said Eric. 'But that doesn't alter the situation with Zena. She's past it.'

'What's Cassandra like?'

'Utterly charming. Funny and warm and all that you could want from a beautiful young woman. Anyway, aren't you going to ask?'

She rubbed her hands. 'Do tell. Are we on?'

'We are. Cassandra has agreed. She said she'll have to work on that husband of hers. He won't be keen, because he's a bit antisocial, she says. You know it's quite possible that he and Zena are both justified in what they say.'

'Oh, well, never mind that. Let's see. I'll ring round tomorrow. Wine and cheese, celery and crackers. No, french bread looks better. Is that enough food or should we have pâté as well? We'll provide the wine, of course. I'll see if the Brooms will come up with some cheese. Zena does bake good bread, but – oh, dear. We can't expect her to come. We'll order some French loaves from the baker and buy some crackers. I'll get a couple of the committee members to make pâté. We won't serve coffee. Should we serve coffee?'

'Depends on how much you're going to charge for the tickets.'

She pursed her lips. 'Ten pounds? Don't you think we can get away with ten pounds? I mean, everyone is going to be absolutely dying to see inside Gorham House. Oh, and you must ring Warwick and ask him if his grandson will print the tickets on his computer.'

Eric frowned. 'Ten pounds is rather a lot. I'm not saying we won't get it, but maybe it would be a good idea to wait until we hear from Cassandra. She said she would speak to Leo and if there was any objection, she would ring me on Monday.'

'I can't do that, Eric. We want to hold the party on September the twelfth and time is racing on. We must get going. Why should he object, for heaven's sake? He's probably flattered silly by being asked to hold a charity do. It's their entry into the community. We're making it possible for them to meet loads of people!'

The Hebards heard nothing from Cassandra, so on the Monday Kitty decided to telephone, but received no answer the entire day.

The date for the wine and cheese party was growing near and Kitty was very worried. On Tuesday morning as soon as Eric had gone to Colchester to do some shopping, Kitty got into the family Range Rover and drove to Gorham House. She was intrigued to see the old place close to, and astounded that it was still standing, given that no work appeared to have been done on it since the war. She felt a shiver of excitement. The party was bound to go with a swing, because everyone else would be as curious as she was herself.

Leo opened the door. 'Good morning, Leo. Another hot day, but we do need rain, don't we? I'm so grateful to you for holding our little party and I've come—'

'What the hell are you talking about?'

Kitty sucked in her breath, sensing disaster. He filled the doorway and she realized that she was not going to be invited to cross the threshold. 'The wine and cheese party for my charity, Save Our Hedgerows. On September the twelfth. Cassandra said we could have it here.'

'*She what?*'

Leo whirled round, searching for Cassandra. Kitty had seen her hiding behind a pillar in the hall, but the girl looked so terrified that Kitty dared not draw her into the conversation.

'I thought it was all settled. Seven o'clock on September the twelfth. We'll do all the work. You don't have to do anything.'

'It's not on, Kitty. I've no intention of entertaining anyone in this house. I want my privacy. Besides, we'll be away on September twelfth. Going to London for a few days.'

Tommy the Turk, busy taking off forty years of grime from the inside of the hall windows, heard every word. He felt fleetingly sorry for the pretty little wife and gleeful that he had accepted the job of cleaning the windows. The Fat Man would be interested in what he had to say.

There was nothing Kitty could do. If he wouldn't invite her inside, she could hardly plead her case effectively. And Cassandra was choosing not to back her up. Vowing never to have anything to do in future with rough Londoners, she said a curt goodbye and heard the door close behind her before she reached her car.

Returning home, she moaned to Eric about Leo's rudeness, then rang Warwick to say that the party was off, so the tickets his grandson had printed were of no use.

'Try the Brooms,' said Eric. 'It would be a shame not to have the party. We could make five hundred pounds if we got a really good turnout and some decent raffle prizes.'

This seemed such a good idea that Kitty rang immediately, received instant agreement from the generous Brooms, and the planning began anew. The tickets were now to cost just five pounds, because as Kitty said, everyone had already seen the Brooms' home.

Later, Eric rang Warwick to ask if Warwick's grandson would print new tickets. Warwick was an old man and had been a student of human behaviour for many years.

'It's a disappointment, not seeing the inside of Gorham House. But just think, Eric, no-one has seen it for decades, so we're no worse off. I'm sure my grandson will be happy enough to print the tickets. He loves that computer more than he loves his wife. Understandable enough. Well, you've met her.'

Eric, who knew young Coral very well, dared not comment. She was a difficult woman, but then, she had married into a difficult family. He passed on the good news to Kitty who began drawing up an invitation list.

Tommy was eyewitness to as vicious a family fight as he had ever heard, which began as soon as the Range Rover had left the grounds. He had felt sorry for the missus when she was hiding behind the pillar looking pathetic. But he soon saw that his sympathy had been wasted. For such a pretty, frail-looking thing, she had a vicious tongue, but fortunately no accuracy with missiles.

'You're a shit, Leo,' said Cassandra, coming out from behind the pillar. 'I wanted that party. You don't let me do anything.'

'If you wanted it, why did you hide? You silly bitch! You leave me to do everything just so you can look the sweet little wifey. Grow up, Cassandra. I'm tired of your play-acting.'

Cassandra launched herself at him, her hands clawed. He caught her by the wrists before she was able to do damage to his face, but she carried on a stream of abuse in a hysterical voice that made Tommy's blood run cold. Breaking free of Leo's grasp, she reached for the decorative plates displayed on a side table and began hurling them at her husband. None hit him, though the fragments of one gave Tommy a crack on the shin.

Not surprisingly, Leo Midnight was no match for her. He ended up by saying that he would think about having the wine and cheese party, but it would have to be held on the twenty-fifth of September. She wanted to go to London, didn't she? He had to see his dear old mother. Cassandra could have a few days to herself, stay in a hotel, live it up. That stopped her in her tracks. She'd do it. That would be just fine. Suddenly the spitting, plate-throwing, screaming harridan had turned back into the sweet young wife.

Tommy, having laboured for two days, could begin to contemplate the end of his window-cleaning. He would hurry on down to Canvey Island and speak to the Fat Man. He had more or less memorized the contents of the house, had seen that there was nothing transportable of any great worth, and had walked the grounds when he had his lunch. Tommy knew that the theft of garden ornaments was a growth industry. He knew also that large statues were usually stolen to order. But it didn't have to be that way. There was room for enterprise, especially when he could see his way clear to taking four huge statues, called, the gardener had told him, the Four Seasons. It was going to be all right. Tommy was experienced. He knew what would be necessary.

Leo relied on the Internet to provide him with a link to the real world. His e-mail requesting guidance brought the reply: 'Yes, why not?'

Next he visited the web site of the Charity Commission. Save Our Hedgerows was listed and seemed to be in order. Still, his cautious nature urged further digging.

That evening he went for a drive alone. He found the Hebard house but drove right past, looking for the nearest pub. An hour spent chatting to the locals helped him to feel that a wine and cheese party would be relatively harmless and would buy him some domestic peace cheaply.

The next day at eleven o'clock, he telephoned Kitty. 'Hello, Kitty? Leo Midnight here. Look, you can have your wine and cheese party at Gorham House, but not on September the twelfth. We're going away for a few days as I told you. Make it September twenty-fifth. Cassandra is very keen on the party, but I've told her not to get involved with the preparations. OK?'

Kitty spluttered something, murmured her thanks and was just about to ask for a meeting when Leo hung up.

'He's agreed! Leo Midnight! September the twenty-fifth. What are we to do now?' she asked Eric. 'We can't hold two parties so close together. I'll have to ring the Brooms and tell them it's off. How embarrassing.'

'I'll have to ring Warwick and ask if his grandson will print a third set of tickets on his computer. I don't know if I can ever face that young man again. The least we can do is give him and his wife a couple of tickets.'

'And Warwick, oh, and the Brooms. I just hope we sell more tickets than we give away.'

The next day the Hebards were treated to a visit from Cassandra and suffered something akin to shell shock, so horrified were they by her account of Leo's violent temper. They were now thoroughly afraid of the man and wondered if the volatile Midnights would still be together on September the twenty-fifth.

Felix rang Greg on the Friday night and challenged him to a round of golf the next day.

'Since the women are going shopping together tomorrow, I thought you and I might get together.'

Greg swallowed hard. 'Harriet is going shopping with Edwina? She didn't tell me. I got the impression she was going alone. I'd love to go but I've got to babysit. Can't get out of it. If you're playing, come round afterwards for lunch. I'll whip up something.'

Felix said that he did wish to play and would see Greg around one o'clock. They hung up and Greg sat back on the settee and closed his eyes.

'Oh, God,' he thought. 'I'm in deep shit.' Fortunately, Harriet was at the supermarket with the children. He would have fifteen minutes to pull himself together. He was not a fool and he knew his wife very well. It would do no good to threaten her. Best to say nothing and pray for her good sense.

Almost a week earlier, they had been watching television together late at night. It was an old film in black and white and Greg was bored. Harriet, however, was taking great interest, if only to criticize.

'Oh, look at that. Another coincidence. He just happens to meet her on a train out of thousands of people. I've caught dozens of trains from Bishop and not seen anyone I know, only later to discover that there were two or three people on it from just around the corner. Crazy coincidences spoil a film.'

'Coincidences happen,' he had said.

'Oh, yes? Name one. Go on, name one.'

Stung, Greg had said, 'All right. Felix transfers to Homestead and a year later Cassandra

Midnight turns up in town and she used to be his girlfriend. How's that for a—'

She had turned to him, her eyes huge. 'That beautiful girl was a girlfriend of Felix? My mum pointed her out to me the other day when we went into Homestead. Oh, my God! Oh, how fantastic! Oh, I can't believe it! When? How long ago?'

'Ages ago. I believe he was eighteen and she was sixteen. Something like that.'

Greg couldn't believe he had been so foolish as to let out such a secret. In vain did he beg her to remember that this was something Felix had told him in confidence. She must not say a word about it to anyone, but especially not to Edwina.

'Especially not now he's screwing her,' he had ended lamely. It turned out Harriet had not known that either.

As he sat on the settee, contemplating the end of his friendship with Felix, he examined his own part in his downfall. 'I've probably got brain disease,' he said aloud. 'That's the only possible explanation.'

On the way to Colchester, Edwina and Harriet were nervously prone to talking over each other and laughing too much and too loudly. But after half an hour they relaxed and the atmosphere in the car was less strained.

There was to be a dance at the golf club in October and it was to be a black-tie affair. Felix had asked Edwina to come with him. Therefore it was necessary to buy something suitable. Edwina thought that she would probably have been wiser to visit the shops on her own, but it was certainly more fun to pick out a dress with another woman, someone who could be relied on to speak the truth about the gown's suitability. And she could certainly rely on Harriet for a frank opinion.

'We'll park at Williams and Griffith and shop there, at least first,' said Harriet. 'Then I'll show you the rest of Colchester. It's a lovely town, the oldest in England. Would you enjoy that?'

'Very much,' said Edwina. 'Thank you for coming with me. I've been looking forward to visiting Colchester, but it would have taken me ages to find my way around.'

It being Saturday, the town was packed. By the time they had managed to find a place in the multi-storey, both women were impatient to start shopping. Harriet led Edwina to the clothing floor and they began fingering the racks feverishly.

'Look,' said Edwina. 'This nice black evening skirt could be teamed with a glittery top.'

'Mmm,' said Harriet. 'I don't know. Anyway, try it on.'

They squeezed into the changing room and Edwina put on a rather shapeless cap-sleeved top made entirely of silver sequins and viewed herself in the mirror.

'I look like a pregnant snake!' she cried, and Harriet laughed so much she fell against the wall.

'No, dear, you look like the grandmother of all pregnant snakes. For heaven's sake, Edwina, buy something modern and youthful. Let me get that black velvet dress we saw. You'd look good in that. Hang on. I won't be a minute.'

She left the changing room before Edwina

could protest and quickly returned with the dress draped over her arm. Naturally, it looked terrific on Edwina and was just what she should buy. And naturally she was annoyed that Harriet had chosen it.

Later, Harriet also picked out a pair of black, strappy sandals to go with the dress, then wanted to choose a necklace for her friend. This was going too far. Edwina could not allow herself to be dressed entirely by Harriet Squiller.

She insisted she had a necklace that she wanted to wear. Actually, she didn't have anything appropriate, but her mother had tried in vain to persuade her to take her grandmother's pearls with her when she left home. Thinking that she would never get the chance to wear them, Edwina had refused. She now decided that she would telephone her mother this very afternoon and ask to have them posted.

As Edwina was removing the new dress and putting on her trousers and blouse, Harriet moaned about her lack of cash.

'I can't afford to buy anything new for the dance. It'll have to be the red chiffon. I can still get into it. You've no idea how expensive children are. Be warned. Do you mind if we go across the road to M & S? I've got to buy some underwear for the kids. What do you want to do for lunch?'

'Oh, let's just go to a hamburger place. I used to work in one, you know. Just for a few months before I got a place in an estate agent's. It wasn't all that much fun, I can tell you.'

They had no choice but to queue, time enough for both of them to wonder if they should go somewhere else. But the customers were being served very quickly and they decided to stick it out.

They managed to find two seats squeezed next to a large family of young children. Harriet bit into her hamburger. 'Children are a terrible expense. I mean, there's no money left over. I'm going to start on a course in floristry at Bishop college and one day open my own shop. It will make a big difference to us when I'm earning, but Greg is furious. He wants a hausfrau. I've got the shop all picked out. It's been empty for ages. I'll paint it pink with those flattering lights like they use in the supermarket to make the meat look bright and juicy. I'll specialize in weddings, of course.'

'Why, that's wonderful. Have you always been interested in flower arranging?'

'I've never done any, but it always looked like fun.'

Edwina frowned. 'But surely, if you don't just live to arrange flowers, if you haven't been reading about it and experimenting with flowers for ever, how can you expect to stick a course in floristry? You will have to eat, sleep and drink flower arranging. It will be really hard.'

'And exactly what do you mean by that?' Harriet raised her hamburger and took a vicious bite. 'You're trying to put me down, just because I haven't been to college. What do you know about floristry? Trees aren't the same as flower arranging. Did Greg put you up to saying these things? I'll bet he did.'

'No, of course he didn't put me up to saying it. I didn't know about your course until you told me just now. Take it from me, Harriet. I've been there. I know how hard it is to complete a course. And I had been interested in trees since I was fourteen. Studying takes a huge amount of commitment. You'll be surprised. And you have a number of distractions that a younger student wouldn't have – Greg and the children and your house. What you're taking on is really enormous. I hope you've thought this out.'

For a full minute Harriet didn't speak, then in a strained voice she expressed herself succinctly. 'I don't think I care to hear any advice from someone who had to go to college to learn how to use a chainsaw. Now then, do you want dessert, Edwina? They've got hot apple pie.'

Edwina shrugged. 'Yes, I'll go up and get them.'

Harriet scrambled to her feet. 'Oh, no, I'll go. I'm finished. I think the uneducated person should be the one to go up to the counter. Don't you? Wouldn't want you to sprain your brain. We can settle up when I get back.'

She strode off, leaving Edwina to regret having given any advice at all. She knew she was right, however. Harriet was a pea-brained woman and probably would not stick the course. Florist, indeed!

The queue at the counter was five deep, but the time spent waiting had not lessened Harriet's fury. 'There we are, two apple pies and two coffees. Be careful. Those pies are hot on the inside.'

She placed the cardboard container of apple pie and a styrofoam cup in front of each of them, smiled brightly and sat down. Edwina began nervously clawing in her purse for some small change. She had no idea how to get on good terms with Harriet again. She was also not sure she wished to smooth things over. The silly cow should learn to take criticism.

Harriet took a bite of pie, burned her mouth, took a sip of coffee, which was equally hot, and blinked back tears of pain. 'That was stupid of me.'

'Are you all right?'

'Perfectly, thank you.'

The silence lengthened as Edwina bit into her own pie, only to have it dribble onto her jacket. This was too much aggravation. 'I'm never coming here again! Next time I eat out it will be on proper plates with proper cutlery. It's all my fault for suggesting we eat here.'

'Funny,' said Harriet with a brittle smile. 'What a coincidence. I was just thinking the same thing! You know, Greg and I were talking about coincidences the other night. They happen all the time.'

'Really?' Edwina felt uneasy, wondering what her companion was leading up to.

'We were watching this old film and I said it was so unbelievable because of all the coincidences. You know the sort of thing. The killer meets the heroine on the train. The detective arrives at just the right moment to prevent the villain from killing her. And Greg said so what, coincidences happen all the time. For instance, Felix came to Gorham a year ago. A few weeks ago the Midnights moved into Gorham House and it turns out the wife is an old girlfriend of his!'

Edwina carefully picked up her coffee and took a small sip. 'He never mentioned it.'

Harriet shrugged, her eyes never leaving Edwina's face. 'She's a married woman now. But it is a coincidence, isn't it?'

'Yes.' Edwina's fragile confidence was slipping away. 'What's she like?'

Harriet shrugged. 'Tall, skinny, long blond hair. Perfect features, from what I saw. Could be a model. He was with her. The beast. Terrifying man. Anyway, Felix is a very attractive man. He's had a few girlfriends since he moved here, I can tell you. There was a WPC at Homestead. She's been transferred. Very ambitious. I never liked her.'

'And the girl who was killed the other day.'

'No, not really. They didn't hit it off.'

Felix had been willing to mention the girl with whom he had not hit it off, but made no mention of the beautiful Cassandra. The day had been spoiled. Edwina wanted to go home as quickly as possible. Harriet, she realized, had a spiteful tongue and a sixth sense for discovering one's fears and insecurities. It was a gift of sorts, but in future she would be avoiding the wife of Felix's best friend whenever possible.

However, they both wanted to keep the lines of communication open after the unpleasantness in the restaurant, so on the way home Harriet recounted some of her adventures as a secretary working for the police. Edwina found this very amusing and was at pains to say so.

By the time they reached the steep High Street at about half past two, they were feeling quite friendly towards one another. It was market day, but many of the traders had packed up and gone home, leaving a few parking spaces at the top of the hill. Suddenly Harriet jerked the steering wheel, crossed the line of traffic to a chorus of car horns and parked at right angles to the road.

'There!' she said. 'Looking in the window of the gift shop! See them?'

'Are they the Midnights?' asked Edwina, but she knew they were. Such exotic beauty was not common in the small market town. Who else could be quite so exquisite as the acclaimed Cassandra? And she had a look of sweet innocence. Edwina's eyes strayed from Cassandra as she forced herself to study the face of her nemesis. Leo Midnight was indeed a terrifying beast. Tall and angular, blue-chinned and sour-faced. She shivered. 'She's certainly . . .' she swallowed. 'She's certainly beautiful.'

'They say she's foul-mouthed.'

'No!' said Edwina.

Harriet laughed. 'I don't believe it either. Just somebody's sour grapes. I must get home. Greg will be fed up on his own with the kids.'

Unaware that Felix was with Greg, Harriet dropped Edwina at her bungalow. They parted on the best of terms, Edwina having decided quite sensibly that it was not Harriet's fault Cassandra Midnight was so incredibly beautiful.

She needed a few moments to gather her thoughts and recover a little of her confidence before telephoning her parents. 'Hello, Mum. How are things?'

'Very well, and how about you, dear? Still happy with your job?'

'Oh, yes.' She certainly didn't intend to embark

on a catalogue of complaints. Her mother had still not given up hope that Edwina would one day see the light and become a teacher. 'I'm really enjoying it. Mum, you remember Grannie's pearls that you wanted me to bring with me? Well, I've been invited to a dance in October. I've just bought this gorgeous dress and I wondered if you could post them to me.'

'Who are you going with?'

'Oh, Mum, he's extremely nice. A policeman. He just lives two doors down from me.'

'I see. Are you serious about him?'

'Oh, why must you do this? I know a policeman isn't good enough for you, but I'm lucky to have a boyfriend at all. He's handsome and decent and everybody likes him. Will you send me the pearls or not?'

'Calm down, Edwina,' said her mother in that superior, high-pitched voice that could be so infuriating. 'I fail to see why you must be so prickly with me. I just asked, perfectly civilly, who you were going out with. I have nothing whatsoever against policemen and I hope to meet him one day. If, that is, you're still going out with him by the time we come to Essex. What colour is the new dress and what sort of neckline does it have?'

'Black. It's got a scooped neck and very short sleeves.'

'Not too revealing then. In your case, that's wise. There are several pieces of your grandmother's jewellery that I will send and you can choose.'

They managed to pull back from their usual sniping encounters and discussed family affairs for five minutes before Edwina remembered that she had some news. 'I've been asked to give a talk about trees to the children of a local primary school.'

This did please her mother, who wanted to know how many children she would be speaking to and what was the academic standard of the school.

'I think you will see,' said Mona Fairfax, 'that you have a natural gift for talking to young children. We're going to make something of you yet.'

'I want to be in arboriculture, Mum.'

'Yes, yes,' said her mother wearily. They soon said goodbye.

She spent Sunday with Felix, but as he was referee in a soccer game at the recreation ground, she had to be satisfied with sitting with Harriet and Greg and their children on the sidelines during much of the afternoon. It was a surprisingly exciting game, but football bored Harriet, so she talked about or to her children during the entire match. Edwina was coming to realize that she could not escape Harriet if she were to continue to see Felix. Yet there must be a way to neutralize this difficult woman.

Her work was beginning to affect her life quite seriously. Joining Felix at his home on Sunday night, she could not sleep and tossed next to his huge frame for several hours. As was his custom, he rose early and made a fried breakfast, but Edwina couldn't even bear the smell of the food, much less consider eating it. She drank a cup of coffee, said she was not hungry and left his house at half past six to return to her own.

When she first came to Bishop, she had been eager to get to the office each day. But on this Monday morning she found it almost impossible to drag herself to work.

John Blue was waiting for her. 'Good morning, Edwina. You look as if you've had a very busy weekend.'

'Quiet, really. I've been thinking all weekend about getting my papers in order.'

He laughed. 'What a good idea. I think I should mention the matter of the hundred-year-old oak on the Elton Magna road. It has been decided that it can come down.'

'I know nothing about this,' she said. 'What? Where?'

'The council wants to widen the road at that spot. There have been too many crashes just at that point. The road sort of curves around the tree and it's on a blind bend. There's nothing for it but to let them take it down. I put a six-month emergency preservation order on the tree, but the time is up. The democratic process has been followed and we lost. The plan is to approach quietly and take it down on the twentieth. There have been a few objections as you can imagine, a small band of locals and travelling trouble-makers. I've been invited to speak to a meeting that's to take place in someone's home. I'm sure you will appreciate that I have other things to do, but this is a job you could take on. Go along and explain to them that not every tree can be saved. There is the broader picture to consider. We make our recommendations but the committee is not bound to follow them. Can you do that?'

'People should drive more carefully. It's

criminal to chop down a tree that has lived there peacefully for a hundred years just because there are a few reckless drivers around.'

'I know,' said John. 'On the other hand, I would not like to be the innocent driver coming from the other direction when some fool speeds round the corner on the wrong side of the road. I'll give you the name and telephone number of the woman who is organizing the meeting. And Edwina, try to be tactful. Give them our reasons, our thinking, but don't call them fools, will you? There's a good girl.'

Later that morning, she dialled the number she had been given. 'Yes, I'm Doreen Dunne and I live on the Elton Magna road close to the tree that is due to be cut down on the twentieth. I'm so pleased Mr Blue is sending you to talk to us, Miss Fairfax. A few of us are getting together tonight to discuss what can be done to stop this monstrous act. Perhaps we can convince you of the rightness of our cause.'

'I'm pleased to come, but you don't have to convince me of anything. I'm on your side entirely, believe me. I'm just coming to explain to you why there is nothing further we can do.'

'Aha! A new recruit. We must do something, my dear. Wait until you see the people we've recruited. Some of those eco-warriors. I can't imagine what they'll be like. Probably smell up the house for a week. Of course, they don't really care about trees the way we do, but they have nothing better to do than make trouble and that's what we want. Now, here's my address . . .'

Edwina wrote down the number and said goodbye. She didn't know how she felt about that evening's meeting. Could she gently encourage them all to stir things up, to delay the felling, while not getting into trouble with John Blue? Yes, she decided, if she were clever enough. The prospect cheered her up enormously and she set to clearing her paperwork with a will.

CHAPTER SIX

Prunella Jenkins and Claris Binns were coming for coffee and Zena didn't know if she was pleased or not. Rising early as usual, she had baked some shortbread which had not turned out as well as she would have liked. So annoying! She had washed up the mixing bowl and utensils while the shortbread was baking. Now she had to get everything out again. This time she would make fairy cakes. Surely they couldn't go wrong.

The early morning fairly flew, and she still had not put a fresh towel in the loo when the door knocker gave a hesitant thump-thump. Why did they have to be so prompt?

'Good morning, Prunella. Dear Claris, come in.' They all kissed. Zena, touching her cheek to Prunella's, could not help noticing that the Fu Manchu moustache was gone. In its place were two drooping strips of reddened skin. So Claris had repeated the cruel remark! And who was the more cruel, Zena wondered, herself for having said something unkind behind Prunella's back, or Claris for having repeated it?

'Do go into the sitting room. I'll just fetch the

coffee.' She left them to find chairs which were neither too low nor too soft and returned to the kitchen which was in a state of chaos. Pressed for time though she was, she had the forethought to load everything onto a trolley. Her arms were so weak these days that she didn't dare try to carry a heavy tray.

'What a beautiful day, Zena,' said Claris with a loud wheeze as the trolley squeaked its way over the carpet. 'I was just saying that if we don't get rain soon we're going to have a lot of dead trees.'

Zena loved the dry weather. 'It's good for some, though. The farmers have all got their harvest in. I can't remember, do you take sugar, Prunella?'

She looked directly at Prunella who stared back blankly. Prunella placed her left hand over her ear. The hearing aid whistled. 'I'm wearing it, but—'

'Do you take sugar?' bellowed Zena.

Prunella flinched. 'No, thank you. I don't know why I didn't—'

'We have some news for you,' said Claris. 'Don't we Prunella?'

'What?'

Claris leaned over to pat her hand with patronizing affection. 'I think your battery is weak.'

'Oh. Battery, did you say? I think I have another. I'll just put on my specs and look in my—'

Prunella opened her handbag with shaking fingers and began poking about in its murky depths. Zena, looking over her shoulder, spotted the printed card and bubble pack that held the batteries and impatiently removed it from the bag. Prunella winced. Claris put the battery into the hearing device before handing it back to Prunella who eventually managed to insert it into her ear.

'Now then, I can hear perfectly.'

Zena turned away slightly. 'Fairy cake?' she murmured softly.

'Pardon?'

'Would you like a fairy cake?' bellowed Claris. Prunella flinched, then nodded her head. The little cakes were served, the milk was poured and they all settled back for the first taste of the coffee.

'Will you excuse me?' Prunella struggled from her chair.

'Turn right in the hall. It's at the far end,' said Zena curtly. Claris and Zena watched as Prunella tottered out of the room.

As soon as she was out of sight, Claris sat forward in her chair, replaced her cup and saucer on the trolley and glared at Zena.

'I've known you for nearly eighty years and I don't suppose we've had a serious quarrel in all that time, but I cannot let your behaviour pass as if it were unnoticed. You've behaved despicably to that poor woman. Have you no compassion?'

'I hate to see the signs of old age. I hate it! I don't want to get feeble and I don't like seeing it happen to others. Anyway, I didn't tell Prunella she had a moustache. I presume that was you.'

'I had to. I didn't want her coming here looking like Fu Manchu, did I? I didn't know what you might say to her.'

'She's burned her lip.'

184

'So she has. Listen to me, Zena, and heed my words. There are only two attitudes to take to old age. You can laugh about it or you can cry. What you cannot do is ignore it. Time marches on. There is no escape. Personally, I'm willing to laugh at it. I've had a good life. I've been lucky to live so long. God willing, I intend to live a little longer. And I have no difficulty being patient with Prunella. She helped me through some dark times when we were younger. It would not have occurred to me to approach you.'

They heard the toilet flush and fell silent as Prunella made her way back to her seat.

'Your coffee will be cold,' said Zena. 'Shall I pour you some fresh?'

'No, thank you. I like it this way. How attractively you have done up your loo, Zena. All those shells! You're very clever.'

'Thank you. They belonged to James. I just glued them onto various things.' Zena drank her coffee, unable to bear the sight of Prunella's growing frailty.

'As I was saying, Prunella, you and I have some news.' Claris smiled maliciously at Zena. 'Mr and Mrs Midnight are to hold a wine and cheese party for Save Our Hedgerows. I don't know how Kitty Hebard persuaded them, but she did. It's on the twenty-fifth. I don't suppose you will want to go, although we three could go together. I'll buy another ticket, if you like. They're ten pounds which I think is very steep, but they won't have trouble selling them. Not when it's a chance to get a look at Gorham House.'

'You're going?' asked Zena incredulously. 'You two are actually going?'

'Come with us,' said Prunella. 'That would annoy the Midnights, but they couldn't stop you.'

'No, thank you. No doubt I'll be able to hear the festivities from my bedroom. Sound travels amazingly well around here. I often hear their pop music. Very annoying.'

Prunella laughed. 'I don't have to worry about such things. I just take out my hearing aid and I can be perfectly comfortable.'

Claris laughed, too. 'There are some advantages to getting old.'

'Oh, yes, many. I wouldn't want to be a girl again, always worrying about what was the right thing to do and what was not permitted. Much more comfortable now. And I've had a wonderful life.'

Zena said nothing, but her thoughts were in turmoil. She had surely had a better life than either of them. She and James had travelled widely, entertained constantly and spent their money without too much thought about the future, simply because they could afford to be a little extravagant. So why couldn't she feel that she'd had a good life?

Because she had lost two daughters in different ways, that was why. Because she had lost a wonderful husband. On the other hand, Prunella must have been positively delighted when the vicar passed away! He had been a frightful bully. Zena could not remember an occasion when he had spoken to his long-suffering wife in a gentle way. He had snapped at her when she was slow, rolling his eyes and inviting others to laugh with him at her stupidity. Zena had, on one occasion, told him right out that he was boorish and cruel, but this had done Prunella no good at all.

Prunella and Claris chatted on a number of topics and Zena made absent-minded contributions, but she was consumed with dismay about the coming wine and cheese party. Everyone she knew, everyone she had known for fifty years or more, would be attending a party in the home of her enemy. She was being deliberately excluded. Kitty had not telephoned to tell her about it, because Kitty knew she would feel betrayed. Yet why had Leo Midnight agreed to open his house for a charity which Kitty had founded, unless she had asked him to do so?

At a quarter to twelve, a taxi arrived to take Prunella and Claris home. Neither could afford to run a car and had to rely on taxis, buses and trains for transport. Zena remembered her manners and waved them off with every expression of goodwill, thanking them for coming, saying how much she had enjoyed their company. Only a lifetime spent in doing and saying the right thing enabled her to hide her bitterness.

The day stretched before her. She had been abandoned by all her old acquaintances and her closest friends. She was too frightened to venture out in her car, except when it was absolutely necessary. For these occasions, she had devised a little scheme which was to wait until the blaring pop music was turned off at Gorham House, then, assuming the Midnights had gone out, dash to the car and speed down the drive. Of course, this was not a foolproof method. Yet more often than not she reached the Elton Magna road without spotting one of their flashy cars. The trouble was, each foray left her emotionally drained. Leo and Cassandra Midnight were destroying her life.

As she stood in her doorway, feeling the late summer heat upon her, the sound of a chainsaw pierced the silence. Stepping back inside, she closed the door, then picked up the phone. She knew Edwina's office and mobile phone numbers by heart. Once more she would express herself succinctly on the subject of Leo Midnight. She was quite sure that if she made life sufficiently unpleasant for Edwina, the girl would do something about the Midnights. Later, she would telephone Felix and complain about their driving. So far her tactics had not borne fruit, but she couldn't think of anything else to do.

Several days later, Edwina drove to the evening protest meeting which was in a housing development close to a large roundabout outside Bishop. These detached houses had been built recently, perhaps completed within the past two years. It might well have been necessary for a few hundred trees to be removed to make way for the houses and roads, but the residents wouldn't know that. Developers built houses to make money. They sold them quickly because members of the public needed homes.

The residents of this development were perhaps escaping from less leafy surrounds in London, hoping for a new and better life. And now they wanted to be sure that no other trees were cut down. They wanted to prevent others from coming to join them in the destruction of the rural landscape.

Edwina was cynical about the Not In My

Backyard types, but their energy and commitment could help to preserve whatever was left of the countryside. She was prepared to use them for a noble purpose.

And, as her hostess had warned her, they were prepared to use eco-warriors for their purpose. Several grubby New Age types were filling the pink Dralon three-piece suite, their boots dropping dollops of clay onto the white carpet. Meanwhile, the middle classes, residents of the estate, perched uncomfortably on straight chairs.

Mrs Dunne greeted her warmly and introduced her to the company. They were an impressive crowd. She counted twenty-five people crammed into the modest living room.

'Do the council know you're here?' asked one of the eco-warriors. He had blond hair twisted into a version of dreadlocks and wore several earrings on one ear lobe.

'I have been sent here by the council to explain to you that we did all we could to save this oak, but we were overruled. We went through the full democratic process and—'

'To hell with the democratic process,' said blondie.

'Shut up,' lisped the girl with the stud through her tongue who was sitting next to him. 'Let the lady finish.'

Edwina swallowed hard and looked around the group. 'That is the council view. My own may differ from it, but that is what I have been sent here to tell you.'

There was a knowing laugh. 'So you'll help us?' asked Mrs Dunne.

'Well . . . that is, there's nothing I can do. My

189

boss, John Blue, put an emergency tree preservation order on the tree six months ago. He had to give way—'

'We don't believe in giving way,' said blondie. 'We believe in fighting the bastards.'

'That's telling them, Duggie.' The girl had the most amazing haircut. The left half of her dirty brown hair was chopped off next to her scalp, possibly with a knife rather than scissors, the rest was in curls. 'We know how to deal with them people.'

Those on straight chairs were looking rather uncomfortable. 'I'm sure you do,' answered Edwina. 'But I've never heard of anywhere that you have succeeded in getting a major road project stopped.'

'Maybe not, but we've cost the contractors a packet sometimes.'

A middle-aged man in a grey suit leaned forward on his chair and angrily confronted the eco-warriors. 'You have not cost the contractors anything. They put the cost onto the council, money that could be spent on social services and other things.'

'If you don't want to be here, Charles . . .' said Mrs Dunne with a fierce frown.

'But I do want to be here. I, too, am concerned about the loss of a one-hundred-year-old tree. A protest must be made, publicity must be generated. I believe, in the long term, such democratic action makes the authorities think seriously about what they are going to do in the future.'

'When the tree fellers are due to start work we can make a protest, get into the papers, get some publicity,' said Duggie. 'That's what we want.'

'That is exactly what we want,' said Charles. 'But no violence, no getting the bailiffs out. That costs taxpayers' money. Of course, since you lot don't pay taxes, that won't bother you.'

'Hey, Edwina,' said Duggie. 'Will you back us? Will you be there?'

'I do sympathize. I could come along to see how the protest is going.'

A cheer went up. Wine was served and everyone began to plan how they would organize the protest, who would climb the tree, what other means of causing a nuisance would be employed. Charles's voice could barely be heard above the general chatter. He was, noticed Edwina, distinctly unpopular even with his fellow residents.

They needed more than plans for protesting at the site of the tree felling, however. They needed a pep talk from Edwina. She felt they wanted to be worked up, to have their enthusiasm and their hate cranked up to fever pitch. They were already working themselves into a froth, blaming the council for allowing this tragedy to occur. Their insulting remarks about council employees and John Blue in particular embarrassed her, because she could not believe that those who were employed to protect the countryside were really unfeeling Nazis. But she closed her ears to these comments and concentrated her mind on what this assorted band of enthusiasts could achieve.

She told them about the French who were planning to cut down the magnificent avenues of trees that had lined the countryside roads since Napoleon's time, planted so that his troops could march in the shade.

'And why are they planning to cut down the trees?' she asked. 'Because it's been estimated by some fool that thirty per cent of all French road deaths are caused by collisions with trees. They're cutting them down by the hundreds, when the real cause of road deaths is speed and drink and carelessness, in France, as it is here. The trees are not responsible for causing the bad driving and shouldn't be punished for it.'

She wanted to impress on them the importance of preserving every possible tree, so she told them about the Asian longhorn beetle which could well decimate the nations' horse chestnuts, maples and willows. The eight-toothed spruce bug could have a devastating effect on spruces.

Then she treated them to a little lecture on oaks. 'They only begin to produce acorns when they are fifty years old and they provide a home for dozens of bird species, butterflies and insects. They even give a home to some ferns and lichens. They must be preserved.' She paused and looked around, making sure she had their undivided attention. The room was silent. 'And some of them are dying. Look around you the next time you go out for a drive. Many oaks in this region are suffering dieback. It's not an epidemic, not yet, but it can be a serious local problem. Every oak is precious, old oaks are doubly precious. We must save every one we can.'

'I get so upset it brings tears to my eyes,' said Mrs Dunne, 'every time I think about how they're cutting down the rain forest in Brazil.'

Everybody made pious remarks about the rain forest. They probably couldn't find Brazil on a map, didn't know the rate of decimation, wouldn't be prepared to do anything practical, even if anyone had come up with a solution. Edwina took a deep breath, trying to restrain herself. She was always at her worst when she sniffed hypocrisy. Inevitably she saw Mrs Dunne as yet another stupid member of the public.

'Yes, it's shocking. But not long ago, France suffered a terrible storm. Three hundred and sixty million trees were blown down overnight. That's twenty times the number we lost in the '87 storm. Yet nobody seems to care about that. We've lost those trees to the environment, and closer to home as well.'

'That was an act of God,' said Mr Dunne, a handsome man in his forties wearing a suit that could be the twin of Charles's. 'Furthermore, they were going to be cut down one day. They were commercial trees.'

'Managed woodland. There's nothing wrong with managed woodland.'

There was silence in the room. All the enthusiasm Edwina had managed to build was dissipated in seconds by her criticism. She had done it again, unable to refrain from passing an opinion on the attitudes of others towards trees. She suggested a time when they should gather on the twentieth, to which they all agreed quietly. Unable to think of anything more to say, Edwina promised to be present to lend support, made her excuses and left.

Felix understood from the cool replies to his questions that Edwina did not like Harriet. She would not say what had upset her on the Saturday shopping trip, but the day had clearly not been a success. At least, that was what he thought until he happened to see Harriet in the High Street in Homestead. According to her, the outing had been the most tremendous fun.

Felix was confused. He set about introducing Edwina to a large number of his friends and acquaintances. He was very proud of her and wanted everyone to know she was his girl. Yet the more their relationship progressed the more disturbed he felt. Something had happened on Saturday when she was with Harriet that had raised some sort of barrier between Edwina and himself. She was a great girl, decent, dependable and honest and these qualities had become important to him over the years.

He now needed a lover who was as different from Cassandra as possible, someone he could trust with his life. Unfortunately, the presence of his former lover in Gorham made him feel very uncomfortable. For some reason, he felt as if Cassandra were in the bedroom with them. He was inhibited, afraid to say anything meaningful to Edwina, as if Cassandra might laugh at him.

At the best of times, Cassandra had always been unpredictable. Now, in his most depressed moments, he imagined a scenario wherein for some reason she took Edwina aside and told her that he was a violent man. He hoped Edwina would not believe it, but the seeds of doubt would have been sown. Their mutual trust would be damaged.

He was shocked by his previously undiscovered capacity to hate. Having considered himself a mild-tempered person, he now realized that he had simply buried his bitter memories of

Cassandra. Once resurrected, they were in danger of consuming him. Eventually it occurred to him that Edwina might somehow have learned about himself and Cassandra, or, as he would always think of her, Cilla. But no, surely not, for he had told only Greg and Greg would never tell a soul. Would he?

This day, the twelfth of September, had seen his sunny disposition tested to the maximum. He was not on duty, but had been called in the early hours to attend another fatality, this time on the road to Sudbury. A motorcyclist had left the road and died in collision with a tree. Felix had been deployed diverting traffic.

While directing cars and lorries away from the accident, he had plenty of time to think about Edwina and what she meant to him, to think about how far he wished to commit himself to her and, ultimately, to the in-laws from hell. He had complete trust only in his mother and his sister. He couldn't rid himself of the idea that all other women harboured the capacity to destroy him.

When he had a spare moment, he rang her mobile phone and told her to pack a bag, for he wanted her to spend the night at his home. He would cook, or at least prepare, dinner for her and they would have a romantic evening. To his surprise and relief, there was no hesitation in her reply. She would love to spend the night with him.

Shortly after he spoke to her there was a thunderstorm, the first rain for three weeks. The brief storm was quickly followed by a series of minor traffic accidents which kept Felix so busy that he had no time to worry about his private life.

Luckily, the evening was a great success. The air was fresh and cool after the cleansing thunderstorm and his home had never seemed cosier. As they finished their lemon mousse, Felix proposed a toast. 'To Sainsbury's cook-chill cabinet.'

'I'll drink to that,' she laughed. 'It's a pity they don't provide a dishwashing service. It was a memorable meal. Now, you sit down and watch Man United beat Newcastle while I wash up.'

Felix switched on the television, put his slippered feet on the coffee table and sighed with pleasure as he thought how wonderful marriage might be. Edwina brought in the coffee, they cuddled up on the settee and scarcely moved for the next three hours. When at last Edwina said she would get ready for bed, he refused to allow her into his bedroom and made her undress in the guest room.

She returned to the living room wearing her Snoopy T-shirt nightgown and they turned off the lights together. Then, with a flourish, he opened the bedroom door and they were met by a rush of hot air. Felix had lit twenty-five candles of all sizes and shapes and placed them around the bedroom. Edwina, rightly assuming that this was intended as proof of his love for her, brushed away tears of joy.

The flickering candles lent a magical touch to his eclectic collection of furniture. The dust on the old mirror softened the reflected light, bathing the rose-patterned wallpaper in a warm hue, lending interest to the second-hand curtains and even turning yesterday's shirt which lay in a heap on the only chair into part of the decor.

He kissed her tenderly, removed her night-gown, thought better of trying to carry her to the bed and led her to it instead.

'Don't the candles look lovely?' she said. 'I saw a scene like this in a movie and I thought one day—'

'I knew you wanted to light candles the first night we were together, but you will have noticed these are not scented.'

Edwina lay on her back on the bed and closed her eyes. There was such an expression of bliss on her face that he was deeply moved. He lay down beside her and put his hand on one firm breast. She had beautiful breasts, he told her. She was lovely all over, had the most beautiful body. He began to kiss her, each breast, her navel, murmuring lovingly to her all the time, lost in his desire, but aware of her loving response until—

Edwina giggled. 'What is this, *Blind Date*?'

'What?'

'*Blind Date*. You keep saying Cilla something.'

'I—'

She sat up. 'My God. It's a woman's name, isn't it? An old girlfriend. Do I remind you of her? Is that it?'

'No, that is, I must have had her—'

'Harriet told me about Cassandra, but she never mentioned a Cilla. Where does she come in the scheme of things? Obviously you can't get her out of your mind.'

Now he found the energy to get mad. 'Harriet told you? I told Greg in confidence. What else did she say?'

Edwina pulled up the sheet, suddenly conscious of her nakedness. 'Is there more? Anyway, I understand Cassandra was a long time ago. So who's Cilla?'

He sat up with his back to the headboard so that they were side by side but not looking into each other's eyes. It was easier this way. But what to tell her? 'Cilla is Cassandra's real name.'

He heard her gasp and knew she was constructing a totally false scenario.

'I've seen her,' said Edwina. 'Harriet pointed them both out in the High Street that Saturday. She's very beautiful. I'm not surprised you can't get her out of your mind.'

'Yeah, right,' he said fiercely. 'I can't get her out of my mind. She is a vicious woman, a troublemaker. I didn't want to hurt her, but I did want to get out of the relationship when I was eighteen and, believe me, she caused me plenty of heartache. Do you know what she did when I told her I wanted to break up? She hit herself with something, I never found out what it was. Then she took a knife and scratched her arms and face. After that, she went to the police and put in a complaint that I had beaten her up. She caused me more grief than I'd ever known. My dad was dead and Mum didn't know how to handle it all. She went to a solicitor, but I'm sure he thought I had actually beaten her up. You can't imagine what a nightmare it was. After all these years, I thought I was rid of her. I put her out of my mind, just blanked it out and then she turns up in Gorham. People say she's beautiful, but all I can see is the troublemaking. She'll give that husband of hers plenty of grief. Ask yourself what kind of woman lays false claims.'

'But why did you say her name when—'

'Because she's got me bugged, I guess. I've been so worried that you would find out about her that I didn't know what to do. I was afraid to tell you what happened, yet afraid that she would tell you I was a vicious brute. I've been dreaming about her. I've gone over and over it in my mind. I've reminded myself that being falsely accused for a couple of weeks and then getting it all settled satisfactorily is not the worst thing that can happen to a person. It was the shock of it, that knock on the door, seeing a cop standing there asking questions. At least now you know. That's one thing I don't have to worry about.'

She shifted slightly and put her hand on his arm. 'Sometimes a bad love affair can be very damaging. It can leave scars that never heal. I'm going to make it my life's work to erase her from your mind.'

'I was eighteen, for God's sake. I should have been able to put it out of my mind without any help. Listen, darling, please stay away from her. I beg of you.'

Edwina laughed. 'Why on earth should I go up and stand anywhere near such a gorgeous creature? The contrast would be terrible.'

He turned to take her in his arms, but she held him off. 'Shall we do our usual thing? Would you like a cup of tea? Then we'll come back in here and I'll be surprised all over again about the candles.' Felix thought that would probably be a very good idea.

'It occurs to me,' she said, laughing as she got

out of bed, 'that we spend more time drinking tea than we do in bed when we're together.'

'You may be right. But it's special. You're special.' He pulled her back onto the bed and kissed her.

Half an hour later they got up and went into the kitchen, still naked, but now laughing and relaxed. The kettle seemed to take for ever to boil, but it gave Felix a chance to tell her about the time Cilla/Cassandra had gone into the local newsagents with him, had stolen half a dozen Mars bars, then confronted him with them when they were halfway down the street. He had been stumped. He didn't feel he could return them and tell the shopkeeper that his girlfriend had stolen them. Nor did he feel that she should keep them. Laughing and running ahead of him, she had torn the wrappers from every one and dropped the lot onto the pavement. He had found himself picking up stolen chocolate bars and wrappers and stuffing them into litter bins while Cilla taunted him. The next day he had told her he planned to be a policeman.

'And that was the beginning of the end,' he said.

'I had a boyfriend once,' said Edwina. She was seated opposite him at the little kitchen table, and put her bare feet on top of his. 'We went to a really nice restaurant and had a slap-up meal. Then after coffee, my boyfriend went to the men's room and never came back. It cost me thirty-five pounds and took me over the limit on my credit card. I had worked all summer to get some money saved up. I was a fool. Then I made the mistake of telling my mother what had happened. I got a long lecture about finding proper young men to go out with, about being too eager to go out with any riffraff who asked me. I worked weekends for ever to get myself out of debt.'

'I'd never do that to you,' he said.

'I know you wouldn't. You are the most honest and decent man I have ever met, Felix.'

'Would your father approve of me?'

The question was so unexpected that she had no time to think up a proper answer. 'Of course, if you were a chief inspector.'

'Policemen don't count for much, I guess.'

'It's not my father who loves you. It's me. And I think policemen are just wonderful. I always want to live up to your standards, dearest. I want you to be proud of me.'

Deeply moved, he stood up and emptied the remains of his tea into the sink. 'Those candles will be burning down. We'd better go to bed.'

Leo drove impatiently, taking chances that made Cassandra squeal with delight, as they sped down the A12 to London. Despite what he had told her, his dear mother would not catch sight of him on this day. He hadn't seen her for years and had no desire to mend the rift.

Instead, he was going to see the man who was no relation to him, but towards whom he felt all the love he would have lavished on two normal parents. He couldn't wait to see that grizzled red face, the thinning thatch of white hair. He'd throw his arms around the sagging shoulders and do his damnedest not to cry. One day the old boy would be dead. His rock, his anchor, his reason for living would be gone. The thought haunted Leo, but he tried to get a grip on the fear. For God's sake! The old boy was only sixty. He could live for another twenty-five years. Yet the cold fear continued to squeeze his heart. It was foolish, but what could he do?

When a man takes you from hell and gives you a life, when he shows you what love is and what you can become if you believe in yourself, you owe him a debt that can never be repaid. If he asks you to do something, you don't question it, you don't ask yourself if you want to do it. You just say, 'Yes, sir, with all my love.'

He glanced at Cassandra, his expression cold, but she was looking out of the window. Wildly overdressed in a tailored pale blue suit, matching stilettos and clunking gold jewellery, she was apparently comfortable in spite of the heat. 'I've booked you into the Hilton. You've got five hundred quid, but you don't have to pay your hotel bill. I'll take care of that when I collect you the day after tomorrow. Spend, spend, spend. But be ready to come away at two o'clock. Don't keep me waiting.'

'No. Oh, Leo, this is awfully good of you. I'm going to look up a few friends and I'm going to visit all the shops, but don't you think I should meet your mother one of these days?'

'One day. Not yet.' He laughed cynically. 'She's a funny old bird.'

Two days later she was as good as her word, waiting in the elegant lobby with her suitcase and a dozen printed carrier bags around her. They had been separated for only two days, but she looked different, dreamy and without the radiance that she had on arriving.

'I've shopped till I dropped,' she said in answer to his worried query. 'Now I'm tired.' She climbed into the car, waited listlessly until her parcels were stowed in the boot, and soon fell asleep. Thunderstorms had torn across the capital with great ferocity the previous day. The temperature had dropped twenty degrees overnight. Autumn had arrived on September the fourteenth.

Leo was content. He had much to think about and no desire to listen to Cassandra's chatter. He had to get on with his task. He must finish it soon, but there was the wine and cheese party in the way. Straight away afterwards, then. He would do it. He would not let the old man down.

Leo woke Cassandra when they reached Gorham House. She stretched catlike and smiled dreamily at him. 'They've had rain! Look, you can see some water still standing on the drive. You know, it's good to be back. I'm getting attached to this old place. It's going to be fun having the party, isn't it? I can hardly wait.'

She went indoors without waiting to help him with the luggage, and looked around. 'Old Queenie's been busy. The whole place smells of lavender polish and she's done a lot of the jobs she said she hadn't time to get around to before.'

He made a second trip into the hall, piling up everything and planning to take it all upstairs when he had put the car in the barn. He never got the chance.

'Leo, Leo! Them four statues around the pond

have been stolen! Taken away! My God! Oh, it looks awful.'

He sighed. What a fool he had been to have called in that dodgy window cleaner. No-one else could have known they would be out of town. Except, he suddenly remembered, Kitty Hebard and every person she might have mentioned it to.

'Don't worry about it,' he said to Cassandra. 'We'll buy some new, decent ones from a garden centre. They only cost a few hundred quid. Not worth having cops all over the place just to get back some worn out statues.'

'I already called them,' she said. 'What's the matter with you? It's their job to get these things back.'

'You didn't ring 999 did you? It's not an emergency. That line isn't intended to be used to report burglaries.'

The police arrived less than ten minutes after Cassandra's call. And they came in force. Felix was there, of course. Gorham House was on his patch. And Homestead's CID man whose name Leo had forgotten. Sque— something.

'Good afternoon,' he said when Greg approached the front door. 'Sergeant Squeegee, isn't it?'

'Squiller, sir,' said Greg mildly. 'Your gardener tells me the thieves came on the afternoon of the twelfth. They told him they had orders to pick up the statues and clean them up before some party you're having here on the twenty-fifth. Is that right?'

'Right that we are having a party here. Wrong that we ordered the statues to be taken away.

Look, don't bother. They're not worth much. You chaps have got better things to do than chase after four statues I can pick up for a few hundred quid in any garden centre.'

Greg's eyes narrowed. 'Felix Trent, you know, the one you call PC Plod, made a quick call to the environment office. They say the statues have probably been here for thirty years or more and that they may be of poor quality and they may have cost very little. But after thirty years they develop all sorts of lichen and that's the way people with money like them to look. Possibly fifteen or twenty thousand apiece at auction, the council reckons. We think they were probably stolen to order. Are you insured? Because I imagine they're out of the country by now.'

Leo had no idea if he had insurance or not. He would have to check. And he would have to tell the old man why he wanted to know.

Felix slipped through the low door of the lodge and was immediately in the small sitting room. It smelled musty and was crammed with huge old pieces of upholstered furniture, framed pictures, crocheted doilies and old copies of the *Sun* and the *Mirror*.

Reg and Queenie Quayle looked terrified and Felix felt very sorry for them. 'Look, if you were told the statues were to go away to be cleaned, you can't blame yourselves. Cheer up. I know he's a difficult man, but Mr Midnight can't throw you out of your home.'

Queenie wiped her eyes on her apron. 'You don't know what they're like, them two.'

'I've a pretty good idea. Now all you have to do is tell me everything you can about the men who came and their lorry. Can you describe the lorry?'

'No,' said Reg.

'I never saw it,' said Queenie.

'OK. How about the men? How many were there?'

'I only spoke to the one,' said Reg. His hands began to shake, so he plunged them into his pockets and sat down on a straight chair.

'Had you ever seen him before?'

'No,' said Queenie quickly. 'We'd have known he was lying if we'd ever seen him before. They wasn't here no time at all.'

Felix had the deepest affection for his remaining grandparent, although she was now in a nursing home and didn't recognize him. He liked old people and he felt sorry for the Quayles. 'Why don't you brew up and try to relax. There's nothing to worry about.'

They offered him a cup of tea, but he told them he would have to get up to the big house and see Mr Midnight.

It soon transpired that there were few clues. The ground had been baked hard at the time the statues were stolen, but later in the day there had been a thunderstorm. Three-quarters of an inch had fallen in two hours.

All in all, it was an interesting development on his patch. There were seldom large-scale burglaries in Gorham. He couldn't wait to tell Edwina all about it, but hearing about wicked men taking things from gardens seemed to unnerve her.

'They were stolen?' she asked, aghast. 'They drove up in daylight and just took them?'

'Needed a crane, too. They couldn't have lifted them. They told the old couple at the lodge they were being taken away to be cleaned. They didn't suspect a thing.'

'No,' said Edwina. 'You wouldn't, would you? If you saw three men taking away some statues in broad daylight. Will you catch them, do you think?'

'Small chance of that. They're probably out of the country by now.'

She continued to be upset by the burglary. He teased her that she should be used to such things, what with her reading so many whodunnits. She was rather silent all evening. Felix took the opportunity to comfort her, to take her in his arms as they sat on the settee, but she was distracted. This surprised him, as he had always thought of her as being a very robust, even fearless, person.

Edwina could not get the burglary out of her mind. Seeing three men removing the statues had not struck her as being out of the ordinary. Her fear had been that Leo would discover she had been on his property.

Nor was there anything she could do about the crime. To tell Felix what she had seen would inevitably lead to John Blue finding out. She liked John enormously and would never do anything to harm him, his reputation or his section. She was also rather keen not to destroy her prospects with Bishop council by admitting to trespassing. She had no choice, therefore, but to hold her peace and pray that the thieves were soon found.

* * *

It was dark before Leo could get away from Cassandra to check his e-mail for an answer to his query. No, it transpired, there was no specific insurance for the statues. The house insurance had not been updated in ten years. The old man was clearly upset and he wanted the statues to be returned.

'He thinks I'm a bloody genius,' muttered Leo.

Cassandra was sleepy again. He had a sinking feeling that she was on something, but he couldn't worry about that at the moment.

He walked down to the lodge. The lights were out, but he knocked loudly.

'Yes,' said Reg when he opened the door. He had put on his raincoat over his pyjamas and would have looked comical if he weren't shaking so pathetically.

'Get in here, Queenie,' said Leo harshly. She was peering round the bedroom door, but he wanted her fully involved during the next few minutes.

Leo took a handful of the raincoat and dragged Reg over to one of the two low chairs with wooden arms that flanked the fireplace. 'Now then. Suppose you tell me the truth. Who spoke to you the other day?'

Reg could hardly get out the words. 'Window cleaner.'

'Where does he live?'

'Don't know. Never saw him before he came to clean the windows.'

'Who was with him?'

'Two men.' Queenie's face twisted into a grotesque grimace as she attempted to keep control of herself. 'I saw them from the window.'

'One,' began Reg, 'one . . . was Duggie Duncuff.'

'Spell his last name!'

'D-u-n-c-u-f-f, I suppose. I never seen it written down.'

'Where does he live?'

'Bishop, as far as I know.' Reg clutched his chest as if he had a pain.

'Does he live alone?'

'We don't know that!' cried Queenie. 'We've just seen him round for years. As a boy he got hisself in trouble in the town a couple of times. That's all. People say he lives in Bishop. The window cleaner said he'd come back and beat us to a pulp if we talked.'

'But he won't.' Leo sneered at the cringing couple. 'I expect he also gave you some money to sweeten the deal. But I'm not interested in that. You can keep your hush money, your ill-gotten gains.'

He walked out of the lodge, slamming the door behind him. Softly, Queenie began to cry. There was no point in reminding each other that they had been proud of their honesty all their lives. Nor was there any point in discussing the twenty-five pounds which was a wonderful windfall. Placed in the building society, it would be there to provide them with a few days out at the seaside next year.

Leo had no trouble finding D. Duncuff in the telephone directory. A quick glance at his A-Z map enabled him to find the road. He left without informing Cassandra, but he reckoned she would be asleep by this time.

Duggie Duncuff was also asleep, but not for

long after Leo pounded on his door. The young man was wearing blue boxer shorts and a very worried expression.

Leo stepped through the door quickly and shut it behind him. 'I live at Gorham House, Duggie. You know, the place where you stole four valuable statues. Let's go get them back, shall we?'

By the bare bulb that lit Duggie's narrow hall, Leo could see each thought that crossed the young man's mind. *Dare I lie? Dare I try to shove him out of my home? What will happen to me if I tell him the truth?*

'Let's you and me go upstairs while you get dressed.'

'What, this minute?' cried Duggie, seriously alarmed. 'You want to go get them now? They're a long way away, I imagine.'

'That's all right. We can hear what's happened to them together, from your fence.'

Such was Leo's air of menace, Duggie didn't consider further, but went upstairs and threw on a few clothes. No conversation passed between them, except what was absolutely necessary in order for Leo to drive to Canvey Island.

As they approached the Fat Man's lair Duggie grew restive, but Leo was so pumped up with adrenaline that he felt nothing at all except the joy of the chase with perhaps the promise of a little physical contact later on.

The Fat Man proved to be made of sterner stuff than Duggie. Leo would have been disappointed had he shown less aggession. He was, however, as quick as Duggie to see when there was no point in bluster.

'I keep quiet if the statues are returned to my property tonight,' said Leo.

'Can't,' said the Fat Man. 'No lorry.'

Leo looked round. 'That one over there?'

'I'd have to pay to use it!'

Leo smiled. 'Do that.'

'I want a thousand.'

Leo leaned against the caravan door and folded his arms. 'For the statues you get nothing. I'll pay you two hundred for delivery. Don't mess with me. I'm not some rural copper. I'm the Met and I've got plenty of back-up I can call on.'

The Fat Man sighed, nodded his head in agreement and turned to Duggie who would receive the full force of his irritation.

'You, snitch, go knock on the caravan next to the truck. Tell him you want to rent it to return some gear. He'll go with you and he knows where the statues are.'

Duggie didn't ask if he would be paid for the work. He just hoped he would live to tell his grandchildren about this night.

CHAPTER SEVEN

Cassandra burst into his bedroom. 'For God's sake get up, Leo. It's ten o'clock. I looked out the window this morning. It was so foggy! And then when it cleared a bit I could see the statues. They've been returned. Who do you suppose is responsible for that? I thought maybe that's the way the police work. So—'

'So you rang them to find out,' he finished for her. He sat up and tried to clear his head. He had finally fallen into bed at four in the morning and, being so very tired, had actually managed a few hours' sleep free of nightmares. Now, all he had to do was shake the rocks from his head. He was surprised he felt so tired. A better night's sleep than he'd had in years and . . .

'They're here!' cried Cassandra excitedly. 'The police. They're here. Not Felix, though. The CID bloke.'

'Squeegee,' said Leo, putting on his pants. 'I call him Squeegee. It drives him mad.'

He went downstairs, finger-combing his hair on the way, and showed the detective into the room that had once been a handsome library, closing the door behind them. 'Sit down.'

'No thanks,' said Greg stiffly. 'What I have to say to you can be said standing up. You got those statues back with amazing speed. I figure you were in on it for some reason, probably trying to make fools of us. Had to be.'

Leo snorted. 'No, I wasn't in on it and you don't need anybody to make fools of you. You can manage it by yourselves, but I wanted to get the damned things back because I want you buggers off my neck. Since on a bad day I'm ten times better at detection than you are, it really was no problem. Want to know a joke? The statues are just moulded cement. The fence couldn't unload them to his customer. But they left a gap in the garden. Nice to have them back. I've saved Homestead the expense of an ongoing investigation, so now leave me alone.'

'How did—'

'By a little proper questioning. By knowing that the whole goddamned world is on the take. Scratch anybody. You. Me. We're all shit. And another thing, I don't believe everything I'm told. You should try harder to keep an open mind, Squeegee. You're lazy.'

Greg thrust his hands into his pockets, thinking hard. 'The Quayles!' he said suddenly. 'You strong-armed that poor old couple! We don't use your Met ways around here.'

Leo was enjoying himself. He laughed loudly. 'Why, bless you, Miss Marple, I never laid a finger on them. Let it go. But let it be a lesson to you. You've got sloppy.'

Greg was too stunned to argue further. He

213

turned without a word and left the room. Some vague idea of hauling the Quayles down to the station was quickly dismissed. Midnight had, in truth, saved the force the expense of further investigations. The statues had turned out not to be worth much, after all.

He returned to the station and sat down at his desk. He had a dozen burglaries to investigate. Vandals had performed their usual ritual acts of destruction on the High Street over the weekend, and, as usual, no-one had been arrested, because Bishop District Council wouldn't pay for Homestead to have CCTV on the High Street.

Besides the vandalism, a young man was lying unconscious in Colchester Hospital after a drunken brawl at the Pig and Whistle. Then too, the Bishop force was investigating a gang murder and had asked for assistance in visiting a few well-known villains in Homestead. And the paperwork was piling up.

Lazy? Sloppy? Maybe he had been, but he wasn't on the take! By God, Leo Midnight had got that one wrong! Nevertheless, a careful examination of his recent performance left him feeling ashamed. He and Harriet had been rowing a lot. The kids didn't sleep. But never mind the excuses. He intended to tighten up. First, of course, he'd have to work through the humiliation of having his sloppiness pointed out to him by Leo Midnight.

He looked around at the officers in the room. Half of them were women, most of them pretty and young. What's more, he'd stake his life that every man and woman in the Homestead force was honest. They had come into police work because they wanted to do some good. Why had Midnight joined? And what kind of man thinks the whole world is rotten?

There was shouting at the sergeant's desk. Greg looked up in time to see a red-faced, white-haired man in his sixties burst into the room. He was wearing grey trousers with a sharp crease and a double-breasted blazer. 'Where's the detective?'

'Here!'

'Lay off Leo Midnight! You hear me? Lay off him. Leave him alone. You're driving him crazy. He needs his peace. You don't, there'll be trouble.'

Greg stood up. 'Who are you?'

'Superintendent Dixie Dickenson, Scotland Yard, retired.' The old man turned on his heel and left.

For a second or two there was stunned silence, then Greg said, 'Hold the fort, will you, fellas? I'm just going to nip home and change my underpants.'

The shout of laughter that followed could be heard outside in the parking area, but Superintendent Dickenson had already driven away.

By God, thought Greg. I'll find out this time who Midnight really is. Sloppy detective work? I'll know everything there is to know about the bastard and what he's doing in Gorham and I'll know it by the end of the day.

Zena had sat with increasing discomfort in the surgery waiting room for half an hour. She had arrived in good time for her appointment. Why couldn't the doctor keep his side of the deal? She would get up in a minute and tell those receptionists just what she thought. But she felt stiff all over and even to relieve her feelings, she could not get up twice. When her name was called on the loudspeaker would be time enough to struggle from this hard chair.

'Zena Alway,' came the disembodied voice of her doctor. She started, then struggled to her feet and hobbled down the corridor, not acknowledging the Harper woman with her bandaged foot or the Grimsby girl who was probably pregnant again.

'Come in, sit down,' said Dr Schreiber. 'How are you, Mrs Alway?'

'I had a little tumble a few weeks ago. Slid down the stairs. Then last night I tripped over the footstool. I grabbed the arm of the sofa, but sort of swung round and sat down on the magazine rack. Hurt the same places.'

He looked a little uncertain. 'Do you want to show me?'

'No,' she snapped. 'Of course I don't want to show you. But I'll have to bite the bullet, won't I? Take down my knickers. Moon at you.' She began to undress, pulling up the skirt of her dress, taking down her knickers. He saw that her eyes were full of tears, and she kept up a steady stream of gasps and groans.

The bruises from the previous fall had not entirely disappeared, but already her thin skin was discolouring from the new fall. He instructed her to get dressed, then took her through a series of movements to see if she had broken any bones.

When they were both seated once more, he smiled at her and leaned forward. 'Nothing broken. You know, it's not a terribly good idea to live alone when you're inclined to fall. Have you thought about—'

He got no further. 'Inclined to fall? I'm not inclined to fall. It just happened a couple of times, that's all. I've had a lot on my mind. If you only knew what harassment I've suffered from my new neighbours. No-one should have to put up with it. No-one will come and visit me any more because of the Midnights. I'm afraid to go out because of them. The police won't help. That tree girl from the council won't do anything. It's no wonder I've fallen over two or three times. Just thinking about something else, that's all. But I'm not moving into some old folks' home, so don't mention it again.'

Dr Schreiber sighed. 'When we get older, sometimes we—'

'We? We? You're about twenty-five. I'm the one who's getting older.'

He smiled wearily. 'I've known you for ten years, so I'm not twenty-five and I'm going to say what I started out to say, so just be quiet for a minute. You might be helped by taking anti-depressants for a few months. It could help you to—'

She stood up so quickly her head swam. She had to clutch the edge of the desk to keep from fainting. 'I am not insane! How can you say such a thing? You're saying I have Alzheimer's disease, aren't you? Well, I haven't. I'm not mad, I tell you. I come for advice about a few bruises and you try to put me in a straitjacket. That's all the help I get for years of paying my taxes.' She hobbled, grimacing, to the door. 'No, don't touch me.'

Tears bathed her cheeks as she attempted to get the door open. Shrugging off his helping hand, she hobbled back down the corridor, wondering, hoping that he would stop her to tell her he had made a mistake in suggesting pills. And yes, she heard him behind her.

'Mrs Alway, how did you get here to the surgery?'

'I drove, of course.'

'When does your licence come up for renewal?'

She laughed bitterly. 'As you know, I have to reapply every three years at my age, and I've just got my new licence. So there.'

'I'll drop in to see you tomorrow.'

'Humph,' she said. 'I may not be there. I may be driving at Silverstone.'

'Yet another school has asked if we can send someone to talk to the children about trees,' said John Blue. He was perched on the edge of Edwina's desk, smiling gently as one would at an idiot. 'I thought of you as I know you're giving a talk at one tomorrow. You know about schools, I believe.'

'I've been to a few,' said Edwina in a sulk. 'If that's what you mean.'

'I thought you told me your whole family are teachers.'

'Yes, but I didn't absorb it by osmosis. However, it could be fun. It's tomorrow at two o'clock. So you'll know where I am if you need me.'

'Are you nervous? All prepared? A hall full of young schoolkids can be daunting.'

'I'm not nervous at all. And I've been around

218

schoolkids and schools for ever. I think I'm pretty well prepared.'

She managed eventually to get rid of him and immediately began planning how she would manage to attend the protest about the oak tree.

The phone rang. 'Hello, Edwina Fairfax speaking. How may I help you? You want to know about Lyme disease? No, madam, it is not caused by lime trees. It's caused by ticks that live on deer. No, it has nothing to do with lime trees. No, we will not give you permission to cut down a lime tree. No, I'm telling you the truth. Lyme disease is not caused by lime trees!' The caller put the phone down and Edwina fumed.

She had come to Bishop council with high hopes and dreams of saving the trees of Essex for future generations. And what had she achieved? A beech tree felled because she wasn't thinking straight, a disaster with the lime tree in Grover's Court, and a hundred-year-old oak that she was not going to be able to save at all, because her own council had been overruled by the so-called democratic process.

Meanwhile, she reckoned she had met or spoken to every nutcase in the district. She had endured abuse from people she had never met, to whom she had done no harm. She had been criticized for doing too much and for doing too little. The complaints against her were often ludicrous, yet she had been instructed to absorb the abuse, to keep cool, to allow herself to be stigmatized as a little Hitler. Edwina was beginning to feel that she did not like the public. Council employees were the butt of everybody's spleen. It was bad enough for her. She knew that the planning officers endured worse. They had only to refuse permission for some dodgy building and they could find themselves stalked and threatened by so-called businessmen.

Fortunately, the Gorham House statues had been mysteriously returned to their proper positions. Rumour had it that Leo Midnight had paid a ransom for them. Whatever the truth might be, she needn't worry about it any more. She had not been seen and John Blue need not be troubled.

Thinking about trespassing on the Midnight property reminded her of the handwritten letter from Leo which had arrived in response to her own. Far from being intimidated by her, his letter was so full of bile, so wickedly clever in getting beneath the carapace of her bravado that she could not look at the single sheet of folded paper in her desk drawer and still breathe normally. The letter and her inability to reply to it caused her endless painful introspection. All she had to do was drive round there and tell him what she thought of him. There was work that needed doing on his property, and she was sure he would one day destroy every tree of value that grew there. Yet she couldn't say so to John, because she couldn't explain how she knew this to be true.

There were plenty of people who had been on the receiving end of Edwina's bluster. She had perfected a technique of appearing to be tough when she had to be, so how had Leo Midnight seen through her act? There was something about him that chilled her. She felt, for no reason really, that he could see right through her and knew that her snappy replies and general impatience with the stupidities of others were just a means to hide her own sense of inadequacy.

She finished the mountain of paperwork, answered a few more questions, then slipped out of the office at a quarter to ten. She had been warned that the police would be blocking off the road so that the tree surgeons could do their dirty work, so she drove to Red Deer Wood and left her car in the small parking area by the picnic tables.

The temperature was in the low sixties, too warm really for the red tartan woollen shirt she had just bought from Millets in Bishop, which she put on over her T-shirt. She also had a knitted hat and a scarf around her neck which would be drawn across her face as she approached the site. Felix might well be present and she didn't want him to recognize her. She was not, she told herself, actually taking part in the protest. She had simply come to observe it.

She walked through the woods, reaching farmland about a mile away. She could see the tree and a few protesters in the distance. They seemed to be outnumbered five to one by police, and they were in two distinct groups.

The first branch was already hanging by a rope, ready to be lowered to a waiting lorry. She jogged along the perimeter of the field and joined two of the women she had met earlier. They looked uncomfortable as protesters, and embarrassed by their lack of aggression.

'What happened, ladies? I thought there would be masses of people.'

Mrs Dunne, dressed for her new life in the country in headscarf, tweed skirt and shiny stout shoes looked at her bleakly. 'Last night the son of one of my neighbours was riding his motorbike along here. He lost control, left the road and hit that very oak tree. He wasn't killed, but he did get a serious head injury and a leg broken in two places. I remember very well what you said about it not being the tree's fault, but opinion has changed around us. My husband has completely changed his mind, for instance. He won't support me in this. People felt it was inappropriate to turn out today. I mean, his mother was at the meeting, for God's sake! I think you spoke to her. So I just said I would come to report on what's happening.'

Edwina looked up at the seventy-foot tree, its knurled old trunk and its leafy branches which had been home to thousands of little creatures, witness to many injuries and had provided shade for a hundred years of farm workers. There were oaks in the area suffering severe stress, but this one was not among them. This tree was healthy and probably would have lived for a few hundred years more, if allowed to.

The whine of the chainsaw set her teeth on edge and she left Mrs Dunne to pick her way over to the half-dozen eco-warriors who were standing apart, recognizing them all from the meeting in Mrs Dunne's house. They seemed downhearted and she assumed this was because the press had not bothered to turn out. There would be no ego-inflating publicity from the loss of this old tree.

Felix had recognized Edwina from two hundred yards away. She had a way of striding out, her arms swinging from her broad shoulders, her narrow hips encased in tight jeans. He had never seen the tartan shirt before, but she was unmistakable. Did she actually think she could fool people with that scarf around her face?

'What's Edwina doing here?' asked WPC Sally Flynn.

'Probably just come to keep an eye on what's happening,' answered Felix, but wondering the same thing himself.

Sally laughed. 'Oh, sure. That's why she's wrapped a scarf around her face. She's come to protest. I'll bet she climbs the tree any minute now. You'll have to get her down, Felix, climb up there and carry her down in your arms.'

At that moment, Edwina reached the six scruffy young men who stood uncertainly with hands in their pockets, not sure whether to give the police some abuse or keep quiet. She had seen Duggie when she was still some yards away and had not, at first, recognized him. His hair was now cut in what was known as a number one. Shears had left him with virtually no hair at all. She shook hands with each one, including the man she knew to be a thief, and they all crowded round her, grinning.

'I didn't recognize you, Duggie. What with the new haircut.'

He ran a hand over his head. 'Yeah. I'm in disguise, ain't I?'

Edwina stole a glance at Felix, feeling sick with guilt. Maybe she should have spoken up about the stolen statues. On the other hand, this young man had his heart in the right place, even if he did seem to be a trifle stupid. She didn't want to be responsible for anyone going to prison. To be locked away was a terrifying thought. She didn't think she could bear it for more than a day.

'I see those toffee-nosed gits didn't turn up. They ain't really interested in trees,' said Duggie.

Edwina laughed. 'Strange that you should say that.' She didn't tell him that they held the same opinion of him, nor that she thought they were all hypocrites.

'My God!' said Sally. 'They really are on the same side. Is she allowed to do that? Protest against her own department?'

'I don't know.' Felix studied the men. 'Anybody know the names of these chaps?'

'Not local, I dare say.' Sally straightened her jacket and squared her hat. 'I'll ask some of the others.'

'I thought you were going to turn out in force today!' exclaimed Edwina to the blond one. 'Where is everybody?'

'This is just, like, one tree. I mean, it's on its own. You can't protect every tree, not when there are terrible atrocities afoot. Everybody's down in Hampshire where they're going to cut a bypass right through a beauty spot, can't think of the name of it. A few of us turned out today to show solidarity, and look what happens. The soft types couldn't be bothered. Probably afraid of getting mud on their shoes.'

'The son of one of the women who was at the meeting was badly injured here last night. That put them off.'

He was unimpressed. 'That so? Ah, it's not worth it. I'm off in a minute. My God, it's only one tree compared to what the bastards are planning in Hampshire. It's not worth getting any aggro from this lot just for one tree. Look at 'em. So scared of us they've called out every copper in East Anglia. I might go down to Hampshire tomorrow.' He turned to his mates, who looked bored. 'What about you lot?' They shook their heads, muttering about being busy. These were hardly committed conservationists, just layabout friends of Duggie, and their lack of commitment disgusted Edwina.

'They certainly outnumber us,' she agreed. 'Well, I think this battle is well and truly lost. I can't stay long either. I guess I shouldn't be here.'

Sally returned to Felix. 'The only man anybody recognizes is the blond one, Duggie Duncuff. He lives in Bishop. Been in trouble since he was ten, but never anything very much. Takes odd jobs. I expect they've all got form, did we but know it. You know the type.'

'Don't I just,' said Felix grimly and walked over to join Edwina.

'What do you think you're doing, coming out here? You're protesting against your own department. You're embarrassing them.'

'They won't know unless you tell them, Felix. I'm in disguise. Anyway, I can always explain to John that I came to see what was happening. Try to understand that this is important to me. They've tried the democratic process and it didn't work.'

'The democratic process worked perfectly. It's just that the tree huggers lost. You've endangered your job for nothing. Even the local papers haven't bothered to turn up.'

She looked around quickly. 'Nobody recognizes me, do they?'

'Everybody recognizes you. I recognized you from two hundred yards. My God, Edwina. Never take up a life of crime. You're not cut out for it. You must leave. Tell your *friends* goodbye.' He walked back to join Sally and two PCs from Elton Magna.

Duggie took a step back from her as if she had an infectious disease. 'I bet you gave him our names!'

'How could I? I don't know your names. Go away if you want to. There's nothing to do here.'

The young men turned and slouched towards their transportation, a white van parked a quarter of a mile away.

Felix and Edwina did not spend that night together. Both eager for a little privacy in order to think, they found excuses for the separation, exaggerated their commitments elsewhere and parted to brood about the scene at the tree felling, and their very different attitudes to it.

The next day Edwina made her way to the primary school and was met by the headmistress, Mrs Scott, who led her into the gym where sixty children were seated on the floor. Two chairs faced them, one of which was offered to Edwina. She sat down, fiddling with the three-by-five cards on which she had written her speech. Mrs Scott remained standing, preparing to address the children, while class teachers leant against the wall, their eagle eyes daring the children to rebel. Edwina was familiar with the look, an attempt by a civilized adult to impose her will on unpredictably uncivilized children, who wildly outnumbered and largely ignored her.

Mrs Scott began to speak. A few messages, a few admonishments, a short lecture on how lucky they were to have Miss Fairfax come to talk to them.

In the front row of five-year-olds sitting cross-legged on the floor one little girl began to cry. Those on either side giggled as they scrambled to put some distance between her and themselves. A teacher arrived and took the child by the hand, lifting her to her feet, leading her away from the damp spot on the floor. The caretaker arrived with his mop. Mrs Scott finished speaking and turned expectantly towards Edwina who stood up and cleared her throat, attempting to control a sudden attack of nerves. She had, she remembered too late, never spoken in public before.

'Hello, everybody. I've come to talk to you today about trees in Essex and about woodland. Now, here in Essex we have woodland cover that is considerably below the national average.'

The murmuring of sixty children, never totally silenced, grew a little louder. Teachers began moving along the ranks, pointing a finger and looking stern here, having a word with an unruly child there. 'Approximately three point five per cent of Essex is covered by ancient woodland. Now, what is an ancient woodland?' No-one seemed inclined to offer any sort of answer. She was losing their attention and had hardly begun to talk. 'Ancient woodlands are the ones which have been in continuous existence since before

227

the year 1600.' Noise was reaching a crescendo. Edwina raised her voice by several decibels. 'Hornbeam, sweet chestnut or sometimes small-leaved lime are the dominant species.' She stuffed her index cards in her pocket. Several of the more alert children thought she had finished and couldn't believe their luck.

Edwina smiled. 'But the best way to learn about trees is to go out of doors and look at them. You have some wonderful trees in the grounds here. We've got to get outside on this beautiful day and look at them!'

She had caught the teachers by surprise, but there was probably an element of relief, as well. One pretty, very young teacher was already pushing the double doors open so that the children could leave the gym. Several others were intent on an orderly exit.

'What a good idea,' murmured the head-mistress to her, and they all went out onto the lawn where the grass was still green and the sun shone brightly on the first of the changing leaves.

The children ran about joyfully for several minutes, but they were soon crowding around her wanting to know what they should do. She sent the youngest children in search of leaves which she promised to identify. She handed each one a large plastic bag and said they could collect a variety of leaves and put them into the bags, then paste them onto coloured paper and write the type of tree underneath each specimen.

Some of the older ones were sent off in small groups to measure the trunks of the largest trees. From her capacious rucksack she produced half a dozen surveyors' tape measures and plenty of graph paper. Trees should be measured at a height of about four feet, she told them. Also, she wanted every tree marked on a general plan. She told them that the largest oak recorded was forty feet around and was a thousand years old. They must hunt for large species.

When all the children had a project and had run off to get started, some of the teachers asked her questions about the trees on their own properties or those in the school grounds which looked unhealthy to them.

With the exception of the cloudburst on the twelfth of the month, the weather had been dry for weeks, although markedly cooler. East Anglia was basking in a memorable Indian summer and Edwina wanted nothing more than to be out in it. She leaned against an oak and chatted to the headmistress for half an hour as the children were given a surprise break from their normal studies.

They approached her in small adoring groups, dragging her off by the hand to explain something or to be impressed by what they had found. At the end of the free period, the headmistress gathered them together and told them to sit on the ground, before handing over to Edwina.

She took them through a dozen different leaf shapes, gratified to see that large numbers of them recognized every leaf. She asked for their figures on tree girth and estimated the age of each tree. They cheered when she pointed out the oak that was three hundred years old.

Eventually they had to be returned to their classrooms and Edwina was sad. She had not expected to enjoy the occasion so much, but found it was the perfect restorative after dealing with adults. Why did people have to grow up?

Reluctantly she returned to her desk at the council offices where John Blue quickly joined her. 'I've heard all about it, Edwina. You were apparently very good with the children. Incredibly, there have already been two more requests for you to speak at schools. Good news travels fast. Want to do them?'

'Of course. It was very satisfying.'

'We've found out what you do well, haven't we? I'm glad. I think you should build on that.'

'I see.'

'You are a good ambassador for trees. Unfortunately, the council can't afford to employ a tree ambassador on a permanent basis. You have a one-year contract. Time enough to sort out what you want to do. I'll always be available to offer advice if you need it.'

She sat at her desk without moving, breathing shallowly as if by saving her breath she could prolong her working life. She had hoped he would be so impressed with her that he would offer her a permanent position. Instead, he had made it plain that she must move on after her contract was finished.

When the feeling of humiliation had given way to panic, and the panic to despair, she gathered her papers and left the building. She had no idea what she was going to do next. She didn't even know what she wanted to do next. She had counted on being given a permanent, hazily defined job with the council. Although the situation had been explained to her most carefully, she hadn't taken in the fact that John Blue felt no responsibility beyond her brief work experience. The thought of moving away was too much to bear.

What of Felix? Not only would she have to move away from him, she would have to tell him about what she regarded as her failure. Then she would see how disappointed he was in her. Edwina Fairfax is not good enough to hold down a job, just as her parents always knew.

There was one visit that she absolutely had to make before the end of the day. Two men had been quarrelling about a hedge of *cupressocyparis leylandii*. This was not the usual quarrel wherein the neighbour wanted the owner to cut down the hedge. In this case, the owner had cut it down and the neighbour was furious.

The request for a visit had reached her just before she went off to talk to the children, but the two neighbours were still outside, still shouting when she arrived over an hour and a half later. The rear gardens backed onto each other and were no more than ten yards long and half that width. The stumps of fifteen trees marched along Mr Curteis's back fence. Branches and twigs covered half his ground. Leaning against the side fence was the tree feller, one foot resting on his chainsaw. It was Junior Hargreaves, and he gave her an insolent smirk and the two-finger sign as she approached.

'Mr Curteis?' She held out her hand to a man in his late forties with receding black hair and a paunch that sent his trousers in a detour below the swelling.

'This has nothing to do with you. I guess I can

231

cut down a hedge in my own garden if I want to. You people are power mad.' He shook hands, however.

'Now you're in for it!' cried his neighbour, apparently trampling his own plants in his determination to get next to the boundary fence. His face was red and he had a two-day growth of beard, due to laziness not trendiness, she decided.

'Mr Scarlet? You rang my office?'

'I did. Look what this vandal has done. Look at it. He can see right into my lounge window now.'

She looked skyward, squinting. 'The back of your house faces south, Mr Scarlet. This hedge must have cut out a lot of light. How tall was it?'

'Twenty feet,' said the men simultaneously.

'And in terrible condition,' added Mr Curteis. 'It was three-quarters dead.'

'It did its job.'

'Yeah, and what was that?' asked Curteis of his neighbour. 'Keeping everybody from knowing what you get up to?'

Through the sliding doors of the Scarlet lounge, Edwina could see Mrs Scarlet looking anxious. Mrs Curteis was in her kitchen looking equally worried.

'How long have you two known each other?'

'Fifteen years,' said Curteis.

'Then, Mr Scarlet, you must have been here when the hedge was planted.'

Scarlet nodded. 'Six years ago.'

'You must have been staggered when the hedge grew so quickly.'

'He was always asking me to trim it,' said Curteis.

Edwina thought for a moment. 'Dig out these roots. Plant another hedge and keep it trimmed to ten feet.'

The council ran a mediation service for just such crises. She thought she had displayed the wisdom of Solomon, but neither man was happy. Curteis didn't want to plant another hedge. He wanted to grow some flowers. This was the perfect spot to do so. The rest of his garden had too much shade.

Mr Scarlet, it turned out, not only wanted another hedge, he wanted Curteis to be brought to court and fined. In fact, he would be satisfied with nothing less.

The men began to shout. Curteis pushed Scarlet in the chest. He was a head shorter and considerably thinner. Nevertheless, Scarlet swung his fist at his neighbour, connecting with Curteis's upper arm. They bellowed like walruses and almost simultaneously reached for each other's throat. In this, Scarlet was at a great disadvantage. Edwina attempted to get between the two men, aware that wives were descending from both houses, adding their cries to the general hubbub. Even at the height of the scrum, she wondered whether there would now be four combatants or if she would have some help in quelling the fight. In the end, she took an accidental blow to the nose that caused it to gush blood, and had to retire from the fray feeling dizzy and sick.

Four people were now shouting at each other, getting physical with the occasional shove or slap. Junior Hargreaves leaned against the boundary fence and laughed loudly.

Edwina reached into her shoulder bag and extracted half a dozen tissues with which she tried to stop her nosebleed. She was standing alone, an island of silent misery in a sea of abuse, when suddenly the four neighbours turned as one and fell about her with wounding words.

'If you council people would mind your own business, there wouldn't be all this trouble,' screamed Mrs Curteis. 'Jim Scarlet wouldn't have had anybody to ring and tell on us.'

'The men could have had a duel instead,' said Edwina with the tissues pressed to her nose.

'They would have sorted it out,' said Mrs Curteis. 'You cause trouble, you do. Always looking for something to complain about. Is this what we pay our taxes for? Bloody busybodies. What use are you? Our money should be spent on schools and roads and the NHS.'

'You're just a waste of money.' This from Mrs Scarlet.

'Go on,' said Mr Curteis. 'Piss off. You're trespassing. I didn't invite you here. You've got no right.'

Edwina's nose was throbbing. She urgently needed to get some more tissues, and her own house was just half a mile down the road. She decided to go home and nurse her assorted injuries, both mental and physical.

Her bungalow was a refuge, a haven of peace and quiet, but also a lonely place where she had to confront the day and what it meant to her. She put a few ice cubes in a tea towel and lay down in the bedroom with the cold pack pressed against her nose. She would have liked to take a couple of aspirins, but it was too much effort to get up again.

No sound from outside penetrated the walls to disturb her, and within a few minutes she was asleep. Several hours later, the jarring sound of the doorbell caused her to sit up far too quickly. The ice had melted, carrying bloody water onto her blouse and the bedspread. Outside, it was getting dark.

'Edwina! Are you in there?' It was Felix.

'Coming! Coming! Just let me turn on some lights.'

'My God! Your nose is swollen,' he said when she had opened the door to him. 'What happened? Were you climbing? Have you had it seen to?'

'No, no. Come in. I got between two men who wanted to fight about a hedge. It's nothing serious, but a blow to the nose always hurts.'

'Was it intentional? Do you want to put in a complaint?'

'No, I don't,' she said vehemently. 'That's the last thing I want to do. These two neighbours deserve each other and will have to sort out their differences.'

'The council shouldn't be involved in hedges.'

'Thank you, Felix,' she said dryly. 'Everybody already knows that, but as a service we will on occasion mediate.'

He came into the living room and turned on a table lamp. 'Come over here and let's see your nose. Are you sure it isn't broken?'

Obediently, she raised her head so that he could examine her face, tap the nose gently, tweak it and pronounce it unbroken, so far as he could tell.

'Come on, I'll buy you dinner. Are you hungry?'

'Not particularly. And I'm certainly not going out looking like this. However, I'm afraid I've nothing in the fridge to cook.'

'Well,' he said. 'Two choices. I could go out for a takeaway or we could just about make it down to the supermarket before it closes to pick up a couple of steaks.'

'Oh, steaks, please. I've got frozen chips. We'll get some fruit. Or an apple pie.'

He smiled at her, then impulsively kissed her gently on the nose. 'Are you coming with me? You don't have to. I'm quite willing to go alone.'

'No,' she said. 'I'm coming. We're unlikely to meet anyone we know at this hour.'

She switched on the oven so that she could put the chips on when they returned, locked the front door and jogged up the road to Felix's car. He drove with his usual care and consideration, so Edwina was convinced that they would not arrive before the store closed.

Chapter Eight

Homestead had two supermarkets, neither as big as the out-of-town giants, but convenient for residents. The Co-op was situated in a small cluster of shops just off the High Street and boasted a generous car park. After hours, it became the perfect place to leave one's car when dining out at one of the local restaurants.

The evenings were drawing in, but it was still possible for Zena to drive her car to the Co-op and walk up the hill for a meal in daylight. She usually ate at six thirty, finishing by a quarter past seven, so that she could drive home while it was still light.

This evening, however, she was delayed. The music blaring from Gorham House had continued well past seven o'clock, forcing Zena to hover near her car door, anxious to be off, but afraid of encountering the ogres. Finally she decided to brave it and made her escape at a quarter past seven. It was after eight when she returned to her car. The supermarket was closed and the car park was eerily deserted, except for a lone vehicle.

Leo had been urging Cassandra to get a move on for the past half-hour. He fancied a curry and it was nearly eight o'clock. 'Turn off that bloody music, will you?' he shouted up the stairs. 'It's driving me crazy. Come on, Cassandra! I'm hungry.'

Clumsily, she manoeuvred the stairs in high-heeled platform shoes. 'I don't know why I bother to dress up for Homestead. No-one dresses up. I wish you'd sell this fleapit and move back to London.'

He looked her over. She was wearing a new black satin suit with a short skirt that barely covered her bottom and a jacket that had difficulty meeting across her chest. Her shoes were silver, as was her handbag. He thought she looked terrific, and she was right. Her expensive clothes were wasted on the locals. 'See that you don't spill any curry on that suit. I like it. Maybe you'll wear it a few more times before you throw it to the back of the wardrobe.'

'I won't throw it away if you like it,' she said warmly. Flicking her hair back, she adjusted the jacket to show a little more cleavage, then looked up at him with a provocative grin.

'You're impossible,' he laughed. 'Come on. Let's eat.'

Felix and Edwina parked as close as they could get to the supermarket, but it was obvious that the place had already locked its doors. One other car stood in the car park.

'That's Zena Alway's Rover,' said Felix. 'Maybe she's in the store and they'll let us in, too.'

'Do you recognize every car of every resident?' asked Edwina.

'Not every one, but I do know a lot of them. Hurry. We may make it.'

They trotted up to the double doors of the supermarket, but they were locked, although they could see several employees at the far end, filling shelves. They went round to the far side where there was a tea shop, but there was no-one around, and Zena was definitely not inside the store.

'What now?' asked Felix. 'Do you fancy a curry?'

'What? Looking like this? We might see some-one we know. I wouldn't mind going out of town. A hamburger will do. The bump on the nose has caused me to lose my appetite.'

Headlights came on in the car park as they rounded the corner of the store. 'Zena ought not to be driving after dark,' murmured Felix.

Before Edwina could reply, a sports car turned into the drive leading up to the car park, its headlights piercing the gloom, and Felix muttered, 'Damn! It's the Midnights. They'd better not give Zena a hard time or I'll be on to them.'

With a roar, the car swept onto the tarmac and drove straight up to the store, parking with a muffled zoom in a space in the row directly behind the Rover. The Midnights climbed out of the car, shouting ironic greetings to Zena.

'Got a date, have you, Zena?' called Cassandra. 'Found somebody as old as you are? Better turn in that moth-eaten wig.'

The old woman gasped. For years she had been

under the impression that no-one knew she wore a wig. Her hair was thinning; it seemed the sensible thing to do in order to remain looking smart. Even Claris had never mentioned it.

'Stay here,' said Felix to Edwina. 'This has gone on long enough.' He started towards the two cars.

Zena experienced a terrible pain in her head as if it would soon explode, a feeling unlike any other she had ever known. Shaken by uncontrollable anger, she released the brake, put the car in reverse and jammed her foot down on the accelerator. The car shot backwards and connected with a loud crunch, buckling the low front end of Leo's car.

'Zena!' yelled Felix, breaking into a run.

'Stop it, you stupid bitch!' screamed Cassandra, as Zena drove forward.

'She's going to do it again! Get out of the way!' shouted Leo to Cassandra. They were both standing on the tarmac. There was nothing he could do to move his precious car away from further damage.

Zena reversed again, this time keeping her foot on the accelerator, as if to push the sports car out of the car park altogether.

Leo saw Felix and shouted to him to do something. Felix reached Zena's car and grabbed the passenger door, but it was locked. She had once more pulled forward. There was nothing he could do to stop her making another assault on the Midnight car and prudently he let go of the door handle.

Leo was furious. A terrifying man at the best of times, he now looked satanic. Edwina wished she could help stop Zena from destroying her own car as well as Leo's, but fear of the ogre kept her rooted to the spot. She could not force herself to move from the shadows where Leo might see her. Instead, she admitted to herself that she got a vicarious thrill from watching Zena ruin his precious possession. Cassandra, she realized, was swearing loudly, every bit as foul-mouthed as gossip said she was.

On her third foray, Zena's car locked with the sports car. She turned off the ignition with shaking fingers and attempted to undo her seat belt. Felix opened the door, reached across to unclip the seat belt and helped her out.

Extending her wrists towards him and ignoring the bellowing Midnights, she said in a quivery voice. 'It's a fair cop. I'll go quietly. Put on the cuffs.'

Felix took a deep breath as he studied the lined face, now defeated by emotions too great for her to cope with. 'Are you hurt? You could have got a whiplash injury, you know. Don't hold out your wrists, dear. I'm not going to cuff you.'

'Oh, Felix,' she whimpered.

With much swearing and many threats, Leo bounced on the locked bumpers and finally disengaged his car from Zena's.

He turned his attention to her. 'You stupid cow! You evil old harridan! What do you think you're playing at? I'll sue you for every penny you've got. That's if I don't wring your neck here and now.'

Her anger abated, Zena felt drained and very afraid. She shrank against Felix who put his arm around her narrow shoulders.

'Shut your foul mouth, Midnight. She's old enough to be your grandmother.'

'Yeah?' Leo stepped close to Felix and looked into his eyes. 'Well, my grandmother just bashed the shit out of my car. If you think I'm going to let this bitch reduce it to rubble and get away with it, you've got another think coming.'

'You've been harassing her for weeks. She snapped, that's all.'

Leo slapped his forehead and turned away slightly. 'Aha! I've got it now. All the good citizens of Gorham pay you to see that they never have to suffer the consequences of their misdeeds. That's how it works, is it?'

'Of course it isn't. I'm not in the Met, you know. We don't take bribes around here.'

Leo, usually so well in control of his temper, now lost his cool. Grabbing a handful of Felix's jacket, he brought the shorter man up to his face. 'I suggest you take that back, sonny.'

Seeing Leo's frustration and quivering anger, Felix sensed he had a slight advantage. Brushing Leo's hand away, he half turned to Zena and said quietly, 'I really don't want to arrest you, my dear. I understand the provocation you've suffered. Of course you will have to pay for the repairs to Mr Midnight's car. But whether or not I arrest you depends on the gentleman. And his kind heart, of course. It's up to him. I have a feeling he will prefer to forget this incident in order to keep his name out of the papers. He does not want to go to court and give evidence against you. And I don't think he will be suing, either.'

Smiling slightly, Felix turned and met Leo's eyes. The two men stared at each other for several seconds. Cassandra was silent, looking at Leo in some surprise, but not attempting to influence his decision.

'Send me the bill for the repairs,' said Zena. 'I won't argue, whatever it is.'

Leo rubbed his chin. 'All right,' he said at last. 'It's going to cost a packet. I don't want any fuss. This old bag should not be driving. She's a menace and you'll regret your soft heart one of these days, Plod. You're a poodle of the middle classes. My guess is, one day you'll do something that pisses them off. Then wait for them to remind you who pays your wages. But, OK, I'll save you the paperwork. It's your funeral. Come on, Cassandra. We'll have to go home and get the other car. If the engine still goes.'

He went to his crumpled car, revved the engine a couple of times, then ordered Cassandra to get in. Edwina, still standing in the shadows, and Felix, with his arm around the shaking Zena, watched in silence as the car rattled away.

When they were gone, Zena collapsed against Felix. 'It felt good,' she whimpered. 'I'm not sorry I did it. I'm glad. It felt so good. Can you understand that? Oh, but will you get into trouble, Felix?'

He looked around as Edwina joined him. There were no witnesses. No-one had come out of the supermarket to see what was going on. The employee car park was way over on the other side of the store. No houses overlooked the area.

'There are no witnesses so I don't think I will get into trouble. I knew Midnight wouldn't want to get tangled with the law. But now, it's more important than ever to stay out of his way, you know. He's a vengeful man. And you must never tell anyone what has happened. Do you understand? Never tell anyone. Get your car fixed out of town. I'm sure you realize that you can never claim on your insurance for this damage. Pay to have it repaired and then forget about tonight.'

Edwina examined the damage to the Rover. 'This car hasn't suffered too much, not like the sports car. Shall I drive Zena home? You can follow.'

'All right,' said Felix. 'But for God's sake, drive carefully.'

He waited until the two women had reached the car-park drive, then quickly entered his car and drove away. He was filled with misgivings. He should have arrested Zena. She was not safe on the roads, but he probably would not be able to make her understand that she should give up driving. And by refusing to charge her, he had lost the power to force some common sense on her. He must try to convince her that she should take a taxi in future.

As if his failure to arrest Zena were not bad enough, he had also made a serious enemy of a dangerous man. Furthermore, he had behaved far below his own high standards. Now all he could do was pray that Zena didn't recount the incident to the entire town. Or to Claris and Prunella, which was the same thing.

Edwina and Felix spent over fifteen minutes with Zena in her home. She drank a large sherry and assured them she would be all right. It was now half past eight and they were both very hungry. Felix drove them to McDonald's seven miles away and they ate in silence, until Edwina spilt hot apple-pie filling on her jacket.

'This place is costing me a fortune in dry cleaning! Oh, Felix, let's go back to my place. I'm whacked.'

'You're also wounded. It's been quite an evening, hasn't it? I just hope—'

'Oh, darling, I don't want you to get into trouble!' she cried. 'You should have arrested her.'

He shrugged. 'I know. I made a mistake there, but Leo Midnight makes me do things I wouldn't do otherwise. I don't know why I let him bug me. I wanted to win, you see. Wanted him to back down. I knew he hoped I would arrest her, so it became stupidly important not to do so. Greg always says you've got to cover your backside. Play it by the book. But I felt sorry for Zena. That London bastard has been driving her crazy. The thing is, she's not within walking distance of anywhere. She needs her car. So once again I've been a poodle of the middle classes, like the man said.'

'Don't let him get you down. Now tell me. What if your inspector does find out that you didn't report Zena's road rage?'

'I'll be in trouble. Not dismissed from the force. At least I don't think so. But Zena won't tell. When she calms down, she'll realize that to talk about it will mean losing her licence. And the Midnights, for some reason, don't want to make a splash. I'm keeping an eye on old Leo and he knows it. He's up to something. I just wish I knew what it is.'

*   *   *

Felix was determined to introduce Edwina to as
many people as possible as soon as possible, and
the best way to do it was to throw a party. As he
had never given a serious party in his own home
with properly prepared food and paper napkins,
he was quite excited about it. Two weeks before
the date he'd decided on, he bought two large
pads of paper, some felt tips and twenty-five
invitations, then went to Edwina's house so that
they could make plans.

'You're not going to invite twenty-five couples
are you?' she asked. 'How will you get them all
inside your house? We'll be standing on each
other's heads.'

'Rubbing elbows makes a party go with a
swing. Anyway, I'm only sending out twenty-five
invitations and some are singles. Not everyone
will be able to come. I hope.'

She looked at him fondly. 'I hope we're not
going to make all the food ourselves. I'll do it if
you want me to, but I'd rather not.'

'Get in caterers, you mean. Wouldn't that be
rather expensive?'

She shook her head. 'No need for caterers. You
go to one of the big out-of-town supermarkets
and order their special party trays. Cold meats.
Indian delicacies. I don't know what else. They
have a catalogue. Choose what you want and
then you pick them up on the day of the party.
Simple.'

'That's brilliant. And what about the drink?'

'Get it delivered by the off-licence or put it
in the back of your car. They'll advise. Shall I
do the ordering from the supermarket while you

organize the drink, Felix? I think that would be the best way round.'

He agreed and they both wrote on their new pads that Edwina would order the food and Felix would order the drinks. They decided to have red and white balloons, so that had to be written down against Felix's name. Then Edwina told him that his house needed a thorough clean. He doubted it, but she was adamant. She would clean the house, while he collected the food on the day of the party.

So far, they had not used more than one page of their pads, but when the discussion turned to the guest list, many pages were ruined. Edwina knew no-one whom she wished to invite, John Blue being considered too old to enjoy a noisy party. After all, he was approaching fifty and had probably not been to a knees-up for years!

On the other hand, Edwina knew just which of Felix's friends she did not wish to get to know better. These people, it turned out, were the very ones whom he felt he must invite, because he worked with them and felt they could not be excluded. The list grew to sixty, was cut back to fifty-six and accompanied by a little prayer that at least a quarter would have prior engagements.

On the Saturday morning of the party Edwina came early to Felix's house, found the vacuum cleaner under the stairs and gave the carpets a thorough going-over. Felix was extremely neat personally and always looked terrific in his uniform, but his housekeeping left a lot to be desired. She tidied every room and gave the kitchen the cleaning it had desperately needed for the last month or more. After she had thrown out everything that was past its sell-by date, the fridge was almost completely empty, leaving plenty of room for the supermarket trays.

Felix meanwhile went to the supermarket to pick up the party supplies, the plates of cold meats, the trays of smoked fish, the samosas and dips, the tiny sausage rolls and meat pies and the selected cheeses and crackers, all made up attractively and arranged on foil trays by the supermarket. He was tremendously impressed with Edwina's choice and the way the food had been artistically arranged. He returned to his house with the boxes, but even the newly cleaned fridge wouldn't take more than half of them, so they had to carry the rest to Edwina's house.

Forty-eight people had accepted their invitation and he hoped that they would be hungry. Above all, however, he knew they would be thirsty, and despite his best intentions, Felix had been too busy to order the drink. He kept this fact from Edwina, convinced that he could sort everything out very quickly and she need never know.

Party-giving was hard work, but they were both enjoying it so much that they seemed never to stop laughing. He did not want to spoil the mood by telling her that he had let the side down.

Wisely, they had also invited the couples who lived on either side of Felix. Edwina had already been introduced to them and had made a good impression. The Falcons were in their fifties. He was a builder. The Cravens were retired; they surely wouldn't stay long. But he hoped that by inviting them he had stopped them from being aggrieved about the noise. Fortunately for neighbourly relations, they didn't intend to play music, because Edwina hated it and Felix wanted everybody to talk as much as possible to her. He called it Edwina's coming-out party.

At one o'clock Edwina suggested that they stop for something to eat, but Felix said he was too busy and escaped before she had time to wonder what was so urgent. Nevertheless, he was hungry, so he went to the Prince of Wales for a sandwich, planning to speak to the landlord about drink quantities.

Fred and Tim, those stalwarts of the Prince of Wales, arrived before he had a chance to speak to Jim, so their orders had to be taken first. Jim would not allow two such valued customers to wait for their pints.

'Must talk to you,' whispered Tim, sidling up to Felix. 'Very important.'

'Right, just a moment.' Felix smiled at the old boy. Tim and Fred were forever giving him little titbits of information, convinced that they had a direct line to all the local villains. So far, nothing they told him had ever been of the least value. Nevertheless, he always listened politely and thanked them for their help in keeping Gorham and Homestead safe. 'I've just got to have a word with Jim first.'

Quickly, Felix explained to the landlord that he was having a party for forty-eight people and asked advice about how much drink and what sort he should get in. Jim said he would write it on a piece of paper. He moved off to wait on a middle-aged couple. Fred tugged at Felix's jacket.

'OK, fellas. I'm all ears.'

'We were in here day before yesterday,' began Tim. 'Couple of blokes come in, looking rough.'

'Never seen them before,' added Fred.

'Talking,' continued Tim, 'about a mate of theirs who got into trouble over some statues. Now, we don't know which statues.'

'Could have been anywhere.'

'Right,' said Tim, frowning. This was his story and he didn't like Fred interrupting. 'They mentioned his name, Duggie, but I didn't get his last name properly. Something like Duggan, I think.'

'Could be Dougan,' added Fred.

'Could even be Douglas,' said Felix, straight-faced. 'Thanks for the tip. I'll look into it.'

Jim, now very busy at the bar, thrust a scrap of paper into his hand. Felix ate a ham sandwich accompanied by a half-pint of beer in five minutes as he chatted with the two old men. Buying each of them a pint before he left, he waved goodbye to his informants before driving to the off-licence. Everything went very smoothly, so there was no need to tell Edwina he had been late with his order.

The party went with a swing from the moment the Cravens and Falcons arrived. It was another fifteen minutes before the younger crowd began knocking on the door, giving Edwina ample time to charm the older couples, to discuss the weather, gardening, trees and the best place to buy good English apples.

Greg and Harriet arrived with a bottle of wine and a dozen cans of bitter. Harriet looked very pretty in an electric blue taffeta dress with a little glitter on the neckline. Edwina was relieved that she had eventually decided to wear a black double-layer chiffon skirt that swirled almost down to her ankles, black court shoes and a skimpy black top with narrow straps that couldn't accommodate a bra underneath. She was not accustomed to wearing a skirt, nor to wearing high heels, but the discomfort on this occasion was worth it. She thought she looked as smart as Harriet.

It was one of those parties that hosts dream about, where the guests just clicked with one another right from the start. Even the older people were made to feel a part of the fun. Edwina was having a wonderful time. There was plenty to drink and the men seemed to have sorted it out among them who was going to look after supplies, so that Felix didn't have to spend too much time serving drinks.

It was clear that there was more food than forty-eight people could ever hope to eat. A most satisfactory situation, even if it did mean that they would be eating sausage rolls for breakfast. She relaxed and circulated, pushing her way through the throng, talking to everyone, which was most unusual for her.

Twice she found herself caught up in one of Felix's bear hugs. He would kiss her loudly and the guests would all roar and make crude remarks. It was a fabulous evening, because she had her man beside her and had found new confidence.

There was still the business of where she would work when her contract ran out, but that was months away. She would worry about her future another time when she was calm and could plan coolly. It was certainly impossible to think clearly in Felix's house at the moment.

The guests filled every space in the hall, living room and kitchen, and there didn't seem to be a wallflower among them. She thought it was the first party she had ever attended where no-one appeared bored and no-one was being ignored. At about half past eleven the neighbours said good night and Felix and Edwina saw them to the door. As they closed the front door, Felix was grabbed by the sleeve by a pretty young constable and dragged off to another part of the room. Close by, Harriet was screaming a comic story about her visits to supermarkets to a grinning couple who seemed to be able to hear her above the noise.

Edwina pushed her way past them and headed for the bathroom off Felix's bedroom, anticipating the comparative quiet. Noisy parties were great, but sometimes it was nice to get away. She repaired her lipstick, her mind on the possibility of future parties, perhaps at Christmas. She and Felix would become known for their fabulous do's.

Felix saw Edwina return from the bathroom and smiled fondly at her. His smile drew her like a magnet, but she seemed to be causing some amusement as she passed the guests. At last he saw why.

'Fairfax,' he said in her ear, his arm around her shoulders. 'I'm going to tell it like it is. You've been found out. We know where you've been.'

'Where?' she asked, looking panic-stricken.

'You've got your skirt caught in your knickers.'

There was a howl of laughter as she hastily tugged at her skirt. 'That's the last time I'll wear a skirt! Next time it'll be my flies that are undone,' she cried and joined in the laughter.

'You're a great sport,' he said and kissed her again. She clung to him, her heart so full she thought it would burst.

'It's too good to be true,' she said in his ear. 'Something's bound to happen.'

He kissed her nose. 'Don't be so superstitious. Nothing is going to happen to us. We're soul-mates.'

'Come on, Felix, you can do that lovey-dovey stuff when we've gone.' Harriet pushed the two apart. 'I want to talk to your lover.' She put her arm around Edwina's shoulders and Felix grinned at them both. 'Want to have a lark, just you and me?'

'I don't know, Harriet. Felix and I are aw-fully—'

'Don't fret. I won't take you away from him for too long. Listen, this is absolutely great. I've bought two tickets to a wine and cheese party. And you know what the joke is? It's at Gorham House on the twenty-fifth. It's from six to eight. Will you come as my guest? It'll be a real laugh. I'm dying to see inside that place.'

'Golly, I don't know. They won't be happy to see me. And it was bad enough the last time I went there. I was afraid of getting . . . Still, it would be a challenge.'

Felix was being hailed by one of his old mates and began making his way to the other side of the room, happy that Edwina and Harriet seemed to be getting on so well.

'What about Greg and Felix? Won't they want to go?'

'The men won't go to Gorham House for some reason. Come on, Edwina. It could be fun. Do it for a dare.'

Edwina took a deep breath. 'OK. I'll do it. Shall I drive? I could pick you up at six. It'll only take about five minutes to get there, but we don't want to be the very first ones to arrive.'

'That's fine.' Harriet gave her shoulder a squeeze. 'Got any Cokes? I've had enough alcohol. I'm driving.'

The party broke up at half past two. Felix earnestly begged everyone to leave as quietly as possible. They did try. Yet several taxis were waiting in the road, their diesel engines chugging loudly. With the exception of a prolonged bout of female giggling and the slamming of a dozen car doors, his friends departed like good citizens.

Edwina insisted on clearing up the major rubbish before going to bed, so they finally fell asleep shortly after three thirty. Felix had lost count of how many beers he had consumed and slept heavily for the first two hours, then woke with a dry mouth and a feeling of unease.

Edwina was curled up with her back to him, deeply asleep. He got out of bed and shuffled into the kitchen for a glass of water and a couple of headache pills. He should have taken them before going to bed. And, of course, he should have drunk a couple of glasses of water as well, to prevent dehydration. His bare feet discovered a piece of luncheon meat which had to be scraped off his big toe. The kitchen smelled of stale beer; Jim had been absolutely right about how much everybody would drink. Refilling his glass at the tap, he frowned, trying to remember what had happened the night before.

The look on Edwina's face when . . . Yes, that was it! He had held her close and said, 'You've been found out. We know where you've been.' She had been horrified, no other word for it. Horrified. Then when she found out he was only talking about how she had her skirt in her knickers, she had laughed with relief. Yet what woman thinks that to be so ludicrously dressed is funny? A woman with a genuinely terrible secret, of course. A woman who is relieved that her real secret has not been discovered, after all. And he had dreamed it all again in slow motion!

Leaning over the sink, he splashed cold water on his face, but it didn't help. The images of his dream would not go away, nor would his suspicions. 'I'll not sleep,' he muttered, and went into the living room to open the curtains on the new day. It was so foggy he could barely see across the road.

The bungalows across the way were probably still curtained and silent. Another hour and the Blakes would be up and about. They were fanatical gardeners and liked to be out in all weathers at all times of the year. He wondered what they found to do. True, their garden was twice the size of his, but still . . .

And there was Ned Banter, two doors away. Felix could hear the front door slam shut, although he couldn't see that far through the mist. Ned would have his fishing gear in hand. He'd be gone all day, enjoying himself and at peace with the world. Felix had been fishing with him several times. Ned Banter wouldn't be wondering if his wife of thirty years had betrayed him. No doubts for Ned. Of course there were decent women in the world, it was just that Felix had never found one to love.

'I'll never sleep,' he said again. Another man? Was that where she had been? Some rendezvous? No, not Edwina. He didn't believe it.

She had been up to some mischief, that was it. Edwina had a gift for getting into hot water.

Suddenly he put his hands to his aching head, like a footballer who has just missed a penalty. He remembered Harriet inviting her to Gorham House and Edwina had said . . . what? He racked his brain. Something about her having been there before and she shouldn't have been. Trespassing. She was good at trespassing, but surely she would have mentioned it. They told each other everything. Didn't they?

Gorham House. What's more, if she had been trespassing and had kept it a secret from him, there must be some shameful reason. The robbery. Perhaps she had been there on that same day and thought he would blame her for it. He shook his head. Absurd. But what if she had seen something? That might make sense.

Whatever had happened at Gorham House, he was now certain that she had deceived him in some way. He wondered if he could bear to lie next to her, but he was tired and headed for the bedroom. Against his prediction, he was asleep in seconds, and this time there were no dreams.

'My God! It's ten o'clock!' cried Edwina, getting out of bed. 'Wake up, darling. We're going to Badger's Wood. Remember?' She disappeared into the bathroom.

Like a robot, Felix got up and went into the kitchen to put on the kettle. When Edwina came out of the bathroom, he passed her without a word.

She had made some toast and set the table by the time he was dressed and shaved. She looked up at him anxiously as he sat down. 'All right?'

It was difficult to speak to her. His mind was so full of a vague sense of betrayal that he didn't wish even to comment on the strength of the coffee. Yet what if he was doing her a serious injustice? Perhaps he was wrong. The trouble was, he could only find out the truth by confronting her with his suspicions. If she were innocent, their relationship would be pointlessly damaged.

For some reason, he couldn't bear the idea of challenging her in his own home. They had already planned to go to the woods and there, on neutral territory, he would find out what she had been up to.

'You'd better drive,' he said when they were ready to leave the house. 'I'm probably still over the limit.'

Edwina patted his face and smiled. 'Drink doesn't agree with you, my grouchy bear. You'd better lay off in future.' He ground his teeth.

Badger's Wood was not far away. It was neither famous nor very old, just a few acres of woodland that was being returned to native species, an area that provided a safe walk for those who loved trees. Edwina thought it was very well managed by the Forestry Commission and wanted to talk about it to Felix.

'Walking among the silent trees fills me with a sense of awe and calm. I'm going to come here on my own one day soon to think out my next move. It's clear John Blue doesn't want me. I'll get up at dawn and walk in the mist. "Season of mists and mellow fruitfulness".'

'Yeah,' answered Felix.

They walked silently for about five minutes, then Edwina held up her hand. 'Here's a log. Let's sit down. You poor darling. You really aren't feeling well, are you?'

Felix sat down on the log, but moved away when Edwina sat close to him. He turned and straddled the log so that he could study her face. At the moment, she looked puzzled but innocent.

'Want to tell me anything, Edwina? Still worried about what Leo Midnight is doing to his trees?'

'Yes, of course I am. What's all this about?'

'About your friends at the protest. You know, that pathetic band of eco-warriors who hung about the oak tree. Remember?'

'I remember.' She looked away now, no longer seemingly puzzled but nervously rubbing her hands together.

'Your friend Duggie?'

'Duggie? I didn't know anybody's name.' She looked at the ground, clearly lying. 'Oh, yes. There may have been a chap named Duggie. They were just a grubby lot of layabouts who love trees.'

'You're lying! It's possible Duggie was one of the men who stole four statues from Gorham House, isn't it?'

Edwina couldn't compose her features quickly enough to fool Felix. She did try, attempting a look of innocent confusion, but he knew her too well. For several seconds they stared at one another. Then she turned away and put her face in her hands.

'Try to understand. I was there the day the statues were stolen, simply because I wanted to see what trees were on the property. When I saw the lorry drive up, I hid behind a tree. They were a long way away. I didn't know they were stealing anything. I really was upset when I heard they had actually been stolen. Above all, I didn't want to have to tell John Blue what I had done. But then there was no need. They were returned so quickly. Why should I have said anything to you once they were returned? I didn't want to get involved!'

'Were there three of them?'

'Yes, there were and they had a big lorry with a grabber thing on the back.'

'So you kept quiet abut Duggie.'

'Not the way you mean. I saw Duggie close to for the first time at the home of Mrs Dunne who was supposed to be organizing the protest.' She stood up and paced about on the soft ground. 'I shouldn't have been at Gorham House, of course. I had heard Leo Midnight and his wife were going to London for a couple of days. I needed to see his trees. You don't understand, because you don't care about trees at all. Besides, what was the point of telling you that I had trespassed on the Midnight property when I didn't know Duggie or any of them from Adam? Later, when I saw Duggie at the meeting and recognized him as one of the thieves, the statues had already been returned. There was just no point in getting mixed up in it all. I only did what most people would have done. He's a stupid kid, but his heart is in the right place. I didn't want to be responsible for sending some poor chap to jail. It wouldn't have done him any good. I mean, he would just have got to know a lot of real criminals.'

Felix stood up and took her by the arm. 'There was a point. Leo Midnight made fools of us. He found the statues when we couldn't. Any information would have been helpful. People tell me things all the time, little things that might be of use. But my girlfriend, who only has to roll over in bed to talk to me, keeps silent or else lies to me. That's great.'

He realized that he was still holding her arm and dropped his hand. Edwina rubbed her arm. 'Is that what this is about? I prevented you from looking clever in front of Leo Midnight? Are you going to arrest me?'

'What for?'

'Accessory after the fact or something?'

'No, I'm not going to arrest you. But I just want to know one thing. Was it worth it? Trespassing, I mean. Did you find something so important that it was worth ruining your career and our relationship for? Is there some tree on his property that is so precious that you were willing to sacrifice your future for it?'

She blinked. 'I can't believe it! Is that how you feel? That it's all over between us just because of this? I worried about embarrassing John. It never occurred to me that such a small thing would damage our relationship.'

'I'm a policeman, Edwina. You and I have different attitudes to the law.'

For a long time she said nothing, then: 'The important thing is, you and I have a different attitude to a loving relationship. I did you no harm. I did no-one any harm. And I'll not apologize for it. Come on. I'll drive you home. You probably have a boy scout meeting this afternoon. Mr Perfect. The well-turned out, morally superior PC Trent.' She led the way, putting each booted foot firmly in front of the other.

Suddenly, she stopped and whirled on him. 'How did you find out?'

'Do you think I'm a complete fool? I had a tip-off that a minor villain named Duggie, they couldn't remember the last name, had been involved in taking the statues. Earlier, when I saw you with the eco-troublemakers, somebody pointed out the one you talked to most as Duggie Duncuff.'

'Is that all?'

'Not quite. But if you were a better liar, you might have got away with it. Last night you got your skirt caught up. Remember? I said I knew where you'd been and you looked guilty, then relieved when I told you about your skirt. I knew then you had a secret.'

'My God, the man's Sherlock Holmes. CID material, if I ever saw it.'

'I know you too well.'

'And I don't know you at all. You're a pompous prig, Felix. You deserve every insult Leo Midnight has ever flung at you.'

He might, he told himself later, just might have forgiven her for keeping silent about Duggie. But he could not forgive her for calling him a pompous prig. The suspicion that he was overreacting was already nagging away at the back of his mind.

They got into the car. Felix folded his arms across his chest and neither spoke until Edwina stopped outside his home.

'Felix, I'm sorry. I see now that I should have told you. It won't happen again. Let's not—'

'Goodbye, Edwina.' Felix slammed the car door and walked up the path to his house.

Greg was disgustingly cheerful on Monday morning. Felix would have been glad to avoid him. 'Felix, great party! Harriet had a ball. She looked good and she knew it. I thought Edwina looked absolutely sensational, too.'

'Yes, she did.'

'And a good sport. You're a lucky man. This could be the one, you know. Your lifetime partner.'

'Yes,' said Felix with a sigh. 'She's a good sport. Not like other people. A one-off.'

Greg moved closer. 'Got to talk to you. I've found out about Leo Midnight. All the gen. Knew I could do it if I tried. For a few years he did undercover work, infiltrating a gang of soccer louts. Travelled with them. Dangerous work, really. But he loved it. The old adrenaline rush, I guess. Then the powers that be thought he might have been rumbled. He was at a loose end and decided to apply for child protection work. Well, it's grim, you know, the suffering you come across. Helpless little kids. You see terrible things and you want to put the perpetrators behind bars for ever, then it turns out it's difficult to get a conviction. A lot of times you've got to watch these sadistic bastards walk free, simply because there's not enough evidence to convict.'

'I wouldn't have thought Midnight was the type for that work.'

'It got to him, that's for sure,' said Greg. 'One day they're called to a house and there's a baby dead in its mother's arms. Its brains have been knocked out against a wall. Midnight goes ape. Loses it entirely. It seems he always reckoned his old man had killed his baby sister. Leo had been bottling up his grief and suspicions about his dad all these years and seeing the baby just brought it back to him. Well, his mates pulled him round, calmed him down. Months later, the trial comes up. The mother's boyfriend is in the dock. Leo's afraid he's going to get away with it like so many others and—'

'So he manufactures a little evidence.'

'That's right,' said Greg. 'Of course, the case is thrown out. The boyfriend is free to do it again, but Leo gets a conviction and a suspended sentence on account of his having been mentally unwell and he's out of the force. Within eighteen months he's a basket case. I think he was sectioned under the Mental Health Act at one time. When he surfaces again, he's got some money but he's not doing anything to earn it.' Greg smiled. 'It's a mystery.'

'Poor bastard,' said Felix. 'I feel sorry for him. I never thought I'd say that, but I do.'

'Man's got guts. I couldn't go undercover, I readily admit it. By and large, the public know nothing about what some cops risk to keep them safe and they don't care anyway. Yet somebody has to do these jobs. Child protection! Please! I simply couldn't do that, not in a million years. So I admire him, but you've got to keep your emotional distance in police work. Remember that, Felix. Nowadays, Leo Midnight is a loose cannon. No telling what he might be up to.'

'Or else he just wants a little peace and quiet.'

'Felix, the man is living in a house worth three-quarters of a million! Yes, he's brave. But also he's not working, yet he's rich. OK?' He rubbed his chin. 'And wasn't there some retired cop who came in to give me hell about him? Let's not lose our sense of proportion.'

Later, those words came back to Felix. Mustn't lose our sense of proportion. Is that what he had done? He was sitting in the living room of his own home, alone, having cut himself off from the first woman he had felt he could trust. He had thought he loved her, for God's sake! Yet she had been the biggest liar of them all. He couldn't get the sense of betrayal out of his mind. Protecting a criminal just because she didn't want to admit she had been trespassing! She could have trusted him. He could have treated her as an informer, somebody whose name was never mentioned.

And yet . . . He sighed. Another part of his mind was busy congratulating himself for his perception, for having put two and two together. For there was no doubt about it. He had leapt to a conclusion, let his instincts take over just like Greg often did. And just like Greg, his instincts had led him to the right conclusion. There was a certain satisfaction in his unravelling of the mystery. He couldn't help but feel a little smug.

The clever policeman who had shafted his own love life out of a sense of duty.

Zena rang Edwina. It was the first time she had called in five days, so she felt rather virtuous. But the day was going to be a long one. It threatened to undermine her sanity and she felt that only Edwina would know what she was going through.

'Edwina?'

'Hello, Zena. How are you?'

'You sound tired.'

'Went to a big party last Saturday.'

'But that was almost a week ago! You're too young to be tired. There's to be a party tonight. Did you know? At Gorham House. I'm not going. Everybody's going and I was invited. But I could hardly turn up on the doorstep, could I?'

'Hardly,' said Edwina. 'Close your windows and turn up the telly. Can you hear the noise from Gorham House?'

'If they're playing their pop music. They wouldn't dare do that tonight, though. I shall be in my recliner watching a film.' She didn't add that she might also walk down to the boundary fence with her binoculars. 'Edwina dear. I must ask you a question. Do you think confession is good for the soul?'

Remembering her recent encounter with Felix, Edwina felt that her whole life would have been better if she had confessed to the trespassing. 'Oh, yes, I do! It's wrong to keep . . . things to yourself. I know I will always regret not having confessed . . . but never mind. Yes, you're right. Confession is good for the soul.'

Zena said goodbye after thanking her young friend for clearing her mind. Almost immediately she rang for a taxi, saying she wished to go to the police station in Homestead.

Five minutes later, Edwina realized with horror that Zena had probably been talking about confessing to her road rage. She was going to tell the inspector! She must warn Felix! Dialling his mobile she puzzled that she received no reply. It seemed the mobile had been switched off. Or run down, more likely. She would have to ring the station, although she didn't want to do so.

Felix was out when Zena arrived, but as soon as he came into the station Greg told him that Zena Alway had been in the inspector's office for the past ten minutes.

'I wonder what that's about?' said Greg.

Felix was sure he knew and wondered what would happen next. Dismissal? He couldn't think calmly, but he knew it was out of his hands now. His life was going to hell in a hand basket.

The door opened, Zena came out and walked right up to Felix, smiling sweetly. 'I had to do it, dear. Edwina told me confession is good for the soul. Bye-bye. Mustn't keep the taxi waiting.'

She had just left the room when the inspector came over to Felix. 'I want to see you. Now.' He was not smiling.

The phone rang in the station and since he was nearest, Greg picked it up.

'Greg? It's Edwina. I must talk to Felix urgently.'

'He's in with the inspector, Edwina.'

'Oh, God! Has Zena been in?'

'She just left. Shall I tell Felix to phone you?'

'No! You mustn't! Promise me not to mention it. I beg of you, Greg.'

'For God's sake, woman,' he said, laughing. 'I promise. I'd love to know what's going on around here.'

'Yes, well, I can't tell you. Bye, Greg.'

'Do you want to tell me about it?' asked Greg when Felix re-emerged.

'Not really. But perhaps I'd better. Anyway, I'm still a policeman. Thought I wasn't going to be. Got off with a bollocking.'

Over a beer and a sandwich, Felix told Greg about the incident in the supermarket car park. He explained why he had not reported the incident. He told the story in a highly coloured fashion, doing his best to give Leo Midnight a sinister motive for refusing to make a statement, but even to his own ears it sounded stupid. Greg, he could tell, was not impressed.

'Well,' said Greg at last, shaking his head. 'You run true to form. I keep telling you to do everything by the book. Cover your own backside. Nobody is worth losing your job for. I agree she's a nice old lady. I like her, but elderly drivers like Zena can endanger life. And nobody who gives in to road rage should be allowed behind the wheel of a car. My God, she could have injured one of them! She expected to be punished for what she did. Couldn't you tell that? It was like a cry for help. Yeah, that's it. A cry for help. She wanted to be stopped from driving.'

'I didn't see it that way. She's not within walking distance of anything. I thought—'

'I'd like to be a fly on the wall at Gorham House tonight.'

'Why?'

Greg looked at his friend in surprise. 'Didn't Edwina tell you? There's to be a cheese and wine party for Save Our Hedgerows.'

'Oh, I know all about it,' said Felix. He rubbed his chin, pinched the bridge of his nose, then closed his eyes for a moment. 'That's what started my other trouble. Me overhearing Harriet invite Edwina to that damned wine and cheese.'

CHAPTER NINE

Harriet opened the door of Edwina's car and slid onto the seat. 'Isn't this exciting! What are you wearing? I've just got on a navy suit with a red blouse. You're not dressed up, are you? I'll die if you are. I can't wait to see what Gorham House is like. And the evil Leo Midnight. Everybody is talking about him. Ooh, this is a lovely car. Mine's an old banger. Do you know the way?'

'Oh, yes. I've been past it a few times on my way to Zena Alway's place.'

Harriet laughed. 'Greg is furious that I'm going tonight. What about you? Did Felix try to stop you going?'

'I don't see Felix every day. There's no need—'

Harriet gasped with pleasure. 'You've had a quarrel! We guessed. Well, Felix was a bit peculiar with Greg. Tell Auntie Harriet all about it. Come on, Edwina. Confession is good for the soul.'

'I wonder sometimes.' She stole a glance at her friend. 'Have you heard anything about Zena Alway?'

'So that's it! Greg says Zena confessed all to

our dear inspector and when she came out of his office she walked up to Felix and told him in front of everybody that you had advised her to confess.'

'Oh, God! I didn't, I swear it. I didn't know what she was talking about when she asked me if I thought confession was good for the soul. I was thinking about myself and it didn't occur to me until a few minutes after she hung up what she planned to do.'

'Then you called the station and spoke to Greg.'

'I wanted to warn Felix. Greg didn't tell him I'd phoned, did he? Oh, Harriet, say he didn't.'

'He had to! Felix was livid and Greg felt that was unfair. He said you had obviously called to warn him that Zena was on her way. I mean he knows Zena is old and tends to put her own interpretation on things.'

Edwina took the corner of the Gorham Road too fast for comfort. 'You know, Harriet, there are four people in my relationship and that's two too many.'

'You've made a mess of things on your own. I don't see what further harm Greg and I can do. So now that there are four of us involved, why don't you tell me what the quarrel was about? I might be able to say something helpful. Confess, now.'

'There's nothing to confess. We just decided to cool it a little.'

'All right,' said Harriet, stiffly. 'I can take a hint. You're not going to talk about it. I mean, I saw the way you two couldn't leave each other alone the other night at the party. My God, he was all over you. Now you expect me to believe that the two of you have just decided to see less of each other.'

'It's none of your business, Harriet.'

'Right, it's none of my business. Turn here! You almost missed it.'

'No, I didn't. I know where I'm going.'

'I doubt it,' said Harriet. She opened the door as soon as the car drew to a halt on the large drive and walked to the front door without waiting for Edwina to lock up.

As the day approached for the wine and cheese party, Leo and Cassandra had experienced an unexpected but powerful sense of pride in their large home. Cassandra had ordered six huge arrangements of autumn flowers from the florist, the sort that fan out in all directions from tall wrought-iron stands. She had discussed these with Leo, but on impulse ordered six additional smaller arrangements for side tables in various rooms, and charged them all to Leo's credit card.

The glowing yellow and bronze chrysanthemums together with autumn foliage brightened the old house enormously and blended in with the colour scheme, since every room seemed to consist of dark brown, cream, washed-out red and faded sage green. All the huge table lamps had been fitted with hundred-watt bulbs to attack the gloom, and there was a log fire in the large fireplace to drive away forty years of damp and mouldy recesses. So fierce was the fire, Leo was afraid the heat would drive the punters out of the room. He had already told Cassandra that he would not be putting on more logs.

'We'll have to let it burn itself out. Besides, I've got better things to do.'

Cassandra wrinkled her nose. 'At least it's getting rid of the musty smell. What are we going to do this winter? There's no central heating in this bloody place.'

'I don't know. It would cost a fortune to have it put in. I wouldn't have it in all forty rooms.' He didn't say that he had no intention of living in Gorham House for many more weeks.

'Maybe it would be better to sell it, Leo. Let's move back to civilization.'

He looked down at her, taking in the low-cut clinging black dress. It had three-quarter sleeves which was not typical of Cassandra's style. She liked little straps across her smooth shoulders and the maximum amount of cleavage. It crossed his mind that she might have worn it to cover up needle marks on her arms, but he quickly put that thought away. He didn't want to know about any drug habits she might have and was happy to assume that she was not into anything.

'You're going to knock spots off every other woman tonight. I hope you know that.'

Her grateful smile lit up her face as she reached up to plant a kiss on his mouth. Without thinking, he pulled her to him and for several minutes lost himself in her generous kisses. He was aware that the Quayles, who had come in to help with the dishes and the serving, were nearby, but he didn't care who saw them.

Cassandra gasped, fighting for breath. 'Oh, Leo, you got to remember your manners. People will be coming any minute.' She stepped away and straightened her dress, then ran her fingers through her hair. 'I'll bet my lipstick's smeared. I'll just go upstairs a minute.' She headed towards the stairs, then turned to him. 'By the way, you look really smart. You see, I told you grey trousers and a navy blazer would be just right.'

He held out his arms and did a twirl. 'I feel like a prat, but if you say it's right, I'll not worry.'

So it was that he was alone in the hall when the Hebards and other members of the committee arrived. They bustled in with hampers of food, asking the way to the kitchen, exclaiming over the old Aga, the wooden draining boards, the rough cream-painted cupboards that looked as if they had been knocked up by an apprentice carpenter.

'I don't suppose this kitchen has changed in fifty years,' said Kitty. 'I do hope you won't modernize it too much, Leo.'

'You can count on me,' he said. 'I won't modernize it too much. We have, however, got a modern fridge, to which I hope you won't object. And the Aga is on in case you want to heat anything up. Thank God the weather has turned colder. That damned thing never goes off and sometimes we couldn't stand to be in the kitchen, if it was a warm day. I've hired some glasses and some cups and saucers. But I see you've brought some as well.'

'Oh, that's wonderful. We'll use yours. Perhaps Queenie will wash up for us afterwards.'

'We have planned to put out the food in the dining room,' said Eric. 'Do you want to show me the way?'

'The dining room?' said Leo blankly. 'You

want to go into the dining room? I guess I didn't think. It hasn't been aired, you know, and I don't know when anyone last ate in there. We eat in the kitchen. Look, the hall's big enough to house a small army. Maybe we could have the food set out there.'

'I'll tell you what,' said Kitty kindly. 'We'll go and look at the dining room and see what would be best.' Leo knew she was determined to see as much of the house as possible.

He led the way, switching on the dim wall lights over the sideboard. The entire committee of three couples crowded through the door to stare at the dining table which could easily seat sixteen people. It was not Leo's idea of a beautiful table, being made of very old planks polished to a hard finish.

'It's magnificent!' breathed Kitty. 'That table must be three hundred years old. And worth a fortune. I hope you have it insured.'

'Surely the chairs aren't valuable. They're falling to bits.'

'Oh, don't—'

'I know,' said Leo, cynically. 'Don't have the room modernized too much. I hope you don't feel the same way about the plumbing. That hasn't been touched for forty or fifty years either.'

Kitty smiled at Leo. 'You know, people want to see your home. That's why we've had no trouble selling tickets. It is a real treat to be in a house that hasn't changed for so long. The dining room does smell musty, but believe me, no-one will mind that. Do let's put the pâtés and cheeses in here.' Leo shrugged. 'If you light a fire in here it will soon be bearably warm. And how about bringing in one of those nice arrangements for the middle of the table? I saw one that's made up entirely of yellow and gold flowers. That would be perfect.'

'I'm a dab hand at fires,' added Eric. 'Show me some logs and a bit of kindling and I'll get going.'

At six o'clock the first guests arrived, two women in their eighties who looked as if they were afraid he might eat them. They introduced themselves as Claris Binns and Prunella Jenkins.

'I've brought something for the raffle,' said Mrs Jenkins. From her large black handbag she produced a small box of bath cubes. Leo looked at them in surprise. The box looked a little dusty, a little crushed at the corners. He thought she must have had it since the end of World War II. Kitty rushed up and took the bath cubes from her with exclamations of pleasure and gratitude, leading Prunella over to the table where the other raffle prizes were displayed.

Claris Binns leaned confidentially towards Leo. 'I couldn't stop her from bringing them, poor dear. I remember when she won them at a fund-raiser in St Bartholomew's. Her husband was the vicar. It was at least ten years ago. I see they've got a big bottle of champagne as a prize.'

'Yes, that's from me. I had to make some contribution. They aren't going to need the bath cubes, so perhaps your friend could take them home. There are a dozen prizes already and I'm told others will be bringing things for the raffle.'

'We couldn't hurt Prunella's feelings that way. Kitty will say all that is appropriate, I'm sure. Such a lovely woman. You've made a contribution all right, Mr Midnight. Save Our Hedgerows is going to do very well tonight. Half of Homestead and all of Gorham will be here, just to get a look at this old place. Your predecessor was a recluse, you know.'

'That's what I would like to be,' he said. Claris Binns laughed politely, thinking he had made a joke.

His neighbours, the Brooms, were members of the committee and had come with the Hebards. They were friendly, but, like everyone else, old. Leo decided that Cassandra would easily be the youngest person present on this night. Also the most beautiful. Also the best dressed.

She had joined him by the time two attractive young women stepped through the open doorway to introduce themselves.

The dark one with dimples walked up to Leo and held out her hand, ignoring Cassandra. 'Hello, Mr Midnight. I'm Harriet Squiller and this is—'

'You're not Squeegee's wife, are you? Detective Sergeant Squiller?' He looked over her shoulder. 'Is he parking the car?'

'He's not coming. He doesn't like you. How do you do, Mrs Midnight.' She kept her eyes on Leo as she shook hands with Cassandra.

Leo laughed. 'So you brought a friend.' He looked at Mrs Squiller's companion, who wore a pale green suit that fitted her a little more loosely than Cassandra chose to wear her suits. She was a pretty mid-blonde for whom a little peroxide would do wonders. She had a pleasant face and beautiful skin, despite the fact that she was for some reason suffering an attack of nerves. He put

276

her down as the athletic type and immediately lost interest in her.

'I'm Edwina Fairfax, Mr Midnight.' No smile from this young woman and the name sounded familiar.

'My God, the demon of Bishop council! The lady who sends me nasty letters about my trees.'

'The lady who receives yours.'

'Well, well, you're just a cheeky kid,' said Leo, looking her over rudely. 'You're welcome here tonight. But don't you come onto my property in daylight. You won't be welcome then.'

'You will have to give in one day, you know. I've got the law on my side.'

'I'll fight you to the bitter end. I don't like busybodies. Bureaucracy grinds so slowly, I probably won't be here by the time you get legal permission to invade my land.'

'Oh, Edwina, I've heard about you,' said Cassandra. 'You're Felix Trent's girlfriend, aren't you?'

'Yes, I am, but—'

'You're just his type.' There was a snorting sound from Leo and Cassandra made a little moue. 'But she is, Leo. Felix likes the outdoors type. Oh, do come and look over our house. You don't mind, do you, Mrs Squeegee? Leo will introduce you round. He likes you.'

Leo laughed, but Harriet looked very unhappy. 'Come on,' he said. 'What's your first name again?'

'Harriet, but—'

'Let them go. When Cassandra gets a bee in her bonnet there's no stopping her. Kitty, this is Harriet Squiller, wife of Detective Sergeant

Squiller. I'll bet she doesn't know anyone here. Wrong generation. Will you show her round?' Without waiting for an answer, Leo turned away and resumed his duties at the door.

Kitty was carrying a tray of assorted cheeses in each hand and looked very harassed. 'Here,' said Harriet, kindly. 'I'll take one of those trays. I know a few people here, so you don't really need to introduce me round. The Midnights are weird, aren't they? Cassandra Midnight just whisked my friend off to show her round the house and I wasn't invited.'

'How galling. However, I'm too grateful for the opportunity to come here to dare to comment on their personalities.' She smiled at Harriet. 'But I have been thinking my thoughts! We're putting the food in the dining room. Wait till you see it. It's fascinating. You know, I believe I've seen you at the newsagents in the village. You have two young children, haven't you?'

'Yes, they get me down sometimes but they are delicious. Oh, it smells in here!'

'I know. Just put the tray in the middle of the table. Ordinarily I wouldn't put food in a musty room, because it spoils the appetite. Yet most people bought tickets just because they want to see the house, so we must get them into as many rooms as the Midnights will allow. Come on, I'll give you a little guided tour. Wait till you see the kitchen. It's a hoot.'

'Come upstairs to my room,' said Cassandra, urging Edwina up the stairs. 'Isn't the hall gloomy? I mean, Lincrusta painted brown. I'd never heard of Lincrusta, have you?'

'No,' said Edwina. 'What is it, a sort of embossed lining paper that you paint over?'

'That's what Leo says. Personally, I prefer the back staircase. It's painted cream, so you can see your way, but the stairs are steeper. I've never been in a house that had more than one set of stairs, have you? And the paintings are all so dark, sometimes it's impossible to make them out. Take a peek at the bathroom.'

Cassandra pulled the cotton cord and a single bare bulb lit up a large, chilly room tiled in black and white. The medicine cabinet had a broken mirror, the pedestal washbasin was cracked and heavily stained by generations of hard water. The bathtub, which stood on ball feet, was enormous with high sides.

'I think I prefer the bathroom in my little bungalow. It's very cosy. I presume you'll have this all taken out and replaced with something modern.'

'Leo won't even talk about having central heating put in! I want to go back to London. We're townies. We don't belong here. I hate crowds of people I don't know, don't you? We'll have to go down sometime, of course, but first we can have a nice little chat in my bedroom. I was mad about Felix when I was a teenager, but I guess he'll be happier with you.'

'How old was Felix?'

'I was sixteen and he was eighteen. I was his first girl. Did he tell you that?'

'For a long time he didn't even tell me he knew you. I guess he thought I'd be jealous because you're so beautiful. I heard it from Harriet. After that, he did tell me about it.' Edwina paused. 'In fact, he told me all the details.'

'Oh, Lord.' Cassandra opened the door to her bedroom. 'Well, I guess I can understand that. Still, I would hate him to say anything really bad about me. I was naughty, but I was only a kid. My mum abandoned me outside Boots the chemists when I was three weeks old. I could have died, but a bobby on the beat found me. I would have been glad to be adopted, but it was difficult then. Anyway, I spent the first sixteen years of my life in foster homes. Twelve different ones. Nobody liked me and they weren't prepared to give me a chance.'

'Oh, you poor dear. Still, you've done very well for yourself. I hope you will be happy ever after. Did you meet your husband shortly afterwards?'

'No, I met Leo ages later. A few years ago, I met the most wonderful man. Carl and I were just made for each other. His family hated me, but we didn't care. He liked to go scuba diving. We went out one day, he went overboard while I stayed on deck and I never saw him again. His body was washed up two weeks later.'

'My God, how awful!'

Cassandra squeezed her hand. 'When I met Felix I was in my last foster home. I was going to have to make my own way and I thought Felix and I would set up home together. It would have been so nice. Then he said he wanted to break up! Wanted to be a policeman, of all things. It was terrible. Can you understand that? It was like being left outside Boots all over again. So I got even. Felix has never forgiven me. He's hard. Have you noticed that about him?'

'Yes, I have as a matter of fact.'

'After Carl died I had some bad times, believe me. So don't judge me too harshly and promise me you won't talk about me to Felix.'

'I do promise you. It's all in the past.' Edwina smiled at the beautiful Cassandra. She felt sorry for this terribly thin little thing with her huge eyes and a way of walking that spoke of exhaustion.

'Look at this door,' said Cassandra, pointing to splintered mahogany around the lock. 'You can tell it's been knocked around a bit. By Leo, actually. He does have the most terrifying temper. It's chilly up here. I don't know what it's going to be like in the winter.'

'You could get some oil-filled electric heaters. They're very efficient. This is a pretty room. Did you have it painted?'

'I made Leo do it. And the bed is new, of course. I like pale green and lemon yellow. It brings the summer indoors. Isn't the house enormous? God knows why we're here. I didn't even have a say in where we came to live. One day he just said he'd got a house and to start packing. I mean, it's fun living in such a big old place and everybody wants to know us because we live in Gorham House, but I still want to move back to London. I'll be safer there, I think.'

'Safer?'

Cassandra sat down on the quilted satin bedspread and hugged herself. 'There's things I've got to say to you. Because of Felix. Because we've both loved him at one time or another. Sit down. I knew I'd like you straight away.'

'I don't want to intrude,' began Edwina,

thinking of Harriet who was probably fuming downstairs. 'I mean, shouldn't we join the other guests?'

'They won't miss us. I know I lied about Felix hitting me, but I'm not lying now when I tell you that Leo hits me often. Never anywhere you can see. No bruises to make people think bad of him, but sometimes . . .' She began to cry, reached over to the bedside table and took a tissue from the box. 'You mustn't tell Felix. Promise me! There's nothing the Bill can do about it. I try to be real nice to Leo so he won't hit me, but he drinks, you know.'

'Look, Cassandra,' said Edwina, who had no trouble believing the worst of Leo Midnight. 'You must leave him.'

'How can I? I've got no money. He just doles it out a little at a time.'

Edwina opened her small bag, certain that she had put her chequebook inside. 'I'll tell you what, I've not got much money, because my job doesn't pay very well. But I can spare two hundred pounds.'

'Oh, Edwina!' Cassandra caught her up in a fierce hug, and the tears began to flow again as Edwina found her pen. 'I've got friends in London,' Cassandra assured her. 'I could go to them as soon as I get the chance.' She leapt from the bed. 'You're the best friend I've ever had.'

She almost skipped across the huge room to rummage in a drawer of her dressing table. 'I want you to have this scarf. It's just right for your colouring. And it'll go with that suit. You could tuck it into the neckline.' She held out an exquisite scarf of deep red devoré velvet.

'Oh, I couldn't, Cassandra. I couldn't take it.'

'It's a good one. Cost me a hundred and fifty quid.' Edwina gasped and, Cassandra, seeing her mistake, added, 'Leo bought it. I picked it out and he paid with his credit card. Please take it. Tuck it into your handbag and think of me when you wear it. Now, I think we'd better go downstairs.' She took the cheque from Edwina, waved it in the air to make sure the ink was dry, then hid it in her underwear drawer.

Claris and Prunella held their glasses of white wine close to their mouths and took frequent sips, attempting to look animated and at ease as they sat by the fire in the drawing room. Other guests had moved away because the fire was too hot, but the two elderly women found the fierce heat comforting. They looked around the room, commenting on the dingy paintings, the bronze table lamps with their cracking parchment shades, the oriental *objets*. The hum of other voices reached them from a distance of twenty feet and neither could make out what was being said, but Claris came to her own conclusions about the guests.

'Everybody looks so elegant, don't you think?'

Prunella put her hand to her bad ear until the hearing aid squealed. 'People elegant?' she asked. She smoothed her tweed skirt and buttoned up the green cable-stitched cardigan. 'Yes, they all look very prosperous and smart, but not that Cassandra Midnight.' She wrinkled her nose. 'I thought that black dress was a bit tarty, didn't you?'

'I agree,' said Claris, mouthing the words. It

was the simplest way to communicate with Prunella. Her own brown wool suit had seen better days, but only she knew that the gap between button and buttonhole on her skirt band was bridged by a large safety pin. 'Kitty Hebard always looks so smart. She knows just what to wear and just how much flesh to expose. That two-piece is silk, you know. I saw it in the window of the Larger than Life shop. The label said two hundred and fifty pounds.'

Prunella gasped. 'No outfit is worth that much money. I mean, I wouldn't pay that much, even if I could afford it. There are more important things in life.'

'You know,' mused Claris. 'I came here nearly fifty years ago when Mr Cartwright's mother died. He had been in love with Edith Fortesque. Hetty's grandmother.'

'I never knew that!' Prunella moved a little closer to her friend.

'You must remember that you had married and moved away. A lot happened in the forty years you were moving around.'

'Forty-five,' said Prunella. 'We left when I was eighteen. But I've been back for nearly twenty years. No-one mentioned it to me. And Mr Cartwright was still alive then. In fact, I saw him in Colchester one day. I used to think he was the handsomest man, but I was only sixteen . . . Hetty's not looking well these days. I'll bet she's glad her grannie didn't marry Mr Cartwright. Edith was much better off with her solicitor.'

'Oh, I don't know. She might have inherited this place.' They gossiped for a few minutes more, remembering the long-dead and speculating about those they scarcely knew. Finally Claris struggled to get up from the low chair. 'Everybody's going in to get something to eat, I think. Come on, Prunella. I want to get there before it's all gone.'

'This is without doubt the stupidest cooker I have ever seen,' said Leo when Kitty bustled into the kitchen. 'It's hot all the time, day and night, a terrible waste of gas. The ovens are amazingly deep and you can't control the heat.'

'You may welcome the constant heat of the Aga this winter. What have you got there? Oh, Leo, you are so generous.'

He stood up from the hot oven with a baking tray of small cocktail sausages in his gloved hands. 'I don't know why you say that. We've only donated some French bread, a magnum of champagne and some cocktail sausages. I'm sure others have given more. The Brooms, for instance.'

'Well, yes, they did buy the wine. Very generous of them. But what about all your flower arrangements? The florist must have been here all day.'

'No, she finished at noon.'

'Well, I'm sure there was no change from six hundred pounds, but the flowers just bring the house to life!'

Leo had his back to Kitty, taking out another tray of sausages from the depths of the Aga. This gave him a couple of seconds to take in her words. Six hundred pounds? He hadn't thought to ask Cassandra how much the flowers would cost. And it had never occurred to him to set a limit. Where the hell was he going to get six hundred pounds for flowers? Cassandra was a serious drain on his limited resources, always spending where he least expected. Turning, he vowed to get the business finished as quickly as possible. They must leave Gorham House while he still had a few pennies left.

'Look, Kitty, I can imagine what the scrum is like in the dining room. Why don't you go ahead with those two baskets of bread. I'll put cocktail sticks in these little buggers and put them on a platter, if I can find one. Cassandra's disappeared with Miss Bossyboots from the council, but I can manage here.'

'Well, if you're sure. I'll be back shortly.' She left the kitchen and Leo found three decent white earthenware dishes and transferred the sausages to them, then began to stab each one with a toothpick.

The noise out in the hall was overpowering. A hundred people had paid a tenner for the privilege of seeing Gorham House, too many for comfort, so he was glad of a few moments on his own in the kitchen. It was not to last, however. He heard footsteps, but didn't turn around as Edwina walked up to the scrubbed wooden table and bent towards him, searching his face. Her own face was red and she crossed her arms in the way people did when they wanted to accuse you of stealing their sunbeds.

'Well?' she said.

'Well?' he replied. He could see she was itching for a fight and he was equally determined that she would damned well not look at his trees.

'I knew you were lower than a snake, but it never occurred to me you would sink to beating your wife!'

He was so taken by surprise that his eyes filled with tears as he blurted out, 'It was in my sleep! I'd had a nightmare! Anyway, she kicked me out. Divorced me, so—' At that point, he realized from her startled expression that she knew nothing at all about Janie. 'Oh, you've been listening to Cassandra's fairy tales. I've never hit her in my life. Also, we're not married.'

'She said—'

'Cassandra will say almost anything. Hasn't PC Plod told you that? A few years ago I had a sort of nervous breakdown. Locked away for three months. My wife took an unsympathetic view of things and her dear mama urged her to leave me. I swear to you that I'm all right now. Cassandra is safe, except from her own vivid imagination.'

'I—'

'I suppose you'll tell this all over Gorham and Homestead.'

'No, I—'

'Here,' he said, thrusting a bowl of sausages at her. 'Take those bloody things into the dining room. I'd like a minute or two to pull myself together. You gave me quite a turn. And while we're at it, I'll cut off any branches of my trees I feel like cutting. Understand? They need trimming. They're mine and I'll do as I please.'

A dozen replies came to mind, but his anger and his brusque dismissal of what she had taken to be the gospel truth undermined her. Meekly, she took the sausages. She had to say something, but while she could now see how the deceptively delicate Cassandra had lied to her, she was not at all sure that she could believe everything Leo said. He looked unstable. Cassandra had said she was afraid of him. By challenging Leo, Edwina was convinced she had made life harder for Cassandra. 'I'm sorry. That is, I didn't mean to pry. Honestly.' She sighed, being careful not to meet his eyes. 'I'll just put these in the dining room.'

'Well?' Harriet clutched her arm as Edwina left the dining room. 'What is the house like?'

'Old. Decrepit and not very interesting. I wouldn't take it if you gave it to me, not unless I had the money to fix it up. Harriet, I've got to talk to you. The most terrible thing has happened. Oh, God! We'd better leave.'

'Don't you want to wait for the raffle?'

'No, I didn't buy any tickets, and I've had my one drink. I can't drive if I've had two. It goes right to my head. Also, I can't stay here and talk to people. I just need—'

'Excuse me,' said a tall man in his forties. He was wearing a pinstriped suit and gleaming black slip-on shoes. 'We haven't met. My name is John Hurst. You visited my home to see our avenue of cherry trees.'

'Oh, yes. I remember. How are they getting along?'

The tall man looked at her sternly. 'They have all died, thank you.'

'Oh, God.' She knew she should not have suggested putting the trees to further stress in the heat and drought of August. They had survived five years in their restricted quarters and would have lasted a few months longer. She should have told the Hursts to water them regularly and wait until the trees were dormant in the autumn before replanting.

'I – I'm sorry,' said Edwina miserably.

The tall man nodded slightly, then walked off.

'He seemed terribly rude. Is that what your job calls for?' asked Harriet. 'You are certainly not in the mood for a party. You're right, we'd better go. No need to say goodbye to anyone. Besides, I'm still starving. Let's go to a pub and have a bite to eat.'

'Not the Prince of Wales!'

'No. You're not up to facing Felix, are you?'

'I should not have replanted one of Mrs Hurst's trees. I was showing off. I should simply have pointed out that they had all been planted in their containers. The council is willing to offer general advice. It's better than just looking in Yellow Pages and happening to get a cowboy, but we're not supposed to get so involved. The weather had been hot and dry and I knew in my heart it was too early to replant! Let's get out of here before something else happens.'

Five minutes later they were seated in a quiet corner at the Pig and Whistle and Edwina settled down to tell her friend about Cassandra. 'She's really a pathetic little thing. She's hollow-eyed and doesn't look at all well. She told me that Leo hits her and she's terribly afraid of him. She even showed me where he broke the lock on the bedroom door to get at her. She wants to leave him, but until she can she feels she's got to keep on his good side. I suppose that's why she's so friendly towards him in company. I did what I could for her, gave a few pounds, but—'

'There's more to this story, isn't there?' asked Harriet. 'What have you done?'

Edwina sipped her orange juice, making no reply.

Harriet glared. 'You went downstairs and bearded the lion in his den, didn't you? I saw you coming out of the kitchen.' Edwina bowed her head. 'My God, woman. You really are a busy-body. He could have killed you. Greg always says you have to be careful about cases of domestic violence. There's a lot of sexual politics mixed up with it. You can't jump to conclusions. What did you say to him?'

'I walked right up to him. He was in the kitchen fixing some little sausages, and I accused him face to face of beating his wife.' Harriet gasped. 'If you're surprised that I said it, you should have seen *his* face! He was gobsmacked. And then his eyes filled with tears. I swear to you they did. He said it was only once and he was having a nightmare and anyway his wife had divorced him. Then he realized I was talking about Cassandra and he pulled himself together. They're not married. He said she has a vivid imagination and he had never hurt her. I didn't know what to say or do, so I took a dish of sausages into the dining room.'

'Felix is not going to be pleased,' said Harriet quietly. 'Neither is Greg. You shouldn't have got involved. That's all that happened? Nothing else?'

Edwina shook her head, avoiding her friend's steady gaze. Leo's remarks about continuing to cut down his trees would not interest Harriet. She knew she could never tell John Blue that she had trespassed on the Midnight property, not only because it would be an embarrassment for the section, but because the wicked Mr Midnight would do his best to make trouble for the entire council if he found out about it. It had seemed such a clever idea at the time, but it was not too much of an exaggeration to say that her sly action had ruined her life.

The food was served and the two women were silent while taking the edge off their appetites.

Greg and Felix sat back in their chairs at the station and looked at one another. 'I'll bet the girls are having a high old time at the wine and cheese thing,' said Greg at last. 'What do you want to do this evening? They won't be back until after eight, and they will probably have stuffed themselves.'

'On cheese? I doubt if there will be enough for two energetic hungry women to eat. Listen, Greg. I've been so busy all week, I haven't had time to follow up my lead. The one I told you about. Gorham House statues. I know they're back where they belong, but I'd just like to check this one out. Let's go over to Bishop and scare the pants off Duggie Duncuff.'

'An armed robbery, a suicide, a pair of very destructive drunken twelve-year-olds and a dozen accidents. Haven't you had enough? However, it's a good idea. Catch him at an off moment. Of course he might be at the pub. Wouldn't want to tackle him in front of others. Got to get him on his own.'

Felix looked at his watch. He was tired. During the week he had also freed a lorry driver whose vehicle had been hijacked. The poor man had been left tied up on the verge of a little-used lane in Gorham and was very agitated after two hours. It was a happy chance that Felix had happened to drive down the lane. Nothing he had done during the week would make an interesting event on a good cop show, but it had all kept him busy.

Later in the week, he had fetched two twelve-year-old girls from the pub after they were too drunk to stand. The landlord was now in trouble and these two cases alone had involved a lot of paperwork. Then there had been the robbery three blocks from his home. He had realized that the car parked in the driveway of the Hemmings' home was not their car. The lights were out in the bungalow, but a little investigation had shown him a torch being used behind the closed curtains. It had been eleven o'clock when he spotted the thief and two in the morning before he finally fell into bed.

But he still had an appetite for more. 'Yes, let's sweat him a little. It's a quarter past six. He won't have gone out drinking yet, surely, or he might even be back from the pub. Do you have to babysit tonight?'

'No, Harriet's mum is doing the honours. Let's go.'

At half past six they knocked on the door of Duggie's house and congratulated themselves on finding him at home, apparently alone. He stood in his bare feet, old jeans following the line of his belly, his many tattoos exposed by his singlet. Greg flashed his warrant card. Felix was in uniform. The two men seemed to come as a horrible shock to Duggie, yet he stepped back from the door meekly enough, so that Felix and Greg could enter, before leading the way down the narrow corridor to the small, messy kitchen.

'I've been expecting you. Like, I knew this would happen. It's been a nightmare. I mean I haven't been able to sleep. I want to get this over. I mean, come the end of September, you're going to find out anyway.'

Felix and Greg hid their surprise and said nothing, aware that their luck was in this day. Keeping very still, they waited silently. Duggie, they guessed, was going to confess to a crime they didn't know had been committed.

'Start at the beginning, Duggie,' said Greg sweetly when the young man appeared to be so distressed that he couldn't go on. 'But first, why don't we all have a nice cup of tea and sit down in the lounge.'

Duggie looked grateful for this small act of kindness and hurried to put the kettle on. 'I know I'm in trouble, but it must count with your lot if I co-operate.'

'And give us names,' said Greg.

'Yeah. Well, they'd do the same to me if they had the chance. I've never been to prison. Just a few minor convictions, you know. This was the biggest thing . . . and it wasn't my fault . . . you know, not my idea at all. Well, later what we did. That was my idea, but we didn't mean . . . aw, hell. It was Tommy the Turk. We met him in the pub in Bishop. Me mate and me. Mel. After it all happened, I've not seen Tommy in the pub. As for Mel, he's got relatives in Wales. Tommy is sometimes a window cleaner and he was taken on by the owner of Gorham House to do the windows inside and out. He said there wasn't much worth having indoors, not that could be lifted easily. Not anything worth breaking in for, but there was these statues in the grounds and he happened to hear the owners was going away for a few days. Tommy wanted us to steal a lorry with a grabber the next day.'

Duggie's story so far was somewhat confusing. Greg and Felix could guess that someone had ordered the Gorham House statues to be stolen. They knew that the house must have been looked over by someone with criminal intent and a window cleaner who was not known to Leo was a likely candidate. They were surprised that Leo had allowed the man indoors, but kept that thought to themselves. Duggie had started to talk and it seemed he could not shut up or slow down.

They contained their excitement as the young villain got to the part of the story where they all drove down to Canvey Island. Felix was taking notes, but Greg never took his eyes off Duggie.

'And then,' said Duggie, 'the Fat Man told us to get rid of the grab lorry. I thought it would be a good idea if . . . It was all my fault, not Mel's. I want to be fair about that. We went to this house where I had helped put some urns and things in the garden. The family's away all of September and they don't let the post office deliver the mail or have the regular gardener in or anything. Frankly, it pisses him off that they don't trust him. Well, now they will know they should let him hang around when they're away.'

'Where did you go and what did you do there?' asked Greg, quietly.

'We drove back to the walled garden and let out the grabber so we could remove the statue in the middle. But I forgot to put down the legs and the bloody lorry fell over on its side! It's still there. When the family come back, they'll find it.'

Felix realized he had been holding his breath. He let it out slowly, stealing a glance at Greg. 'I think you'd better show us where this house is, Duggie.'

'Yeah,' he said morosely, then looked up brightly. 'I am co-operating. You can see that, can't you?'

Eric Hebard rang a hand bell that he had brought along for the purpose and in the slight lessening of noise that this caused, attempted to tell one hundred chattering guests that the raffle was about to be drawn.

'And we have some lovely prizes. Twenty-five in all. So get out your tickets. I just want everyone to know that we have sold two hundred pounds' worth of raffle tickets and since all the food and wine has been donated, we've made a thousand pounds on the tickets as well!'

There was a loud cheer as Cassandra was invited to draw the tickets. The magnum of champagne went first, followed by seven bottles of wine.

'How many raffle tickets did you buy?' Claris asked her friend.

'Two. They were fifty pence apiece! I couldn't afford any more. Ten pounds for one ticket to a wine and cheese party was outrageous. The tickets should have been five pounds and raffle tickets ten pence each.' Prunella held her two tickets tightly in her fist, cocking her head and listening carefully. When there was a slight lull, she turned to Claris. 'How many did you buy?'

'Ten. I felt I had to—'

'But you've spent so much! I'm not made of money—'

Claris patted her hand. 'I know, dear.'

Prunella's face registered pain each time a number and colour were called that was different from pink, three-oh-nine and blue, five-two-six. Claris knew she desperately wanted to win something. Any little prize would make Prunella feel that she had enjoyed a wonderful evening. But it was not to be.

'And there is just one prize left,' called Eric. Interest in the raffle had waned and people had started to talk among themselves. 'Pink number two-oh-seven!' Eric shouted, and Claris looked at her tickets in amazement.

'It's me!' She glanced at her friend whose eyes now held tears. 'I'll give you the prize,' she hissed and began to push her way to the prize table. There, in lonely state, were Prunella's bath cubes. She picked them up, turned to the crowd and waved them triumphantly. There was an ironic cheer.

'Congratulations,' said Prunella when Claris returned to her side.

'Oh, well. Why don't I give them back to you so that you can donate them to another charity raffle? Those cubes have helped raise a lot of money for good causes.'

Prunella snatched them and thrust them angrily into her handbag. 'I'd like to go home now.'

'The taxi won't be here for another ten minutes. Why don't we see if there are any more of those little sausages left? But wait, Mr Midnight is going to say something.'

Leo had taken advantage of the raffle draw to pull himself together. He had his temper under control, but Edwina's sudden attack had brought back a host of bitter memories. As usual, he wanted to lash out, to hurt someone else, as he had done ever since he could remember.

'Ladies and gentlemen, I am new among you and had never heard of Save Our Hedgerows. So I made a few enquiries. Now, it's obvious you raise a lot of money, but the general feeling in the neighbourhood is that this charity was set up just as a fighting fund against the Hebards' neighbour, farmer Wilkinson. I need hardly remind you that this sort of thing is against the requirements of the Charity Commission. What has the poor man done, other than to take out a few yards of old hedging? He was prosecuted and paid his fine. He should be left in peace. Money raised by a registered charity shouldn't be used to fight the neighbours, even if—'

'That's not true!' cried Kitty. 'We're going to do good work!'

'That was a despicable thing to say!' said Eric fiercely, but Leo just looked at him calmly.

'Are you accusing the charity of a criminal activity?' asked a slightly hysterical woman. Leo shrugged. It was more effective not to answer. From the corner of his eye he could see Kitty Hebard's stricken face.

A murmur of embarrassment among the assembled crowd rose to a swell. 'This is hardly the time!' shouted a male voice at the back. 'And certainly not the place!'

Following his lead, others chided Leo for his remarks, but it was too late. For the Hebards the evening had been spoiled. Kitty was in tears. Eric's face was so red he looked as if he might be about to explode.

Leo shrugged. 'Just thought I'd mention it.'

'Oh, Claris!' said Prunella. 'I'm so glad we didn't miss this. It's about time Kitty Hebard got her comeuppance. Our taxi will be here by now. Let's get him to take us up to Zena's!'

It was nine o'clock before Greg and Felix were free to visit Gorham House. They had been staggered to see the old lorry lying on its side in the garden of The Hoo. By the light of their torches they saw a pile of old bricks that had once been a mellow wall, and flashing their beams on the statue of a naked woman, could see the straps still round her ample hips. Duggie had talked non-stop for half an hour, but he was silent now.

They took him to the station where he was invited to make a formal statement, then contacted the gardener who worked at The Hoo. He seemed to be both angry that the beautiful garden had been damaged and pleased that the owners had got their just desserts.

'They should have trusted me,' he said triumphantly. 'This is going to cost their insurance company a pretty penny – if they're even insured for garden ornaments.'

The gardener didn't think there was a keyholder and he had no idea if any members of the family lived nearby. News of this disaster would just have to wait until Mr and Mrs Smithers returned home on September the thirtieth.

Nevertheless, there was a lot of paperwork, and Mel and Tommy the Turk, as well as the Fat Man, had to be interviewed if and when they could be found. That was work for others, however. Greg and Felix had been working for thirteen hours and were due for a rest.

Visiting Leo Midnight would be, they both felt, therapeutic. They wanted to see his face when they told him about their coup.

They walked through the still-open front door, nodding a greeting to the Hebards. Kitty was crying and jumped when she saw them.

'Did he send for you? Has he accused me of a criminal offence?' she asked. 'Could he sink so low? I haven't done anything wrong. Not really. Or if I have, I didn't realize it.'

'Nobody called us, Kitty,' said Felix. 'We came to tell Mr Midnight about the men who stole his statues. Do you know where he is?'

'No, and we don't care,' said Eric. He and Kitty went out the front door, laden with cardboard boxes. The Brooms, following on behind, shook their heads sadly at the policemen.

They found Leo in the kitchen smoking a cigarette and drinking a glass of wine. 'We've got the names of all of them,' said Greg without preamble. 'Duggie, Mel and Tommy. Even the Fat Man.'

Leo stood up. It was clear he was not in the best of moods. 'Can't wait to nick the working classes, can you? None of your nice, friendly locals. They can do what they like. Bash up cars . . . My God, Felix, I'd love to see how you'd treat an old dearie from the East End if she gave in to a fit of road rage.'

'That was wrong,' said Greg quickly, 'and Felix has been reprimanded for it. I understand Zena Alway's house is up for sale, and she has already sold her car. She'll soon be out of your hair. And, of course, you'll be out of hers.'

Leo shrugged, reached for two more glasses and indicated that the men should help themselves. They declined.

'You think you were clever, getting your statues back,' said Felix, trying to keep calm, which was difficult in the face of Leo's open contempt. 'But these men were busy that day. They went to another property and tried to steal a large statue. Did quite a lot of damage.' There was no need to tell Leo about the lorry falling over. Felix and Greg had been hard pressed not to laugh when they heard about it, and Felix certainly didn't want to give Leo anything to laugh about now.

'You know,' continued Felix, shrugging off Greg's gentle touch on his shoulder. 'It's OK to be happy. Just because you aren't, doesn't mean others can't be. It's all right to have been born to parents with a bit of money, to have had a happy childhood. It's not a crime. And these people are entitled to protection under the law. You'd like us to leave them to fend for themselves. But we try to look after people who live in isolated areas. They're very exposed and they're frightened.'

Leo stood up and faced the men across the scrubbed surface of the table. 'What I think,' he said quietly, 'is that you're not dry behind the ears, Felix. The force won't let a lad of your age stay in Gorham. One day you're going to be transferred. Then you'll find out what policing is all about. How will you cope when the people you are supposed to be helping hate your guts, but are scared of their neighbours every day and night? They would rather beat each other half to death than call for help. You will have to protect their kids from their drunken rages, until the kids are old enough and mean enough to give you something else to worry about. And the law-abiding ones would fall over in a dead faint if you dropped in for tea. But you won't have time for that. You'll be too busy trying to keep the lid on the violence. And just like the toffs around here, when they're pissed off they'll remind you who pays your wages.'

Felix started to speak, but Leo hadn't finished.

'It's nice here. Everybody loves you and you love everybody. What a cosy situation. But will you love police work where nobody loves you? That's the test.'

For several seconds no-one moved or spoke. Then Felix nodded. 'I guess you're right. We know you are a brave man, but we get the feeling that you hate the force more than anybody out there. Why do you try to undermine us?'

Leo gave a world-weary shrug. 'Would you believe me if I told you that I just want a quiet life? The Lord only knows what I was doing having tonight's party here. It seems I just can't learn to keep my mouth shut among all these middle-class shits with their charities and their do-gooding. I'm looking for peace. Inside of me and outside of me. And nobody's going to let me have it.'

Cassandra had been in her room for several hours when Leo finally dragged himself up the stairs. He had drunk two bottles of wine, but it hadn't helped at all. He still felt like shit. He stood under the shower for five minutes, put on a clean pair of underpants and flopped wearily into bed. He was asleep in seconds.

He woke in a panic and looked at his watch. He'd been asleep for forty-five minutes, that was all. Forty-five minutes of sleep during which he had relived that first time when he met the old man. The dream was Felix's fault, saying what he did about it being all right to have been born into a family with a bit of money, to have had a happy childhood. Leo had not thought about that day for a long time. The old man had found him at King's Cross, cold, wet, hungry and in mortal danger. The odds were against his reaching twenty in one piece, and he had been scared.

The old man had talked to Leo quietly and persuaded the boy to come home with him for a meal and a change of clothing. That was when Leo had discovered that there was another world, parallel to his own, but so different.

The old man had introduced his wife, a smiling motherly woman who was probably every bit as old as his own mother. Yet she looked years younger. Her eyes told you nothing about terrible things she might have witnessed. And it occurred to him that she had not seen terrible things, that she had lived for forty or more years happily unaware of the misery that dwelt just a few miles away. And then there was their little boy, five years old, flaxen-haired and happy. Trusting. Ready to give his love to this older boy who was a complete stranger.

Within hours it had been decided that Leo would stay with them. The kid hung around him or ran his errands, offering unconditional love. These people he soon chose to call Mum and Dad gave sanctuary and encouragement. They taught him to believe in himself, how to reach his potential. Yet he never felt like one of them, never felt a true part of the family. He couldn't swallow his bitterness about the bad years, his grief for his little murdered sister. The old man understood. And even his understanding annoyed the young Leo. Why did some people have it so sweet while others, like Cassandra and himself, were born damned?

'Why can't I stop thinking about it? What am I going to do?' he moaned aloud. And suddenly, irrelevantly, he knew what he was going to do. He was going to go into Cassandra's room.

He got out of bed and padded silently down the corridor. He did knock, but he didn't wait for a reply, crossing the room quietly, whispering her name.

'Cassandra?'

She stirred. 'Leo? What? Is something wrong?' Then as she came fully awake, the sexy voice replaced the sleepy one. 'Are you coming to bed?'

'Can I?'

'Sure.' She made room for him, reached out and touched his arm. 'You do love me, don't you, darling?'

'Yeah.' What he wanted had nothing to do

303

with love. He couldn't love her, but he could crave her beautiful body. He slid down between the sheets and drew her to him, kissing her until they were both breathless and sweating.

'Say it.' She breathed the words against his neck.

'What?'

'Say you love me, Leo. Say it.'

Anything. He would be willing to say anything at this moment. So he said he loved her, and with that ritual out of the way, he took her, just managing to rein himself in, not to be too rough.

For the second time that night, he slept instantly. For the second time, he woke in a sweat. This time the glowing red numbers of the electric clock told him that he had enjoyed four dreamless hours. He had to thank Cassandra for that. But then he remembered and shivered. He might have dreamed. He might have hurt her. And what then for the old man's plans? PC Plod would be all over him. He got up and crept back to his own room. Cassandra had not stirred as he left her.

CHAPTER TEN

This day had seemed to go on for ever. Zena imagined the bustle and excitement at Gorham House, tried to remember what it looked like on the inside. Had they brought in new furniture or painted some of the rooms? How she longed to be attending the wine and cheese party! If only her pride had not stood in the way. As six o'clock drew near, she felt desperate to share some of the pleasure of such a grand party. Everyone would be there, people she had known most of her life. And probably no-one would comment on the fact that Zena Alway had chosen to stay at home. In desperation, she decided that she would be there, in a way. She would spy on them.

She put on her short blue coat and her sheepskin-lined boots and stepped out into the mellow night armed with a small flashlight and her binoculars. The ground could be tricky leading down to the boundary fence. The grass was long and often concealed little hillocks which were just high enough to trip an old lady. She knew, too, that a mole had been active in this part of the garden.

Gorham House was lit up like a Christmas tree, but that didn't mean she had a clear view of the people inside. In fact, she could tell nothing about the evening party, except that there were an amazing number of cars bouncing their way up the unmade road, their lights swinging wildly each time they hit a bump or hollow.

After about half an hour there was no room for more cars in front of the house and they were directed by unseen hands onto the lawn. She wondered how many people would come and longed to know who among the town's society would turn up.

It was very dark, being overcast, and the temperature had dropped considerably since she first came outside. Nevertheless, she felt she must see more. The boundary fence was made of chestnut paling for most of its length, but she remembered there was a section further along that consisted simply of posts and two lines of wire. Switching on her torch once more, Zena stumbled to this section and managed eventually to get her small, brittle frame threaded between the wires.

She was now on the Midnights' property and the thought of it fired her blood. She felt as if she had achieved something very important, although she couldn't imagine what excuse she would give if she happened to be discovered.

The ground beneath her feet was treacherous, so it was almost inevitable that she would fall. Her coat caught on thorns. She turned to free herself, took an incautious step back into a deep depression and fell heavily onto her right side.

The shock and pain of it made her cry out, but

there was no-one to hear. She assumed she had broken her hip, because that was what happened to old ladies who fell badly. She remembered Mrs Grogget who had lived down the road from her parents. When Zena was eight, the old lady fell and broke her hip. She was put to bed and three weeks later died of pneumonia. In those days, that was the accepted fate of the bedridden.

Distantly, the voices of new arrivals to Gorham House drifted up to her, but she would quite literally prefer to die than to be found trespassing on Leo Midnight's land. Her curiosity about her neighbour's party now seemed extremely foolish.

Nothing for it, then, but to crawl back up the sloping ground to her own front door. She thought she could manage it by pulling herself with her arms and using her good leg occasionally for purchase. She calculated that she was halfway between the two houses. She had a couple of hundred yards to traverse in some way, and could have cheered when she managed to slip beneath the bottom wire of the boundary fence. The lights of her little cottage beckoned as she paused in her struggle to get her breath. If she stopped to rest, however, she felt she would never have the strength to resume. So she took half a dozen deep breaths that left her light-headed and pressed on.

It took her the best part of an hour and she reached her own front door in a desperate state, only to find that she had left it open. The entire house was cold. The fire in the living room had probably gone out, but she didn't think she could get that far in any case. She would try for the kitchen with its warm Aga.

Now that she was in a place of safety, she took stock of herself and realized with relief that she could not possibly have broken anything. Congratulating herself on her strong bones, she credited her years playing netball for their toughness.

She had dragged herself all the way, but on reaching the hall was able to pull herself upright by holding onto the hall stand, and realized that she could hobble painfully, inch by inch, her breath rasping in her chest. She was so tired she wanted nothing more than to fall asleep, but dared not settle into her recliner before cleaning herself up a bit.

The filthy coat was removed, accompanied by whimperings of pain, and dumped on the floor of the hall cupboard. She went into the small downstairs loo and studied her face in the mirror, only to confirm that she looked desperately tired and ill. Despair visited her suddenly, now that she no longer needed to summon all her energy just to survive. She sat down on the toilet lid and wept.

'It's over,' she said. 'I must move into . . .' She couldn't speak the words 'nursing home' aloud. They were the equivalent of saying 'I must move into my coffin.'

Finally she washed her face, dried it gingerly because of the many scratches she had sustained, then, in a last gesture in defiance of injury and old age, reached with a shaking hand for a lipstick she kept on a nearby shelf. The smear of red ran immediately into the fine lines around her thin mouth, but she was cheered nevertheless.

The knock on the door startled her and made her heart pound painfully. Struggling to rise, she opened it to find Claris and Prunella standing before her beaming with good cheer and glowing health.

'What's happened to you?' exclaimed Claris. 'Are you ill?'

'I fell in the garden, but I'm all right. Come in. Send the taxi away. You can ring for one later.'

'Good idea!' Claris went off to speak to the driver.

Prunella gave her old friend a sharp look. 'You could do with a cup of tea. I know it's your house, but you must let me prepare it for you. And a couple of paracetamols.'

'Yes,' said Zena wearily. 'I'll just go and sit down in the living room, but I'm afraid the fire has gone out.'

Caught between joy at their arrival and a strong desire to go to bed, Zena relaxed and allowed events to take their course. Claris put some logs on the fire. Prunella brought in tea, painkillers and a bottle of sherry with three glasses. They wrapped her in a knitted lap rug and bathed her scratches with disinfectant, all the while regaling her with a description of who had been to the party and how the house had appeared to them.

'I'm sure there's a Holman Hunt on the wall,' ended Claris. 'But Prunella thinks it is probably just a cheap copy. And the mirrors are all pitted, with the frames in need of renovating. I didn't see the kitchen, but I'm told they've not done anything to it.'

'They raised about twelve hundred pounds,' added Prunella. 'But the best part was after the raffle. We nearly missed it. If the taxi had come earlier—'

'Leo Midnight gave a little speech,' cut in Claris excitedly. 'Basically, he just said that Save Our Hedgerows was a registered charity that was only interested in harassing the Hebards' neighbour. You know, the farmer. Can't think of his name.'

Zena roused herself. 'Wilkinson. Ever since he took out that straggly old hedge on the south side of his lower field, the Hebards have been at daggers drawn with him. They've slandered him to every person in the village. Kitty set up the charity and raised the money, but the committee haven't done anything worthwhile except print leaflets about how farmers are villains for grubbing out hedgerows.'

'In her two-hundred-pound dresses,' muttered Prunella.

'She's a good woman,' said Claris stoutly. 'Lots of people don't like their neighbours. The Hebards aren't the only ones. Kitty works tirelessly for all sorts of good causes.'

Zena was beginning to feel very much better. 'On the other hand, most people don't set up a charity to annoy the neighbours. But I thought everybody knew that the whole thing was motivated by spite. Wilkinson is a farmer of the old school. Farms a hundred and fifty acres himself and cereal prices have collapsed. He's just trying to keep the old wolfie from the door. Same as anybody else.'

'I believe you can't dig up a hedge nowadays.' Claris felt strongly about ecological matters. 'Wilkinson shouldn't have done it. They took him to court.'

Prunella poured herself another glass of sherry. 'She always wears the most *expensive* clothes to church.'

'It must have been devastating for her,' mused Zena. 'There's nothing worse than being humiliated in front of those whose opinions you value. What a terrible thing for that man to do. If he thought she was cheating or something, why didn't he tell her privately?'

Claris nodded. 'He was drunk, for one thing. Prunella dear, do you think you should have a third glass of sherry? I mean, it's none of my business, but you did have two glasses of wine at the party.'

Prunella held up her glass defiantly. 'She probably spends more on clothes than most men can earn in a year. No, I shouldn't have another glass of sherry, but I'm going to. Cheers.'

Suddenly it struck Zena that she was very fortunate. Any woman who had two like-minded friends with whom she could gossip must consider herself blessed. It was not her custom to make such an admission, but then this was a strange night. 'I'm so glad you came to visit me. It was very kind of you, because, you know, I was feeling very lonely. And frightened, too, after I fell. What good friends you both are.'

With this encouragement Prunella and Claris sprang into action, offering to help Zena up the stairs to her bedroom, to make her a hot-water bottle, to lay out her breakfast.

Zena resisted. 'No, my dear friends, I dare not go upstairs for fear I will not be able to get down again in the morning. I'll sleep on the couch over there.'

Then the two friends had to bustle about, bringing down bedding, helping Zena to get undressed and into her nightgown, filling a Thermos of coffee for her.

'I hate to leave you alone tonight,' said Prunella while Claris was phoning for a taxi. 'But we'll both be round tomorrow morning at nine. Don't try to do too much. Wait for us. You know, you could afford to move into The Breakers. You're an active retired person. Healthy, really. You'd have your own apartment in that beautiful old house, but you'd be looked after. Cleaning and meals and things like that. Company, too. They're very nice. I visited Anne Witherspoon there many years ago. The flats are expensive and I couldn't even think of moving there, but you could afford it.'

Zena thanked her for the suggestion. The Breakers was most definitely not a nursing home. Smart people lived there in some style. Zena liked the idea. Moving into The Breakers was not at all like ordering one's coffin.

'Oh, we almost forgot,' said Claris, coming back into the room. 'We have a little present for you, haven't we, Prunella?'

Prunella, for once alert and able to hear every word, immediately opened her handbag and withdrew the pink box of bath cubes which she placed in Zena's unresisting hands. 'We won them, dear, and thought of you.'

Zena sighed with pleasure and her eyes filled with tears. They kissed her goodbye when the taxi arrived, and she fell asleep seconds after the sound of the engine had died away.

*   *   *

It was hard to appear to be cheerful when one's heart was broken. Edwina had never been good at hiding her feelings. After Felix had been so scathing about her character, she felt as though nothing mattered. He had made her see herself as she really was, as she appeared to her father. Sly, stupid and totally lacking in public spirit.

It was hard even to walk out of her front door and expose herself to the contempt she felt she deserved. Everywhere she went, people asked her what was wrong. Why was she so sad? She said she wasn't feeling well, and that was certainly true in a way.

She had a job for the moment, but increasingly she felt that any post involving the public was not what she wanted. This was a difficult thought to cope with. After all, she had defied her parents to take the course at Capel Manor, telling them that she wanted nothing more in the world than to work with trees in the public sector. Besides, she did not believe in quitting. She believed in carrying on to the bitter end, until she had won through. Edwina Fairfax was not a quitter. She would try, try, try again.

When a request came in saying, for instance, that Mr X in So and So Street wished to trim an overhanging branch from his chestnut tree, it was Edwina's job to visit the street, examine the branch and later write to the owner, telling him if he could or could not do as he wished with his own tree. These applications came in by each post and all of them had to be dealt with. Yet, increasingly, she felt that it was time wasted. Whether the answer was yes or no, the surface of the earth would be basically unchanged. Real problems were not being solved by this careful monitoring of private tree management. It was ironic that some poor householder would be held to account for an infringement of the rules when she knew perfectly well that council workers regularly damaged young trees with their powerful strimmers.

She craved work that was dramatic and important, and, of course, work that never forced her to come into contact with the public. People were fools about trees. The public didn't care sufficiently. Collectively too lazy to find out about trees and their importance to the globe, they were mostly hypocrites.

She really wanted to spend her time with those who were studying to change the face of the Earth. Edwina felt she needed to be in the company of intelligent people with high ideals. Believing she had it in her to make some earth-shattering contribution to the problem of trees in the world, she wondered how she could do it. A little research into possible avenues of activity was necessary. She would have to move away, of course. There was no point in staying in north Essex now that Felix no longer wanted to be with her.

John Blue gave no indication that he thought she could be a famous arboriculturist. He saw her differently, as a good ambassador for the work of the environment department. When requests came in from schools, asking for a speaker, he now always sent Edwina. He praised her teaching skills and her ability to empathize with children. He said she was making a real contribution to the district, but she suspected he just wanted to get her out of the way. He also didn't want to spend his own time talking to children.

Yet she did enjoy it. Afterwards she would often be invited to join some of the teachers in the common room where the talk was similar to the sort of conversations she had heard at home: homework, the odd difficult child, pay and conditions, awkward parents. She felt nostalgic in any common room, because she had visited her parents at school on so many occasions, leaning against her mother's chair or gazing at her dad as he held forth on some educational theory.

Teachers, she thought, were different from the members of the general public whom she so despised. They were intelligent and eager to learn, and so she cheerfully answered their questions about tree matters, although some of the questions were every bit as naive as the telephone queries from unknown callers she dealt with daily.

Naturally she shared in the triumph felt by all teachers at the sight of a shy or slow child suddenly coming to life when they realized they could master a subject. Trees and how and where they grew was a less threatening subject than reading or writing or numbers. Many, especially the little ones, experienced a kind of epiphany right there on the school grounds. The less academic they were, the more easily they seemed to be able to identify trees by their leaves. When they developed this simple skill, other children could admire them, if only briefly.

She was also proud of the fact that she taught them to love trees without teaching them to hate farmers or property developers or politicians.

Time enough for them to develop their own prejudices when they were capable of understanding a little of the complexities of life on an overcrowded island.

She made several good friends and saw a couple of the younger teachers in the evenings, meeting them in groups at pubs throughout the large area of Bishop District Council. But even this small amount of socializing was restricted, because sooner or later they would break off into pairs. Most of them had boyfriends or husbands, while Edwina was achingly conscious of her single state.

A week after the party at Gorham House, she was struck by the thought that Zena Alway no longer telephoned her. Her imagination presented her with a grim picture of Zena lying dead, her body undiscovered. Having finished two visits in short order, she drove directly to Zena's home, surprised to find a For Sale sign at the bottom of the lane.

Zena answered the door looking frail. There were several fading scratches on her face. 'I haven't had a call from you lately and wondered if you were all right,' said Edwina. 'May I come in and chat or are you busy?'

'I'm never too busy to see you, my dear. What on earth would I be doing, anyway? I've sold my car and I've put my house up for sale. Just this morning a young couple came to look around for the third time and they made me an offer. Now I've got to think what I'm going to do, where I'm going to go.'

'You'll be putting some distance between yourself and the Midnights.'

'Yes, thank the Lord. Come into the kitchen,' said Zena. 'It's nice and warm in there. We can sit at the kitchen table, have a coffee and a good old chinwag. So much has happened. Remember you said confession is good for the soul? Well, I've got a confession to make. On the night of the Midnights' party, I wanted to see who was there. I took my torch and put on my boots and walked down to the fence.'

'It was pitch dark that night. No moon.'

Zena smiled. 'That's why I took the torch. Anyway, I got to the boundary fence and I couldn't see much, so I walked along the boundary to where there were just posts and two wires. I crawled through the wires and—'

'But that's the wooded part and it's terribly overgrown!'

'Yes, it is. How do you know that, Edwina?'

Edwina shook her head. 'Tell you later. What happened next?'

'Well, I walked along and like a fool, I fell. Hurt my hip. I thought I might have broken it. It took me almost an hour to crawl back here. You know what I mean, crawling on my elbows and dragging my feet. Like they do in films. I was as good as Arnie Schwarzenegger. I looked a mess and I was exhausted. I never saw who came to the party and forgot I was ever interested.'

'You must have been very frightened. It got pretty cold during the night. You could have died of hypothermia.'

'I thought of that at the time.' Zena placed a cup of coffee in front of Edwina and fetched her own before sitting down. 'Have you ever thought of the upset that couple have caused?

317

They moved into our little community and turned us all upside down. I'll tell you what Leo Midnight has done. He's made us all take a good hard look at ourselves. And we don't always like what we see.'

'I can't blame Leo Midnight for it, but it was because of him that Felix and I split up. He hates me now. Well, they both do. Felix and Leo Midnight.'

'Nonsense!' exclaimed Zena. 'Felix doesn't hate anyone. He loves you. What happened with you and Leo Midnight?'

'You will recall that the Midnights wouldn't – won't – allow me onto their property. But I had to see what he was up to with that chainsaw of his. Do you remember the day the four statues were stolen from Gorham House? Well, I was there that day. I was trespassing, of course. I knew that the Midnights would be away. The funny thing is, I can't remember how I knew. I've a sneaking suspicion that I overheard it at the Co-op checkout. Anyway, I drove over to Badger's Wood and walked through the woods to their property. I found the simple fencing and crawled through just like you did.'

'We're sisters at heart!' crowed Zena.

'I was looking at all the trees and making a note of what was important when I saw the lorry arrive and the men start to remove the statues. I thought nothing of it, I promise you. It never occurred to me that they might be stealing them. My main concern was to avoid being seen.'

'Don't tell me!' cried Zena. 'When you found out that those men must have been thieves, you didn't tell Felix.'

'How did you know?'

'Because I would have done the same. You didn't want to get mixed up in anything and neither would I. Not with the law. Not if I was also breaking the law.'

'It gets worse. Sometime later, I went to a meeting about saving an oak tree that was about to be felled at a dangerous corner and one of the thieves was there. I didn't know his name, but later he came with others to the demonstration. Felix saw me there, saw me speak to the man. A week or so ago, when he got a tip-off that this man had been involved in the robbery, Felix put two and two together and accused me of harbouring a thief or aiding and abetting, or just plain keeping my mouth shut when I could have helped him with his enquiries. I don't know what, exactly, but I certainly must have done something terrible. He said he and I had different attitudes to the law and he was a policeman and—'

'Felix is a bit stuffy. He needs to lighten up. Live a little.'

Edwina laughed delightedly. 'Zena, you are so good for my morale. But Felix is a good policeman.'

'He's no hotshot. He should have marched me straight to the station that night when I damaged the Midnights' car. He didn't even ask if I had ever committed any other driving offences. But the inspector knew. We go back a long way. I was always being pulled up for speeding. Once lost my licence for six months. I was a tearaway after James died.' Zena thought for a moment. 'I was a tearaway before James died.'

'Well, I feel a little better about our quarrel.

Maybe I can convince him that I'm not so bad. If I ever see him again. If he ever comes round.'

'Ring him up and give him what for. There, I've settled your problem. Now maybe you can help me. I've got an appointment to visit The Breakers in half an hour. You know, the stately home that's been turned into retirement flats. That's where I was thinking about moving to, but they look you over, you know. And all of a sudden, I'm nervous. Will you come with me? You could drive me. I'll cancel the taxi.'

'I'd love to.' Edwina was supposed to be working, but she didn't care. Let them fire her. She wanted to offer support to Zena, the woman who had in the space of a few moments made her feel so much better about herself.

'And on the way, I'll tell you what Leo Midnight did to Kitty Hebard the night of the party. Have you heard?'

The Breakers was a magnificent Tudor house set in twenty acres of landscaped gardens. Its public rooms were beautiful and the set of rooms Zena was offered was very bright and spacious. It consisted of a minute kitchen, a bathroom, a bedroom which was larger than the one in her cottage and a very large living room with high ceilings and windows on two sides.

Zena seemed to be a bit overwhelmed. When the administrator left the flat to attend to some other business, she turned to Edwina with tears in her eyes. 'What's the point? It seems to me I've done everything I want to do in this life. Wherever I am, it's just the same over and over. Get up, get dressed, do my chores, watch the television, prepare some food and eat, then go to bed. Only here, I won't even have my usual chores. What will I do with myself? I can hardly go jogging or line dancing or get a job. I'll lose a lot of my freedom, you know, so I'm not entirely sure about moving. It means admitting that I can't look after myself.'

'It also means a beginning. A fresh start with new friends.'

'I like my old ones.'

'Oh, Zena, don't think that way. You don't have to give up your old friends. You'll only be moving a mile away.'

Zena looked around the room which had no furniture, since the previous occupant had already moved out. 'It is a pretty room. My furniture would look very good in here, better than it does at the cottage. It's hard for an old bat like me to take to new ways. To tell you the truth, I'm a bit afraid. What if I don't like it here? What if I don't get on? Sometimes I just wish I could go to sleep and never wake up.'

Impulsively, Edwina gave her a hug. 'You mustn't say that. What would I do without you?'

The administrator returned. 'Your next-door neighbour will be Mr Stuart, Mrs Alway, and he has suggested that we drop in to his flat right now.'

Zena hesitated, putting out a thin hand to clutch Edwina's arm. The younger woman guided her towards the door, determined that she should make the effort to meet someone new.

Mr Stuart's door was open and he was seated at a computer. What hair was left to him was fine and white. He had a beaky nose, a small white moustache that contrasted well with his thread-veined cheeks and a sparkle in his faded blue eyes. He clutched two handsome canes and rose gallantly on frail legs to greet them. 'Do come in! How nice to meet you, Mrs Alway.' His papery hand enfolded her own. 'I was just sending an e-mail. I'm taking lessons in using the Internet. We're never too old to learn, you know.'

He's a gentleman, thought Zena. Someone who hasn't given up on good manners. 'You might not be too old to learn,' she said, 'but I'm afraid I am.'

'Don't do yourself down. You could learn to operate a computer in no time. Older people do very well with a little instruction. Do you know, we've got a higher percentage of silver surfers in Britain than anywhere else.'

Suddenly Zena felt light-headed, due, she thought, to a lifting of responsibility. No more worrying about getting to the shops, maintaining her house and garden, cooking for herself alone. At the same time, pride in her appearance re-turned to her with a rush. She experienced an urgent need to buy a few new dresses.

'On the Internet,' Mr Stuart was saying, 'you can send an e-mail to anywhere in the world for the price of a local call. I've a son in Sydney. I can't get out to see him so much any more and he doesn't come home as often as I would like. But we send each other long letters and get answers within a few hours. It's wonderful.'

Zena's spirits began to rise. The computer screen was glowing a challenge at her, daring her to learn, daring her to conquer it. Perhaps, after all, there was more to life than she had thought.

How exciting it would be to learn something new! To take a few chances, make new friends! Suddenly it all seemed worthwhile and she felt her old fighting spirit return. Mr Stuart had a face accustomed to smiling. She could see all the laughter lines around his face. He was smiling at her now as he praised the quality of the food at The Breakers. She was beginning to feel at home already.

'You know, I think I would like to learn to operate a computer. I might just write my memoirs. I'd like to do lots of new things. I've got a daughter in Kuala Lumpur.'

'Oh, really?' said Mr Stuart. 'What's it like in KL?'

'Haven't been there,' chuckled Zena. 'Haven't done *that*.' She nodded at the computer, now laughing heartily. 'Didn't get the T-shirt!'

For days after his encounter with Leo Midnight, Felix brooded about what the older man had said to him. Midnight had a way of making a person feel bad about himself. Thinking about their angry exchange made him miserable, but he found that the antidote to unpleasant intro-spection was to keep busy.

There was a great deal of hard work involved in tying up the case of the stolen statues, as well as the attempted burglary at The Hoo. It transpired that the owners had used a security system to anchor their expensive sculpture to the ground. This had foiled the thieves, but at the expense of a beautiful old wall. For once the insurance company paid up readily and repair work was quickly under way.

Felix thought he might have been able to take whatever criticism came his way if Edwina had been around to help him keep the confrontation in perspective. He admitted that he had driven her away. As a result, his carefully honed set of values was now under review. He decided he no longer knew what was right or acceptable.

His mother might be a willing listener, as she had been when he was a child. But a telephone conversation struck him as an unsatisfactory way to sort out his thoughts. That left Greg as the unwilling confidant.

As often happened, Felix and Greg went to a pub to have a sandwich lunch. 'It has occurred to me,' began Felix, 'that we're more interested in status and position than in sex.'

Greg nearly choked on his beer. He put the tankard on the counter, grinning. 'I must admit I've never thought of it that way, but I'm sure you have a reason for saying so.'

Felix drank his beer, unable to find a way of explaining what he meant.

'It's that Midnight bastard, isn't it? He's stripped your confidence,' said Greg. 'You're going over in your mind everything he said to you and now you don't know if you ever made a good arrest, ever did anything right. Let me tell you, he's had the same effect on me. But I've been through it. My belief is that this bloke is deeply unhappy, a failed cop who's been sectioned. I mean, he's not quite sane. Let's face it, what he says mustn't be taken too seriously.'

'Maybe not.' Felix finished his pint, but it tasted of sawdust. At the present time, his life tasted of sawdust. He needed to get his chaotic emotions sorted out in his mind, but Greg was not being particularly helpful. It was no good saying Midnight was crazy. Maybe he was, but Felix felt there was probably more than a grain of truth in his criticism. 'He said I'll be transferred one day. He said I need to find out if I like policing even when I'm in an area where nobody likes me.'

'He's got a point. Around here, they do think the sun shines out your arse,' laughed Greg. 'Handsome young copper, always obliging. It must affect your work, all that admiration.'

'You think I shouldn't be so obliging?'

Greg sighed. 'I didn't say that. I just think he may have had a point. All right? Anyway, you'll probably make everybody love you no matter where you're sent. Villains will give themselves up just for the pleasure of your smile. Druggies will decide they can do without a fix after a few words from you. You've got that gift.'

'I want to talk about Edwina.'

'Ah. Now we're getting down to the real problem.'

'I broke up with her because we are incompatible. Edwina was trespassing on the Midnight property the day Duggie and friends stole the statues.'

'I'll be damned!'

'She saw them, but thought they were just taking the statues away legally for some reason. She was more concerned that they shouldn't see her, because she didn't want John Blue and the landscape and countryside section to be embarrassed by her actions. She wasn't bothered about me. When she found out that they had stolen the things, she said nothing to me.'

Greg laughed. 'She kept a secret from you, the naughty girl. No wonder you made that remark about status. If she had spoken to you, you could have made a good bust. So you quarrelled, giving up sex for status. Makes sense, what you said. Pity you didn't think it all through before breaking up with Edwina.'

'It's not funny. Later, she saw one of them at the demonstration over the oak tree that had to come down. Remember that? Well, she could have fingered him then, but she never said a word.'

'She is a bad citizen.'

'You're laughing at me.'

'That, Felix, is because you're laughable. Are you telling me that you broke it off with the love of your life because she kept a secret from you? She didn't want to get involved. She didn't want to feel responsible for somebody going to prison. My God, ninety per cent of the population feel that way. You're not going to change her. You ought to be able to accept her as she is, and I'll tell you why, because she is as close to being the perfect wife for you as you're ever likely to find.'

Felix, more from embarrassment than thirst, ordered a tomato juice. When the glass had been put on the table, he looked at Greg ruefully. 'One thing about you is, you tell it straight.'

'Listen to me. You're having problems about when to be nice, when to be tough, when to listen, when to ignore what you hear. That's because being a cop is not easy. Did you ever think it was? Now you take soldiers. They're told to do this, do that. In a war situation, you can't have every little squaddie deciding for himself whether to advance or retreat. They have to do what they're told without question. But it's different for us. The police have a totally different way of going about things. Each and every one of us is expected to think for himself. Or herself. Every situation that comes up, we've got to think it out. That's why we get it wrong sometimes. We think for ourselves. But then we're not fighting a war in enemy territory. We're on the same side as the people we've sometimes got to nick. Cheer up, man. And make it up with Edwina.'

'Mmm. I guess so. It's a bit difficult. She seems perfectly happy without me. If only she would show some sign of wanting to get together again.'

'I can't help you there, but maybe Harriet can—'

'No, thank you. I'll just plod along in my usual bumbling way. After all, I've got to get sorted out myself. Believe it or not, I really do want to be a good cop.' Felix looked around idly, wondering why he felt so discontented and bored. It occurred to him that the reason was quite simple.

'I'd like to find out what Leo Midnight is up to.'

'If that will make you feel better, we'll do it. I'll make some more enquiries. Why don't you try a few of your informers?'

Normally Edwina cut her own hair, trimmed the fringe, then brought the rest around to the front and whacked off a bit when it got too long. But she decided one Saturday morning that she would go to the hairdressers and have something drastic done.

The change of hairstyle would be an outward manifestation of the change that had taken place within her, as the last couple of weeks had proved to be surprisingly pleasant. She was gaining confidence. Her social life was quite busy, what with going out with a couple of single teachers, playing in a darts team and having an occasional cup of coffee with Harriet. Most surprising of all, these occasions always seemed to be filled with laughter.

It was time for a more mature hairstyle. At Clip U Like, Hedda, the owner, was a tall dark woman in her forties. Edwina had come in for a manicure before Felix's party and had been charmed by the hairdresser's good nature. Hedda was almost a clone of Harriet in that she never stopped talking and had a way of saying the wrong thing, but could later make a good story out of her gaffes. She was just giving change to a customer when Edwina walked in.

A plump, middle-aged woman with a girlish style of heavily bleached hair put a pound tip on the counter. 'Oh, thank you, Mrs Perkins,' said Hedda. 'I saw your son the other day. Lovely young man. You know, he looks a lot like Barry Manilow.'

'What? Oh no, I don't think so. You can't mean my son,' said Mrs Perkins. 'Are you saying Geoffrey has a large nose?'

'No, no. I think Barry Manilow is very good-looking. I don't think his nose is—'

'He has a large nose. You must admit it, Hedda. He does have a large nose. Geoffrey's nose may be a bit longer than some of these snub-nosed boys you see at his school, but he does not have a large nose. I'm surprised you should say such a thing.' Mrs Perkins flicked her blue chiffon scarf over one shoulder and left, slamming the glass door behind her.

Hedda turned to Edwina and gave a comical shrug. 'You know my trouble. Can't keep my big mouth shut. I can't tell you the number of customers I've lost that way.'

'Surely Mrs Perkins will not go elsewhere just because you said her son looks like Barry Manilow.'

'No, but every time she comes in I'll have to listen to another lecture about her son and poor Manilow's nose.'

It took Hedda no time to wash Edwina's hair, or so it seemed. She passed the time by giving her customer a running commentary on her love life which was very funny, but could not possibly be entirely true. Soon Edwina was seated before the mirror and the moment of decision had arrived.

'I think it should be short, really short with just a bit of a fringe.'

'Exactly,' said Hedda. 'Leave it to me. Would you like to look at a copy of *Hello!* while I'm cutting?'

Ten minutes later, Edwina looked up from a riveting article about Posh Spice and David Beckham to find that she had very little hair left. At the back, it curved into her neck like a typical man's haircut. A light fringe brushed her forehead and the rest was about to be blow-dried to give it a bit of a lift.

'What do you think?' asked Hedda. 'Makes you look older.'

'Yes, it does.'

'Well, I don't mean older so much as more mature.'

Edwina began to laugh. 'More sophisticated, perhaps.'

'Yes, and besides, you've got a short neck and – no, I didn't mean that. You're neck isn't short at all, but it is a bit thick and—'

'Hedda! Don't dig yourself in any deeper. I love the style. It's grown-up, just the change I needed. And it makes my neck look longer. Believe me, I shall never go anywhere else in future to have my hair done, if only because this place has the best conversation in town.'

She drove straight to Harriet's house to show off her new look. Harriet was very complimentary. 'That's the way to do it. New hairstyle, perhaps a change in dress. Felix will come running.'

'I didn't do it to impress Felix.'

'I know that,' said Harriet. 'But I've heard all about it. He feels ashamed of himself for being so hard on you. Greg gave him a right bollocking, I can tell you.'

Edwina flung her handbag onto the settee with great force. 'Does everybody discuss my private life? Has Felix been telling the world about my criminal activities? My God, I don't have a life to call my own.'

'You know you love him.'

'I know nothing of the sort. That is, I'm not sure. I'm getting along very well without Felix. I'm a person in my own right. I don't need a man to define me.'

'What? I didn't get that.'

Edwina flopped onto the settee beside her bag. She took a couple of deep breaths, then looked up at her friend and smiled. 'Let's not quarrel. I've got a funny story for you.'

This seemed to mollify Harriet. The story of Hedda the hairdresser comparing a customer's son to Barry Manilow made her laugh loudly. When Edwina reached the part of the tale where Hedda said the new cut made her look older, Harriet laughed so hard that neither of them heard the front door open. When Greg and Felix entered, it caught both of them by surprise.

'Hello, Harriet,' said Felix, but he had eyes only for Edwina.

She smiled at him. 'How are you, Felix? What sort of day have you had?'

'Multi-car pile-up this morning, one fatality, six injured. At half past five David Wilkinson, a farmer, woke me up to tell me his tractor had been driven off in the night. He's deaf and didn't hear it go, but he was convinced the Hebards did it to spite him. So nothing out of the ordinary.' He smiled warmly. 'I can see what you've been doing today. Your hair looks great.'

Greg rubbed his hands together. 'I'm dying for a cup of tea. Come on, woman. Let's put the kettle on.' Harriet leapt up and headed for the kitchen and Greg followed.

'Take your time with the tea,' hissed Greg as soon as they were in the kitchen. 'I think this is it. He'll make it up with her.'

'I'm not so sure.' Harriet reached for the breakfast tea. 'She says she's doing great without him.'

Greg snatched the tea from her and put the

canister back on the shelf, then removed the Earl
Grey. 'Don't fall for that. Every woman is dying
to have a man of her own and Edwina is no
exception.'

Harriet grabbed the Earl Grey canister with
both hands. 'Edwina can't stand Earl Grey. Will
you leave me alone to make the tea? Get the
biscuits out of the red tin.'

'Felix.' Edwina clasped her hands, focusing just
past his right shoulder. 'I want to say I'm sorry
that I didn't confide in you about that young lad.'

Felix tried for a light manner. 'Does that mean
you no longer think I'm such a prig?'

Edwina gave him a saucy look, eager to keep
the reconciliation on a jokey level. 'Oh, I never
really thought you were a prig. Zena thinks you
are a bit stuffy, but I'm not so sure.'

He laughed briefly. 'I'm grateful for Zena's
appraisal.'

Edwina grinned broadly. 'She also thinks
you're no hotshot as a policeman. She has a
terrible driving history and once lost her licence
for six months. She thinks you should have found
out about that.'

'I did,' he said, showing his teeth in a sardonic
rictus that bore no resemblance to a genuine
smile. 'Her friend, the inspector, informed me of
it when he reprimanded me for my kindness to
her. I'm touched that she is so grateful. Doubly
touched that you advised her to see the inspector.'

Edwina was startled by his anger, aware that
the joking conversation was getting out of hand,
yet having no idea how to recover the light-
hearted mood. 'Oh, Felix, dear, you aren't really

stupid enough to think I would encourage her to try to ruin your career! Surely you don't think I'm that evil?'

'I really don't know what to think, Edwina. You've certainly convinced Greg that you're an angel. Clever you. Are you suggesting that Zena is a liar as well as a dangerous driver?'

'I was wrong, Felix.' Edwina jumped to her feet. 'You are a pompous prig. You are also a fool with a big head.'

'Really? Well, just ask yourself this. You don't have to say it out loud, but answer the question to yourself. Would your father think it was right to trespass on someone's land, witness a crime and then not tell the police?'

When Greg and Harriet returned to the living room with the tea tray, the best china, paper napkins and a large plate of biscuits, only Felix was still present to partake of it.

'Edwina, having been as insulting as possible, has gone home. I didn't bother to tell her how rude she was to leave without saying goodbye to you. But then, I don't want to be a pompous prig!'

'Leo.' Cassandra threw the car keys onto the kitchen dresser and sat down at the scrubbed table. 'There's going to be an art exhibition this weekend to raise money for a new village hall. But tonight's when everybody who is anybody goes to see it. There's wine and cheese!'

'What sort of art?' he asked, then before she could answer, 'I should have thought you got your fill of wine and cheese the other night.'

'I believe the paintings are by amateurs. It could be fun.'

'Paintings by amateurs! My God, a fate worse than death. Weepy watercolours of cherry trees and sweet little pussy cats.'

'I still think it could be fun. Anyway, I bought two tickets.'

It was dark when they arrived and parking space in front of the village hall was limited. Leo had to park two streets away, which meant Cassandra was in a foul mood by the time she had walked a hundred and fifty yards in three-inch heels.

The large room was full almost to capacity. Tall stands, their upper halves made of pinboard, were ranged side by side, and cut off the view of three-quarters of the room. Each board held a number of paintings and Leo could see straight away that these were not the sort of amateurs' work he had envisaged. Most, however, were landscapes and flower pictures, not the sort of thing that appealed to him.

'I'll get us a glass of wine. What do you want, red or white?'

'Nothing. I don't feel like anything,' she murmured and wandered off to view the far side of the boards.

Leo went into the ante-room where trestle tables had been set up to serve wine, mineral water and orange juice. He picked up a glass of red wine, then remembered that he and Cassandra had eaten only a pizza for dinner, or rather Leo had eaten half and Cassandra had said she was not hungry.

The cheeses were attractively arranged and

there was a greater variety than had been the case at the Save Our Hedgerows party. Several were local cheeses he had never heard of. He sampled each one, then decided to try them all again. They went so well with wine that he bought another glass and returned to the cheeses, beginning to feel quite pleased that they had come.

'Have you decided which painting you're going to buy?' said a deep voice behind him.

'Which one?' said Leo, turning round to see the weather-beaten features of Warwick Provender, whom he recognized from Kitty Hebard's drinks party. Kitty had been at pains to inform him at the Save Our Hedgerows do that Warwick's grandson had printed the tickets, and Leo had been at pains to say that he didn't care. However, the old boy was nice enough.

'I have most definitely decided not to buy any pictures. They wouldn't fit into Gorham House. Too new. Too clean. Not the house, the pictures.'

Warwick smiled and helped himself to a piece of cheese. 'Would you care to make a wager? You *will* be buying a painting for about two hundred pounds and it will be by the least talented, most handsome artist exhibiting.'

'Cassandra,' said Leo. 'I should have known. Can I buy you another glass of wine?'

'Why not?' said Warwick genially. 'You owe me that for talking to you. You're pretty much *persona non grata* around here after you attacked Kitty. My speaking to you will go some way to restoring your standing in the community.' Warwick was smiling broadly.

'Why does everybody suppose I want to be liked? I go out of my way to make myself disagreeable to everyone and here you are pretending to like me.'

'I do like you, in a way,' said Warwick. 'Like poor old Wilkinson, I, too, am a farmer and sometimes I get a little impatient with the Kitty Hebards of this world. They don't understand what difficult times we're going through. I'll have a glass of red, thank you very much.'

Edwina had made arrangements to attend the art exhibition with Ulrika, the darts player, but Ulrika had been asked to dinner by a man friend and so had backed out at the last minute. Edwina was keeping her distance from Harriet these days, so she came alone to look at the paintings and to marvel at the prices. She couldn't afford to buy anything, but told herself that she had at least purchased a ticket and part of the price went towards the village hall fund.

After studying each picture carefully she walked around to the back of the boards to look at the paintings on the other side, just as if she actually cared what they were or who had painted them. There was no-one present whom she knew and she had about decided to drink her glass of wine and leave when she noticed that the feet of those arriving could be seen below the pictures. She recognized Cassandra's slim ankles and delicate shoes immediately, and began to plan her escape.

Too late! The Midnights went their separate ways, Leo towards the drink and Cassandra apparently coming towards Edwina from the other end of the room, although she stopped long before reaching her. Cassandra had found a handsome man to talk to and would not be putting herself out to talk to anyone else.

Leo left the ante-room to search for Cassandra. As he had been warned, she was talking with great animation to a baby-faced young man in a blue velvet jacket. Warwick was right on all points. The watercolour about which the young man and Cassandra were enthusing was a muddy landscape that could never have been painted from an actual scene. Brownish daubs representing autumn leaves stiffly populated the distance while a few red leaves on a black branch occupied the foreground. And for this the poseur wanted two hundred quid! Why was it the good-looking young men were never the ones with talent?

'Darling,' Cassandra interrupted the artist in mid-sentence. 'This is Blake Conway. He's just the most marvellous painter. I'm buying this picture for my . . . the bedroom. Don't you love it?'

Leo looked at her carefully to see if she was joking. She wasn't. With a sigh, he pulled his chequebook from his inside jacket pocket and scribbled out a cheque for two hundred pounds. 'Very nice. Very autumnal.'

Blake Conway, having made his first sale ever, wanted to chat to the new owner, but Leo had caught sight of Edwina, and left Conway and Cassandra without a word of apology.

As luck would have it, Edwina saw him coming when she happened to be in a corner of the room with no avenue of escape. Two folding chairs had been placed in the corner for those who might be exhausted by looking at all the paintings. The display boards, on the other hand, had been crammed in because there had been a terrific response from artists in the region. There was no quick way out of the corner, so she abandoned the idea and stood waiting for her enemy to reach her.

The sight of Edwina reminded Leo of their last meeting, of how she had managed to surprise him into a confession about Janie. Day by day he spent the better part of his energy hiding the weakness and the shame of his past, then this little thing came along when he was least prepared and brought it all back. He could not forgive her.

He had all but forgotten the latest communication from Bishop council but her downy cheek and huge frightened eyes reminded him that he was very annoyed indeed. It flashed through his mind that this golden opportunity to get his own back had only come about because Cassandra wanted to go to an exhibition of amateur paintings. But he was not in the mood to be amused by coincidence.

He bore down on her, and his height and anger made her shrink into the corner until a chair seat pressed against the back of her legs.

'How dare you put the law onto me, you silly woman?' His voice was low and full of menace.

Edwina winced, gasping for air. 'What . . . what are you talking about?'

'The court order! That's what I'm talking about. Don't tell me you had nothing to do with it.'

'I didn't. Get away from me. I didn't do it. It was John Blue, the head of landscape and—'

'For God's sake, Edwina, grow up.' He leaned one hand against the wall, hemming her in. 'He wouldn't have known anything about it if you hadn't gone whining to him.' Her only escape was to sit down on the chair, but this left him leering down at her.

'White wine, Edwina?' said Felix over Leo's shoulder. He seemed to have come from nowhere, and he was in uniform.

Leo whirled. 'Ah here's your minder, Edwina. Your protector. The man who will save you from men like me, even if he can't protect you from your own stupidity.' He gave Felix a slight push in the chest to make some space for his exit.

'White wine?' said Felix again. Edwina reached for the wine, but her hand shook so much he pulled the glass away. 'Take a couple of deep breaths. You're going to spill this otherwise.'

'He's angry because he thinks I sent him a court order demanding access to his property. But I didn't. It was John Blue. Leo hates me.'

'I doubt if you're the person he hates. Listen, Edwina. Don't mess with him.'

'Mess with him! All I want to do is get away from him. I don't know why he hates me so much.'

'I keep trying to tell you he doesn't hate you. Please understand that what I know about the man I found out through police sources and so I'm not allowed to divulge any information. I'm in enough hot water as it is. So I'll just say that you must make every effort to stay away from both the

Midnights. We think he's up to something bad. Greg and I are working on it. Here you are. I think you can hold this glass safely enough. Take a few sips. You look like you need it.'

'Thank you.' She drank half the glass and, as the alcohol hit her stomach, was fooled into thinking she was all right. 'I must go soon. I've not had anything to eat. Ulrika was going to come with me and then we would have . . . but she's going somewhere else, so I just thought I would slip over and see what there was . . . and it was something to do, I guess. The paintings are very nice but I can't afford any of them.'

'No,' he said. 'Neither can I. But they're nice. How's the job?'

'OK, I guess. Or rather . . . that is, I think it's all right.'

He smiled. 'So, no change there. I'm on duty this evening. Just dropped in to see how the fund-raising was going. This place leaks like a sieve when it rains. I hope they get all the money they need soon. Shall I take your glass?'

She finished the wine and handed the glass to him. They smiled awkwardly at each other, and then he left. Edwina sat for several minutes, fighting back the desire to give way to tears.

It was half past seven in the morning. Edwina was up, but hardly expecting a call from anyone at this early hour on a Wednesday.

'Hello?'

'Edwina, it's Harriet. You've got to help me out. Be a friend.'

'Anything I can do—'

'I'm giving a speech tonight. Large gathering

340

of ladies of the Women's Institute. About two hundred. Will you come?'

'I've nothing else on. I guess I could—'

'The thing is,' said Harriet, sounding harassed. 'Greg was going to come. And now the swine tells me he's got to work. Mum's babysitting. It won't last long and we can have a late supper. I couldn't eat beforehand. It wouldn't stay down, I'm sure.'

Edwina didn't suppose she would be able to eat before speaking to two hundred women, either. 'Poor you. I'll drive. What time shall I pick you up?' Harriet thought six thirty would be about right.

When Edwina arrived, her friend, dressed in a black trouser suit and scarlet blouse, looked very attractive and so nervous she could scarcely sit still in the car.

'This is something new for you, isn't it?' asked Edwina. 'Public speaking? I mean, I never heard you say anything about it before. What are you going to talk about?'

'Oh, just crazy things that have happened to me.'

Meaning, thought Edwina, adventures in a supermarket car park.

'I've never spoken to so many people before. Usually just fifteen or twenty, and during the day. It seems more important and exciting when it's at night. I hope I don't dry up.'

The venue was just two miles away. Edwina turned into the car park and began looking for a space. 'You have notes, surely. Can you make a whole half-an-hour speech out of crazy things that have happened to you?'

'Oh, just anecdotes, you know. Sort of acting out some of them.'

Edwina's heart sank. She thought Harriet had ample experience of talking about herself, but couldn't help wondering if the audience would be amused for half an hour by her stories.

The village hall was buzzing. Every chair had been pressed into service and only the ones at the very back were still empty, but Edwina was shown to the front row where a place had been reserved for Greg. Embarrassed by this special treatment, she hunched down in her seat and waited with increasing anxiety for Harriet to be introduced.

There was a little WI business to be announced, then, very quickly, Harriet was on. Edwina gaped at her friend, hardly recognizing the flighty, occasionally boring, Harriet Squiller. The Harriet who took centre stage was a self-possessed, born entertainer. Holding the microphone confidently, she walked to the edge of the small stage, engaging her listeners immediately by looking directly at them. Her voice was strong and her introduction and first story made Edwina laugh as loudly as anyone.

She relaxed. This was not going to be a cringe-making evening, after all. Harriet, she acknowledged with relief, was a polished speaker.

As the speech wore on, it became more of a stand-up comedy routine, filled with one-liners and crazy, impossible incidents. After the first five minutes, if she had said 'hello', her audience would have laughed, and Edwina would have laughed the loudest.

'And,' said Harriet, halfway through her

allotted half an hour, 'I put on this sequinned top. Very good, I thought, for wearing with a plain skirt. Well, I said to the assistant, "I look like a pregnant snake!" And the girl never cracked a smile, just said, "Yes, madam." I nearly didn't go to the party after that.'

The audience roared. Edwina gasped. It hadn't happened to Harriet. It had happened to her. What's more, the line about pregnant snakes had been her witticism, not Harriet's. She was very annoyed.

There was more to come. Harriet, she told her audience, had once made the mistake of comparing a friend's son to Barry Manilow. Edwina slid down in her seat. How could she ever face Hedda again?

Harriet wound up her routine by recounting the time she had, she said, emerged from the pub loo with the back of her skirt caught up in her knickers. 'Next time I'll wear trousers. I've got nothing to get caught in the flies!'

They gave her a thunderous ovation. Harriet basked in their approval, with just one swift look at Edwina. By the time the clapping had died down and the audience had sung 'Jerusalem', Edwina had forgiven her. She had just seen a masterly performance. And she's my friend! thought Edwina with pride.

Later, while they were enjoying a curry, she said as much.

'You're a good sport,' said Harriet. 'I was worried, but you know that's how it's done. You gather whatever material you can find, wherever you can find it, and you use it. What do you think? Am I good? Would you pay me to come and talk to your organization?'

'You are a terrific entertainer and I would pay you to speak. It's a hidden talent, Harriet. You amaze me.'

'I started in a small way. A friend of my mother's asked me to speak to a senior citizens' club. They seemed to like it and I got a few other offers. But this was my big night and I wanted Greg to be there.'

'Of course you did. I'm sorry he couldn't make it, but his absence was my good fortune. You are full of surprises. Always coming up with something new. And that reminds me. I haven't asked about your floristry course. How is it going?'

Harriet shrugged. 'I quit. On the very first day I realized that everybody else in the class had real talent with flowers. I didn't know the names of any of the plants and I didn't even like touching them. The other students loved it all and knew the names of all of the plant material. I was just an idiot, also older than most of them. I'll work the whole experience into one of my speeches sometime.'

'You quit? You paid to take a course and you walked out on the first day? Harriet, how could you?'

'Oh, you know the old saying. If at first you don't succeed, give up and try something else. See? I was no good at arranging flowers. I didn't like all that preparation with foam and tape and everything. But I'm a natural at speaking. I'm taking it up seriously, you know. I won't make much money, I guess, but Greg says I wouldn't have made any money at floristry. I don't ever want to work for somebody else again, and we couldn't have afforded to buy me a flower shop. This way, I'm doing what I'm good at.'

'Aren't you embarrassed?'

'Why should I be?'

'That people will laugh because you gave up so quickly.'

'I couldn't care less and chances are they won't give it a second thought. You worry too much about what other people think, Edwina. Your parents or Felix or whoever. It's screwing you up. Be yourself. Do whatever you want to do in this life. By the way, are you and Felix back together again?'

'No.' Edwina finished the curry on her plate and helped herself to another poppodum. 'One day soon I may have it out with him. But not yet. First, I have to decide what I want. One good thing has happened. I've proved to myself that I don't need a man in my life. And, truly, I don't want a man. I just want Felix.' She paused to collect herself. 'I love him and I don't have to ask anybody if that is all right. Oh, Harriet, I can't get him out of my mind. Is he all right? He's not in trouble or anything, is he?'

'Course not! You will be pleased to hear that he and Greg have wrapped up the case of the thieves who stole the statues at Gorham House. The villains also had a go at The Hoo, you know. Did some damage but didn't get away with anything. I expect they're blue-eyed boys around the station these days. You ought to give Felix a ring. I'm sure he's missing you.'

'I saw him Friday night at the art exhibition. He bought me a glass of wine.'

'And?'

'And nothing. He said he was on duty, which I could see because he was in uniform, and that's about it. Do you really think I put too much store by what other people think?'

Harriet laughed. 'You're doing it again. It doesn't matter what I think. What do you think? It occurs to me that you've left home, but on the other hand you haven't left home. You've got to cut the old umbilical cord.'

'There's nothing wrong with having a family, is there? Lots of people have one.'

'Perhaps. I mean, of course lots of people have families. But yours is positively damaging. I can't imagine how they got to be that way. But you've got to take yourself in hand. I know you don't like the work you're doing. You're great with kids. All the mums are talking about it. Why don't you go in for teaching little ones? You would make a wonderful teacher.'

'To tell you the truth,' said Edwina slowly, 'I don't know what I think about anything. But I do know I don't want to be a teacher. That, naturally, is the career my parents had mapped out for me.'

'So you don't want to do it in order to spite them? Is that it?'

'No. Even if I was the greatest teacher in the world and they wanted me to be an astronaut, I wouldn't want to teach. John Blue knows I'm all wrong for the job. I had hoped to get a post somewhere in the landscape and countryside section, but I don't want it now. I haven't worked out the terms of my contract. I shall be stuck in this job until next August. At least there's still time to think out my future.

'Oh, Harriet, I do envy you. You've got a great husband, two adorable children and a loving mum. You keep talking about how tied I am to my father, but you don't understand. I just keep trying to please him, hoping that one day he'll say, "Well done." I would be happy then. I could let go. Is that so much to ask for?'

CHAPTER ELEVEN

'Edwina, may I see you in my office for a few minutes?' John Blue was standing in the doorway to that office, a muscular man in his forties who knew more about trees than anyone she had ever met, and must have climbed a thousand or more. Edwina respected her boss and liked him for his patience and humour, but his invitation caused in her a deep sense of dread. She would rather get on with her paperwork than submit to the sort of painful interview she knew she was about to endure.

'Of course, John.' She smiled brightly, trotted across the room and took the chair in front of his desk, noticing as she did so that he was carefully closing the glass door.

He sat down facing her, leaning back in his chair and rested his knee against the desk top, a favourite position of his. 'You're not very happy, are you?'

She shook her head, feeling exactly as she used to when called into the headmaster's study.

'Perhaps we could have a little discussion about your future. You always put too much store by this one-year contract, you know. I was a trifle worried when I heard you had gone so far as to buy a house in the district. Of course, there are positions in council work that might interest you, but there won't necessarily be a job here in Bishop. You do understand that, don't you?'

'I do, John, but I have come to the conclusion that I shouldn't work with the public.'

'That,' he said, laughing, 'is a conclusion we have all come to. But let me just go over the sort of work the council does, both statutory and non-statutory. Stop me when something sounds interesting.'

'All right, but—'

'No, for once, just listen for a few minutes. We have already established, I think, that you don't want to issue tree preservation orders because that means visiting properties and dealing with people. For the same reason, implementing the hedgerow regulations and legislation relating to dangerous trees are non-starters for you.'

'That's true,' she said firmly, remembering the Brooms' beech tree.

'We advise and actually have to approve the landscaping of new developments – what they are going to plant. The developers have to present a landscaping scheme and that is always for me to approve.'

'Am I qualified to do that sort of thing?'

'No.' He smiled. 'You're not qualified for very much, my dear. What we are trying to decide is just which direction you're going to go. So keep your mind open. We also operate a countryside management project in the River Colne Valley and we're partners in a project in the Stour Valley. Does that interest you?'

Edwina rubbed her chin. 'I just want to do something important with trees.'

He thought a moment. 'As part of our country-side remit we also do a grant scheme to encourage landowners to plant primarily native stock. We work with the experts from the Forestry Commission.' He raised his eyebrows questioningly.

'I don't know. It's just trees, you see.'

'Yet you don't want to be hands-on, pruning, planting, that sort of thing.'

'It's not . . .' she looked up at him, silently pleading with him to understand. 'It's not saving trees for the world. I mean, it's just one tree at a time. Oh, I can't explain what I feel.'

John Blue sighed. A placid man normally, he was beginning to feel a certain irritation. However, having started, he was determined to get to the bottom of the enigma that was Edwina Fairfax.

'What is it about you and trees?'

'They're the oldest living things on earth and they're strong and beautiful and non-judgemental and—'

'Ah,' said John, smiling. 'And I'm sure, my dear, they would love you every bit as much as you love them, if they were capable of such a thing. But they aren't. I think you have troubles which have nothing to do with trees or your job. You've got to confront your personal problems before you can begin to decide what you want to do when you leave Bishop. It's only October. You don't really have to come to any conclusion before next spring at the earliest. Then you can begin to make plans. So why don't you just carry on with the work I've given you and do it to the best of your ability? Meanwhile, think about . . .' he waved a hand in the air, suggesting helplessness. 'Whatever.'

Leo had fashioned a huge fire. It was damp and rather chilly outside, but seemed to be even colder and damper in the vast drawing room. They had drawn up the settee to within a few feet of the fire, pulled an overstuffed old chair close up on either side and were determined to stick it out for the evening. A portable television on a nearby table gave them access to all the bad news that Leo could possibly wish to know about, and all the soaps that were Cassandra's preferred viewing. Both of them were tired of sitting on hard kitchen chairs in order to take advantage of the Aga's steady warmth during the long evenings.

Cassandra curled up in one of the chairs, a small blanket over her legs. Leo was stretched full out on the settee, the concise crossword from the *Mail* propped up on his chest with the aid of a book. Crosswords had helped him through some of the bad times. Concentrating on a clue drove out more vivid images, giving him momentary peace. Eventually his steady drinking had palsied his hands and fogged his brain, so crossword solving became more difficult. But tonight he seemed able both to concentrate and to write. The fire had been snapping and fizzing for over an hour and the ferocious heat had reddened his cheeks. As *EastEnders* droned on in the background the crossword went out of focus, his hands loosened on the book and pencil and he slept.

He was aware of warmth on his left side and awoke to the exquisite sensation of Cassandra kissing his chin. He half turned, embraced her and kissed her parted lips. She purred like a kitten and snuggled closer. He put his hand on her breast and they lay in companionable silence.

'Love me?' she asked, as she did so often.

'Mm-hmm.' He couldn't bring himself to utter the lie any more, yet she needed constant reassurance.

He took her left arm, exposed the pale skin inside her elbow where needle marks and bruises were unmistakable evidence of her habit. Then he looked at her accusingly.

'I don't do it often, Leo. I'm getting better, I really am. Don't be mad at me.'

He kissed the arm, fairly certain that this was the truth. Checking his finances, he had calculated that she had taken from him about a thousand pounds, and knew that she had bought her supplies in London. Since their few days there she had once gone off in the car, saying that she was to visit a friend. Heroin would have been the object of her visit; he accepted the knowledge. The truth was, her drugged state suited his present plans rather well. But she would be short of money by now, without a source either of cash or of heroin. He was confident that he could control her habit. He knew why she did it.

Much later, he went to bed in his own room, despite her pouting protests. 'Nightmares,' he had explained briefly. She nodded her reluctant understanding, leaving him wishing he had not offered a hostage to fortune by speaking the word aloud.

Half a bottle of Scotch, consumed like water as he sat on the side of his bed, sent him off to sleep in a stupor. And, as night follows day, so the nightmares followed the drinking.

He never, ever, dreamed about his two years' undercover work with football hooligans who followed the England team all over the Continent. They were hard men, dehumanized, craving violence and booze, knowing nothing else. He despised them, then forgot them once they were no longer a part of his work. Those had been exciting times, however, keeping the adrenaline flowing, so he had sought other challenging work to follow.

His choice, which had seemed logical at the time, was a serious mistake. Recurring scenes of his brief time in Child Protection haunted him. In a few months he had seen more horror than in two years pretending to be a hard man of soccer. Children were traumatized by sexual and physical abuse, unable to express their grief, able only occasionally to act out with dolls the appalling things that had happened to them or to draw pitiful pictures of their suffering.

Inevitably his nightmares centred on the terrible day when they were called to an address in a vast housing estate, a small terrace that was even more run-down than its neighbours. They found a weeping mother, all of sixteen, with a bundle in her arms, her boyfriend, much older, wearing an expression halfway between shock and bravado.

Leo and his mates found out soon enough what

had happened as they went inside the house to a chaotic front room, the stench of dirty nappies filling their nostrils. A baby of three or four months was being rocked frantically in its mother's arms. He pulled aside the blanket to expose a little dead face, the left side of the head caved in. In his dream, as in real life, he felt his gorge rise.

'She wouldn't stop crying,' whimpered the mother. 'She's not been well.'

WPC Kramer, a woman in her forties with considerable experience, had her notebook out. 'Is this man the father?'

The young mother shook her head.

'He do it?' asked Kramer, quietly.

The mother clutched her baby fiercely and began to wail.

'Bashed the baby's head against the wall, did he?'

Leo looked where Kramer indicated. Bloodstains. Brains? Could that be brains? He heard a bellow from the boyfriend, a stream of excuses. And then there was nothing.

He became aware that he was sitting in the squad car. Just sitting. Several squad cars now filled the road. Women stood huddled together to watch, trying to take in what had happened. One older woman was telling a young bobby that she had rung the authorities several times. Why hadn't they . . .

But how had he got into the squad car? He had no recollection of walking from the house to the car. Later, in hospital, they told him that blackouts were common in his condition, the mind refusing to take in any more horror.

Kramer had opened the door, her kindly face wearing a deeply worried expression. 'Leo, can you hear me?' He had looked at her dumbly. 'Why did you say that in the lounge? Why did you say, "Dad, you've killed Sis. You beat her to death."?'

Leo always woke up at this point. He never dreamed about the time he spent in hospital, never relived the terrible days in court when, determined to ensure a conviction, he had claimed that the boyfriend had confessed to other acts of violence against the child. But Kramer had been there. She had known he was lying. Afterwards she couldn't meet his eyes. In the witness box, she hadn't contradicted him, merely said under oath that she had not heard what Leo said he had heard.

Had he been completely in his right mind, he would never have done it. He was an experienced cop, twenty years in the force. He knew that convictions were rare in cases of child abuse, knew better than to give the defence lawyer a chance to wiggle his client off the hook, knew that one lie exposed could help the bastard to walk. Yet an emotion more powerful than reason and experience had compelled him to lie. He had to nail the bastard, put him away for ever, make up for keeping silent when his dad had . . .

Leo sat up in bed, turned on the bedside light and reached for the whisky. He had lost everything. His career, Janie, the possibility of a happy retirement. All that was left to him was to do this one thing for the old man, who was his rock, his reason for carrying on, for not topping himself. But in these last months he had lost his bottle.

No stomach for this sort of thing any more. Leo Midnight was a coward.

Sleep eluded Edwina for many hours, but she finally drifted off at about two o'clock in the morning, only to awaken as usual at seven. However, by this time she knew what she wanted to do. She would go to Badger's Wood where she felt so close to her beloved trees and she would see what answer they had for her and what comfort they could offer.

It was Saturday. She always made up a load of washing on Saturday mornings and changed the sheets. These chores could not be put off, so it was half past eight before she had showered and eaten a cooked breakfast, put fresh sheets on the bed and changed the dirty towels for clean ones.

Much of Badger's Wood was designated ancient woodland, its sixty hectares providing a quiet refuge from the busy world on all sides. No severe frosts had yet occurred to sever all the leaves from their branches, but autumn colour had turned the forest a glorious mixture of gold and russet. Some of the paths were narrow with branches of hazel and ash bending over them, the ground carpeted by fallen leaves.

Edwina parked the car and walked quickly down one of the more mysterious-looking paths, one she had not taken before. Here she could think clearly, she was sure. As she walked she noted the oaks, still in full leaf, the sweet chestnuts, also clinging to their leaves, the redwood grove, an oasis of deep green, and of course the brambles, their fruit mostly rotted or taken by the birds.

She breathed deeply, taking strength from the fresh air. Autumn was a dying time which many people found depressing. Until this autumn Edwina had not understood their feelings, but now she knew. Soon the bleak winter would be upon her and she would have no-one to warm her soul, no-one to say 'Went the day well?' Or, 'Carry on! What you propose to do is wise.'

Up ahead was a clearing and two huge logs had been positioned so that visitors could sit down for a rest. She trotted quickly over to one and straddled it, taking her heavy handbag off her shoulder.

Come next spring, would she still be in Gorham, able to visit Badger's Wood? What a beautiful place it must be then. There were, she knew, two hundred species of wild flowers among the trees. What fun it would be to count them, especially if one had a special friend with whom to share the quest. Not someone who thought coppiced trees were just so many shaving brushes, not someone who thought ancient woodland meant that trees were sixteen thousand years old. In spite of herself, she smiled at the memory and her eyes filled with tears.

Her computer had been her companion of late, the Web her social life. She had surfed a few sites, e-mailed for a prospectus or two and had even made contact by phone. There were possibilities, avenues to explore but—

In the distance, she heard a man calling to his dog. The dog barked in reply, high and youthful. They would be upon her in a second and she resented their intrusion. She had sought to escape, yet the human race continued to pursue her. Couldn't a person be left alone to think? Unable to bear the necessity of saying even a quick, impersonal hello to a complete stranger, she stood up, grabbed her handbag by the long strap and bolted for the scrub, crashing through the clawing thorns until she reached the grove of redwoods once more. She stopped, positioned herself behind a tree and tried to catch her breath. Yet how stupid to run away merely to avoid contact with another human being! It was beginning to be a habit with her.

And then her mobile phone rang, trilling absurdly as she huddled behind a tall tree. The sharp-eared dog barked at the unexpected sound and lolloped in her direction. His master called to him as Edwina finally managed to scrabble through the contents of her bag to reach the phone.

'Hello?'

The dog turned out to be a Labrador puppy. It romped up to her, barking madly and whining, begging for a frolic. The owner, a man in his twenties with a bright red sweater and a pleasant open face, came running as he tried to call the dog off.

She put the phone to her ear. 'Hello? What? Oh, my God. Yes, I'll be there.' She switched off the phone. 'Nice dog, but I'm afraid I can't stay to play. There's an emergency.'

She was actually no great distance from the car, having walked in a circle. She climbed into the car, gunned the engine and reached Barleytwist, the home of the Brooms, in under three minutes.

As she turned down the drive, she looked

up into a tall sycamore and saw Junior Hargreaves hanging upside down from his totally inadequate harness. He was clearly unconscious and needed to be lowered to the ground as quickly as possible.

Incredibly, old Mr Hargreaves was nowhere in sight. Could Junior possibly have been climbing alone? Summing up the situation, she assumed he must have cut off a branch which he had intended to allow to freefall. However, the branch had swung back and struck him on the head. But surely he had not been working alone? Junior was now thirty feet above ground and in grave danger.

She drove onto the lawn just inside the gates, directly behind Felix's own car. He was in casual clothes and she wondered how he happened to be first on the scene. He was in the act of pulling off his thick sweater and she realized he intended to try to rescue Junior himself.

'Don't you dare go up there, Felix!' she shouted.

She opened the boot of her car to fetch her climbing equipment, then began running. Mr and Mrs Broom were standing by, looking worried.

'No, Felix!' she called again. 'You can't go up there. You don't know what to do. It will have to be me.'

'You're not strong enough. He's a big man, for God's sake. Besides, you admitted you're not good at climbing. I can't let you do it. Wait for emergency services. Someone who—'

'It has to be me. Can't you see that? I'm the only one who knows what to do and we must get him down as quickly as possible, before he falls out of that harness.' It was not impossible for a healthy girl like herself to rescue a much larger man, but it would be difficult.

She was already clamping the climbing spikes to her legs for a rapid ascent, shrugging into her harness, putting on her hard hat and gathering the ropes she would need.

'Why is he climbing alone? Where is his dad?' she asked Bob Broom.

'He was here but he got a call on his mobile. We're trying to find him,' answered Bob. 'I don't want you to get hurt. Why not wait until he arrives?'

'Do you want a dead man on your lawn? I'll be glad if he gets here in time to act as ground man, but he probably hasn't climbed in years, so I'm still Junior's best hope unless emergency services arrive in the next few seconds.'

She checked her equipment: sharp knife, climbing irons, topping-down strop, a chest strop and three karabiners. She was sure the rope she had with her was long enough.

'Was this tree to come down?'

'No,' said Bob, still aggrieved. 'It's only a sycamore and spoils the view, but you wouldn't give permission.'

Junior, she saw, was not wearing climbing spikes. Her own would damage the tree, but it couldn't be helped. She ran to the tree and climbed it like a monkey.

Felix didn't want to watch, but couldn't bear to look away. Although Junior was thirty feet above the ground, Edwina apparently needed to be even higher. She reached what Felix felt was too fragile a branch to take her weight, secured her rope and began lowering herself to Junior.

She thought she knew what had happened. Being, as she well knew, a poor workman, he had probably been careless with his directional felling cuts.

The chainsaw and a pruning saw were lowered to the ground. He was mumbling incoherently, but his eyes were closed. She pushed him around until he was upright, then fastened a chest strop to her harness and passed the free end over his left shoulder and under his right arm, attaching the other end to her chest with a karabiner.

The hefty branch, ten feet long and a foot thick, was still dangling from its rope and getting in the way. With her knife she cut it free, shouted a warning and sent it thudding to the lawn below.

Glancing over to the driveway, she saw Mr Hargreaves running towards the tree. 'Take the ropes, Mr Hargreaves,' she shouted. 'Felix, get that junk away from the base of the tree.' The two men ran to do as instructed.

A squad car drove onto the grass and PC Ken Crossley, in full uniform, jumped out and began running towards them. An ambulance appeared in the driveway. Edwina felt ready for the descent.

Murmuring words of encouragement to the recovering Junior, she moved him round until she was straddling his body.

'Don't worry, Junior. I'll have you down in a minute. Just hold on. You're not hurt. It's OK.' Junior mumbled something, opened his eyes briefly, but appeared to see nothing.

Having checked his set of ropes and her own,

she put her right hand on the prusik knot of his rope system and her left on her own prusik system and inched them both towards the ground. She had to keep him close in order to ensure their measured descent, without the danger of becoming separated or of their bumping into other branches as they went down.

Half a dozen pairs of hands stretched out to hold them as they reached the ground. Junior recovered sufficiently to say that he was all right but seeing double.

It took a moment or two for all ropes and harnesses to be taken off, and the paramedics were anxious to get Junior settled, while his father was capable of little more than wringing his hands and crying. He had done all that the ground man could do during the emergency, however, and Edwina hadn't the heart to scold him for his sloppy safety precautions. The authorities would perform that task, and probably withdraw Hargreaves's licence to operate a chainsaw commercially to reinforce the message.

A second squad car had turned up as had a fire engine, and there seemed to be dozens of people milling around on the large lawn, but Edwina didn't notice them. She flung her helmet to the ground and herself into Felix's arms. There seemed to be no reason for either of them to say anything. They clung together, hearts beating furiously as they rocked to and fro for several minutes. Perhaps, thought Edwina, loving did mean never having to say you're sorry.

'Afraid I was going to lose you,' he murmured into her hair. 'I can't forgive myself for the way I've acted during these last weeks.'

'There was never a chance of losing me. We practised aerial rescues every month at Capel Manor. Anyway, I love you so much, I just wanted to get down so I could give you a cuddle.'

'You can do that later,' said Bob Broom, laughing. 'Come inside for a cup of tea. I suppose it's too early for something stronger.'

But first she had to make a statement to the police. The owner of the tree also had a few comments for the police. Bob Broom wanted them to understand exactly where the blame lay. 'Old Hargreaves was supposed to stay and help his son. This wouldn't have happened if he hadn't gone off somewhere.' Mr Broom started to walk away, then turned to clear himself of all responsibility for the near tragedy. 'I have planning permission to carry out this work. You know I do, Edwina.'

She nodded, then bent to unstrap the climbing spikes from her legs. 'You know, a tree surgeon is supposed to wear special trousers, ones that stop the chainsaw immediately it touches them so that there's no chance of cutting off one's own leg. Junior wasn't wearing them, nor a helmet. His harness was old and frayed and had probably belonged to his family for years and years. It's not safe to employ the Hargreaves family, Mr Broom. I know this means robbing them of their livelihood, but they must learn. I have never understood this macho thing that makes men turn up their noses at safety regulations.'

Bob smiled sheepishly. 'Man was made to take chances.'

'So was woman, apparently,' said Felix. Now that she was totally free of all her climbing gear he reclaimed her, putting an arm around her waist and pulling her close to his side. 'I had my heart in my mouth. I always thought that was a cliché, but it really did feel as if I couldn't swallow because of this obstruction in my throat.'

Bob nodded. 'Words won't describe what we felt when we saw Junior hanging upside down. I called Felix first of all, because I have his number handy. He said to call 999, so I did. Then I thought of you, Edwina. I found your mobile number, so in the end you all came.'

Much as they were unwilling to be separated, Felix and Edwina had to drive their own cars home. Felix parked his car in his driveway and ran back to Edwina's where he found the door standing open.

'I'm getting changed,' she called, but just then the telephone rang and she emerged from the bedroom with her blouse unbuttoned.

The call was from the local press who wanted the details of her rescue immediately and made an appointment for half an hour later at the Brooms' to take photos. No sooner had she hung up the phone than it rang again. This call was from BBC East. They were sending a film crew and would meet her at her house to discuss what she was going to wear. BBC Essex radio were the last callers. They did a telephone interview live. Fifteen minutes after arriving home, she was still in her old boots and trousers.

'I'm not going to be photographed looking like this,' she cried, and dashed once more for the bedroom. Five minutes later she emerged wearing a short tartan skirt, green woolly tights and an oversized yellow sweater. Felix said she looked delicious.

When the photographers arrived, they were not pleased. She must put on her trousers and boots and all her climbing gear. Felix was also interviewed, but it was Edwina's day, her moment of glory. She was not anxious for publicity, yet she couldn't help thinking that there would be proof of her achievement, newspaper clippings to be posted to her parents. Validation, she hoped, of herself as a useful person.

All the activity and excitement made two healthy people very hungry, so they walked to the Prince of Wales, which they soon regretted. Everyone had heard of the daring rescue and everyone wanted to buy them a drink. Edwina did not feel in need of any kind of stimulant, being high on success.

Felix allowed Fred and Tim to buy him a pint of beer, because he enjoyed seeing them carefully splitting the cost, counting out the coins as if their futures depended on getting the sum right.

In a far corner sat Mr Hargreaves, looking old and defeated. Edwina went to him to ask about Junior.

'He's all right. Got concussion. My fault. I shouldn't have left him. The council's going to be crawling all over me come Monday. Anyway, thank you for getting him down. He could have died.'

'I've got a great idea,' said Felix as they ate their sandwiches. 'Let's go to London for the weekend. I've tried to raise Greg and Harriet, but they're out of town, apparently. Gone to visit his parents in Eastbourne. So let's pack a few things and take off.'

'Where shall we stay? I mean, we haven't booked. Perhaps we should come back here to-night.'

'No way.' He took her free hand and kissed it. 'We'll stay at the Hilton. It's a big place. Surely they'll have a room. Then we'll see if we can get tickets to something we'd both like to see.'

'Or the flicks.'

'Could do. The sky's the limit.'

The train ride from Braintree seemed magical. Edwina had lost all connection with her ordinary life. She would be appearing on television on Monday evening. She had been interviewed and photographed, praised and fêted. Best of all, she and Felix were together once more, and neither of them had needed to make a humiliating apology. She didn't intend to raise the subject of stone statues, villains or Leo Midnight. She would be very careful to keep this weekend break on a joyful, loving level.

Two hours later they had exchanged the leafy friendliness of Gorham for the Park Lane roar. The view from the hotel window was dazzling. Far below their room on the sixteenth floor the trees of London looked wonderful, a random blend of yellows, browns and reds. For once, however, Edwina was able to allow all the trees to grow in peace, neither worrying about them nor criticizing the way they were being managed. If Felix noticed that the t-word was missing from her conversation, he made no comment. Perhaps he was afraid that this would set her off on another harangue. Fortunately, she felt perfectly capable of laughing at herself on this special day.

On Sunday they went sightseeing on a topless double-decker, queued for Madame Tussaud's, then Felix fell asleep in the velvety darkness of the Planetarium. The play they had seen on the previous evening had been all that any theatre-goer could ask for, and they kept referring to it all day Sunday. The weekend was threatening to be perfect, a dangerous state of affairs, Edwina thought. There ought to be just one small thing that went wrong. She did not trust perfection.

Her superstitious dread was borne out late on Sunday evening. They had found an expensive cocktail lounge which rang to a polyglot of accents and languages. Sinking into dark red leather chairs, they ordered two Cokes at three pounds fifty each and tried to look as if they couldn't care less who was sitting next to them or lounging at the bar or posing in the doorway.

'Have you heard about Harriet?' asked Edwina, watching his face for any telltale change of expression. 'Throwing up her course after just one day.'

'Yes, Greg mentioned it. He was certainly pleased.'

Edwina sipped her Coke. 'But don't you think she should have stuck it out? I mean, if at first you don't succeed and all that.'

'I don't see why. Everybody knew it was a mistake. Harriet has no talent with flowers. I brought her a big bunch of flowers once. Can't think why. Anyway, the best she could do was ram too many of them into one vase. Greg felt there was no point in telling her she shouldn't take the course. Well, he did in fact tell her and they had a terrible row.'

'So now she's giving after-dinner speeches.'

Felix laughed. 'So I'm told. You went to hear her. Is she any good?'

'Brilliant,' said Edwina. 'I guess she found her niche, after all this time.'

'Smart woman. I think I'll have a Manhattan cocktail. Would you like to try one? Remember, there may not be too many weekends in London in the near future.'

She shook her head. 'It's all been terribly expensive, but wonderful.'

Felix gave his order to the waiter who was back with the cocktail in a stubby, thick-bottomed glass in no time at all. They sat in silence, watching the show, the passing parade of all nationalities with but one thing in common: they could all afford the prices.

'I recognize the woman in the doorway,' murmured Edwina, leaning towards Felix. 'She's in *The Bill*.'

'Oh, in that case I won't know her. Never watch it.'

Edwina grinned at him. 'Well then, what about the gorgeous woman across the way? I'd love to have a dress like hers.'

'It's hardly there! Definitely not decent. A few dresses like that in Gorham and the crime rate would shoot up. Still, it would lower the boredom factor.'

Edwina looked down at herself. 'I haven't got the cleavage for it, anyway.'

He laughed, turning to look at the woman again. The dress was black, like virtually every other dress being worn that evening, and cut to the waist.

'How does she keep from—'

Edwina giggled. 'Double-sided sticky tape.'

'You're kidding!'

'It's true. I read about it in a magazine.'

Felix stole one more glance at the woman wearing double-sided sticky tape, then turned to smile at her. 'Gorham would never get over it if you turned up in a dress like that at the Prince of Wales. It's bad enough that you play darts so well. You know, I like living where people dress sort of ordinary. London is noisy and dirty and there are too many people on the pavements, too many cars on the roads. These last few days have been wonderful, but I'll be glad to get home again.'

'Cassandra might wear a dress like that.' The moment the words were spoken, Edwina could have kicked herself for mentioning the woman. She held her breath, wondering what Felix's reaction would be.

'She'd wear a dress like that to milk cows,' he laughed. 'My mum always said she had no idea of what was appropriate, what was the right thing to do, wear or say in any situation. By the way, I called her. My mum. When I went home to get packed. She sends her congratulations.'

'That's very kind, but I'm glad all the attention is over. I know that sounds pretentious, but endlessly repeating what happened changes the whole thing, somehow. Was I a heroine every time I practised an aerial rescue at college? Were we all heroes? It was just something I had to do. It didn't take long and I was never in danger. But talking about it has made those few minutes into some sort of epic. I don't like the way I'm beginning to feel about getting Junior down from the tree. And I can't imagine what this is doing to his self-esteem. He comes out of it as a wimp or a villain. He'll never think of himself the same way again, nor will his friends.'

'You're a modest girl. Nevertheless, I'll bet your parents were very proud when they heard.'

She looked away. 'I didn't tell them.'

'Why not?'

'Oh, I don't know. I guess I didn't want the whole thing spoiled. I could hardly tell them without boasting and—'

'And that would be your father's attitude? That you were boasting?'

'He doesn't like boasting.'

Felix snorted. 'Even when your brothers are the ones doing the boasting?'

'Let's not talk about it. I really don't want to—'

'But I do, Edwina. Your family are twisting you out of shape. You need to put some real distance between yourself and them.'

She picked up her Coke and sucked loudly on the straw, getting a mouthful of melted ice. 'That's what I'm doing, isn't it? Putting some distance between myself and them. I'm on the other side of the country. I don't tell them anything about my work. You can't mean you want me to give up my family altogether. How would you like not seeing your family at birthdays and Christmas and—'

She stopped. The Christmas morning of the year she was ten came to mind vividly. She could see the presents under the tree, so many that she couldn't count them all and never thought of trying. But as the morning wore on and tissue paper and ribbon littered the room, she couldn't help noticing that the boys each had a handsome stack of presents beside them. Robert even had a set of car keys for a second-hand car as part of his booty. Her own pile, neatly arranged, was much smaller.

Silently, she counted them, then raised her eyes to find her father watching her closely. 'That,' he said quietly, 'is to be a lesson to you not to be such a whinge during the coming year as you have been this past twelve months. I'm sick of being told that Robert has had this or Thomas has had that.'

Edwina had gasped, her face burning, but mercifully no-one else had heard. Except Grannie who was very frail, sitting in tight-lipped pain, just occasionally making sniping remarks at her daughter. The boys' Christmas had not been spoiled as hers had, and she knew well that she dare not show any disappointment or hurt lest the punishment continue. Looking at the two CDs, the three books and the cardigan that made up her stock of presents from her parents, she had known that they could still be snatched from her, even on Christmas Day.

Every year since, she had silently reckoned the number of presents she received against those of her brothers. Never again had there been such a discrepancy, but the fear would not leave her. Each year she made a special effort to find the perfect present for her father in the hope of seeing his eyes light up with pleasure. Surely he would

371

forgive her many faults if she demonstrated her generosity by giving him something thoughtful and expensive? If so, he had never shown any sign of it.

'My family are not perfect, but they are all I have,' she said.

Felix, distressed, leaned forward to wipe the tears from her cheeks.

CHAPTER TWELVE

On Monday morning they had to leave London at six o'clock to be sure of reaching Gorham in time to change for work, but the journey proved to be very easy and swift. They made it by a quarter to eight and even had time for a proper breakfast, cooked to perfection by Edwina. At least Felix said it was perfect. Edwina ate little and gave only distracted answers to his remarks. Her head was full of plans.

Felix was at the station right on time, so anxious to have a word with Greg that he could hardly bring himself to be civil when his colleagues praised Edwina and himself for the rescue. But Greg was not at the station, having been called out to a house in Homestead where a substantial cache of cocaine had been found by police when searching for stolen goods. Drug trafficking was rarer in Homestead than in many other towns of similar size, but nowhere was completely free of dealers and users, and the users accounted for a disproportionate number of burglaries.

Frustrated, Felix dialled Jim Horrocks, a Homestead-based estate agent.

'No,' said Jim, 'we didn't handle the sale of Gorham House and the word is, the house was never sold. It was inherited by an elderly woman in north London and lent to the people who live there now. All done through Mr Cartwright's solicitor, Jonathan Gray. If you want any information you might try Jonathan.'

Felix knew Jonathan's number, having used the elderly solicitor when buying his house. At one time he had needed to telephone several times a day, a frustrating business.

'Slocumb and Gray,' said a frail voice.

'It's Felix Trent, Jonathan.' Felix knew it must be Jonathan as Slocumb had recently died. 'I need some confidential information. Who inherited Gorham House?'

'Interesting you should ask. I've been wondering about the Midnights. Old Cartwright's niece, Miss Cartwright, inherited. But she's in her eighties and never intended to move in. She didn't even come to visit the old boy when he was alive or to look over the house once he died. I travelled down to London to see her. She's a bit eccentric, but then all the Cartwrights have been eccentric. She wrote to me to say that somebody would be living at Gorham House for a short period, a few weeks is what she said. After that, I'm to put it up for sale. Told me the name of the temporary residents. Not that it's any of my concern, you understand. Still . . . let me see. Where is that damned thing?'

There was a long pause accompanied by the sound of shuffling papers. Felix took a deep breath. He knew there was no point in trying to hurry Jonathan. The old man was easily flustered. Surely he must retire soon!

'I know I've got the letter here somewhere. Should have been filed, but what with Slocumb dying so suddenly . . . Did I tell you she's very eccentric? What say I call you back later? I've got visitors arriving in a few minutes. Their business might take a few hours. Can you wait?'

'Oh yes. Not that much of a hurry.' Felix hoped this was true. He really needed to talk to Greg before going any further. Greg had contacts and would know how to proceed.

A few minutes later a call came in to say there had been an accident between two lorries on the Gorham Road near Homestead High Street. Felix and WPC Bilton were soon on their way.

Edwina went to work as usual on Monday morning and shyly accepted the congratulations of her colleagues, while basking in John Blue's praise. She dealt with all her letters with great speed, spoke gently to telephone callers and cleared her desk by ten o'clock. Then she made two cups of coffee and took them into John's office.

'A word?'

'Yes, indeed, Edwina. I can see your weekend adventures have had a great effect on you.'

She smiled. 'I would like to take a couple of hours off to visit Writtle College. I've got an appointment with the admissions tutor. I'm thinking of taking an honours degree in horticulture. Just thinking, mind you. I want to ask lots of questions when I get there.'

'A letter from me might help.' He pulled out a

piece of stationery and began to write. 'This is a good decision, you know. I'll let you go immediately if they will let you start this autumn. The term starts next week, doesn't it? Believe me, there are plenty of young people who would welcome a short-term contract like yours in order to get some experience.'

'I know. Forgive me, John, for failing to show my appreciation. I really have learned so much.'

'Mostly about yourself, my dear. Here's the letter. I've not sealed the envelope, just put Edward McDonald's name on the front. No jokes about hamburgers, please. He's sick of them. Good luck.'

Writtle College was just two miles from Chelmsford, a pleasant enough drive in the middle of the morning, but it might not be so pleasant in the rush hour. She found it without difficulty and stopped the car just within the gates. The long red brick building stretched out before her at the end of the drive, half covered in ivy and looking like the perfect centre of learning, with flat, well-mown lawns on either side of the driveway enhanced by a selection of ornamental trees.

At the reception desk she gave her name and said she wanted to see Mr McDonald, then sat down on a blue banquette, quivering with excitement. This was it, the sort of place that made her pulse race. Already she knew she would feel at home here, safe from a confusing world, able to get lost in her studies.

Mr McDonald was a little younger than her father and considerably thinner. He led her through several of the red-painted doors to a small interview room where he read John Blue's letter with escalating eyebrows, then looked up to smile at her.

'Three A's at A level? All in science subjects. We require only two. I must say, you have left it very late to sign up for a course, but we can fit you in. Not, unfortunately, in halls. We have four hundred rooms, but they were taken ages ago.'

'That's all right. I have a house in Gorham. I would commute.'

'Fair enough. It's an honours degree in horticulture that you want, with a view to doing further research, perhaps even to getting a PhD? From what John says in his letter, we will be lucky to have you.'

'He did? Good heavens! I think he's just anxious to get rid of me. I want an opportunity to get my teeth into something really challenging. I'm not cut out for dealing with the public. The happiest time of my life was the year I spent at Capel Manor. Oh, I know that Capel is further education and Writtle is higher education, but the atmosphere is similar. This is where I belong, I'm sure of it.'

Mr McDonald said there was time enough for her to decide what she wanted to specialize in, but there were a wealth of opportunities. The college, he said, had connections with a university in Kenya and there was an exchange of students. Some research was in progress about underplanting of rubber tree plantations in Sri Lanka. Or she might consider biomass production for fuel. The opportunities were endless and could lead to jobs all over the world.

Feeling particularly drawn to this young

woman who so clearly was eager to learn, he suggested a walk around the grounds, all two hundred-odd hectares of them. She saw more handsome buildings than she could count, all built since the 1940s, and here and there modest gardens where students could gather. Student facilities were very good.

She drove home as if travelling on a cloud. She knew how fortunate she was to be signing up for her degree course at the very last moment, and put this down to John Blue's influence.

Greg returned to the station, having been made aware that there had been an accident on the Gorham Road, since traffic was backed up all the way down the High Street. 'Where's our hero?' he asked of no-one in particular. 'As I've heard about nothing else but the daring rescue over the weekend, I'd like to see the man himself. Couldn't reach him on the phone.'

'He and Edwina are going to be on BBC *Look East* tonight,' said the inspector, coming up to Greg's desk. 'Felix couldn't wait to tell us this morning. He's very proud of that girl of his. It was a job well done. Everything went smoothly on our side, too. The Health and Safety people will be crawling all over Hargreaves. About time, too.'

They could hear the duty officer taking particulars of the couple who had been arrested for possessing cocaine. PC Jones's deep voice was a sort of counterpoint to the agitated, high-pitched swearing of the couple.

The inspector went back to his office and a minute later Felix's phone rang. Greg picked it up. 'Squiller here. Oh, hello, Jonathan. Felix is out. Can I take a message? Who? Let me get a piece of paper. Gorham House was lent to a Mr Dickenson for a few weeks, you say? Thank you, I'll tell him.'

Greg was puzzled, but it was time to question the young couple about their half a kilo of cocaine, and there was a stack of forms that needed filling out. He had no time to consider this random piece of information. Vowing to discuss it with Felix as soon as he could, he walked to the interview room.

Edwina had always known that she must never call either of her parents at work. But it was the lunch hour and she felt she couldn't wait. Her heart was singing, all was right with the world and she had to tell the family.

'Hello?' said an angry, breathless voice.

'Hello, Dad, it's me, Edwina.'

'I've had to run all the way down the hall. Heard the phone ringing. Thought it might be important. You, of all people, should know that I don't like to receive personal calls at work.'

'I'm sorry. It's just that everything is so chaotic. I rescued an unconscious man from a tree, but that isn't why I called. I'm leaving my job immediately. It doesn't suit me. I'm going to—'

'Have you gone stark raving mad? Fairfaxes are not quitters.'

'Dad, it was just a one-year fixed contract, after all, and—'

'I told you to get a degree, but no, you never listen to your father.'

'But that's just it,' she said, grateful for a way

into the subject. 'I've signed up to do a degree course in horticulture at Writtle Agricultural College here in Essex.'

'I hope you've learned a lesson from all this. Had to take a practical course, didn't you? You could have studied trees in the first place. Fairfaxes have *brains* and know how to use them. Still, you've learned how to use a chainsaw, so all is not lost. Now you can cut down the trees to count the rings, or whatever.' He paused and she couldn't think of anything to say to fill the gap. She knew he was calculating. 'Now I get it!' He exploded. 'You've called me to ask for money, haven't you?'

'I'll pay you back Dad.'

'On your salary? Don't make me laugh. I'm very sorry, Edwina, but I cannot in all conscience give you any more money. I funded your brothers when they wanted to get degrees. They did well, which was all I asked of them. But you would never take my advice. You chose to defy me. Now that you are in a pickle, a failure at your job and unwanted, you expect me to pick up the pieces. Well, I won't. You are a silly little girl and must find your own way out of the mess you've got into. I am very disappointed in you.'

'Dad . . . Daddy, please don't be angry with me. I don't want to disappoint you. I want you to be proud of me.'

'A funny way you've chosen to go about it. Why didn't you ask our advice? We would have told you what to do.'

'I'm a grown woman, Daddy.'

'You're old enough to vote, which is hardly the same thing. I'm going to hang up now and give you time to reflect. The best thing for you to do now is to come home. We'll let you live here rent free and then we can work out a plan of action. Do you hear me?'

'Yes, Daddy, goodbye. Give my love to everybody.' She could scarcely speak for crying.

Edwina poured herself a glass of wine and, remembering that she had not eaten lunch, cut a piece of Cheddar, pulled the biscuit tin from a kitchen cabinet and sat down to review the conversation with her father. Nothing had changed since she was thirteen and first began to believe that she could think for herself. Since that time, she had struggled against her parents' contempt. She thought she had broken free at last, but knew that she would always be their wayward daughter, no matter how hard she tried to please them. Remembering Harriet's words that she was too worried about what others thought of her, she, nevertheless, wondered if everyone would think she was ill advised to take a degree in horticulture.

Stupid she might be, but she would never be so foolish as to return home to sleep in her old room. She knew that if she were to do such a thing she would die an old maid, looking after her parents during her procreating years, then shrivelling away when there was no-one left to bully her.

The phone rang and Edwina, filled with dread, ran from the kitchen to answer it.

'Edwina, this is Robert! I want a word with you!'

'Hello, Robert. What a surprise to hear from you.' She pulled the phone round so that she could sit on the settee while talking to her brother. This was not going to be pleasant. 'Have you been speaking to Dad?'

'I have and I must say you've got a damned cheek. You used your wheedling ways on Grandma Hopkins until she changed her will and left you seventy thousand pounds. Poor Mum, her only child, got only seven thousand. Then you have the gall to—'

'Grannie told me she never intended to leave anything to Mum. It was all to go to the RSPCA. She didn't change her will at the last minute. It was made out to me when I was ten, just after she spent Christmas with us. Are you saying that I knew enough to persuade her at ten years of age? Mum and Grannie didn't get along, Robert, as you know perfectly well. We could never leave her and Mum alone together for more than ten minutes.'

'Then you have the gall to ring up my father and beg for money. You want to go to college? Spend your own goddamned money.'

'Mum said she didn't expect or want Grannie's money, although I grant she might not have meant it. Anyway, Grandpa Fairfax left you boys very well off.'

'That's different,' said Robert. 'It's customary to leave money to the men in a family.'

Edwina took a deep breath. 'You are quite right as usual, Robert. I will use my own money. Thank you for reminding me that I must not look to my family for support of any kind. Goodbye.'

She hung up on his spluttering reply, then lifted the phone to call Felix's mobile. 'Felix, where are you? Are you alone?'

'Yes, on the Hedingham Road. Is something wrong?'

'I need to speak to you, dear. Meet me at the entrance to Badger's Wood. It won't take me any time at all to get there. I'm leaving now.'

Five minutes later she saw that he had driven well into the visitors' parking area so that the brightly painted squad car was partially hidden. She pulled up beside him and scrambled from the car. He was standing by the picnic table. It needed just half a dozen paces and she was in his arms.

'What is it? You look distraught.'

She clung to him for a moment, gathering her thoughts, considering how she was going to explain. 'I'm not into casual affairs, Felix. I love you and will till the day I die. I will always be there for you, but I need to know how much you love me. I need to know what sort of commitment you're prepared to make. Because I have broken away from my family permanently. My brother is due to get married in January, but I won't be there. I won't be gossiping with my cousins or giving their children a cuddle. I am without family, a kind of orphan, and it's scary. But it had to be done if we were ever to make a go of things. That's how much I love you.'

He drew in his breath sharply, not knowing what he was expected to say. 'I could not ask you to do such a thing. I'll get along with them. I'll be polite. Don't break off . . . I mean, there is nothing I could do to equal such a sacrifice, but, believe me, I do love you.'

She moved away, went to sit on the picnic table, her feet muddying the bench. 'I have left my job at the council. I'm to start a degree course in horticulture at Writtle in a few days' time. I was very fortunate to be able to fix it up at such short notice. But, Felix, dear, I will need money, so I'm going to sell my house. My grandmother left me seventy thousand pounds, which is more than enough, of course. I could find a room close to the college, but I don't know if I could face the loneliness. I want to move in with you.'

'Is that all?' He came to sit next to her. 'Such a small thing to ask, no sacrifice for me. I was about to ask you to move in. I really was. It's what I want most of all, but don't rush into anything. Is this what you want to do? This degree course?'

'Yes, it truly is and I'll probably go on to do a PhD. I won't be earning anything for years and years. But I'll pay my share of expenses, I promise you.'

He smiled and as he did so, he felt a little light-headed. She would be all his, a woman learning to be herself without the distortions that her family had forced on her character. He felt it was right that she should put as much emotional distance as possible between herself and them.

Yet he couldn't encourage her to make a complete break. The thought of never seeing his own mother and sister made him shudder. No, it was too drastic. Many people settled for having difficult families, seeing them only occasionally and trying not to brood on the latest emotional wound in between times. Most people who had a choice chose to maintain contact. Even the notorious Fred West had kept control over his children, because they desperately needed a father, and he and their wicked mother were all the family they had.

'It will be a privilege to have you in my house, Edwina. And you can share my family. As soon as we can, we'll go down to Devon and I'll introduce you. And when you move in I think we could do with your furniture instead of mine, don't you? Or maybe buy some new stuff.'

She laughed, happy to change the subject, to back off from the intensity of the past few moments. 'I'm a pretty good cook and the house has great potential. Wait until you see what I can do.'

'And when we get fed up with our little bungalow, we'll just go to London for the weekend.'

She squeezed his hand. 'It will be wonderful. I'll be studying a lot, of course. I won't be under your feet all the time. When you want a night out with your mates—'

'Forget about my nights out. Just one thing is wrong with all this, Miss Fairfax. Having you will be no sacrifice at all. I'm the one who will have everything to gain. But much as I can see the argument in favour of it, I can't let you cut yourself off from your family for ever. Don't do it.'

She sighed. 'I've tried for years to be a valued part of the family, but they bring out the worst in me. I do the most stupid things when I'm around them and I don't know why. I actually rang my father to ask him to support me while I get my degree. My brother soon rang back to say I should spend my own money. Why didn't I think of that? Why was my first thought to put myself in my father's debt? Stupid! I'll always be in the wrong.'

'Just as a matter of interest, why did you ask your father to support you when you have so much of your own?'

'I've thought about it. I guess I wanted him to say "Oh, my dear daughter, you are so wonderful, let me do this small thing for you." Something like that. When I'm around the family I do the stupidest, most childish, thoughtless things. No, it's got to be a clean break, because they . . . because I . . . oh, Felix, it's just that when I'm with you, I'm as good and sensible as I am capable of being. You show me what I can be. So it's got to be you, if you'll have me.'

For an answer, he took her in his arms and kissed her, until the radio on his shoulder squawked a message requesting his presence at the station. He broke off to reply solemnly that he was on his way, barely able to complete the sentence without laughing, because Edwina was dancing around the picnic table.

Leo looked at Cassandra coldly, trying to separate what had to be done from his lust and the growing pity that he had been unable to stifle.

At about ten o'clock this morning she had gone up to her room, staying for half an hour. He supposed she had mainlined then, the needle driving the heroin deep into a vein. This was the way true addicts chose to take their heroin. Cassandra would want to imitate the bad guys. Yet she had not been injecting for long, he calculated. She still got the brief, ecstatic rush that the addicted users no longer enjoyed. After that,

386

there seemed to be a period of a few hours when she was drowsy but happy. Also, and crucially for his purposes, she was at this time usually hardly more than semi-conscious and unable to concentrate for long.

He looked around the small room, the one Kitty Hebard had called the morning room. Everything was in place. He had built a fire which had soon made the room very warm indeed, sleep-inspiringly warm. He had drawn up two easy chairs, closed the curtains, sent Queenie home an hour early. He looked at his watch, went into the kitchen where Cassandra was sitting in a rocker staring at the old cream-glazed Aga and humming a tune.

'Let's go into the little room. I've built a fire. That chair isn't comfortable, darling. It hasn't got much padding, and neither have you.' He pulled her to a standing position, looked into her eyes, saw the constriction of her pupils, noticed how slowly she drew each breath. Barely functioning. Happy and relaxed. It was now or never, poor bitch.

Greg and Felix met at the station. Greg wasted no time in giving Felix the news that had come in during the younger man's absence.

'The house was rented to a man named Dickenson. Ring any bells?'

'Dixie Dickenson,' said Felix. 'The retired chap from Scotland Yard. Came in here bellowing about leaving Leo alone. That's probably the man. But I don't understand. It's interesting, but it solves nothing.'

'I know.' Greg sat on the edge of Felix's desk.

'But anyway, I rang a mate in London last Friday. He is supposed to ring me back about now. I wanted you to be here so that we can act straight away if necessary.'

Felix went off to get a couple of cups of coffee and when he returned found Greg on the phone. He was writing furiously and making distracted grunting sounds as he wrote.

Greg hung up, looking disturbed rather than triumphant. Perhaps, thought Felix, there was no useful news.

'First off, Dixie Dickenson had a son named Carl. The kid was the apple of his dad's eye, apparently. Of course the old man wanted Carl to be a policeman, follow in dad's footsteps. But Carl couldn't settle to anything. Had half a dozen different jobs and as many live-in lovers after leaving school. Then he meets up with this floozy and she well and truly leads him astray, plus she didn't want anything to do with him becoming a cop. Seems Carl was pretty smitten at first, then he begins to cool. Tells his old man he's going to dump her. Next thing dad knows, the two of them have gone scuba diving, although she's hardly the athletic type, and Carl never comes back. Old Papa Dickenson goes around saying if it hadn't been for – wait for it, Felix – if it hadn't been for Cassandra, Carl would still be alive.'

'So where does Leo come into this? Did Dickenson hire him to pop off Cassandra, do you think?'

Greg grinned. 'Better than that. Leo is Dickenson's adopted son, much older than Carl. He's the son who did what Dickenson wanted. Went into the force.'

'Nevertheless, he's going to kill her, Greg! We've got to get out there.'

Greg shook his head. 'He would have done it by now.'

'No! He needs to find a way that will look natural. Maybe he got her hooked on drugs. I'm sure he plans for her to die of an overdose. She's cottoned on to who he is and she's afraid for her life, so she calls us, pretending he's beaten her up and—'

'Don't run away with all this. I appreciate she meant something to you once and you're anxious to do something to protect her, but—'

'Hold on,' said Felix, smiling broadly. 'She means nothing to me. Edwina and I have patched things up. She is going to move in with me. I don't give a damn about Cassandra, but we can't let him murder her.'

Greg patted him on the shoulder. 'You're getting pretty smart in your old age. Edwina's just the girl for you. Congratulations. Now let's go and have a talk with Mr Midnight.'

'Here we are,' said Leo, speaking softly. 'Sit down here in this old chair. It's funny and rather depressing that everything in this house is brown. And damp, too. But the chairs ought to be reasonably dry after half a day in a warm room. Are you comfortable? Put your head on the back of the chair. Mind if I turn on this lamp? No, don't turn away. I want to look at you.'

'Do you, Leo? Am I pretty?'

'No, not pretty. Beautiful. I always said you're the most beautiful woman in the world.' He paused to let her think about how beautiful he found her. 'Do you think of Carl often?'

'All the time. I didn't used to. Just since you and me, you know what I mean. I can't get him out of my mind, because of you and me.'

'Well, that's a fine thing,' he said gently. 'Here I've tried to make you forget him and love me. Now you tell me you can't stop thinking about him. Clearly, there's no hope for me. What happened the day he died?' Her eyes were closed and she made no answer. 'Cassandra! What happened the day he died?'

'He was going to leave me.'

'He told you he was going to leave you? What did you do?'

She seemed to be in a deep sleep, and he was just wondering how to proceed when she spoke. 'Hit him with an empty oxygen canister.'

'No, he drowned. Carl drowned, didn't he? It was an accident.'

'I strapped the canister on his back and pushed him over. Took the boat back to shore and told them he'd drowned.'

'As simple as that.'

'I loved him. But everybody leaves me, Leo. All my life. Everybody. I can't have that. Got to fight back.' She had opened her eyes to speak these words, but now closed them again. Damning as her words had been, Leo needed more. He waited.

She put the knuckle of her first finger in her mouth and sucked it. 'I thought they'd know right away. But his body got stuck, trapped somehow, and didn't come ashore for ten days. Nobody said anything to me, like I done it,

390

except old man Dickenson. He thought I'd topped Carl, but nobody paid any attention to the grieving father.' She giggled weakly as tears studded her lashes.

Leo sighed. He had done it, got the confession his old man was sure would be forthcoming, eventually. In a mad moment, Cassandra had bashed Carl on the head. By the time the body floated ashore, it was so badly decomposed and eaten that there was no evidence of foul play. Nobody believed it possible, anyway, not even Leo.

For one mad moment he felt intense pity for her, and at the same time self-disgust. He had played on her need for love, her trusting need, had even slept with her, deceived her completely in order to get her confession. Perhaps he could wipe the tape he was making and tell the old man she hadn't—

He had a sudden unwelcome memory of Carl on the day they had met. A golden-haired boy of five with a lisp who had openly worshipped Leo from the start. The kid never showed the slightest sign of jealousy. Here was this big rough man-sized boy moving in to share Carl's home, intent on taking some of the love that his parents had to give.

Yet Carl had been delighted to share, glad to have a brother, no matter how different that brother might be from himself. A surly older brother who would occasionally deign to kick around a ball, who laughed at his attempts at cricket, who monopolized his toys, yet sneered at his good school grades.

By the time Carl was old enough to join the

force, Leo had beaten him to it and was building quite a reputation with his undercover work. Carl had shied off from competing. He had drifted from one job to another. He had sold everything from vacuum cleaners to double glazing to fund his love of sailing. Until Leo had his breakdown. Then, to maintain the family tradition, he had said he would become a policeman. And he would have been good at it, too. Carl had been six feet tall and well muscled . . .

Leo looked over at the sleeping Cassandra. So innocent. So frail. She couldn't possibly have killed Carl in the middle of a row. There was no spur of the moment reaching for a weapon to strike a blow in temper that accidentally killed him. She would have had to sneak up on him, maybe even as he dozed in the sun. Carl would have had no chance to defend himself. And God alone knew how this little woman must have struggled to get the empty canister strapped onto the dead man before pushing him over the side. Determination, not the strength born of panic, had enabled her to complete her task.

Cassandra stirred and opened her eyes. 'It was wrong to kill him, but I can't bring him back and I can't stop thinking about it, Leo. Help me to stop thinking about it.'

'Yeah,' said Leo, unable to think of a sensible, truthful reply.

'And I killed old mother Berkeley, too, but I don't care about that. Anyway I was just a kid, didn't know what I was doing.'

'Who?' His voice was harsh and too loud. He didn't want to startle her. As an ex-cop he knew that people would sometimes make a surprise confession when under no immediate pressure to do so. Sometimes the burden of the secret became just too much to bear.

'I was fourteen. She found out I'd been stealing from her. Said she was going to send me back to the home. People are always leaving me, Leo. It's not fair. All I want is someone to love me. Promise me you won't leave me.'

Fourteen? She had killed before she met Felix. He was lucky to be alive. 'Where did all this happen?'

'Colchester station. Rush hour. The platform was packed. I followed her, came up behind her just as the train was coming in.'

He was finding it hard to breathe. 'And nobody twigged?'

'She didn't scream or nothing. Just fell. I never said I was with her. I was waiting at her house when they came to tell me she had committed suicide. Suicide! I got away with it.'

'That was long before Carl?'

Tears rolled down her cheeks. 'Yeah.'

She had endured a hellish life, probably worse than she had indicated. Yet many had suffered worse and never even considered killing anyone. Her rotten childhood explained her actions. But no-one could condone them.

'Cassandra, are you tired?'

'Yeah, better go up and lie down.' She opened her eyes and struggled to get out of the deep chair. Leo stood up easily and helped her to stand, kissed her cheek because she asked him to, put her head on his shoulder. She looked up at him and smiled drowsily. 'I'm glad I told you. Maybe I can forget now. Get some peace at last.'

'Can you make it upstairs on your own?'

'No trouble. I'll sleep for a couple of hours. Don't wake me up. I'm really tired.'

She went up the stairs readily enough while he stood below, making sure she was out of earshot before picking up the phone in the kitchen.

'Dad? She did it, but a drugged confession won't put her behind bars. She also killed one of her foster mothers, too. Pushed her under a train at Colchester station when she was fourteen.' He paused, listening to the old man as he broke down and sobbed, feeling his heart break for the suffering of his grieving father, wondering if the old man would cry for him if he . . .'Why don't you drive out here and we'll decide what to do. I filmed it all with a camcorder.'

Leo went back to the morning room and played the confession to make sure the camera had worked. He didn't listen to it all the way through, because it was too painful. But the confession was there. No-one could dispute it.

Greg was about to put on his raincoat against the cold autumn wind and a fine driving rain, was ready to leave the station when a call came through that there had been an armed robbery in the village store in Banwell, a small place west of Homestead.

'I'll have to go,' he said to Felix. 'Wait until I come back. Don't confront Leo on your own.'

Together with several of the Homestead force, he ran from the station. Felix watched him from the window, waiting until the two squad cars were out of sight. He was already wearing his waterproof, needing only to pick up his hat and walk out before the inspector saw him. He didn't need Greg. There was business to be settled between himself and Leo.

Leo opened the door and looked at Felix with surprise. 'Hello, did Dixie phone you? My dad?'

Felix pushed past the older man and looked around the hall. 'Why should he have called? Where's Cassandra?'

'Upstairs, resting. What's up with you, Felix?'

'Have you harmed her? Is she alive?'

Leo's face darkened. 'No, I have not harmed her and yes, she is alive. Do you mind telling me what has suddenly got into you? You look like a madman.'

'I have reason to believe that you intend to do away with Cassandra.'

For the first time that day, Leo laughed. 'No, you have no reason to believe that I intend to top Cassandra. Take a deep breath, kid, and start again. What do you think you know?'

Felix headed for the stairs. 'I want to see her for myself.'

'You bloody idiot! Have you no sense? Why would I attempt to kill her today, since I haven't laid a finger on her all these weeks?'

Felix raced up the stairs, taking them two at a time. Leo was close behind. On the landing, Felix was forced to stop and Leo cannoned into him. 'Which room?'

Leo pointed down the hall. 'This way. You're going to give her a fright. Try not to be too much of an eager beaver. OK?'

Felix strode down the hall, opened the door of the room Leo had indicated. At first he thought she was just peacefully asleep. Then his eyes took in the syringe, the rubber tubing, the small empty packets. He hurried to her side, picked up one limp arm and felt her pulse. It was weak and slow. Patting her cheeks and calling her name failed to bring a reaction.

'You've done this!' he cried.

'I didn't, I swear it. But if you ever loved her, let her die now. She killed Carl Dickenson and, before that, one of her foster mothers. Pushed her off Colchester platform in front of a train. Two years before she met you.'

'That's your story.'

'Felix, I filmed her confession! Believe me. Let her go. What has she got to look forward to? Even if she's found not fit to plead, which I doubt, they'll bang her up for ever. She can't face the world without drugs because of what she's done. It's been preying on her mind and she wants peace.'

Felix stood up, shaking with rage. 'I'm not judge and jury and I'm not a murderer.' He rang 999, then placed a call to the surgery and told them that Cassandra had taken an overdose of heroin. Was there a doctor close by who could come? He turned to Leo. 'A filmed confession? I'll bet she didn't know you were taping it. You'll need more proof than that. No, my guess is, if she lives, she'll walk free to do it again.'

Leo shrugged. 'You're a good cop, but there are some things— If my dad gets going on her case, he'll find the evidence. Somebody's here. That was quick. I'll open the door downstairs and leave it open.'

He left the room and Felix looked out the

window in time to see one of the doctors from the surgery, Dr Flawn, heading towards the front door, then he turned back to Cassandra, for once entirely sure that he was doing the right thing.

Leo brought the doctor upstairs. 'Wouldn't you know it,' he said to Felix when they entered the bedroom. 'The doctor has arrived quicker than I would have guessed possible. The poor bitch may live.'

Dr Flawn looked at Leo in surprise, then turned to his patient. 'You're sure it's only heroin, I presume.'

'Yes.'

'Is she physically addicted?'

'I don't think so. That is, I haven't the slightest idea what that means. I don't think she's been taking it for long, if that's what you mean.'

The doctor turned to his case, began removing things. A heroin overdose suppresses breathing and heart rate. He needed to act quickly. 'Get a container of some sort. She may vomit.'

Leo hurried from the room, but was back within a minute with a large flowered basin from the adjacent bedroom. Meanwhile the doctor had injected Cassandra with Naloxone. The basin arrived in time for her to be sick. She opened her eyes.

'Leo?'

'Here.'

'I wanted to die. It's no good. I can't . . .' Her eyes closed.

'You'll be leaving Gorham House,' Felix said as they heard footsteps on the stairs.

'Yes. Not my sort of place, really. I'll go home

and stay with my dad for a while. He's going to need me.'

The paramedics arrived in the room. They and the doctor worked quickly to place a tube down Cassandra's throat and attach an IV drip to her arm before they stretchered her away, saying they would take her to Colchester.

'Will she live?' asked Felix when the paramedics had left.

The doctor looked at the two men and shook his head. 'Naloxone lasts for only half an hour, while the heroin will continue to affect her for six to eight hours. They can inject her again, but I really can't say how she'll do.'

Flawn closed his bag and left the bedroom as two of Felix's colleagues arrived. They said they wanted a statement from Leo. Would he like to come down to the station to make it?

'I will come once my dad has arrived. He's on his way. He's a retired police officer and I'm ex-Met. I think you can trust us to keep our word.'

'Where's this confession you were talking about?' asked Felix.

Leo had no intention of turning over this vital recording until after the old man had heard it. He owed Dixie that. 'What confession? I don't know of any confession. Perhaps my dad will know when he comes.' He smiled sadly. 'Give me an hour or two on my own, for God's sake. It's been a terrible day, maybe the worst. I've had a few bad ones, so I'm not quite sure.'

As Felix turned to go, Leo placed a hand on his shoulder. 'Good work. You'll not fail as I have.' Suddenly embarrassed, Felix's two colleagues left the room and could be heard clumping down the stairs.

'You're too hard on yourself, Leo. We're only human, after all.'

'No we're not! We're cops. Civilians are only human. We've got to be something more. The public expect us to be able to stand up to anything, and we expect it of ourselves. Who wants to be defended from the bad guys by a bunch of wimps? We've got to be strong, and I'm not. But you'll do.'

Felix left, feeling that Leo would have done better had he demanded less of himself. But he would be wasting his time in trying to make this tortured man take an optimistic view of life.

Leo went through Cassandra's drawers, gathering up three pretty nightgowns and a couple of very expensive dressing gowns. She'd need slippers. If she lived, she'd want some make-up. He gathered it all and stuffed it into a piece of Louis Vuitton luggage. He would have it sent to the hospital, having no intention of visiting her there. Whatever the future held for her, she didn't need to look upon her betrayer.

Finally he went downstairs to the morning room and lowered himself like an old man into the chair. He thought he knew now how most ordinary people found themselves in the dock. Just the way he now found himself in such a painful predicament. The old man had asked him for a favour. 'Yeah,' he had said. 'OK, but I'm pretty sure she didn't do it.' And, little by little, he had perpetrated greater deceptions until he had made her fall in love with the instrument of her downfall. He hadn't meant to be so cruel, yet here he was, triumphant as she lay dying.

During Carl's lifetime, he had never met the siren who was apparently leading him astray. After the lad drowned, he had set about meeting her, wooing her, sucking her into his lair, setting the trap that would destroy her. He had been clever, no holds barred, determined to redeem himself in the old man's eyes.

It was a nasty business, deceiving a pretty young thing so completely. He hated having to do it. Yet now that she was out of the house and her perfume was no longer strong in every room he entered, he could see that someone had to be prepared to act ruthlessly. He had done it! Trapped a double murderer. He laid his head against the back of the chair and smiled. He thought he could manage in future without the whisky. That would be a start in the right direction. And to make up for destroying a young life, he might just do something positive for a change. The doorbell rang and he leapt from his chair.

CHAPTER THIRTEEN

On returning to her home, Edwina decided to telephone the estate agent. The sooner she put the house up for sale, the better. The agent agreed. He arrived at her home ten minutes after she spoke to him. There followed an irritating period while he took measurements, asked her innumerable questions, reminded her of the regulations surrounding the sale of a house, and pointed out that although all this had been explained to her as recently as late July, it all had to be said again.

She was impatient and found it difficult not to show her irritation. A cup of coffee for the two of them gave her something to do. He finally finished indoors and was busy hammering a For Sale sign into the lawn when her phone rang.

'Edwina? This is your father calling. We've been making enquiries here. You could go to Pershore. Your brother has contacts there and can keep an eye on you and introduce you to some intelligent people. I've managed to pull a few strings and—'

'Dad! I told you I've registered at Writtle!'

'And I've told you that you can't afford it.'

'As Robert has suggested, and as I should have figured out for myself, I am comfortably off and don't need any money from you. I am going to sell my house and use Grannie's money to fund my degree.'

'And live in digs for three years? No, I think—'

'I'm moving in with Felix.'

'The policeman?'

'Yes, the policeman.'

She heard him snort derisively. 'But he is not, of course, going to marry you.'

'Well, not—'

'It's as I feared. You can only define yourself in terms of a boyfriend. He's nothing more than a token to prove that you're attractive. Can't you see that? You don't know about love, and I'm willing to bet he knows even less.'

'Dad, please. You don't know him.'

'And when your policeman lets you down, where will you run to? Tell me that.'

Edwina took a deep breath. 'Not to my loving family. I've been meaning to call you. Where I go and what I do is no longer any concern of yours. I'm not coming home for Christmas, or ever. All my life you've belittled me. I might have been driven mad if it weren't for Grannie's belief in me. She saw what you were doing. I heard the row you had on Christmas Day when I was ten. As you pointed out the last time we spoke, I am old enough to vote and I vote to live with Felix. He loves me wholeheartedly, and because of that simple fact I am able to do sensible things and to make something of myself. He won't destroy me. I could never please you and I'm no longer going to try. Goodbye, Dad.'

She hung up the phone and flung herself onto the settee as the sound of hammering continued out of doors. It was done. The break was total as she had promised Felix it would be. It felt a bit scary, but not so bad as she had imagined. There were not enough happy memories to dwell on, so the sense of freedom was more powerful than the sense of loss. She thought for a moment about her dear grandmother who had known she was dying all those years ago and had made plans to protect her only granddaughter.

Edwina still couldn't understand what she had ever done while growing up to bring such contempt upon herself, but that was no longer important. Self-pity must be consigned to the past. Her future lay with Felix in East Anglia, where she had friends and even, she dared to think, a few people who admired her. The knowledge made her feel strong, and the feeling of strength left her with no option but to attempt to slay one more dragon.

Standing up from the settee, she waved good-bye to the estate agent through the picture window, picked up her short navy coat and the heavy bag which was her constant companion and left the house.

It was no distance at all to Gorham House, but driving there represented something very important. The old man at the lodge tried to stop her, but she simply waved to him and drove past, parking her car finally by the steps to the front door.

The sound of the bell was still echoing within when the door was flung open. 'Dad!' cried Leo. Then he saw who was standing on the step and his face fell. 'Oh, it's you.'

'I'd like to have a word with you, Mr Midnight.'

'It's a bad time.' When she showed no sign of moving, he ran a hand through his hair and sighed deeply. 'Look, Cassandra has taken an overdose of heroin. No-one can say if she'll live.'

'Oh, God! I gave her the money to do it! I gave her two hundred pounds.'

'Enough for a few hits, but—'

Edwina took a step back. 'Did she want to get away from you that much? Were you so awful to her that she would rather be dead?'

He gave her a sour smile, shoving his hands into his pockets. 'It's herself she was trying to get away from. I'm not a villain, Edwina. I used to be with the Met and—'

'The Metropolitan Police? You were a policeman? Does Felix know?'

'Yes, you funny person, he does. Cassandra killed my adoptive brother. She confessed to me today, which is what I have been trying to get from her all these weeks. What's more, two years before she met Felix, she killed one of her many foster mothers. Felix was lucky to get away with a few false accusations.'

'Oh, I . . .' She rubbed her forehead. When she was driving to Gorham House, everything had seemed to be so simple.

'So you see,' he continued, 'this is no day to be talking about trees. I'll be leaving here as soon as my dad arrives, anyway.'

'Yes, I can see it is the wrong time. But you'll be gone tomorrow, so I've no choice but to settle my business now.'

He marvelled at her single-mindedness. He had just told her an horrific story about a woman who was at death's door, a tale of murder and deception. But the kid could think only of trees. Yet he could see she was wound up. Her 'business' was important to her. 'Oh, what the hell! Just let me get my mobile in case the hospital calls.'

He was gone no more than thirty seconds. When he returned she stepped up to him warily, as if she were entering a lion's den, took him by the upper arm and gently led him down the two stone steps, as one might with a frail old man. She heard his soft chuckle and played up to his amusement.

'You don't know how wicked I've been, Mr Midnight.'

'You don't know what wickedness is.'

'I know about trespass, however. I trespassed on your land.' She stopped and pointed to the huge conifer on his front lawn. 'This, sir, is a wellingtonia. Magnificent tree. It must be about a hundred feet tall, yet its roots may be only two feet deep. For some reason wellingtonias can often withstand great storms.

'And that magnificent magnolia by the gateway, which you never saw in bloom because you arrived too late in the year, can also withstand tremendous winds. Some of your pines blew down in the great storms of '87 and '89, and nobody bothered to cut them down. They have provided a home for lots of insect life, but they do look unsightly.'

'I was trying to tidy things up, but you and the old bat didn't like it.'

'You don't know what you're doing, that's why. Chainsaws have only been with us since the Fifties, but ignorant people have certainly been able to do a terrible amount of damage with them.'

They walked past the neglected pond still guarded by four stone statues. He smoothed his hair as a gust of wind sent a flurry of crisp leaves swirling about them. 'My God, but it's miserable at this time of year in the countryside!'

They walked past a very old apple tree, its canopy reflected on the ground in fallen and rotting apples. They were on rising ground now, the act of walking putting a strain on their thigh muscles.

Edwina, young and fit, had to stop and wait for Leo. 'This was once a great arboretum, possibly planted to celebrate the last centenary. Who will plant trees here for the twenty-first century?'

'Don't fret about it. The house is going to be sold. Somebody will come here and prettify the place and hold grand parties and live the sort of life that this house has always known.'

She flung her arms wide and turned a full circle. 'But you're lucky to have lived here for a few weeks. What a privilege!'

He laughed at that. 'You think so? Give me London every time. The siren sounds, the screech of tyres, even the violence and the street rows. People actually engaging with one another, actually living. In London, you're stuck for choice with restaurants and cinemas and theatres and nightclubs, and if you absolutely have to see a tree, you can go to a garden. This place gives me the creeps. The only sounds you country types could manage for me was the beat of the occasional military helicopter. The silence is driving me crazy.'

Edwina felt a sudden hollowness in the pit of her stomach as Leo's recent remarks sank in. Cassandra was dying. He had tricked her into incriminating herself. 'She loved you! Cassandra, I mean.'

'So you've brought your thoughts round to something other than trees? Good for you. It's not healthy to be so obsessed. As for Cassandra, her love can be lethal. I told you. No-one is allowed to leave Cassandra. She shoved her foster mother under a train, because the poor woman was about to send her back to the home. No, she didn't love me. She needed me, which is not quite the same thing. I played on that need and I betrayed her into confessing. I'm not a nice man, Edwina. But you can't let a woman like that run around loose, popping off anyone who annoys her.'

'You were clever at it.'

'It's what I do best, God help me. My only talent.' He stopped to catch his breath. 'You might feel better about it if you had ever met Carl, my adoptive brother. He was thirty-one, hadn't found himself yet, but was getting a hell of a kick out of life with his sailing and scuba diving. He told her he wanted to break up. He had finally decided to join the police like his dad wished. So she hit him when he didn't expect it with an oxygen canister and pushed him overboard. Should I have let her go?'

'No, it had to be done. I just hope that—'

'Felix doesn't have to do that sort of thing? I assure you, in the police force it's not encouraged.'

'And what will you do now?'

'I've got no stomach for deceiving people any more. I plan to live with my old man until he gets over all this. Then I thought that I might do a little voluntary work with druggies. I understand them, you see. I've some idea why they do it and I might be able to help some of them to get a life.'

'That would be wonderful. They say people's lives are ruined by drugs like heroin. That would be good work.'

'Want to hear something funny? Some say it's easier to get off heroin than what used to be the housewife's drug of choice, valium. Maybe I should go around visiting housewives and—' He laughed at the absurdity of it, then stopped suddenly. 'Do you mind telling me what the hell I'm doing out here?'

'I wanted to point out the tree I hid behind when your statues were being stolen. Just over there, that chestnut.'

Amusement smoothed some of the strain from his face. 'You saw them taking the statues? Let me guess. You had no idea they were being stolen.'

'None at all, but I soon heard all about it. However, I didn't want to get involved. It would have been very embarrassing for John Blue if a member of his staff had admitted to trespassing. So I said nothing, not even to Felix.'

'In towns, people see things all the time that they don't want to tell the police about. It didn't make any difference to my getting the statues back. Forget it. Can we go back now?'

He checked his phone to make sure it was working. She knew she had very little time left to engage his thoughts.

'Not yet. There's another tree I want to show you. It's not much further. You're out of breath. You'll have to get into shape.'

'You're probably right, so make this quick before I pass out. By the way, when did you stop being afraid of me?'

'When I stopped thinking of you as the demon king and started thinking of you as a human being. Besides at one time you reminded me of my dad, and I'm afraid of him.'

'Your father!' He had trouble seeing himself as the father of a grown woman. 'I'm not a human being. Don't be fooled.' Yet he was amused, grateful for any distraction.

'Look at that!' she cried. 'That branch broke off before you had finished sawing through. Then you just left the snag, a potential site for disease. Oh, look! See that yew tree? It's been crowded by other trees for years and has grown tall and straggly, but yew trees can grow to be three thousand years old under the right conditions. Some people believe churches have been built on sites that were dedicated to older religions, because of the presence of ancient yews, but there's no archaeological evidence for it. Nevertheless, yews in a churchyard can be much older than the church. I can't explain it.'

They came to a clearing with but a single oak tree in it. Nothing remotely like a tree grew within a hundred feet of it in any direction.

'This is it. This is the prize of all the trees at Gorham House.'

'That tree is dead. It's only got leaves on one side and it's rotted away in the middle. It's the ugliest tree I've ever seen. I was going to cut it down but it was too big for me. You're not saying that this old thing—'

'This old thing, as you call it, is thirty feet round. I believe that the arboretum was designed to go around it in a way, to show it off. A hundred years ago they knew that it was something special.'

'If it's not already dead, at least it's dying.'

'It needs work doing on it,' she admitted. 'The cement that was put into it to help it go on living would not be used nowadays. It's lost a huge branch there on the west side which it would not have done if the props were still in place.

'But you're missing the point of this tree. When Henry VIII cut off Anne Boleyn's head, this tree had been growing here for perhaps fifty years or more. When the armada threatened England, this tree was getting on. By the time Napoleon was rampaging across Europe, this oak was a venerable tree and would have been appreciated and treated with reverence by all who saw her.

'She has withstood the First and Second World Wars, the storms of '87 and even an ignoramus with a chainsaw. You don't have to love her. You just have to leave her alone.'

Leo looked at the tree in awe, then his old cynicism returned. 'You can't know it was here in Henry's day.'

'Yes, we can. There are ways. The trouble is, the Cartwright family were recluses and they owned this property for a hundred years, so nobody living around here now remembers the tree. I found out about it because I trespassed. It's wrong to trespass and might have cost me my job, but I'd do it again. I've been a mess at the council. I'm too impatient with the public and I get annoyed that everyone doesn't share my passion. But I did this. I found this tree and I saved it. Now that I've told you, I can tell John Blue what I have done and the Gorham House oak will be plotted out in the county records and cared for and loved for maybe hundreds of years to come.'

'So now you've done what you came for. All these weeks you've wanted to confront me and tell me about my oak before I did away with it. I must have scared the hell out of you for you to have stayed away so long. But you overcame your fear and I am impressed. I'm always impressed when people believe in something so much that they will fight their personal demons to do the right thing. It occurs to me Felix is a lucky man. Now, can we go back, please? My dad is due any time and I want to be there to greet him.'

They walked briskly back in companionable silence. Edwina wondered if he felt as much at peace with himself after getting Cassandra's confession as she did after securing the oak's future. Mission accomplished.

They rounded the corner of the house in time to see a red Mondeo drive to a halt. An elderly white-haired man got out. Leo began to run, and the two men embraced without a word, both unashamedly in tears.

She walked to her car, not looking at the loving

411

pair, trying not to think of her own father. There had never been a bond between them like the one that sustained these two. But she had Felix and her new life was just beginning. Nobody ever said life was perfect.

The phone rang seven times in Edwina's living room before the answering machine switched itself on. There was a pause while her message was relayed, then a tense, tinny voice echoed round the empty room.

'It's Dad. Look, darling, I may have given you the wrong impression. We don't want . . . we never meant . . . that is, your mother and I want to visit you, meet this Felix. We never intended . . . oh, God, Weena. Please give us a call.'

THE END

THE PARADISE GARDEN
by Joan Hessayon

Fran Craig, impoverished, pretty, and approaching forty, had a son she was trying to put through university, a mother constantly whining for financial assistance, and a charming but feckless ex-husband who wasn't above conning her out of her hard earned money if he had the chance. Fran was trying to support herself as a garden designer, but the going was tough – until she met the new owner of Gosfield Hall.

Richard Dumas, self-made American millionaire, gave Fran the unprecedented sum of £10,000 to redesign the gardens of his stately home. He also gave her unstinted admiration and not a few expensive dinners and Fran, finally goaded into revolt by all those using her as a payroll, decided she was going to try and net the wealthy American as a husband. But as she and Richard got to know each other, as she steadily dipped into his £10,000 to pay her debts, something unexpected happened. Fran found she was beginning to care for the man she planned to cheat. It took a boardroom takeover, a trip to Italy, and the creation of a paradise garden before Fran's problems began to be resolved.

0 552 14692 7

THE HELMINGHAM ROSE
by Joan Hessayon

Joyce d'Avranche had always been the poor and ignored member of the d'Avranche family of Helmingham Hall. Her childhood had been one of hardship, and over her dead mother hung the disgrace of an old scandal. Then, when the legitimate heir went missing on the Amazon exploration, Joyce was brought to Helmingham and told she could well be the new owner of the beautiful old house and garden.

Almost at once she fell in love with it and wanted, more than anything, to possess it. But her background had not prepared her for the running of a huge estate. Everything she did was wrong and her only friend was Rose, wife of the head gardener. Rose, too, had sorrows to bear. Barren, in spite of her longing for a child, she sublimated her sadness in the gardens of Helmingham, concentrating all her energy on the breeding of a new rose – the Helmingham Rose.

As the two young women watched the gradual unfurling of the perfect flower, so their own lives moved towards maturity and unexpected happiness.

Joan Hessayon continues her magnificent sequence, begun in *Capel Bells*, of combining a house and garden which actually exist, with the breeding of a new flower to create a fascinating and evocative novel.

0 552 14535 1

CAPEL BELLS
by Joan Hessayon

Charlotte Blair had worked hard all her life. Raised amongst the porters and street sellers of Covent Garden, she had achieved unusual success for a woman in 1911 – her own flower shop. It was unfashionable, in a poor part of London, and made only a small profit, but Charlotte had a secret ambition, to become one of the great floral decorators of the period, transforming the ballrooms and grand houses of the aristocracy.

When she was bidden to Capel Manor for her first floral assignment she fell in love with the house, but – cruelly – fate snatched the commission away from her before she had even begun. It was several weeks later that she learned Capel Manor could be rented and, borrowing every penny she could, she moved her business to the beautiful old house, believing that this would give her an entry into the great families of the neighbourhood.

Beset with every problem, cheating gardeners, the crooked plans of her old friends in Covent Garden, and the return of Matthew Warrender, the owner of Capel Manor, Charlotte fought to realize her ambition to become the most famous floral decorator of her time.

0 552 14220 4

A SELECTED LIST OF FINE NOVELS
AVAILABLE FROM CORGI BOOKS

14058	9	MIST OVER THE MERSEY	*Lyn Andrews*	£5.99
14609	9	THE BLIND YEARS	*Catherine Cookson*	£5.99
13915	7	WHEN NIGHT CLOSES IN	*Iris Gower*	£5.99
14449	5	SWEET ROSIE	*Iris Gower*	£5.99
14537	8	APPLE BLOSSOM TIME	*Kathryn Haig*	£5.99
14538	6	A TIME TO DANCE	*Kathryn Haig*	£5.99
14567	X	THE CORNER HOUSE	*Ruth Hamilton*	£5.99
14770	2	MULLIGAN'S YARD	*Ruth Hamilton*	£5.99
14686	2	CITY OF GEMS	*Caroline Harvey*	£5.99
14820	2	THE TAVERNERS' PLACE	*Caroline Harvey*	£5.99
14220	4	CAPEL BELLS	*Joan Hessayon*	£5.99
14535	1	THE HELMINGHAM ROSE	*Joan Hessayon*	£5.99
14692	7	THE PARADISE GARDEN	*Joan Hessayon*	£5.99
14603	X	THE SHADOW CHILD	*Judith Lennox*	£5.99
14772	9	THE COLOUR OF HOPE	*Susan Madison*	£5.99
14822	9	OUR YANKS	*Margaret Mayhew*	£5.99
14693	5	THE LITTLE SHIP	*Margaret Mayhew*	£5.99
14658	7	THE MEN IN HER LIFE	*Imogen Parker*	£5.99
14659	5	WHAT BECAME OF US	*Imogen Parker*	£5.99
14752	4	WITHOUT CHARITY	*Michelle Paver*	£5.99
14753	2	A PLACE IN THE HILLS	*Michelle Paver*	£5.99
10375	6	CSARDAS	*Diane Pearson*	£5.99
14655	2	SPRING MUSIC	*Elvi Rhodes*	£5.99
14715	X	MIDSUMMER MEETING	*Elvi Rhodes*	£5.99
14671	4	THE KEYS TO THE GARDEN	*Susan Sallis*	£5.99
14747	8	THE APPLE BARREL	*Susan Sallis*	£5.99
14744	3	TOMORROW IS ANOTHER DAY	*Mary Jane Staples*	£5.99
14785	0	THE WAY AHEAD	*Mary Jane Staples*	£5.99
14640	4	THE ROMANY GIRL	*Valerie Wood*	£5.99
14740	0	EMILY	*Valerie Wood*	£5.99